THE LITTLE BLACK BOOK KILLER

FIONA WALKER

Boldwood

First published in Great Britain in 2025 by Boldwood Books Ltd.

Copyright © Fiona Walker, 2025

Cover Design by Rachel Lawston

Cover Images: Rachel Lawston

Map Design by Fiona Walker

The moral right of Fiona Walker to be identified as the author of this work has been asserted in accordance with the Copyright, Designs and Patents Act 1988.

All rights reserved. No part of this book may be reproduced in any form or by any electronic or mechanical means, including information storage and retrieval systems, without written permission from the author, except for the use of brief quotations in a book review. This book is a work of fiction and, except in the case of historical fact, any resemblance to actual persons, living or dead, is purely coincidental.

Every effort has been made to obtain the necessary permissions with reference to copyright material, both illustrative and quoted. We apologise for any omissions in this respect and will be pleased to make the appropriate acknowledgements in any future edition.

A CIP catalogue record for this book is available from the British Library.

Paperback ISBN 978-1-83561-952-0

Large Print ISBN 978-1-83561-951-3

Hardback ISBN 978-1-83561-950-6

Trade Paperback ISBN 978-1-80656-019-6

Ebook ISBN 978-1-83561-953-7

Kindle ISBN 978-1-83561-954-4

Audio CD ISBN 978-1-83561-945-2

MP3 CD ISBN 978-1-83561-946-9

Digital audio download ISBN 978-1-83561-948-3

This book is printed on certified sustainable paper. Boldwood Books is dedicated to putting sustainability at the heart of our business. For more information please visit https://www.boldwoodbooks.com/about-us/sustainability/

Boldwood Books Ltd, 23 Bowerdean Street, London, SW6 3TN

www.boldwoodbooks.com

For Susie and Richard, two of life's loveliest champions, with heartfelt thanks.

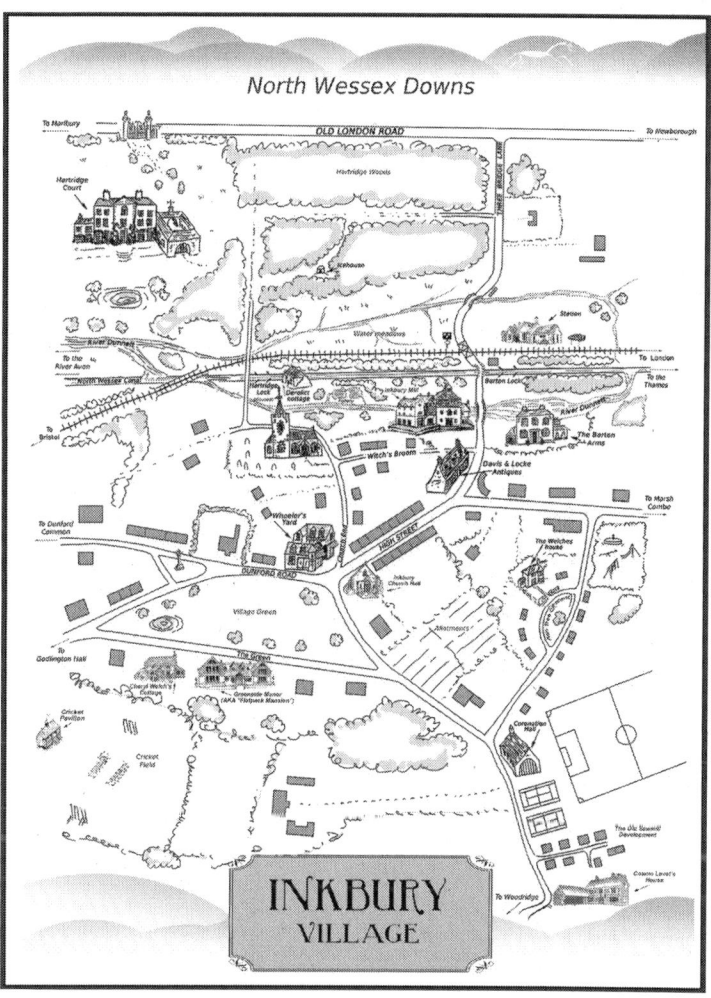

PROLOGUE
PHOEBE

'Imagine your life of crime on primetime, Phoebe my dear!' Dennis said expansively, powering his glossy red Range Rover along the Old London Road towards Dunford.

'It's good of you to think of me,' Phoebe told him. Frank Sinatra was crooning 'Luck Be a Lady' on the car's stereo. It felt auspicious.

She was enveloped in a cloud of Acqua di Parma as Dennis leant closer to confide: 'I'm so well connected in broadcasting, it's criminal not to help you out – pun intended!' Guffawing, he beeped his horn at a crow pecking at roadkill in front of them. 'If this comes together, I shall insist upon a credit.'

White-haired and mahogany-skinned, veteran television producer Dennis de Lacy was an old-school charmer who believed in pre-digital networking.

Phoebe had been introduced to him by her friend Juno, whose mother was enjoying a renaissance as a celebrity cook on Channel 5 thanks to fiancé Dennis's genius in attracting older viewers. Now he was determined to bring Phoebe's whodunnit novels to the small screen.

This evening, he was taking her to swanky lifestyle destination The Priory at Dunford to introduce her to one of the channel's high-flyers.

'Lucia Vance is Middle England's go-to murder mystery producer,' he briefed her now, 'and she's hungry for fresh blood. *Leapt* at the chance to meet up while she's staying at The Priory for a conference. Ever been there?'

Phoebe said she hadn't.

'Overpriced but the grub's terrific. A skip across Dunford Common from the fast train to Paddington. Media types like Lucia love it. Knew her when she was a humble runner at the Beeb. She's always looked up to me,' he bragged. 'I've told her you write fiendishly clever whodunnits with TV Choice Awards written all over them. You'll soon be famous, I predict. *And you're a sleuth in real life, a gift to publicity!*'

Phoebe hummed vaguely at this. Shying away from self-promotion was bad news for a novelist in search of a television deal, as husband Felix had pointed out when he pep-talked her earlier. Working in the film industry, Felix was wise to screen rights acquisition and the elevator-pitch urgency needed to make an impact. This meeting could be transformative, they'd agreed, and she owed it to her family to do her utmost to sell herself.

Close friends Juno and Mil were equally vociferous in support, sending rallying WhatsApp messages which she now read on her phone. *Knock 'em dead, gorgeous* from village pub landlord Mil, and *Life is for living* from Juno, the person who had instigated their mystery-solving side hustle.

It was true that, with their help, Phoebe had recently been instrumental in tracking down the culprit behind the deaths of the village postman and a local socialite, and before that a crooked art dealer who had washed up in the River Dunnett.

The experience had formed an alliance they'd nicknamed the Village Detectives. The others were already eagerly looking for a new case, their shared WhatsApp group constantly pinging with new messages from ever-alert Mil reporting yet more suspicious goings on in Inkbury.

Phoebe switched her phone to Do Not Disturb. This evening, she must focus on Lucia Vance. It was a golden opportunity.

Life is for living. She repeated Juno's mantra in her head as she pulled down the sun visor to check her reflection, the cropped gunmetal hair with its white streak tamed and sculpted for once, bright green eyes framed by a rare application of make-up, the anxious scowl in need of a hasty reset.

Phoebe's bright smile held strong when Dennis swept her into the turreted former home of an order of sixteenth-century monks, its cloisters now a glass-sided bar serviced by staff in tailored burgundy livery.

Most of the tables were occupied, conversations buzzing, the atmosphere urbane and animated.

Dennis was already waving to faces he recognised. 'These are my people! No sign of Lucia yet, so let's circulate you.' He made Phoebe sound like a pamphlet.

Having ordered cocktails from the bar – wild strawberry mojitos to match his Garrick Club tie – he whisked her off on a table-hopping tour, landing first on a group of older men on sofas by an unlit fire whom he hailed as old friends. There followed introductions to a procession of Nevilles and Colins, Nigels and Ians that Phoebe couldn't hope to keep up with, after which Dennis spirited her around the room at warp speed, more names swapped, and not just those from the broadcasting convention. It was a well-worn Wexshire joke that Dennis inevitably knew almost everybody at a local gathering, but Phoebe had never seen this borne out so manifestly as here in the bar at The Priory, where he wasted no time making his handshaking, air-kissing, never-forget-a-face mark. She soon found herself introduced to a local entrepreneur, two professional footballers and even a member of the waiting staff: 'If it isn't Doc Green's daughter home for summer! Still studying technical wizardry at Imperial?'

Navigating back to the bar for a fresh brace of mojitos – his a mocktail this time – he briefly introduced her to a Wexshire landowner perched there with the hotel's owner, then it was back to the table-pinball, where Phoebe was spun between movers and shakers out on the sunlit terrace, amongst them a man sitting alone, sporting an admirably retro 1980s mullet, mirrored sunglasses and leather flying jacket.

'Wayne, my dear chap! Are the TV men trying to get you to invest? Phoebe, meet another local business genius. You're all here this evening!'

Wayne lowered the phone he was speaking into and flashed his veneers, his accent creamily local. 'All right, Dennis, mate. I'd've come somewhere quieter if I knew all you knob-twiddlers would be in.'

'I'm just here for a quickie, old boy.'

'Ha!' Barrel-chested, with a lot of gold jewellery and a bawdy chuckle, Wayne stood up to shake his hand. 'I heard you had a new ladylove. Hello, darling.' He turned to plant wet kisses on Phoebe's cheeks. 'I'm meeting my best girl here too.'

'Phoebe's with me on a professional footing,' Dennis corrected. 'My fiancée Judy is at home.'

'You dirty devil!'

Dennis laughed gamely while Phoebe smarted, watching Wayne sit heavily back down. He was noticeably unsteady. She wondered if he was drunk. On the table, his phone was still on a call, a disjointed voice barking faintly from it. 'Hello? Wayne? You there?'

Wayne made no effort to pick it up, instead looking woozily around the courtyard. 'My date's late. Bloody hope she looks like her pic—' Something caught his eye behind them. 'Dear God, please don't let this be her.'

Waving for attention, a large, frowning woman in a boxy black suit was bearing down on them through the tables.

'Oh, here's Lucia!' Dennis waved back. 'Do excuse us!' He steered Phoebe away, whispering aside, 'Bit of a player, Wayne, but it always pays to do lip service to big-money investors. Lucia, my darling! Looking *sensational*!'

Still wiping Wayne's lip service from her cheek, Phoebe summoned her bright smile again to meet Middle England's go-to murder mystery producer, who had a handshake like a can crusher.

'I've got five minutes, then I'm having dinner with Paramount,' Lucia announced gruffly, checking her watch before marching them to a nearby table. 'Dennis tells me you write books that might make good TV?'

'I hope so.' Phoebe fished in her bag for some copies of her novels Dennis had suggested she bring along, placing them in front of Lucia. 'I have two different series. The Dorothy De'Ath mysteries are cosy and upbeat, based in the Yorkshire Dales in the 1920s, featuring an aristocratic flapper and her maid investigating—'

'Done to death, not interested, next.'

Phoebe tried not to react, forging on: 'I also write crime thrillers as P. F. Sylvian. Those are edgier police procedurals set in the eighties and based around here.'

'Pretty area, like it. Edgy retro's on point. What's the hook?'

'*Great* writing is the ultimate hook, dear Lucia!' Dennis

stepped in smoothly. 'Loveable characters, brilliant plot twists, beautiful scenery. Middle England at its finest! America will *adore* it!'

Tutting, Lucia shook her head. 'Blow off those moths, Dennis. We need a USP: minority representation, a cultural diaspora, identity and divergence. Mental health and menopause are old news' – she eyed Phoebe beadily, daring her to question one middle-aged, middle-class white woman sitting in a boutique hotel dictating ideological trends to another – 'but cancer's still hot, along with financial hardship, public cancellation and ageing isolation. I'm looking for an authentic voice, lived experience, a *hook*.'

Finding her recent lived experience pithily summarised, Phoebe looked from her to Dennis in shocked silence.

'Phoebe is a detective herself!' He jumped in before she could demand exactly how much Lucia Vance knew about her personal life, and how.

When Dennis started enthusiastically describing the cases she had recently helped crack, Lucia interrupted impatiently to ask Phoebe whether the murders in her novels were based on personal experience.

'Absolutely not,' Phoebe said before realising that this was the wrong answer. Lucia was already scooping all the books into her tote bag as though sweeping aside crumbs and asking Dennis about erstwhile BBC colleagues.

Fight for this, Phoebe reminded herself. *Your family need this. You have the USP. Life is for living.*

Yet she was still too aggravated to trust herself to speak. Her own cancer survival, her family's financial struggles, her career cancellation and her loneliness remained deep, painful wounds she couldn't bring herself to pimp for profit.

Taking a few deep, quiet breaths, she watched a waitress

hurrying through the cloisters with a tray of glasses, another carrying a champagne cooler the other way.

At a table nearby, eighties throwback Wayne had clearly remembered his phone conversation and was chuckling away into his mobile. He caught her eye over his aviator shades and winked.

Then he promptly face-planted in his aperitivo olive bowl, leaving Phoebe almost grateful for the distraction.

Her companions barely paused for breath between name-drops, not noticing the drama at first. Not even when a waiter rushed across to help Wayne, beckoning urgently to a colleague for assistance.

Leaping up, Phoebe found herself part of a small posse surging towards the table and quickly realised she would be of most help keeping everyone back while the first-aid-trained staff member put Wayne in the recovery position.

'Is anyone calling 999?' she asked, turning to address the crowd urgently, and then – spotting at least half a dozen people were doing so simultaneously – she insisted all but one stop. 'The rest of us need to stay back, okay?'

She glanced over her shoulder to see Wayne being carefully laid down on his side, a rolled-up serving apron under his head. His face was an alarming shade of grey, his eyes rolled back and bloodshot.

The woman on the line to the ambulance service handed her phone to the first aider so he could talk to the call handler. In a panicked voice, he explained that every indication was that this was a heart attack: 'He's not breathing and I can't feel a pulse!'

Phoebe realised that several bystanders were now filming everything on their phones.

'Stop that!' She stepped in front of one furiously.

To her relief, the phones were all lowered.

Behind her, the first aider had started administering CPR.

More hotel staff were coming out to the bar's courtyard, led by a manager who asked guests to move through to the library bar where they would be served a complimentary drink.

'Don't tell me,' said a gruff voice beside Phoebe, 'you're going to announce who the murderer is when everyone's gathered there?'

Turning, she found Lucia Vance thrusting out a hand to shake hers with another can-crushing squeeze.

'Gotta split' – she nodded curtly – 'can't keep the Paramount boys and girls waiting. Good to meet you. You certainly bring the drama.' With a cool glance at Wayne, she marched off.

Joining the exodus towards the library bar, Phoebe met Dennis returning from the gents', tugging his crisp shirt cuffs to straighten them after washing his hands. 'Sorry to dash off like that, dear girl; dicky prostate waits for no man. I've already bid farewell to Lucia. I think that went rather well, don't you? Wayne all right now?'

'I'm afraid not.' She shook her head. 'Looks like he's had a heart attack.'

'I'm sure he'll bounce back in no time. Another strawberry mojito to celebrate our collaboration?'

But Phoebe had no desire to stick around amid such upset, asking instead if Dennis minded taking her home.

'Of course!' He cast a baleful look towards the library, where the excited courtyard drinkers were now noisily knocking back free cocktails. 'Judy will have the hot tub revved up. I tried to persuade her to come along, but she says television types are frightful bores these days.'

The ambulance arrived while they were walking back to the car park, paramedics leaping out to hurry inside.

Minutes later, it overtook Dennis's Range Rover at speed as he and Phoebe headed back to Inkbury on the Old London Road, rushing Wayne to Wexshire Royal Infirmary, blues and twos flashing.

'You're going to put this evening in a book, I take it?' Dennis asked cheerily, pulling the Range Rover back out into the carriageway after letting it past.

Frank Sinatra was blaring 'Mack the Knife' from the stereo.

'Unlikely.' Phoebe had briefly contemplated making Lucia Vance a cold-blooded assassin in her next novel, but now she repeated Juno's *life is for living* mantra in her head. 'There wasn't a murder, for a start.' She added a quiet prayer that poor Wayne pulled through and got to meet his 'best girl'.

Ahead of them, the blue lights were fading from sight.

Through the car speakers, Frank was singing about a body on the sidewalk oozing out life.

'There is just one strange thing.' Phoebe thought about it.

'What's that?'

'Wayne's date. She didn't turn up, did she?'

1

JUNO

Black Box's 'Ride on Time' was thudding through Inkbury Church Hall as Juno pumped her arms and waved her glowsticks, their two colourful points all that her sweat-blurred vision could distinguish. She could no longer see the Clubbercise instructor onstage or hear her shouting through a headset over the music. Her own heartbeat pounded loudly in her ears.

She guessed the class was supposed to be side-stepping, because Cheryl Welch kept barrelling into her, panting hard.

'I'm dying!' gasped Cheryl. 'If I peg it right here, Juno, it's an open and shut case for you and the Village Detectives! My cousin did it!' She pointed to the stage where their instructor was lifting her knees to her elbows at speed.

Juno would have pointed out that she was likely to die first, but she was too puffed out to speak as Underworld's 'Born Slippy' kicked in and they all started running forwards and backwards, crossing and uncrossing the glowsticks overhead.

Clubbercise – a frantic hour of dancing to nineties rave anthems in a darkened room – could purportedly burn six hundred calories in one session. Braver participants wore dayglo Lycra, which shone brightly in the UV lights.

Juno's fluorescent pink cycling shorts and yellow smiley-face vest bobbed like a buoy through the dark sea of bodies.

Small, rotund and enthusiastic, Juno's attempts at getting fit were stalling in direct proportion to her addiction to pastries from the village deli, but she loved the sociable side of exercise classes, and they were a great source of Inkbury intel. Not that the Village Detectives were currently investigating anything; writer Phoebe was wrapped up finishing another fictional whodunnit while her filmmaker husband Felix edited his latest movie; landlord Mil was rushed off his feet in the pub; and Juno was getting work fit by testing her limits with techno and glowsticks.

Right now, those limits were under threat of being exceeded. She only realised their instructor had told them all to take five when she tripped over two ladies who were lying down to recover.

'I think you can stop!' Cheryl called across to her, hands on her knees, the group around them panting heavily.

Juno lowered her glowsticks and waited for her vision to stop tunnelling. The music had switched to the slower, trancey 'Drifting Away' by Faithless.

She joined Cheryl's knee-clutching huddle, gasping, 'See – you're still alive!'

'Take more than dance music to kill me,' Cheryl puffed back, reaching for her water bottle, ''specially not when I'm about to get it on in the Aegean.' She laughed throatily.

Part of Inkbury's notorious Welch family – a matriarchy of leggy seductresses with high muscle tone and minimal self-doubt – Cheryl was Juno's romantic inspiration, and she liked to think they had a lot in common. Two single mums in search of second-chance love, both were age-defying adventurers with hard-partying pasts.

'That's the spirit, ladies!' Their instructor, Beth, had joined them. Cheryl's dreadlocked blonde cousin gave an encouraging whoop before adding a Millennial, 'Glasto, mud, Groove Armada, no phone chargers!'

'No phones at all in our day.' Cheryl raised her water bottle in Gen X solidarity. 'Ibiza '89, off our tits at Amnesia, Pete Tong!'

'Millionaires nightclub, Croydon, Dave Lee Travis!' A slender figure sprang into the group as Debra Bass placed a pink-taloned hand on Juno and Cheryl's shoulders, dayglo leopard print and bleached teeth gleaming. 'That's where I met my Rich. It was love at first sight, girls!'

The others melted hastily away, leaving Juno and Cheryl stapled in place by ten long pink acrylics as Inkbury's village czarina held court.

'We're so lucky to have each other, me and Rich,' Debra trilled in her singsong voice. A diva self-believer with no dimmer switch, Debra had what Juno's gamer son called 'main character energy'. Husband Rich Bass had a matching supply. They could power their own grid.

'Never take love for granted, ladies.' She pulled the two women closer. 'It can vanish in a... heartbeat.' Clicking her fingers next to their ears, she lowered her voice. 'Take poor Wayne Baxendale. Dropped dead last week. Heart attack.'

'Wayne is dead?' Cheryl's mouth fell open.

'He was on the phone to Rich at the time, waiting for his dinner date, saying he thought he'd found love again. Next moment, gone!' The fingers clicked again. 'His last words were "this Rioja tastes corked".'

'Was this in The Priory at Dunford?' asked Juno, realising it might have been the incident she'd heard about from her mother's boyfriend Dennis. Her friend Phoebe had been there too, although she'd typically played it down. 'He *died*, you say?'

'*Totally* unexpected. So much to live for. Could almost be a case for you, Miss Marple.'

Juno's detective instincts quickened. She itched to ask more, but Debra was still talking: 'Wayne was the life and soul, eh, Cheryl? Big charmer, that man; never settled. Used to be in business with Rich, investing in local startups. One made *serious* lolly,' she told Juno, waggling a huge diamond solitaire ring as evidence. 'Cheryl's ex-hubby was in on that. Wayne bought himself a vintage Ferrari to celebrate, I recall,' she sighed sadly.

'Womanising bastard.' Cheryl gave Juno a knowing look.

'Don't speak ill of the dead, babes,' Debra scolded.

'I meant my ex, Russell, and I only wish he was,' Cheryl sighed, then covered her mouth in horror. 'I'm so sorry, Juno, I didn't think—'

'It's fine!' Juno reassured her. 'Being a widow doesn't stop me remembering the urge to empty the vacuum in his pants drawer.'

'That's why I'm so lucky to have Rich,' Debra beamed from one woman to the other, the Botox and lip filler making her smile look stuck on, like Mrs Potato Head. 'Thirty-five years we'll have been married this summer.'

'Wow!' Juno led, nudging Cheryl.

'Yeah, congrats.'

Staying married to uber-ego Rich Bass took hardcore loyalty. They exchanged another look.

'Is that silver?' asked Cheryl.

'Silver wedding anniversary is twenty-five.' Juno knew it without thinking. 'Thirty-five is coral.'

'Rich is taking me to Dominica,' Debra told them, straightening the rungs of glittering solitaires on her tanned, manicured fingers. 'The Champagne Reef.'

'Sounds like another eighties nightclub!' joked Juno.

'Apparently, the coral bubbles away under a turquoise sea like Bollinger. And I know what you're going to say – "but Debra babes, you're only just back from the Seychelles", and you're right!'

'I wasn't going to say that,' Cheryl muttered.

Debra pretended not to hear. 'He spoils me rotten, does my Rich.'

'How heavenly,' Juno rushed on. 'You two ladies make me green with envy, jetting off with your gorgeous men!'

'So who's this new boyfriend, Cheryl?' Debra got several suggestive octaves and key changes out of the question.

'Early days.' Cheryl flashed a wry smile.

'He's whisking her off to his luxury villa in the Greek islands,' Juno boasted for her.

'How did you meet?' Debra demanded beadily.

'Through friends.' Cheryl gave Juno a look that forbade dissent. They both knew 'Hot Rod' had been a match on Dapper and Discreet, an exclusive online dating service Cheryl described as 'midlife mojo's best kept secret'. She was helping Juno to join up, but insisted she keep mum.

'He sounds divine,' Juno sighed wistfully.

'We'll find you a man, Juno babes,' Debra promised, hoicking down the leopard-print leotard which was giving her a wedgie. 'Shame about poor Wayne passing; you two might have made a nice match.'

Cheryl snorted with laughter. 'You're *kidding*?'

'Wayne just needed the right woman by his side.'

'Or the right cardiologist.'

'He had a big heart, it's true.'

'And more exes than a maths equation.'

'Could one have taken revenge?' Juno asked, still in detective mode, picturing charming Wayne breathing his last amid the nocellara stones, his belly full of Rioja and cyanide. 'He'd just found love again, you said. She must be devastated.'

'Never turned up.' Debra sniffed sadly. 'Whoever she might have been. Like I say, girls, never take love for granted. Which Greek island is it you're going to, Cheryl?'

'Santorini.'

'Brave.' The filled lips pursed. 'Aren't you put off by the seismic tremors?'

'I'm actually hoping the earth moves.' Cheryl smirked.

'Rich never disappoints in that department, I'm happy to say.' Debra admired her plastic talons. 'He's my personal JCB!'

Again, Cheryl caught Juno's eye and they had to look swiftly away to stop themselves giggling.

The trio swigged from their water bottles: long-married Debra, newly wooed divorcee Cheryl and widowed Juno, who envied the other two their romantic holidays if not their rivalry. Debra wasn't usually such an apologist for her boorish, bulldozing husband, but she was also highly competitive, and Cheryl was looking amazing, a dewy loved-up glow kissing her round cheeks, the big blonde mane sun-streaked and glossy.

'I can't believe you're going to miss my housewarming party,' Juno grumbled to her. 'You could have brought Rodney along, introduced him to us all.'

'Rodney, is it?' Debra got another suggestive key-change from the word. 'What's his surname? I might know him.'

'You won't. He's a very private person.'

'Poor you, how dreary.' Debra sniffed, flouncing off to join the diminishing loo queue, leotard riding up again.

'Bitch,' Cheryl muttered at her retreating back. 'I don't know why you're nice to her. Everyone in the village hates her.'

'I'm nice to everyone,' Juno pointed out, although she remained secretly rather in awe of Debra's steely brio.

'That's why you deserve love,' Cheryl told her warmly, adding in an undertone, 'I've done you that personal referral to join the app like I promised. It fast-tracks you past the waiting list. Did you get the link? I sent it last night.'

'Thanks.' Juno flushed.

'Honestly, don't hang about. One minute Rodney was a Dick Dastardly avatar called Hot Rod sharing light bulb jokes, the next he's swept me clean off my feet. Now I'm off to the Aegean, and I have Dapper and Discreet to thank for that.'

'Do you want me to feed your cats while you're away like last time?'

'River's house-sitting.' Cheryl pulled a mock horror face. 'Feeding the cats is the only thing that'll get him off his computer chair.' Her twenty-year-old son – just a couple of years younger than Juno's boy Eric and similarly tech-mad – drifted back and forth from doing something clever at a university. 'Don't change the subject. Have you logged in yet?'

'I'll take a look later,' Juno promised, grateful to hear the music switching to the loud electronic bam-bam-bams and 'no-no-no-no's of 'No Limit' as their instructor bounded back onstage, headset on once more, clapping her hands high above her dreadlocks to call them all back into action.

The truth was Juno had filled in her details on Dapper and Discreet with indecent haste, excitedly awaiting a match, which Cheryl had promised would be superfast. She'd since checked it hourly. So far, there'd been nothing.

* * *

When the class finished, Juno determinedly didn't check her phone again. Instead, she joined the small group of Clubbercisers who always recovered with a round of iced spritzers in The Barton Arms.

It was a glorious high summer evening, golden light spilling warmly though the village's narrow lanes as the women walked to the pub together in a shoal of hot Lycra, their breathless talk focused on Cheryl's whirlwind romance.

'It's a dream come true!' Cheryl led them along the pavement like Donna leading out a skipping dance procession in *Mamma Mia*. 'I thought I'd never feel sexy again when River's bastard dad walked out on us for his bit on the side.'

'That was so hard on you,' one of the others cooed.

'Harder on River.' She slowed her walk, hugging herself and looking up as a group of swifts screeched past overhead. 'Dropped out of school halfway through his A levels, wouldn't come out of his room, just lived on the internet and games console. His mental health nose-dived.' Her voice shook.

Putting an arm round her, Juno – whose clever, introverted son's reaction to family trauma had followed a similar pattern – felt a deep pang of empathy. 'I'm so glad you're both in a better place now.'

'Thank you, my darling, and we are.' Cheryl hooked her arm around Juno too and marched her onwards, back in upbeat ABBA mode. 'River's still glued to a screen, but he's doing well in his first year at uni and he's madly in love which helps. Xanthe's a lovely girl... *They* are a lovely person,' she corrected. 'I haven't lost a son, I've gained a...'

'Person!' Juno helped, wishing her own son had found love with a soulmate. Eric's first child was imminent, its mother determined to go it alone. Juno's grandmotherly role had been sidelined to googling his paternal legal rights.

'River and Xanthe both insist I deserve some fun,' Cheryl danced onwards, 'so they're right behind me going away. I can't wait, ladies. I've not slept for thinking about it! Wait till you hear what Rod has planned.'

Listening to the promises of naked swimming, mountain-top kisses and the best sex of Cheryl's life, Juno's jaw slackened even more jealously. Maybe Dapper and Discreet was the answer.

In need of a drink and a real-life friendly face, she put on a spurt of speed along Three Bridge Lane, arriving in The Barton Arms bar ahead of the others to order the first round from landlord Mil.

'How's my favourite sleuth?' he greeted her.

'Sweaty.'

'Glowing.'

A handsomely battered and flirtatious ex-rugby pro almost as broad as he was tall, Mil was one cornerstone of the unofficially named Village Detectives. Together with friends Felix and Phoebe Sylvian, the foursome had already uncovered the real culprits behind a trio of suspicious village deaths. And just like Juno, Mil saw cases everywhere.

He leaned closer, voice dropping. 'Eager for a new investigation?'

Mil could read her like a book. Juno secretly hoped Dapper and Discreet matched her with a man just like him, only closer to her in age and perhaps slightly less fond of practical jokes. In her wilder fantasies, she saw Mil and herself as Mulder and Scully from *The X Files*, David and Maddie from *Moonlighting*, and she loved feeding him suspicious snippets she'd picked up.

'What have you got?' she whispered.

'Graveyard Ravers,' he said, glancing round to ensure nobody was eavesdropping, but the pub was quiet and her

Clubbercise companions were noisily gathering chairs outside on the decked terrace overlooking the river.

'What are the Graveyard Ravers?'

'Someone keeps dressing up tombstones in the churchyard in party gear. The churchwarden's doing her nut. I put it on the WhatsApp chat earlier.'

'I didn't see, sorry.' She unlocked her phone to check.

There was a notification from Dapper and Discreet. She had a match!

'Still on Bumble, are you?' Mil teased. 'How many times have I told you I'm your dream man?'

'This is a different app' – she quickly minimised it – 'and who says I'm not secretly hoping the man of my dreams won't sweep me off my feet at my housewarming party?'

'He's going, is he?' Mil looked nonplussed, clearly not realising that she might mean him.

'First man I asked.' She'd invited the Village Detectives WhatsApp group before anyone else.

'You meet him on that new dating app?' he asked jealously as he lined up the spritzers.

'Not his thing,' she said, trying to catch his eye, but he was looking broodily across at the pub's near-empty restaurant, where teenage waitress Courtney was slyly watching TikTok on her phone.

Taking a swig of her spritzer, eager to change the subject, Juno urged, 'Tell me everything you know about these Graveyard Ravers. They're dressing headstones up in party gear, you say? Bit macabre.'

'Knew you'd be straight on it!' Face brightening, Mil leaned across the bar, lowering his voice. 'It started last month – when the schools broke up, take note – and they've struck twice so far, both times late at night. My money's on village kids, although some of the gear's quite kinky, the churchwarden said. Undies and stuff.'

'I'll see what I can find out,' Juno promised. 'Meanwhile, I might have another interesting case. What do you know about Wayne Baxendale?'

'Yeah, I heard he'd died, poor sod. Not suspicious, is it?'

'Probably not,' she said cheerfully, taking another big swig of spritzer. 'But it *was* sudden, and I get the impression there might be a few dancing on his grave.' As she said it, she felt an unexpected chill run through her. Must be the cold drink, she reassured herself.

Eyes sparkling, Mil leaned yet further across the bar and whispered, 'You might be onto something, now you mention it.'

'What makes you think that?' she asked excitedly.

'Baxendale took over as village cricket captain this year,' Mil told her, 'not that he lived in Inkbury, plus golf was more his game. The skipper before him was a weekender, but at least he took it seriously, still does. Only Rich Bass is chairman and pays for everything, so what he says goes, and he crowbarred in his crony Wayne as captain to ensure he gets selected to bat first, even though neither of them could hit a ball if it was sitting on a plate. Plenty round here had their backs up about that.'

'Wayne had enemies here in the village then?'

'Not many left on the cricket team to count, if I'm honest. I've been on it since I was twelve – even came back to play matches when I was touring with Wexshire Warriors – but it's not what it was. Now this. Big match at the weekend, too.'

'I heard Wayne was quite the womaniser.'

'Don't know much about his personal life. Like I say, he lived outside the village, and he never drank in here. Loved his classic cars, I know that much. Had a place over near Marlbury with more garages than rooms.' Mil leaned even closer so their foreheads were practically touching. '*Could* it be murder, you think?'

'Gut instinct says it's worth finding out more.' Juno nodded, thrilled at the prospect of another collaboration.

'I'll ask around,' he promised, squaring his big shoulders so heroically, she had to remind herself firmly that he was far too young for her.

Juno jumped as her phone let out a distinctive 'I say!' – the notification sound effect she already regretted allocating to the Dapper and Discreet app. Flustered, she clutched it to her chest. 'Great, we're on the case! Although, to be honest, I shouldn't be thinking about suspicious deaths right now, or Graveyard Ravers even.' She was secretly, guiltily far more eager to escape to the ladies' to look at her match. 'I'm focusing totally on' – love, romance, whirlwinds, age-appropriate lust – 'my housewarming party!'

'About this party...' Mil cleared his throat and raised his scarred eyebrows, rugged smile at its most beguiling.

'*Nobody*'s dying at my party,' Juno promised.

'I might not make it.'

'Okay, so one person may die,' she said darkly.

It was a prediction that would prove uncannily accurate.

2

PHOEBE

'You caught the killer again, Lady Dee! The Dingledale Ladies' Reading Circle is free from the Library Steps Ripper! I don't know how you do it, milady.'

'Three parts clever reasoning to one part intrepid spirit, Annie, and a big splash of instinct. Which reminds me, we must have passed the yardarm by now.'

'Shall I ask Benson to mix your usual, milady?'

'And bring my cigarette box, will you? Just no cyanide this time!'

'That,' Phoebe told her two small dogs as she typed THE END beneath the final line, 'is bloody awful.'

Phoebe always hated first drafts. The perfect garden she'd pictured in her mind whilst writing was inevitably reduced to scrubland on the page; much weeding, pruning and replanting would be required before it was ready to share with readers.

Yet she'd been in this position enough times to derive a certain glow of satisfaction, not least because her timing was immaculate. Juno's party was tonight, and Phoebe had promised she would be more sociable. Now she could also be celebratory.

'Let's go for a run,' she told the dogs, who were already ahead of her, crowding the door eagerly, their morning outing postponed by Phoebe's denouement.

Grabbing her phone, Phoebe turned off Do Not Disturb and took a screenshot of the final page and sent it to Felix, hoping it would help spur him through his own creative marathon in a London edit suite, frantically trying to shave forty minutes and an MPA age classification off his latest project to secure an American distributor.

She ran out beneath the grand stable yard arch and on into Hartridge Woods, along the wide, shaded bridleway ride towards the river and canal. In her pocket, her phone vibrated with two days' worth of backlogged messages landing as it found signal again on the grassy bridge over the River Dunnett.

Phoebe climbed the padlocked gate with its 'Private – Hartridge Estate' warning sign and walked down onto the old lock island, long abandoned now the water-levelling mechanism was decommissioned, its lock keeper's cottage derelict.

Wriggling between the gate bars behind her, the terriers raced past to burrow through the tall nettles and willowherb into the cottage. It was one of their favourite spots.

Phoebe had shown the tumbledown cottage to Juno not long after she'd arrived in the village, naively suggesting it might be the 'doer upper' project her friend was looking for. But the Hartridge Estate was currently mired in inheritance disputes after the death of its previous owner, and its trustees wanted nothing altered until it was resolved. Which meant this secret corner would stay as it was for the foreseeable future.

The old mooring in front of the cottage was amongst the prettiest in Inkbury with its views across the village's water meadows to the church beyond. This private inlet wasn't accessible to the many passing narrowboaters to tie up. Its quietness was one of the reasons Phoebe liked it so much.

Perhaps it was no bad thing Juno wasn't transforming the lock keeper's cottage into her dream thatch, she reflected. A social animal, Juno loved nothing more than throwing her doors open, cranking up the Britpop and inviting the village in.

Phoebe looked at the phone messages while she was catching her breath.

> My housewarming party tonight, don't forget!!!
> Bring grog!

She tapped on it, replying with a quick thumbs up.

It was Juno's third reminder that day, she noted, this one followed by:

> Weather looks iffy, argh!

She gazed along the sun-soaked towpath of the North Wessex Canal and up to a spotless blue sky; even Phoebe's hard-wired pessimism would struggle to summon a black cloud.

But ever-buoyant Juno wanted her guests to have fun rain or shine, asking now:

> Do you have a pop-up gazebo? I'll deck it with fairy lights!

> You don't have a garden.

> Going to use the courtyard if crowd gets too big.

> How many people have you invited?

> I'll ask Mil.

> Mil knows how many people are coming to your party?

> He's bound to have some awnings and stuff for the pub. I'll keep you posted.

Phoebe had no great desire for an update on the purveyance of a gazebo but decided not to share this. Instead, she pocketed her phone and broke back into a run to catch up with her two terriers who had abandoned the cottage to bound along the lock island bank towards the old Hartridge Estate fishery.

As a part of her conscientious effort to be more sociable, Phoebe was determined to be a better friend to party-loving Juno, who had recently moved back to her native Britain after twenty years in the States and was eager to build a tribe. They'd partied together back in the nineties when Phoebe had been the up-all-night hedonist, as Juno was fond of reminding her, although they'd not been close back then.

The more she was getting to know the lively, generous woman with whom she'd been little more than a passing acquaintance in their twenties, the more Phoebe sensed Juno's unending positivity was a side-effect of all the trauma she'd bottled up, her natural effervescence and concern for others masking her own cares. Losing her soulmate and husband, Jay, had affected Juno deeply. The humour that had once paid her rent as a stand-up comedian was more urgent these days, covering fire to her fast-beating heart. Like the frantic friend-making, her urgent quest for love, and even her fascination with solving crimes, it struck Phoebe as a clown's mask, shielding a more mournful resting face.

But Phoebe also knew how much this party meant to Juno, and if that meant putting on her own squeaky red nose and curly wig for a night, so be it. After failing with her metaphorical sandwich board and roller skates at The Priory the previous week, it mattered a lot to get this right for her friend.

Life is for living, she reminded herself, having repeated the well-worn mantra often since that night, particularly after learning just a few days ago that Wayne Baxendale had never regained consciousness.

Phoebe was so deep in thought she ran further than she intended, passing Valence Lock, a popular tourist spot where the River Dunnett and the North Wessex Canal joined forces to flow on towards Newborough.

The seasonal pop-up champagne bar and plunge pool there was doing great Saturday trade, beautiful young things splashing about in designer wet wear.

Not wanting to stop and pant in front of an audience, Phoebe pounded onwards with the dogs beneath the little road bridge and past the car park there, back into open country again, passing a long line of moored narrowboats before eventually pausing by a broken footbridge. There, she gulped for air, waiting for her heartbeat to come down, grateful for its fast, thrumming reminder that she was alive and kicking and could still out-run her twenty-something self even if she could no longer out-party her.

Across the water, she could just make out the grey shoulder of one of the wartime pillboxes that were dotted along the North Wexshire Canal, constructed there as gun positions in case Hitler invaded Britain by coming up its waterways. Nowadays, it was just armies of pleasure boaters who advanced en masse along this peaceful stretch, the putter of engines closing in on her from both sides, along with the swish of rapid oars as a group of kayakers swept into view, talking noisily.

Watching them pass, she called Felix, who remained a seasoned party animal.

It went through to voicemail.

Still breathless, she left a message: 'I hope the edit's going well. Let me know which train you're getting. Can you pick up some wine on your way home to take to Juno's bash? My bike has two flat tyres and I refuse to buy overpriced paint stripper from the village shop.'

Then she turned to run back the way she'd come.

By the time Phoebe had retraced her steps to the village outskirts, waiting by the gate to the bridge for the terriers to check out the old lock keeper's cottage again, Felix had replied with a curt text:

> Late back tonight, if at all. Buy paint stripper.

Phoebe gritted her teeth irritably, flicking onwards to a new message from Juno who reported that Mil had several gazebos but no time to bring them to her:

> He says he's working this evening! I am livid.
> He's dead to me.

Three lines of angry emojis followed.

Surprised, Phoebe stomped across the grassy-topped old canal bridge before cutting along the footpath known as Witch's Broom to The Barton Arms, which Mil ran with older brother and chef, Albie.

The riverside pub was quiet, just a few afternoon drinkers

out on the terrace that overlooked the bubbling Dunnett to the still canal alongside it. Landlord Mil was on the phone, his kind, craggy face frowning in concentration.

'What's this about you missing Juno's housewarming?' demanded Phoebe.

Mil waved at her to be quiet. '...Celiac... vegan... nut allergy... yes, I've got all that... Eight o'clock, sir, no problem!' He ended the call, cheek dimples deepening guiltily as he told Phoebe, 'Albie's on holiday with the family. Like I told Juno, I can't get away. It's just me and a temporary chef tonight. Even Courtney's let me down, saying she's going round to a mate's.' His teenage waitress – a fiery member of the Welch clan – was notoriously unreliable.

'So, come after last orders. Knowing Juno, the party will only just have got going.'

'Big village cricket match tomorrow,' he grimaced. 'Our old skipper's coming back for it especially and he's on our case to get an early night. He's a mean bastard.' His hangdog look was overplayed.

'Since when did a big game stop you partying?' she scoffed, wondering what he was really avoiding.

'You haven't met this captain. Ask Felix, he knows him. And he's playing too.'

It was the first Phoebe had heard of it. She suspected her husband had forgotten. He was consumed by work right now.

That's when it occurred to her that Mil's hard-grafting, conscientious sports professional act could be a ploy to score more runs than Felix tomorrow. The two men were absurdly competitive. Either that, or Mil had a surprise planned.

'You'll have to party hard enough for the rest of us,' he was telling her ruefully.

'I'm a lightweight; I won't last past ten.' She'd been hoping to make that nine. 'We can't let Juno down, Mil. Felix will be there for her, no matter how late.' She'd make certain of it.

She would have liked to add how worried she was about their friend, but loyalty and good manners prevented her.

And Mil, like Felix, just saw the social butterfly who brightened up Inkbury's social scene.

He looked notably more enthusiastic now he thought Felix was prepared to break team orders. 'Bound to be a wild night. I'll try to show my face if I can.' He glanced down at his reservation book and blew out through his lips doubtfully.

'That's the spirit! Hollow legs before wicket,' Phoebe encouraged, remembering to ask, 'Can I buy some wine from you?'

He produced a brace of bottles. 'On the house for a fellow Village Detective. Talking of which, have you found out any more about our late cricket captain's suspicious death yet?' When she looked blank, he clarified. 'Wayne Baxendale?'

'Wayne wasn't murdered, Mil. He had a heart attack. I witnessed it. If the coroner had any suspicions, they'd have called for a police investigation by now.'

He looked unconvinced. 'The Case of the Graveyard Ravers is still unsolved.'

Phoebe gave him a long-suffering look. 'The what?'

'I messaged the Village Detectives WhatsApp group about it a few times. Juno's already on it.'

'We're not detectives, Mil.'

'We've solved crimes. Juno's designed a logo and everything.'

Phoebe was reluctant to make investigating Wexshire's criminal underbelly a regular thing. Especially not if that involved finding out who was dressing up the oldest church gravestones in plus-size ladies' underwear. She had so far studiously ignored Mil's WhatsApp messages, photographic evidence, video footage and voice notes.

'They struck again last night,' he told her darkly. 'Two basques and a feather boa on the Hopkins sisters' stones from the nineteenth century. The churchwarden wants to put up a hidden camera.'

'Good plan.' She slotted a bottle under each arm. 'I'm certainly not dusting for fingerprints.'

'Take the forensic tent with you, at least.' He produced an enormous, wheeled holdall almost as tall and broad as he was, explaining it contained a pop-up gazebo they used for occasional private events in the pub beer garden. 'Drop it off with Juno on your way back?'

'It weighs a ton,' she complained. 'You could hide a walk-in wine fridge in here.'

'Or a dead body...?' Clutching his chest and rolling his eyes, Mil feigned a slow gurgling demise, one of his favourite tricks.

Leaving him sprawled hammily across the bar, eyes gazing lifelessly up at the hanging tankards, Phoebe hauled the packed-up gazebo around to Wheeler's Yard, where Juno was in her flat above a closed-down vintage shop, counting hired glasses in a state of high angst. 'What if nobody comes, Freddy?'

'Of course they'll come.'

Only Juno called Phoebe 'Freddy', an obsolete nickname from her twenties, when she and Juno had moved in the same circles and partied every weekend.

A small, round ball of blonde-bobbed energy, Juno radiated warmth, and not just because she was constantly menopausal and pink-faced. She'd been just the same in London in the nineties, before she'd married American photojournalist Jay Mulligan and moved to New York. The comedian-turned-blogger still loved nothing more than to bring joy and tell tales. This flat was her new Jackanory set, filled with bright colours. Juno was renting it while she looked to buy somewhere locally, her life crammed into a three-roomed apartment.

Phoebe marvelled at its rare tidiness, the furniture pushed back to the walls, throws folded away. A discarded cushion caught her eye, the entwined V and D printed on it familiar. 'Isn't that the Village Detectives logo you designed?'

'All done!' Juno swung around and dropped the empty glass box over the cushion before Phoebe could stoop to pick it up, smiling brightly. 'Now I need your help, Freddy. I'm horribly short on men.'

'So I heard from Mil. But who needs eleven sober ones obsessed with hitting leathery balls?'

'What are you talking about?'

When Phoebe explained about the cricket match embargo, Juno's big grey eyes widened with horror. 'Is that why Mil's not coming? Who is this captain? I have a very female-centred guest list. Those missing cricketers could totally wipe out my testosterone factor, and let's not forget the umpires. This is desperate! I'll put the word out.'

Picking up her phone, she fretted through her contacts and WhatsApp groups. 'Even my son isn't coming.'

'Is Eric on one of his...?' Phoebe didn't know the correct terminology for the strange, competitive world Eric Mulligan occupied. All she knew was that Juno's only child had dropped out of a lucrative GCHQ traineeship and was currently floating round on a houseboat playing competitive video games for a living.

'ESport tournaments,' Juno finished for her. 'He does it all the time. Making a fortune by all accounts, although you wouldn't know it, and he's clearly in complete denial that he's about to become a father.'

The reason that Eric had dropped out of GCHQ was because he'd got his much older boss pregnant, the brief affair now over. While sanguine Eric was chill about this as all things, Juno was finding the fallout hard to handle. Not only was the baby unlikely to feature much in hers or Eric's lives, but the prospect of becoming a grandmother sat badly with her renewed quest for youthful love and abandon.

It was another reason Phoebe feared this party was an ill-timed displacement activity to mask Juno's rising panic. She'd given up a busy, fulfilled life in Brooklyn to come back to England and look after her son and her elderly mother, only to find one off grid and the other on fire; Juno's mother had found love with silver fox Dennis.

It worried Phoebe that Juno had so far done little more about finding work than daydream about starting a detective agency. Like her lacklustre love life, it was far easier to fantasise a fresh start than enact one. Juno needed income to stop herself burning through the money from selling up in Brooklyn, but she complained that she wasn't qualified to do anything much except crack jokes, not all of which landed.

Throwing parties was a familiar artform, by contrast, although her guest list was X chromosome heavy.

Juno was still scrolling her phone's screen furiously. 'Why do I know so few men? I used to know lots. Is it a midlife thing?'

'A single woman thing, maybe,' Phoebe suggested.

'I'd invite all my Bumble matches if I hadn't deleted my account. There were plenty of those. This new dating app I'm on only offers one at a time.'

'I thought you'd given those up?'

'Men or apps?' She looked up with a deflecting smile.

'You told me you wanted to try dating in the wild again, after what happened last time.' An unfortunate experience with a serial philanderer she'd met online had almost landed Juno in deep water recently.

'This is super exclusive. Cheryl from Clubbercise met her millionaire through it' – she looked up dreamily for a moment – 'and he's whisked her off to his Greek villa. It's called Dapper and Discreet.'

'The millionaire's villa?'

'The app.'

'Sounds like a concierge service.'

'I suppose it is, for midlife romantics. Oh!' She covered her mouth guiltily. 'I'm not supposed to tell anyone about Cheryl.'

'I'm in too deep now,' Phoebe deadpanned. 'Spill.'

'It's very hard to join – there's a waiting list and a selection system – so Cheryl helped me jump the queue with a member referral. Men are only allowed in if they're worth a packet, but it's easier for women.'

'This has scam written all over it,' Phoebe warned. 'Run a mile.'

'It's legitimate, I promise – it's recently been bought by one of the dating app giants like Match. But it's all a bit weird. Everyone has cartoon avatars with masks on and usernames like Shadow Rider.'

'I repeat, run a mile.'

'It's weirdly sexy. Think masked ball meets Marvel.'

'What are you?'

'Curvy Kitten. Here's my avatar.'

Phoebe studied it in alarm. A voluptuous cartoon version of Juno winked back, wearing cat ears and falling out of a red bustier. 'This is practically hentai.'

'There are limited design options. You only get to share real pics from your private gallery when you've exchanged a qualifying number of DMs. It's all fiercely monetised. Male members must buy credits to send messages.'

Phoebe laughed drily. 'Male member being the operative word once the private gallery's open, I'm guessing. What about women?'

'Oh, everything on the app is free for us.' Juno beamed, then looked at the screen doubtfully. 'That's actually a bit sketchy, isn't it?'

'How many matches have you had so far?'

'Just one, Green Man, a food-loving financier and Arctic Monkeys fan. He sent a wink yesterday – that's free, I think. I messaged last night saying I'm looking for laughter, cuddles and a thatched cottage. I'm still waiting to hear back.' She looked wistfully at the phone again, then squeaked as it lit up and started to buzz.

'Is that him?'

'No, it's my second reminder that I'm late for my pre-party pamper appointment next door.'

Juno was a loyal supporter of her neighbouring beauty salon whose treatments and makeovers she plugged on her popular Mother Love blog in exchange for a hefty discount.

She'd started to flap again, panicking afresh as she looked from To Do list to phone screen to wall clock. 'It's a promotional thing with an Insta Live, so I can't let her down. Oh, heck, I can't believe it's past four already. I must collect the nibbles from the deli before they close! And I haven't set up the karaoke or tested the disco ball! Not to mention trapping Kevin Bacon the cat in my bedroom. What's happening to me? I used to be good at throwing parties!'

To Phoebe's alarm, big tears were forming in Juno's grey eyes, her limitless good humour for once up against a wall.

'Let me help.' Phoebe put a steadying hand on her shoulder. 'I'll start by going to the deli for you.'

'Oh, would you? You're a life saver. Autumn, who works there, has my order set aside – she's the barista with blue hair – and I'll give you some keys so you can bring it all in here.' She reached for her handbag, fishing out a set. 'If you see Kevin Bacon, will you shut him in my room? Also, how good are you at putting up pop-up gazebos? It'll need fairy lights and maybe some seats if the deli can spare some of their café chairs?'

Phoebe held on to Juno's warm, round shoulder a little longer. 'Calm down, enjoy yourself. It will be wonderful.'

'Freddy, I love you, but I haven't scheduled time for pep talks.'

They set off across the sunlit Wheeler's Yard together, watched by Phoebe's terriers who were still tied up outside the vintage shop, both now flat out in the shade of two planters spilling with purple lobelia.

The pretty cobbled courtyard had once served Wheeler's Butchers Shop, which still boasted in black lettering on its gable wall that it had first purveyed the finest meat in Wexshire in 1837. Its old outbuildings had been converted into artisan retail units, some with accommodation above: a beautician, florist, framers and the quirky vintage goods shop above which Juno lived, Mr Benn's Favourite Emporium. Tucked behind Church End in sleepy Inkbury, most struggled for trade compared to the bustle of nearby market towns like Marlbury and Newborough. Many villagers barely knew of their existence. By contrast, eager proponent Juno was a one-woman loyalty scheme.

As Juno swung excitedly through the door of the beautician's, Phoebe headed round the corner to Inkbury's smart little deli, a cottagecore confection of striped awning and arty Aboards offering in-season produce, its shelves lined with overpriced organic Wexshire fayre, its café serving Spanish lattes and herbal teas to the few villagers who had the time and money for it. Juno was on first-name terms with all the staff, but Phoebe never shopped here. Its tooth-breaking artisan bread cost almost as much as an amalgam filling.

The girl at the counter wore silky football shorts and a faded, oversized Wham! t-shirt, and indeed had hair the same bright azure as raspberry bon bons, matched with multiple piercings and sleepy painted eyes. Two equally languid student types were draped on barstools nearby, gazing at their phone screens whilst chewing impassively on cinnamon swirls like cattle on cud, flakes snowing down on the marble countertop. Phoebe guessed Autumn's friends were taking advantage of an end-of-day lull to make sure the leftover breakfast pastries didn't go to waste.

'We were going to carry the party food round to Juno's place in a bit,' Autumn told Phoebe when she introduced herself, her voice a lethargic drawl that could make a shopping list sound faintly ironic.

Juno had predictably ordered enough trays of food for a wedding reception.

'We'll help you take them now though, if you give me time to lock up,' Autumn offered, summoning her friends who groaned good-naturedly. Like Autumn, they looked as though they'd be more at home in thirties Berlin or a seventies artists' commune than sleepy little Inkbury.

One was heavy-lidded with a beautifully insolent pouting mouth and Lord Fauntleroy blonde curls; the other had a choppy black on-trend pixie haircut, shaved eyebrows and an amused, red-painted sneer that reminded Phoebe of her own almost four decades earlier. She also felt sure she knew them from somewhere.

'C'mon, Xanthe, you can't refuse to carry anything that's not vegan,' Autumn badgered as Pixie-hair slid reluctantly from their stool, grumbling.

'River promised me the disaffected Inkbury Genzees still hung around in graveyards, not in delis playing packhorse.'

'You know full well we do!' scoffed the boy, who must be River.

Phoebe took note, thinking about the Graveyard Ravers.

'Only at weekends,' tutted Autumn, explaining to Phoebe, 'Xanthe's a backwoods hermit these days, but they grew up here.'

'They forsook us!' River put an arm around them.

'Until you found me again and brought me home.' Xanthe laid a long kiss on his Cupid lips, humming indulgently before they went full-tongue snog. Soon, River was wearing most of Xanthe's lipstick.

As they kissed on, Autumn cleared her throat, whispering to Phoebe, 'PDAs give me the ick, but they're still very new to the best-friends-to-lovers vibe. I like your tee.'

Phoebe looked down, realising she'd thrown on an old Royal Blood tour t-shirt of Felix's to run in.

'I can hum more of yours.' Phoebe nodded at Wham! Like Autumn, her own daughters wore more of her generation's pop icons on their chests than their own.

'Bet I can hum just as many.'

'Let's not test it.'

They shared a smile and Phoebe felt a pang of longing for her sensible, sardonic, sleepy-voiced daughters, currently working and studying overseas.

'You're Juno's writer friend, aren't you?' Autumn asked as

they all walked to Wheeler's Yard together carrying trays. 'The one who helped her find the postman's murderer?'

'That's right.'

'And you live in the big house across the river?'

'Yup.'

Food trays rattling, the other two quickly closed in, Xanthe demanding, 'The stately home?'

'It's not ours,' Phoebe deflected vaguely. It wasn't very stately either; a crumbling empty country pile she and Felix were house-sitting for his distant family while its late owner's estate was settled.

'Isn't your husband some sort of movie producer?' asked foppish River.

'Something like that.' Phoebe found people's interest inevitably transferred to Felix with indecent speed.

But to her surprise, the beautiful youth cast her a sceptical sideways look from beneath his heavy eyelids. 'Dying art, movie-making – gaming is the future. We all want to have narrative autonomy nowadays.'

'You have a point.' Her narrative autonomy longed to be starting on its edits instead of herding snacks for Juno.

Skirting past the excited terriers, she led Autumn and her friends into the old shop below Juno's flat, leaving the trays of food on the disused counter. Hiding behind it, the cat Juno had adopted with her rented flat was hissing through the windows at Phoebe's dogs.

'Hi, Kevin,' said Autumn, stooping to stroke the black and white mog.

'I think he's usually friendlier,' Phoebe said as Kevin puffed up like a two-tone pompom and shot behind a wicker bookcase. The she remembered too late that she was supposed to whisk Kevin Bacon to the safety of Juno's bedroom ahead of the party.

There was another hiss as the cat shot out from behind the bookcase and, dodging Phoebe, disappeared into the clothes racks of vintage fashion.

'This place is so dope.' Autumn was admiring an original 1977 *Star Wars* poster. 'We used to come here a lot once. Shoplifting, mostly.'

'The guy who ran it was a total pothead,' River told Phoebe.

'Are there going to be any drugs at Juno's party?' Xanthe asked hopefully, trying on a rainbow bucket hat.

'Rescue Remedy, Rennies and HRT,' Phoebe predicted. 'Are you coming?'

'I promised Juno I'll pop by,' Autumn sighed, picking up a pair of John Lennon-style dark glasses from a stand on the counter and trying them on. They suited her pretty, heart-shaped face perfectly. 'Should I bring anything?'

'Men.' Phoebe glanced across at the girl's two friends, both fascinatingly androgynous, one wrapping round a feather boa while the other shrugged on a sequinned waistcoat. Surely they were prime suspects for the Graveyard Ravers?

Then she reminded herself she was not playing detective.

'Sweet.' Autumn was admiring her reflection in an old pub wall mirror that was advertising Bacardi Breezers. 'I am up for that.' She looked over the rims at her friends. 'What about you two? Nothing else going on in this backwater.'

'We've got plans.' River blew Xanthe a smouldering kiss, donning a fascinator and Elvis shades while they slipped on mirrored Aviators and pulled out a phone to take a selfie of the three of them pouting and mewing, 'Can we have these clothes as thanks for helping you?'

About to say no because they weren't hers to give, Phoebe

changed her mind. 'Pop up a gazebo for me, and they're yours.' She'd slip a tenner in the charity pot on the counter, she decided.

While they were all unfolding the great metal frame and dragging the canvas roof over it, she asked the trio if they knew anything about the voluminous lingerie and party clothes appearing randomly on the church's oldest gravestones.

'No idea!' they chimed so perfectly in chorus that she was certain they were lying.

3

JUNO

Juno loved hosting parties. When she'd lived in New York, she'd thrown plenty, her legendary BBBs – Bacchanalian Brooklyn Bashes. This was her first on British soil in over twenty years, and she had one strict house rule.

'Just nobody get killed tonight!' she told the crowded room cheerfully.

It was still early, but her little apartment was bustling, all the seats taken, voices rising and falling, glasses clinking. Her tympany! So what if it was currently more like a Jane Austen tea party than rock and roll orgy? Things would hot up later, she reassured herself.

On the sofa, Phoebe was wedged between Juno's chatty mother, Judy, and her octogenarian friend Pam, both under strict instruction to keep her from bolting home too soon. Antisocial Phoebe hated parties, making Juno doubly grateful she'd been amongst the first to arrive, even if she did look as though she was nursing an abscess in a dentist's waiting room.

Lucky to get a seat, thought Juno cheerfully, grabbing a bottle to top up guests' glasses, starting with her own.

Her party had been in full swing for just over an hour, and a gratifying number of people were here in her little rented flat, its stairwell and the shop below.

'This is quite some soiree, dear child!' crooned her soon-to-be-father-in-law Dennis, stepping forward, bouffy white hair gleaming like a silk turban. 'Such an *eclectic* guest list.' He was brandishing a platter of savoury beignets in one hand and a bottle of prosecco in the other. A social butterfly with waspish determination, Dennis had appointed himself co-host. 'Seeing as you don't have a chap to do it, eh?'

'I'm on the case with that, Dennis. No rush.'

Juno refused to let her romantic ice age cast a chill over her housewarming party, although she was alarmed that her amorous ambitions seemed to be a running theme; perhaps her guests had misinterpreted her last-minute shout out for more male invitees?

'Juno, girlfriend, we were just saying we must get you that man you keep banging on about! How's online dating going?' came an air kiss from one side as a blonde Welch siren breathed in her ear, 'Did you sign up on that app Cheryl recommended?'

'Midlife mojo's best kept secret?' Juno scoffed, although the truth was she'd checked it ridiculously often today.

'We all call it the millionaire app but keep it to yourself, remember,' the blonde whispered, putting a finger to her pouty lips. 'Shh!'

She moved on, and Juno tried to remember which Welch siren she was, the prosecco already muddling her head. They all looked like former Gladiators, and she knew Mil had gone out with several of them. He had a soft spot for Welch women, she reflected grumpily, suspecting he wouldn't use a staff shortage and a Sunday cricket match as an excuse to miss one of *their* parties.

Which made her even more grateful for dapper discretion.

Thrillingly, Green Man had messaged her while she was in the beautician's salon, a full-credit, paid-for DM, albeit just seven words long.

> Passing through Wexshire tonight, are you free?

Which was typical of Juno's luck. The one night she was committed! She'd hummed and hawed about inviting him to her party before deciding against it. She needed him to ask her more about herself before scoping her immediate availability. So she'd replied with a flirtatious emoji wink and *next time*.

'Early days!' she told Dennis brightly, hoping he hadn't heard her midlife mojo slip. 'I'm following all leads.'

'Keep investigating, darling girl.' Dennis winked before leaning in to offer canapés to the occupants of the sofa.

'Juno, is it true you're starting a detective agency here?' asked Pam, selecting a beignet.

'Wild rumours,' Juno said vaguely, although out of the corner of her eye she was alarmed to spot that Phoebe had again unearthed one of the cushions bearing the logo she'd designed for the Village Detectives and was examining it with interest. She thought she'd hidden all the promotional merch.

Hurrying downstairs to the shop below with her bottle, Juno sensed a pre-tsunami shockwave rippling through her guests there, a collective intake of breath, a sudden hush and then...

'We're *here!*' There was a cacophony at the door as two new arrivals made a noisy entrance like a holiday camp Redcoat double act determined to ramp up the fun.

'Debra! Rich! Welcome!' She rushed to greet Inkbury's self-styled power couple, the Basses.

Debra was dressed in her usual leopard print, plumped Mrs Potato Head smile grimacing from the waxy Botox mask. Beside her, Rich leered in white linen, mahogany tanned and wrinkled, like a paper-wrapped pepperoni with googly eyes pinned on.

'Babes! The fun has arrived!' cried Debra, sashaying up to Juno brandishing a champagne jeroboam before whispering in her ear, 'I am getting *trolleyed*. Rich is driving me *mad*!'

Although Juno rather enjoyed Debra's brazen energy at Clubbercise classes, she'd quickly gleaned that she and her retired businessman husband were almost universally loathed in the village. Some locals unkindly called them the 'Basstards'. Despite being relatively recent incumbents – which in Inkbury meant this side of the Millennium – the Basses had muscled their way onto every local club committee, from which they micro-managed the community with the fierce entitlement of an HR department. When they weren't sautéing in Factor 8 on a far-flung sunbed, Wexshire's pushiest couple could be found shouting at one another in their much-extended mock-Georgian gin palace overlooking the Green, which disapproving neighbours had nicknamed Flatpack Mansion.

Such cruelty made Juno just want to embrace them all the more, although they could be rather abrasive.

'I can't believe you live somewhere like this!' Debra shrieked. 'What *is* this place? It's like Steptoe and Son!'

Other party guests were already shrinking back towards the walls, Juno noticed, as the new arrivals poked at the shop displays and clothes rails.

'You need a better gaff, sweetheart!' boomed Rich, giving

Juno a lusty squeeze. 'This place is diabolical. We'd better find you that thatched cottage PDQ.'

'I'm rethinking the affordability of that,' she admitted.

For all their brashness, Juno rather admired the Basses' non-stick joie de vivre, the fact that they were community-minded and splashed their considerable cash on local good causes. They were also what her mother snobbishly called *nouveau riches*, which to Juno's mind made them excitingly racy, glitzy and forever eighties.

And having Rich here doubled her man count.

'You're looking very tasty tonight, sweetheart. Shame I'm on a diet.' He was still squeezing, making Juno's generous cleavage rise like soufflés. He'd once been something big in kitchens, she gathered, before selling his company for a fortune and retiring to the Home Counties to fashion himself as a Wexshire investment dragon. With his gleaming wire wool quiff and hard, appraising eyes, his was anodised self-confidence.

'*Watch out*, Juno babes, my husband's incourage— incorrige — a randy sod!' Debra sneered as she ripped into the champagne foil with long gel nails.

'I love younger women,' he growled in Juno's ear, 'especially beautiful ones.'

'Flatterer.' Juno played along whilst subtly trying to extract herself from the clinch.

'Debs tells me we need to set you up with a fella.' Rich still hadn't stopped squeezing. 'She can't help playing Cupid. Gotta have a soulmate.'

'Last one died!' Debra popped the cork loudly.

For a moment, Juno thought Debra meant Jay, and a vice of pain and hurt gripped her throat so tight she couldn't speak.

'Wayne!' Debra reminded her husband. 'I was going to fix

him and Juno up on a blind date, remember? Only he met that woman online he was obsessed by.'

'Great bloke, Baxendale. God rest him.'

'Wayne Baxendale?' Juno jumped on the name gratefully, realising they meant the friend who had keeled over in a Dunford boutique hotel, witnessed by Phoebe and Dennis. Her imaginary spyglass was already poised. 'I heard it was very sudden?'

'Yeah. Told me he'd got a hot date and then, phut!'

'You don't think that's suspicious at all?' she asked lightly.

'Don't worry your head about it, gorgeous,' Rich told Juno's breasts. 'He's no good to you now, and Debs tells me you need a man with plenty of get up and go, eh?' With a Carry On cackle, he gave her another squeeze.

Starting to feel claustrophobic, Juno reminded herself to be less loudmouth about her barren love life. She must wean herself off making it her new comedy turn. Much as she longed for an old-fashioned hero – one strong and fast enough for Bonnie Tyler to hold out for 'til the morning light – that was no reason to make a song and dance about it. And men like Rich inevitably saw it as an invitation to play panto villain.

Beside him, Debra's taut face was now looking a lot less friendly, her Mrs Potato Head smile now upside down.

'We do actually know someone, don't we, Rich, babes?' she said as her husband reluctantly let Juno go. 'Grant!'

'You'll need ear protectors,' warned Rich.

'My brother used to be in a band,' Debra told Juno. 'He's *very* rock and roll.'

'If you like shoe-gazers.' Rich chuckled, checking his phone, which was chirping with notifications.

'Depends if we're talking Louboutin or Birkenstock,' Juno

said vaguely, spotting Phoebe sneak past with her vape, giving both Basses a wide berth.

Debra gave a gratifying cackle of laughter. 'Hilarious! You and Grant are made for each other, aren't they, Rich?' Realising her husband was now too busy looking at his phone to respond, Debra pulled Juno closer, confiding, 'My little bro's a man's man – builder, likes a pint, looks like Danny Dyer. Makes beautiful traditional-style homes.'

'No profit in it,' Rich sneered, still scrolling his phone.

'He's a true craftsman,' Debra sighed, admiring one of the many big solitaire diamonds adorning her thin, tanned fingers. 'And you can't buy love, can you, Juno, babes?'

Rich pocketed his phone and cupped his wife's much-lifted face with his hands, his own many chunky rings like golden knuckle dusters indenting her tight skin. 'Not a love like ours!'

Both Basses laughed, Rich's hooded eye gleaming, Debra's false lashes batting.

'Don't you ever forget it, Rich,' she growled in an undertone.

'More than my life's worth!' cackled Rich. Still harrumphing happily, he took the jeroboam and headed off to hail fellow villagers with overbearing bonhomie, repeating: 'More than my life's worth!'

'Never a truer word,' Debra breathed, rolling her eyes. Then she turned to Juno brightly. 'You *must* meet my little brother Grant, babes. You'll cheer him up no end. He's been ever so sad since his separation.' She lowered her voice, looking pained. 'You remember how tough it is.'

'I'm widowed,' Juno reminded her, feeling angst spike, her eyes automatically seeking out Phoebe through the open door. She was edging across Wheeler's Yard towards Church End and escape.

'Shame,' Debra sympathised absently. 'When did he die, your fella?'

Heart racing now, Juno felt her throat tighten as it always did when asked about Jay, the uncertainty of it all stifling her, that vice at her throat once more. 'A while ago now.'

'So it's time to have some fun!' urged Debra, looking round. 'Not many fellas here.'

'Blame the village's puritanical stand-in cricket captain and a grudge match tomorrow,' muttered Juno.

'It should be poor Wayne captaining, not him.' Debs's Botoxed forehead strained with the effort of looking sad. 'You have no idea how devastated Rich is that his friend's passed.' She pretended not hear the boom of laughter from her husband across the room. 'Wayne had so much to look forward to. But that man always lived in the fast lane, babes. "Bring the party" was his motto. He and Rich are very alike in that way.'

'No pre-match curfews when Wayne skippered then?'

'Rich is playing tomorrow,' Debra revealed conspiratorially, glancing across at her husband again, 'but we paid for the new pavilion and I do the teas, so nobody tells him he can't let his hair down the night before a game.' Eyes narrowing, she watched him pouring champagne into the all-female guests' glasses in exchange for a kiss. 'More's the pity.'

Then she let out her bright bell of a laugh, fluffed her hair, rearranged her leopard-print cleavage and turned to look around the shop. 'Is your sexy film director friend from Hartridge here yet?'

'Felix is coming later, but his wife's already here and she's fabulous. Do you want me to introduce—'

'Oh, no need to bother her. Look, there's Bethany!' She whisked off.

Juno hurried outside to top up Phoebe's glass. The sun was

dropping out of sight beyond the roof above the florists' shop, the party fairy lights starting to sparkle magically. 'You're not leaving?'

'Of course not.' Phoebe looked longingly out to the lane before pointing back at Mil's pop-up gazebo glowing with its firefly strings of lights. 'I'm just enjoying the festival vibe out here.'

'Alone?'

'Moths will gather to the flame, just you watch.'

'You promised you'd be more sociable, Freddy. Come inside and let me introduce you to the Basses,' Juno urged. 'Debra's dying to meet you.'

'No, she's not,' Phoebe deduced succinctly. 'Something's up, isn't it?'

With her big, heavy-lidded green eyes, beaky nose and full curling mouth, there was an air of the vintage aristo about Phoebe, Juno always felt. Her long-necked, androgynous beauty belonged to another era, one in which she'd have crossed remote deserts on an Arab stallion or flown Tiger Moths solo across vast oceans. Tonight's sleeveless camel polo neck and white chinos had strong Amelia Earhart vibes.

Phoebe was also one of the most insightful and fearless people Juno knew. Which was why Phoebe had clearly guessed Juno wasn't enjoying this party as much as she should.

Realising she hadn't brought her own glass out with her, Juno swigged straight from the bottle, reluctant to admit the truth. That she kept thinking about Jay, about forsaking their little Bay Ridge house for an English village flat with a paranoid cat and a shipping container crammed with memories. But Juno couldn't bring herself to admit that to Phoebe whilst standing out here with party guests still arriving and her game face on.

They had another shared interest that would deflect her attention.

'Detective itch,' Juno told her.

'Probably midges.' A cynical eyebrow lifted. Yet the way Phoebe had her arms folded right now, sucking in one cheek, eyes creased in concentration, was classic Freddy on a case.

'You feel it too!' Juno realised with relief.

'Mmm.' Phoebe wrinkled her noble nose as she thought about it. 'I have a hunch they might strike again tonight.'

'Another murder!'

'Who said anything about murder? They're headstones. It's a bit late to suggest foul play.'

Juno realised her mistake. 'You're talking about the Graveyard Ravers, aren't you?'

Before Phoebe could answer, a group of new arrivals spilled in through the gates: pub quizzers and members of her book club, Clubbercise ladies, more Welch family members and two elderly village stalwarts, Ree and Bernard Cole. Another man, Juno realised gratefully, as Bernard waved a bottle of homemade wine at her.

Raising her own bottle in a cheerful welcome, Juno whispered urgently to Phoebe, 'I have a bad feeling about tonight, Freddy.'

'You have guests to greet.' Phoebe stepped beneath the awning's shadow.

'What about our detective itches?'

'Do *not* scratch. I'll keep watch out here.'

4

PHOEBE

For the next hour, as more villagers arrived at regular intervals to cram inside Inkbury's old vintage shop, Phoebe remained outside gathering her 'moths', the vapers and the smokers standing in the lowering sun or clustering beneath the gazebo, chatting and chuckling while those inside burbled in tight queues for the stairs, food, drinks and the loo.

'Bit stuffy in there,' said Ree Cole, hurrying out with a cigarette packet. A wiry village sage known for her technicolour allotment and plain speaking, she grumbled, 'I thought Juno was an original raver. I've been to livelier WI cake sales. Only the Basses are partying hard.'

'Probably why everyone else is wall-flowering,' said one of the book club crowd.

Juno was constantly drawn outside too, pink cheeks toned down by the cooling night air as she welcomed arrivals, topped up glasses and grabbed a chance to mutter increasingly inebriated asides to Phoebe. 'Still just five men, average age sixty. I don't think anyone's having much fun.'

'It's what my girls call "chill",' Phoebe reassured her.

'That's what Alexander the Great died of,' Juno sighed, helping herself to more fizz before turning as another group came through the Wheeler's Yard gates, calling back, 'Don't go anywhere, Freddy. Stay alert!'

Bestowing welcoming whoops and hugs upon each new arrival, Juno accompanied them inside to pour them a drink and introduce them to others before she hurried back out to rejoin Phoebe on the cobbles, whispering for her to be their eyes and ears. 'What have you found out so far?'

'The village knitting circle are making festive tree waistcoats to decorate the lime trunks along the High Street, but I don't think they're our Graveyard Ravers. Did you invite *all* the village?' Phoebe watched another couple troop in.

'I hope so,' Juno said eagerly. 'I'm gathering suspects. I need your gut instinct, Freddy. Hello! Welcome!' She leapt into hostess mode once more.

Phoebe felt the Graveyard Ravers hardly merited this level of surveillance. But she sensed that Juno's detective itch had less to do with a rash of suspicions than finding Inkbury didn't party quite like Brooklyn. If Juno was feeling as homesick as Phoebe suspected, she needed her friend to have her back. Bitter experience had taught Phoebe that life's lemons weren't best served in party cocktails.

She longed to be home. Every fibre of her being craved solitude, books, tea, the radio, a leisurely message exchange with her daughters, sister, or old friends that required no small talk and no standing around in high heels. She wanted to close her eyes in Hartridge's cavernous silence and idly imagine a day when her home would once again be her own, a blissful point in the future that she had to trust was approaching at greater speed than her demise.

Like Juno, Phoebe was disorientated to find herself living on shifting sands this far through life. The twenty-first century had been far less kind to her than the twentieth. In recent years, finding her health, career and home all under terminal threat had made Phoebe reluctant to party like it was 1999. She wasn't shy, nor remotely misanthropic. Phoebe liked people; just not en masse, perfumed and eating finger food. She quietly adored Juno who, for all her bluster and fuss, was deeply kind. But much as she appreciated Juno's mantra to dance like nobody was watching, Phoebe preferred to do so at home, safe in the knowledge that they really couldn't be.

'Got a light?' It was Zadie Welch, one of the village's glamorous Amazonian tribe, at least two of whom Phoebe had spotted at the party, homogenous in their blonde, wise-eyed beauty.

Phoebe had spoken with Zadie a few times when investigating the death of art dealer Si Locke, who had briefly been Zadie's lover. Another of her many exes was Mil, who remained fiercely loyal to Inkbury's sugar-hipped, sharp-talking Tank Girl. This evening, dressed in one of his old rugby club's shirts, denim hotpants and biker boots that showed off her glossy brown legs, it was easy to see why she still held such sway over him and other male villagers.

'I'm off home in a minute,' she told Phoebe. 'Came with my kid sister, but it's not my scene. Besides, I can't take Rich Bass; he's such a creep. No idea why Juno invited him.' She checked the time on her watch, an oversized men's chronograph. 'You up to much? Still snooping, I hear.'

Earthy, hardworking and better than the sum of all her ex-partners, Zadie was a useful finger on the pulse of Inkbury's shadier side, and she had a firm grip on the scruff of its disaffected adolescents' necks through her teenage kids.

She could help with Juno's detective itch, Phoebe reasoned,

telling her, 'We're looking into whoever is dressing up the church graves.'

'Hardly a crime.' Zadie looked away, puffing on her cigarette. 'What about Wayne Baxendale's death? Pegged it a couple of weeks back, didn't he? All a bit dodgy, Juno says. I heard you were there with him.'

'I was in the hotel bar,' she said vaguely, wondering what exactly Juno had been saying.

'No disrespect, but I'm not shedding any tears.'

'You knew him?'

'Wayne was even creepier than his mate Rich.' Zadie shuddered. 'Always out cruising in those old throwback cars of his. Used to come in the garage where I work, smarming about calling me "Juicy Fruit" and telling me what he'd like to do with me. Kept mistaking me for my little sister, and when I put him right, he just said he couldn't tell us Welches apart because we're "all slappers".'

'He said that?' Phoebe was shocked.

'Okay, so maybe he said "cheeky minxes" but it means the same thing. People round here are too quick judge my family, but it's dirty old bastards like him and Rich who should be called out.'

Phoebe would have liked to ask more, but Ree Cole was bustling back out with a refilled glass and her cigarette packet, and Zadie made for the lane, muttering that she wasn't 'hanging round for that old bat to give me another earful about my lad and his mates'.

'Always a live wire, Zadie!' Ree told Phoebe. 'All the Welch girls are. No discipline growing up; they ran wild; their children are as bad.'

Which rather proved Zadie's point, Phoebe felt.

'It's her boy and his gang who keep vandalising the church headstones if you ask me,' Ree went on in a loud whisper.

'What makes you say that?'

'Well, they're the sort, aren't they? Wear hoodies, swear non-stop, spit like llamas.' She launched into a rant about Inkbury's feral teenagers.

Half listening, Phoebe envied Zadie her escape, once again overwhelmed by an urge to run home, especially when Ree changed tack and tried to persuade her to give a talk to the WI. 'You might even sell a few of your books.'

Phoebe promised she'd think about it, casting hastily around for a change of subject: 'Did you know Wayne Baxendale at all?'

'Not from the village.' Ree pulled a disapproving chin into the folds of her neck. 'I used to do cricket teas with a lovely group of local ladies, but the Inkbury CC went to pot after the Bass-tards took over and made him captain.' She launched into another rant, this time about corporate lager sponsorship and Debra's flaccid crustless sandwiches.

Phoebe listened politely, relieved when Ree finished her cigarette, unwrapped a Glacier mint and apologised that she must go and check on Bernard. 'He's keeping score at tomorrow's match and his IBS will flare up if he eats too many party snacks.'

Before long, the little group of gazebo smokers had dispersed to top up and catch up, leaving Phoebe playing solitary sentry to the gate once again. She could hear a Blur track playing in the shop, now just as jam-packed with villagers as the flat above it. Juno was a natural befriender, a collector of people as well as objects, her life – and home – overcrowded. Phoebe doubted Juno would ever fit in the thatched 'doer upper' cottage she dreamed of unless it had an aircraft hangar attached for storage.

There were more figures coming through the Wheeler's Yard gateway. Stepping back further beneath the gazebo, Phoebe recognised two of the languid youngsters she'd press-ganged into helping her erect it earlier, and who she'd suspected of being Graveyard Ravers. Bored university students home for the summer to earn money waiting tables were far more likely culprits than village hoodies to Phoebe's mind.

She watched them closely as they paused in the arched entrance. Huddling together, heads close, they were studying the glowing screen of a phone.

Both melted back to the lane when a pouting, dishevelled blonde came out of the shop, lighting a cigarette and pulling her own phone from a small, embroidered handbag. Phoebe recognised Zadie's pretty younger sister, an unlikely fitness instructor.

Not noticing Phoebe, the blonde Welch siren tapped at the screen with a long glittery gel nail, wandering out of sight behind the florist's van.

Moments later, a tanned older man in expensively branded sports casuals stepped out onto the cobbles, shouting into his mobile with a gruff, self-important bark. 'Hello? Hello?... Where? Hello? Say that again... What, *now*?'

This had to be Rich Bass, she realised.

Phoebe's own phone vibrated in her pocket, distracting her. It was a message from Felix:

> Almost done. Might catch up with some mates at Soho House and crash there. Be back in time for brunch.

'Hello!' Rich was shouting on the step. 'No, I haven't bloody read it. You know I don't text! What?'

Phoebe, who did text, was too busy typing an angry reply to Felix to pay him much attention:

> It's Juno's party. Come home tonight or I will kill you.

That usually did the trick, but just to be sure, she added:

> ...and I'll cut up your cricket whites. You'll be going in to bat dressed like a doily.

Then she added a PS for good measure:

> Juno thinks there might be a murder tonight. Let's prove her wrong.

5

JUNO

Juno was losing her sense of time, head spinning from too much fizzy wine, the heat inside her flat making her dizzier still. When she hurried back outside and found Phoebe's moths had flown, she panicked her friend had slipped away unnoticed. Then she spotted a faint glow in the shadow of the pop-up gazebo. Phoebe was typing into her phone.

'Thank goodness! I have intel!' She hurried closer, whispering, 'More than one local source has confirmed tonight that Wayne Baxendale was a notorious business shark and serial shagger with a *lot* of enemies including The Priory's head chef, who owed him a stack of money. Could it be no coincidence that is also where he died?'

'Almost certainly pure coincidence.' Phoebe looked up from her screen.

'I thought you shared my detective itch, Freddy?' Feeling woozy, Juno caught hold of a gazebo strut, the whole structure swaying.

'About the Graveyard Ravers, maybe.'

'But I really do think Wayne might have been *murdered*.' She mouthed the word to avoid being overheard. Then she realised she had said it out loud after all. 'Oops.'

Phoebe regarded her levelly. 'You've had too much prosecco, haven't you?'

'Jus— eep!' Juno's protest was cut short by a ripe hiccup. 'Now I'm out in the fresh air, you know, I do feel just a *tiny* bit tight.' Plastered, she realised giddily. 'Overdid the bubbles trying to liven up the atmosphere in there. It's as dead as poor Wayne Baxendale.'

'*Not* funny.' Phoebe was reading an incoming message.

'Sorry. You're right. Please tell me that's Felix to say he's on his way?' Juno swallowed down another hiccup. 'I *still* only have five men, although Rich Bass is packing enough machismo to fill Stringfellow's.' She pointed across at the leathery retired kitchenware magnate who was standing on the shop's step shouting into his phone that he couldn't hear whoever was at the other end.

'I guessed that must be him.' Phoebe glanced up at him, narrowing her eyes.

'We need Felix's cool.' Juno realised she was swaying again, and grabbed hold of the gazebo which started swaying along too. 'He's not working all night, is he?'

Handsome, charming Felix had been uncharacteristically tetchy and unshaven of late when he was around, which wasn't often. Although vague on detail, Juno was aware his current movie was over budget, had an issue with its distributors and was proving a post-production nightmare.

'The edit suite is booked until ten' – Phoebe pocketed her phone again – 'after which he's promised he'll be on the last train, especially now I've reminded him about tomorrow's cricket match.'

'Isn't this team curfew ridiculous? Rich Bass says the stand-in captain is a little Hitler,' Juno lamented, watching him stomp back inside. 'I really think they should have postponed the match out of respect for poor Wayne.'

'And your party,' Phoebe said with a wry smile.

Juno was too squiffy for irony. 'I can't believe Mil might not even come tonight, and Felix won't be here for *hours*. The Village Detectives should *all* be here. There might have been a' – realising she was almost shouting, she dropped to a whisper – 'murder!'

'Do you want there to have been one?' Phoebe asked matter-of-factly.

'What sort of a question is that?' Juno was deeply hurt by the insinuation that she had a macabre death wish. 'It's my itch.'

'You don't think it's a bit far-fetched imagining a man you've never met – who died from a heart attack in front of multiple witnesses – was murdered?'

'Put like that...'

'So Wayne Baxendale was a bit of a bastard, but he wouldn't be the first arsehole to enter asystole, would he?'

'No.' Juno felt too crushed to ask what asystole meant.

'It's a complete flatline cardiac arrest,' Phoebe enlightened her. 'Almost inevitably fatal.' Then her face softened. 'Yet despite all that, I trust your itches.'

'You do?'

'They're oddly infectious.'

Juno smiled gratefully, feeling strangely emotional. 'Oh, I wish all the Village Detectives were here! You, Felix and Mil.'

Glancing up at the flat's windows framing multiple chattering silhouettes, she realised that they were the three people she cared about seeing most tonight. Her squad. 'This party is to celebrate our success.'

'Yes, I spotted the branding.' Phoebe bit on a smile, eyebrows lifting. 'You don't think having VD emblazoned on your soft furnishings sends out the wrong message?'

'Perhaps I got a tiny bit carried away,' Juno acknowledged, grateful she'd hidden the coasters, mugs and tote bags. 'And I *know* I need a proper job, but trust me, it's a *nightmare* over fifty when you've done nothing but stand-up comedy and blogging since your twentieth-century degree.' She turned to see a slender, blue-haired figure in combats and a leather corset loping in through the Wheeler's Yard gateway. 'Autumn, darling! Can I have your job at the deli when you go back to uni?'

'They hardly ever pay me!' Autumn laughed, her crazy-coloured double buns jiggling as she bounced along on thick rubbery boot soles. 'Ask the boss here.'

Then Juno's jaw dropped. Because behind Autumn was a man. And *what* a man.

Thunderbolts.

Tunnel vision.

She didn't recognise him from the village. With peppery hair, dimpled chin and an apple-slice smile, he was just Juno's type.

Autumn started to introduce them. 'Juno Mulligan, this is—'

'Cosmo Lovat,' he said, lifting his Ray-Bans from the bridge of his straight nose to reveal searing blue eyes. His aura was pure mature metropolitan machismo, from those square shoulders through narrow hips down to his size twelve Chelsea boots. Even his name sounded like an action hero, Juno realised giddily.

'You two are so going to get on!' Autumn predicted, her voice lacking irony for once.

'Sorry to gate crash.' His hand shook Juno's, strong and confident.

'My gate is wide open,' she swooned. 'I love the deli.'

'So I've told him.' Autumn nodded eagerly.

'Shame I'm never in there.' The blue eyes twinkled into hers.

'Don't blame you with those prices,' murmured Phoebe.

Noticing her friend had her sardonic face on, Juno made a flustered introduction. 'This is Freddy, I mean *Phoebe* Fredericks, I mean *Sylvian* who is—'

'Felix's lovely wife.' Cosmo turned, smile deepening the dimple in his flinty chiselled chin. 'At last. We all thought he was keeping you locked up.'

A cross expression replaced the sardonic one. 'Perhaps I was keeping Felix locked out.'

Juno could tell Phoebe was bristling at being husband-named.

Smile fixing, Cosmo seemed uncertain what to make of such dry humour.

'Phoebe writes brilliant books!' Juno told him.

'Good to hear,' he told Phoebe. 'Your Undomestic Goddess column was my guilty pleasure way back in your heyday.'

Phoebe looked even more prickly at the suggestion her heyday was long gone. 'How do you know Felix?'

'Through Inkbury CC's First Eleven.'

'First four, you mean,' corrected Autumn, amused, 'plus whoever else can be blackmailed or bullied into making up numbers. Our village cricket team has a captain problem,' she explained to the others.

'The incumbent one just died, sadly,' Cosmo took over

briskly, 'and so his forerunner's been drafted back in. *Very* competitive skipper.'

'So I hear!' Juno turned to beam at him, holding up the prosecco bottle she was carrying to refill guests' glasses. 'And I probably shouldn't offer you any of this! I gather he's a ridiculous old fuddy-duddy about players getting early nights before a match.'

'I am.' Cosmo smiled briefly, the blue eyes developing icy chips.

'You're the captain?' Juno stuttered, mortified.

'Used to be. Acting captain now.'

'He's hardly ever in the village any more!' Autumn scoffed.

'I'm mostly in London these days,' Cosmo explained, 'although I still have a house here.'

'And a business,' Autumn reminded him. 'Which Juno loves. We all look forward to her coming in to make our day because she's the GOAT, which is why I wanted you to meet her, remember?'

Cosmo's handsome smile was looking even more fixed.

'I'm being a terrible hostess!' Juno overplayed the bonhomie, hoping he hadn't misinterpreted the 'goat' thing; Gen Z slang could be tough to navigate. 'Let me offer you both a drink! Something soft, I take it, Cosmo?'

'Hardcore for me,' Autumn drawled.

'Thanks.' Shooting Autumn a tetchy look, Cosmo turned to Phoebe again. 'I gather we have good friends in common, the Seaton family.'

'Oh, I haven't seen them in ages!' Phoebe's face lit up. 'How are they?'

'Show me to a beer.' Autumn took Juno's arm, marching her away and murmuring, '"Old fuddy-duddy" is priceless; he thinks he's still so relevant.'

'I'm sure he is.' Juno glanced back, mortified she'd just been a drunken klutz.

'He likes naff nineties indie, Ricky Gervais and being pompous about cricket, politics and the ULEZ,' whispered Autumn. 'He's only acting uptight because I told him how gorgeous you are, and now he's seen it for himself he's tongue-tied. Give him five minutes.'

Juno felt a rush of grateful affinity, reluctantly abandoning the handsome gate crasher with Phoebe to lead the way inside, where the party atmosphere was at last livening up, the chatter at high volume, bass beats thumping through the floor as personal space was forgotten and drunken dancing began. Debra had annexed the old karaoke machine that Juno had set up and was now singing 'Like a Virgin' on an echoing microphone, whilst glaring at her husband, with several of the Clubbercise ladies 'ooh ooh-ing' on backing vocals.

'Please tell me there's someone else under forty here.' Autumn stood in the shop door, scoping the mature crowd. 'That is tragic.'

'Oh, there are some youngsters!' Juno promised, grateful that she hadn't arrived during the line dancing to 'Achy Breaky Heart'.

A leathery figure swaggered up, dissipated white smile flashing.

'Juno! Bubbles for the bubbliest hostess!' Rich was once more in possession of the jeroboam, distributing champagne and largesse, his hooded eyes on the hunt for gratification. They trailed their way slowly up Autumn's young body. 'Summer, darlin'! How's your dad?'

'It's Autumn and put your male gaze away, mate. You can ask him your—'

'Great party, shweetheart!' Rich wasn't listening, turning to fill Juno's glass, his seedy focus landing on her cleavage once more, like a wasp on sliced ham.

It was hard to tell if he was slurring or doing a Bogart impression, but Juno – who couldn't forget Debra boasting that her husband scored record innings while she served winning teas in the pavilion – felt it best to warn him in a stage whisper, 'Our puritanical village cricket captain's just arrived!'

'Acting captain,' Autumn demoted.

'Forgive me, young lady, but that man is a bellend.' Rich chuckled, trapping the big champagne bottle under his arm so he could top up his own glass. His phone started ringing as he did so. 'Better get this. Expecting an important call. Excuse me, ladies. Hello... *Hello?* Yes, it's Daddy. Hello?' He headed back outside, champagne splashing in his wake.

Juno watched him, momentarily baffled by the 'Daddy' because as far as she was aware, Rich and Debra had no children.

'Bass-turd's so cringe.' Autumn shuddered. 'Comes in for a caramel latte most mornings, says he likes drinking Cosmo's profits.' She took Juno's hand to lead her through the shop. 'Those two hate each other.'

'So Cosmo owns the deli?' Juno asked breathlessly as they made their way through the throng. Their progress was hampered because she kept pausing to ensure her guests had full glasses and good company.

Herding her along like a sheepdog, Autumn explained, 'It's not his primary business. He bought it for his wife as a project, but she wasn't interested.'

'Where's she?' Juno asked as they queued to get upstairs behind slow-moving Bernard Cole and his walking stick.

'Holly died eighteen months ago.'

'That's tough.' Juno felt a painful stab of empathy.

'She was a bitch,' Autumn said in a flat voice.

'Still, it must be hard on him. The first year or so is the worst.'

It had been seven years since losing Jay, but Juno wasn't sure she'd ever be over it. She wondered if Cosmo also threw parties on landmark dates to blot out the loneliness, then wished he was having a giggly night in with close friends. Did he also cry in the bath and have a recurring dream that his wife was still alive, she wondered. Perhaps he, too, carried his dead spouse's old business card tucked amongst his bank cards and driving licence.

Jay Mulligan
Photojournalist
New York

Maybe it should come as no surprise that his absence kept hitting her afresh again, tonight of all nights. Jay. Was. Gone. The planet around which her own had once orbited, along with their one precious moon.

'My son Eric was supposed to be here,' Juno told Autumn over-brightly as they climbed the stairs. 'I'd love for you to meet him, but his eSports team's through to a grand final tonight.'

'That's gas! Who does he play for?'

While Juno usually found anyone over thirty needed a careful explanation of her son's money-making pro-gamer side-hustle, Autumn was straight onto it. She started chatting about a friend who wanted to be a games dev as Juno led the way to the kitchen where an ice bucket was filled with bottled beer. Juno was grateful that there were some youngsters upstairs, hurrying to introduce Autumn to the funky mechanic couple she relied upon to keep her on the road.

The three beautiful young things chatted easily, fast to bond, and soon sharing delighted laughter over a ludicrous but loveable repeat customer with two cars currently in for repair, first a racy Mini she'd owned for two days before pranging it on a driveway, '...and then her mother's hatchback ended up in the River Dunnett!'

Juno, who was that customer, caught herself slipping into a stand-up routine – 'My motor insurance premiums include therapy sessions!' – but it was gratifying to keep them in stitches.

'*Don't* tell my dad that story,' Autumn warned her, wiping her eyes. 'He has beef about stuff like that, and as if you hadn't noticed, I'm trying to set you two up.'

Juno was confused. 'Who's your dad?'

'Duh, Cosmo?'

'Cosmo's your *father*?' Juno gaped at her.

'Didn't I say? I thought you realised. I just assume everyone knows I'm the deli nepo-baby. Sorry. When Dad said he'd be in Inkbury for cricket this weekend, I insisted he had to be my plus one tonight. I've been badgering him all summer to come and meet you.'

Realising she was deemed a worthy match for Autumn's own father, Juno perked up even more. She just needed to make up for a poor first impression. 'I must take him out that soft drink and some nibbles.'

Autumn put a hand on her arm.

'Thing is' – she lowered her voice – 'I haven't told Dad about you being an amateur detective. But you should know what happened to my stepmother in case he says anything.'

'Was her death... suspicious?' Juno asked, her detective itch flaring like prickly heat.

Autumn glanced across at the mechanics who were

selecting fresh beers and pretending not to listen in. 'Holly drove into a wall at high speed the morning after her fortieth birthday party.'

'How awful!' Juno gasped.

'There were no witnesses, no other vehicles involved; they found nothing wrong with the car. It was brand new, a birthday gift from Dad. She was crazy hungover, but the postmortem found she'd been legal to drive. The coroner recorded an open verdict, although Dad's always blamed her party DTs and bougie birthday wheels, hence he doesn't drink any more and now drives an ancient banger with a top speed of fifty.'

'That "banger" easily does a ton,' corrected one mechanic. 'A 1982 Merc SL convertible. Beautiful. We used to service it when Mr Baxendale owned it. Looked after all his vintage cars.'

'Wayne Baxendale?' Juno squeaked in recognition.

'He was our best customer.' The other heaved a rueful sigh. 'Loved his eighties classics. I remember him saying he'd sold his Merc to a mate.'

Juno's prosecco-diluted mind was still on a go-slow as she struggled to cram more pieces into her Wayne Baxendale puzzle. Could Holly's death somehow be connected to his?

Before she could make any sense of it, Dennis sprang into her little group with an oval serving dish. 'Can I interest anyone in a meatball slider or cauliflower popcorn?'

'Yum.' Autumn took one of each. 'These aren't from the deli.'

'Judy made them,' confided Dennis, pointing at Juno's mother. 'She doesn't trust that place.'

'Can't blame her.' Autumn nodded earnestly. 'They employ slave labour.'

'Good grief, really? Did you hear that, Boppa?' Dennis called to Judy on the sofa. Moments later, the blue-haired student was sitting beside the one-time TV cook, regaling her with deli counter scandal. Perching on each arm, the mechanics listened in.

Leaving them all chatting – and hoping her own three-a-day Danish pastry deli habit wasn't mentioned – Juno helped herself to more prosecco, taking the bottle with her for good measure. She then hurried back downstairs with it and a non-alcoholic beer for Cosmo, passing Debra belting out 'Born to Run' with opera diva emotional overload on the karaoke, her backing troupe miming running on the spot.

Out on the cobbles, she took a few gulps of fresh air, wishing she could stop the courtyard spinning. She shouldn't have had that extra fizz.

That's when she heard Cosmo Lovat snarling at Rich Bass just a few feet away:

'Don't bother turning up for the match tomorrow!'

'Frightened I'll score more runs than you, little man?' Rich was laughing, jeroboam nestled in one arm like a sleeping toddler. 'The club chairman always opens. You know the deal.'

'I'm not selling out to that.'

'You can't buy talent like mine, sunshine.'

'Not even from a pound shop?' Cosmo mocked. 'I heard you and Debra are so down on your uppers over at Flatpack Mansion these days, you get your little blue pills with Green Shield Stamps.'

'That dates you, Lovat!' Rich laughed louder. 'Never could keep up with the times, could you?'

'I'm not the one paying to keep my dirty secrets up in the cloud.'

'And you'll crash and burn if yours ever comes out, little man!' Rich cackled. 'Crash. And. Burn.'

'Go to hell, Bass-tard!' Cosmo looked like he might punch him.

'Guys!' Juno interrupted, reeling towards them. 'There are delicious nibbles, cocktails and mocktails upstairs! Also karaoke, vintage fancy dress and even board games—'

'Get losht, Juno shweetheart,' Rich told her in his Bogart slur.

'You need to sober up,' hissed Cosmo, which Juno thought rather gallant until she realised this might be directed at her, not Rich.

Focusing hard on walking in a straight line, she joined Phoebe, who was under the pop-up gazebo with her vape, flanked by a brace of old-school smokers. To one side, a roll-up glowing between her lip-fillers, was Juno's Clubbercise instructor, the hippy-chick cousin of Cheryl's with dreadlocks, a Welch siren whose name Juno was too squiffy and hyped to remember. To her other was Ree Cole from her book group, sneaking yet another drunken ciggie while husband Bernard wasn't looking. All three were watching the altercation on the cobbles.

Juno edged closer to Phoebe, enunciating carefully under her breath, 'I'm sure this isn't just about Rich drinking the night before a cricket match.'

'Stop scratching that detective itch,' Phoebe reproved, watching the men circling one another trading insults, 'although Cosmo's a testy sort, isn't he?'

About to agree that Cosmo Lovat was very tasty indeed, Juno realised her mistake and said nothing, watching him bark across the cobbles that there was no way he was fielding Rich tomorrow.

Rich was swinging the jeroboam like a cricket bat now, demonstrating his superior stroke skills.

'I wonder what it's really about?' Juno mused.

Earwigging in, Ree Cole reported eagerly, 'Those two have never stopped locking horns. Bernard says it's because they're both ultra-preeners.'

'Vain, you mean?' asked Juno.

'Business ultra-preeners!'

'Entrepreneurs,' Phoebe deciphered. 'Which means it's probably about money.'

'Or sex.' The hippy chick fitness instructor held up her phone like a Regency fan to shield her mouth, leaning towards the other women and speaking behind it. 'They're a pair of rutting old stags.'

Still shamefully struggling to remember her name, Juno tended to agree. Circling each other like two bare-knuckle boxers working out where to land the next punch, the men were now deriding one another's bowling.

'You give us more no balls than a eunuch colony, Bass!'

'Your googlies fall short, Lovat!'

'Is *this* the real grudge match, I wonder?' murmured Phoebe, watching Rich sneering at Cosmo about his weak spin.

'No, that's Inkbury versus Upper Lambford tomorrow,' said Ree. 'Always brutal. St John's Ambulance draft in extra volunteers.'

They all fell silent as Cosmo howled, 'You won't get away with it, Bass-tard!'

'Wanna bet?' Rich laughed uproariously. 'I do what I like round here, Lovat-boy, and don't you forget it!'

Juno started to panic that they were really going to physically fight as she watched Cosmo pacing ever faster, one fist smashing into the opposite palm, ignoring the jeroboam swinging close by.

Grabbing Phoebe's hand, she drew her urgently towards the two men. 'You must stop them before someone gets hurt!'

'Why me?' Phoebe dug in her heels. 'You're the hostess.'

'They just ignored me. You have more authorit-*eep*' – she hiccupped – 'and you're not as squiff-*eep*.'

'I've had at least four glasses of fizz.'

Then they both jumped as, wrenching the jeroboam of champagne from Rich's grip, Cosmo tried to smash it on the cobbles. But it landed intact, rolling away to slop bubbles everywhere.

'You'll suffer for this, Bass-tard!' Kicking the big bottle as he passed so it spun like an oversized teenagers' truth game, Cosmo marched out through the gates and off along the lane.

'Well, that's a relief,' Phoebe sighed, slapping Juno's back to help her stop hiccupping.

Holding her breath to swallow them down, Juno hurried forward to help as Rich lurched to retrieve the revolving jeroboam, which was still glugging out its contents.

'Waste of posh grog.' He wiped the neck with his sleeve, then shook his head before starting to pour the rest into a flower trough. 'Makes them sway prettily.'

'Don't throw it away!' The dreadlocked blonde fitness instructor hurried over to tug the bottle from him. 'I'll drink it.'

'D'you sway prettily too?'

'You know I do,' she purred.

'Then I'd better fetch you another a bottle, darlin'!' He gave a throaty laugh, patting her backside.

'You're a devil, Rich Daddy!' She weaved away with the jeroboam, pulling her phone out to take a selfie with it by the fairy lights before typing something on screen, no doubt updating her socials.

Relieved the high drama was over, Juno decided she should do the same for her Mother Love blog. At least her hiccups seemed to have stopped, although holding her breath had done nothing for her tipsy clumsiness. She pulled out her phone to capture some crowd shots, starting by inadvertently videoing her own eye.

She then tried to take a photo of Phoebe, but by the time she'd pressed the shutter, Phoebe had ducked out of shot, retreating beneath the gazebo to rejoin the smokers. She always hated being photographed.

Juno snapped Rich Bass instead, grateful for the chance to be nosy. 'You and Cosmo got very heated back there.'

The leathery face creased into a downturned smile, gaze falling straight to her decolletage. 'The man's a bellend, like I say. Should never have helped him. He owes me big time.' His phone started ringing before she could ask more. 'Hello?... Hello! *Yes, I can hear you!* Hang on – need a bit of quiet...' He swaggered out into the lane.

Juno took a few more photographs before losing interest and rejoining Phoebe. 'I wonder what the beef between Rich and Cosmo is really about?'

'None of our business.'

A thought struck Juno afresh. 'What if Wayne's death is connected to Cosmo in some way?'

'Why would it be?'

She beckoned her aside to whisper urgently, 'Tonight I learned that Cosmo's wife Holly died in a high-speed collision last year, after which Cosmo bought *Wayne Baxendale's* car. Then Rich booted Cosmo out as cricket captain and replaced him with close friend Wayne, after which Wayne dropped dead.'

'So?'

'The two deaths might well be connected, don't you see?' Juno's mind was racing: was hunky Cosmo in danger too; or was he the danger? *'This* has to be our next case!'

'Juno, we don't need a "next case",' Phoebe whispered back. 'Especially not one involving men like Cosmo Lovat or Rich Bass. The egos would take too much heavy lifting. Besides which, this is a village. People regularly buy each other's motors and play competitive sports. They rarely kill one another's friends or wives over it.'

'You said you trust my itches.'

'I do, but tonight you should be letting your hair down, having fun, singing us a song,' Phoebe sighed. 'This is your housewarming party.'

'It's already more than hot enough inside,' Juno grumbled, glancing at the shop, from which she could hear a group of her guests zig-a-zig-zigging the Spice Girls' hit on the karaoke. She was getting increasingly irritated by Phoebe's uncharacteristic live, love, laugh soundbites, which she sensed might well be a result of those four glasses of fizz. She herself was fast sobering up again, the feeling of dark foreboding returning. She needed more bubbles. 'Perhaps I should just pop in and let Autumn know her dad's left. You keep watch in case he comes back and lamps Rich.'

But when Juno hurried back through the shop to the stairs, her path was blocked by her elderly mother making her way slowly and noisily down, assisted by Dennis. 'It's no good, Pusscat, I must go home. Need to be close to the china frog, you understand.'

A few steps ahead of Judy, clearing the way, Pam steered Juno aside to explain. 'Nobody can go to the lavatory because someone has been locked in there almost twenty minutes.'

'Awful gut rot!' Judy called as she picked her way down. 'Must have accidentally eaten something from the village deli. Oh, there's karaoke down here! I would have done my Aretha Franklin if I'd known. Too late now! Fetch the car, Doobee!'

Before she could dash upstairs to determine who was barricaded in the loo, Juno found herself trapped in a long round of noisy, kissy farewells, obliged to listen to her mother saying how many guests had enjoyed speaking with her, 'apart from my own daughter who I've barely seen all evening! That blue-haired girl is sweet, isn't she? Told me all about her father looking for love again. He sounds quite the catch.' She shared a lusty wink.

When they'd finally got Judy into Dennis's shiny red Range Rover, Pam squeezed Juno's shoulder and winked. 'You bright young things can party without us oldies to worry about now.'

Waving them off, Juno briefly savoured being thought of as a bright young thing, although in truth she doubted their departure dropped the average guest age below fifty.

Which meant there were a lot of bladders under threat.

She hurried up to the locked loo, which she'd now quite like to use herself.

'Hello, it's Juno here.' She knocked gently on the door. 'Is everything okay?'

There was a long, loud raspberry sound from the other side, which she hoped was somebody blowing their nose. The alternative could ruin her party hostess reputation, as well as that of the deli.

'Are you unwell?' she asked the door. 'Can I get you anything to help?'

She heard sobbing.

'May I come in?'

A lot more nose-blowing ensued before Juno was admitted entry. Inside, she found Debra Bass with a bottle of vodka and panda eyes, giving it the full soap opera diva in an exaggerated stage whisper: 'He's gone too far this time! I am going to kill him, babes! I mean it.'

'Are you talking about Rich?'

'Who else? I just heard from Michelle who heard from Lindy who was told by Gemma that her mum spotted him on the treadmill in the David Lloyd yesterday. Rich said he was at the driving range!'

'Right.' Juno nodded, trying to keep up.

'He's been *working out* at the *gym*!'

'Isn't that a good thing, health-wise?'

Shaking her head vehemently, Debra downed a hefty swig of vodka, closing her eyes tightly to swallow it before taking a deep, shaking breath. 'Don't tell anyone, Joo babes, but Rich isn't the paragon he makes out. He was having extra-marital relations until very recently.'

'Really?' Juno tried to sound surprised.

'Not for the first time. He has a *very* high libido. Powerful men often do.'

'Gosh.'

'Rich had promised me all that was behind him – and we've both taken steps to spice things up in that department – but as soon as he started on the skinny jabs, I guessed he was at it again. It's the same every time: always on his phone, deleting his messages as soon as they're sent or read, goes online incognito, smells better than usual, and *works out at the gym*.' She took another swig and grimaced. 'Our holiday in the seashells, I mean she sells, the Seychelles, was supposed to be a reset, and I thought we'd put on a united front tonight, but he's still got that look. He keeps checking his phone, jumping on every call. I think it's the same woman. I can't bear it. It's not over at all.' She broke into racking sobs. 'They're back together!'

'Are you sure? Have you any proof?'

'Oh, I always know.' Debra mopped her eyes with her wrists. 'First thing tomorrow, I'm calling our solicitor.' Hiccupping, she eyed the empty bathtub forlornly. 'What will happen to the dog though? Bullet is our baby!'

'Maybe have it out with Rich first?'

'You're right,' Debra said in a small, tight voice. 'But I won't believe he has mended his ways until he swears on his *life*.'

'Good for you. Get out there and tell him you want to talk to him.'

'Are you *mad*?' Debra squeaked, red eyes blinking fast from the mascara-stained Botox mask. 'I can't let anyone see me like this! Half the village is here. Tell Rich to come up, will you, babes?' Then she added in a far deeper growl, 'Or I'll kill him.'

Slipping out of the bathroom and apologising to the small queue waiting outside that it was still occupied, Juno went in search of Rich.

Downstairs, the karaoke had been appropriated by retiree busybody Bernard Cole and Oscar from the antiques shop, both dressed in Panama hats and dark glasses, performing 'Soul Man' to an eager, clapping crowd.

There was no sign of Rich.

Nor was he outside, where Wheeler's Yard was now hosting more than just the smokers and vapers as guests spilled out onto the cobbles to party al fresco. Beneath the light-festooned gazebo, Phoebe had attracted her many moths again, all chatting animatedly, fumes rising. The jeroboam bottle stood beside Ree Cole like a dog sitting at heel as she beckoned her in. 'Join us, Juno!'

'Has anyone seen Rich Bass?'

'Didn't he say something about going to fetch more champagne?' said one of the group.

'He kept shouting into that phone of his,' said Ree.

'Saw him heading off along Church End,' said another.

Gnawing her lip, Juno turned urgently to Phoebe to

breathe, 'Loo siege situation going on inside with repeated death threats,' before asking the group: 'Did you see anyone leave with him?'

There was no sign of Cheryl's hippy-chick cousin who had called him 'Rich Daddy', she realised. 'Where's thingamabob, the fitness instructor? She's one of the Welches. Beverley or Britney maybe?'

'The tarty young one with the big mouth and dreadful hair?' asked Ree.

'That's her!' Juno said without thinking.

'If you mean me, I'm here,' growled a voice, a familiar dishevelled blonde stepping forward, roll-up in hand, eyes bright with offence, 'and it's Bethany.'

Juno felt her cheeks flame, furious with her boozy tongue and foggy brain.

'No, not *you*, Bethany! You're not Beverley!' she fudged, catching Phoebe's arm and drawing her aside to confide, 'I need your help, Freddy. I can't get Debra Bass out of the bathroom and I must wee. Also, you're right, I'm obsessing about murder. And I'm drunk, only I thought drinking fizz would make me happy, but I keep wanting to cry and forgetting people's names. And I'm no good at throwing parties any more.' To her mortification, big fat tears started plopping out.

'You're a brilliant hostess,' Phoebe reassured, cupping her cheeks with her hands and sweeping them away with long windscreen-wiper thumbs. 'It's a great night. Everyone's loving it. *I'm* loving it.'

'Really?' Juno studied the bright spots of colour in her friend's high cheeks, the clever green eyes phosphorus with good humour, and realised she was telling the truth. Was the only person not enjoying her housewarming Juno herself, she wondered?

'Let's spring Debra out,' said Phoebe, leading the way.

In the shop, Oscar was now singing Frank Sinatra. Some guests were ballroom dancing, others were playing board games. Bernard was tackling a jigsaw puzzle. Vintage clothes had been raided from the rails, along with all the dark glasses from the till counter display. Juno prayed her landlord would forgive her for a bunch of nostalgic middle-aged party anarchists going rogue.

Upstairs she leant against the wall to catch her breath, wishing she'd eaten more and drunk less, while Phoebe shooed the queue away from the bathroom door before addressing it matter-of-factly. 'You must come out now.'

Another long nose-blowing raspberry came from the other side.

'Where's Rich?'

'We can't find him.'

'Then I want to go home,' Debra said in a small voice between sobs. 'Is there a back door?'

'There's only one way in and out.'

'I must not be seen!'

'We could smuggle her out in disguise,' Juno suggested to Phoebe in a low voice. 'There's a lot of retro gear in the shop.'

'Don't be ridiculous,' Phoebe muttered back before addressing the door briskly. 'I'll walk you home, Debra.'

It opened a fraction. 'I'd like the disguise, babes.'

Debra looked dreadful, wobbly and half-focused, the Botox mask and Mrs Potato Head smile rigidly fixed in place, her thick eye make-up now dispersed across her nose and chin like bruising.

'*Nobody* can see me like this, understand, but I won't wear anything from that horrid shop.' The sound of whoops and laughter from downstairs made her step back.

'I have a headscarf and some dark glasses you can borrow,' Juno offered.

'Are they designer?'

'Absolutely!' she bluffed, dashing off to pull a shawl from a side-table lamp and fish around in her bag for her oversized Jackie O shades. As she did so, she felt heart palpitations and panic grip her once more, the same sense of foreboding that had mugged her all night.

'You okay?' Phoebe asked.

Juno was shocked to find the backs of her eyes hot. *Please, not the tears again.* What fresh menopause hell was this?

'I'm more worried about Debra,' she whispered.

'I'll take care of her. You look after your guests. Enjoy your party.'

'I don't think I like parties as much as I used to, Freddy.'

As she said it, there was a great roar of noise from downstairs. Male voices. Whoops and cries. Swearing. And a familiar bellowing Wexshire burr: 'Where's the sexiest detective in Wexshire? Juno!'

'It's Mil!' Juno realised delightedly, hurrying to the top of the stairs to look down. A swarm of wide striped shoulders greeted her.

Men!

Lots of men.

She recognised several faces – along with cauliflower ears and broken noses – and turned back to Phoebe, elated. 'He's brought the local rugby team with him!'

At this, the bathroom door slammed shut again.

Juno stared at it guiltily. The noise downstairs was getting rowdier. 'I just hope none of them have weak bladders,' she panicked.

'Go down and greet them!' Phoebe urged. 'I'll sneak Debra out.'

Juno hugged her gratefully. 'Promise you'll hurry back? We can sing a karaoke duet: "Psycho Killer" or "Smooth Criminal" maybe?' She was already halfway down the stairs. 'Your choice!'

Much later, Juno would wish she'd suggested anything but those songs.

She'd been tempting fate.

6

PHOEBE

Getting Debra Bass out of the bathroom took all of Phoebe's steely wile and most of the rest of the bottle of vodka.

Thankfully Juno's remaining guests were too distracted by a quintet of strapping rugby players blasting out the Backstreet Boys' 'Everybody' on the karaoke to notice her smuggling a head-scarfed woman past them through the shop.

Reeling home, resembling the plastered ghost of Princess Margaret in dark glasses with a fake Hermes scarf knotted under her chin, Debra drunkenly recounted the story of her husband's affairs to Phoebe as they walked. There had been many. She was already at double figures by the time they passed the war memorial.

'Rich saystheymeannothing, that he's jushtalwaysrandy.' Her voice was flat and slurred, the words blending together. 'I think he's turned on by all the secrecy, but they destroy me.' She veered off towards the duck pond and Phoebe steered her back.

'He usetogo on these boysown golfingtrips with Wayne. To Thailand, youknow? I tries to turnablineye, but in then I had toputastopit. Snotlike his handicap improved and he got terribly prickly heat. Oops!' She turned a heel and lurched into Phoebe.

'I'd do anything forthatman, babes, *anything*! You don't want to know the lengths I've gone to to fulfil his sexual fantasies. Let's just say I never thought I'd get the baby oil out of the Egyptian linen, and we'll leave it there.'

Phoebe hoped Debra didn't regret confessing all this by morning, or better still, she didn't remember their conversation at all.

The Basses' house was impossible to miss, being the biggest, the newest and the only floodlit one amongst those skirting the village green, like a luxury yacht moored amongst old sailboats. Phoebe knew some locals called it Flatpack Mansion, but she rather admired its garish splendour.

It took Debra four attempts to enter the right electric gate code. Then she couldn't get her key to fit in the front door lock, so Phoebe took over and opened it.

Whilst lit up from the outside, inside was in darkness. A very yappy dachshund greeted them in a light-up LED disco collar, a beeping alarm warning somewhere behind him.

Rich was clearly not back yet.

It took Debra even more attempts to input the alarm code. 'Shtayandhaveadrink!' She cannoned through an archway into a cavernous kitchen, where she approached a wide American fridge in a drunken zig-zagging line, like a dressage horse.

'Maybe I can make you a cup of tea?' Phoebe followed reluctantly.

But Debra was already extracting a bottle of rosé. '*Never* have caffeine after lunch, babes.' Swinging off a wall cupboard handle, she wrenched it open and stared at the glasses inside.

'Bah!' She closed the cupboard and lifted the bottle to her lips, not realising the screw top was still on it.

Phoebe searched around for a kettle.

'There's a blingwartap,' Debra said vaguely, putting the bottle down and picking up a framed wedding photograph.

Translating drunk-speak, Phoebe located the boiling water tap.

Debra was still looking at the photograph, enunciating her words more carefully: 'You know, I was a beauty queen when me and Rich met? Miss England, second runner up, 1982. Only just turned eighteen. I could have had anyone. Rich was MFI kitchen salesman of the year. I told him I wouldn't marry him until he made a million, so he did. Took him eight years, mind you. He'd be nothing without me. He hates it when I tell him that, but it's true.'

Setting the picture down, she picked up one of Rich on a jet-ski, which she hurled across the room, followed by one of herself and Rich playing golf somewhere sunny, and Rich shaking hands with Boris Johnson. She picked up another and jabbed a finger into its line-up of men in suits. 'Like I don't know what they got up to on those business trips, him and Wayne, God rest him. Investment Angels, they call themselves. Ha! They put the sin in bloody syndicate.' She lobbed the picture over her shoulder and selected another of the village cricket team, Rich manspreading at its centre, smile matching his whites. 'He's so selfish expecting me to turn a blind eye to all his goings on!'

The picture joined the others across the room.

'Everybody knows! It's humiliating. Poor old Debra, playing the loyal wife, putting up with his wickedness. You don't think I hear them gossiping behind my back at the parish council and the open gardens and those bloody cricket matches. Well, I've had enough, you hear. *Had enough!*'

With a manic laugh, she reeled back to the fridge and started unloading its contents, lobbing them around. 'I'm in charge of cricket teas tomorrow! Thassa a joke. They can eat it after I've jumped on it!' She stamped on a wheel of cheese, inadvertently skewering it with her heel, and then slumped into a chair, holding her head. 'Feeldizzee.'

The yappy dachshund skittered across the tiled kitchen floor to snuffle after the spoils, delighted at this turn of events.

Phoebe managed to shut the dog in a utility room to stop it gorging on duck pâté and smoked salmon, then started gathering up what food she could rescue. 'You feed the cricketers exceptionally well.' She detached the cheese wheel that was still spiked on Debra's shoe heel like a jouster's ring. 'Isn't this Epoisses?'

Debra looked at it with a half-closed eye, then groaned. 'Thass for our lunch. Rich loves smelly cheese. I forgot we already took the cricket stuff over to the pavilion earlier. Rich doesn't like it cluttering up the kishen.' Bending over and groaning, she pressed her forehead to her knees. 'I need to go to bed.'

Phoebe poured her a large glass of cold water: 'Drink this first.'

There was a yap from the utility room.

'Bullet needs to go in the garden for his weewee.' Debra stood up shakily then sat down again.

'I can do that before I go.' Phoebe offered her a hand up.

Debra took it. 'Juno's right about you, babes. I don't know why everyone round here says you're such a stuck-up bitch. Take no notice of what they say. You're a diamond.'

'Very hard, diamonds.' Phoebe smiled tightly.

'We should stick together. They hate me too.'

Debra leant heavily against her as Phoebe saw her to the bottom of the stairs. 'You, me and Juno mushgo out for a girl night soon!'

'Of course.'

'Love Juno. We've gotta find her a nice man. I'm going to introduce her tomybrother. Don't let her sign up to that awful dating app, will you? Half the villagesonit. Dappy something.'

'Dapper and Discreet?'

'Thassit!' Debra's nails dug deep into Phoebe's arm. 'Tell me she's not on it, babes?'

'I can ask,' she said carefully.

'I was glad when Rich sold his share.'

'He had a share?'

'Startup capital. Swat he does. Wexshire Enterprise sex-sects-somethingorother. They investinallsorts, but I din like that one. Sunromantic. My baby brother's a catch, tell Juno that!'

Phoebe promised she would.

'I'll be fine from here.' Debra grabbed the newel post and lurched upstairs with the help of the banister, pausing after a few steps to ask in a small voice, 'You won't tell anyone what I said to you about Rich, will you? About the affairs?'

'Absolutely not.'

Debra gripped the banister, posing for her Norma Desmond moment as she looked over her shoulder, wet-eyed.

'You must know what it's like, babes,' she said. 'Your Felix strays a lot, doesn't he?'

'What makes you think that?'

'Everyone says so. Common knowledge in this village. You and me both, eh?' With a sob, she tripped her way upstairs.

Phoebe gritted her teeth as she watched to make sure Debra

got safely to the top. This was why she distrusted villages. And villagers.

She went to the utility room to let the yappy dachshund through a back door, stepping out behind it and finding herself on a mock-Italian veranda, beyond which stretched a vast floodlit garden. Coloured LEDs, trained on statuary and water features, changed hue every few seconds in a strange, silent outdoor disco show. A swimming pool gleamed through a gap in a laurel hedge, and a tennis court glowed further on, all lit up like a country club.

Phoebe pulled out her vape and wandered across the velvet-smooth lawn. The gardens backed onto the cricket field. She could see Cassiopeia's W-shaped constellation over it, recalling that Poseidon cast her up there as punishment for being vain. She hoped Debra wasn't being punished by Rich for still bragging about being Miss England second runner-up in 1982. An ageing wife harking back to her former glory was uncomfortably familiar territory to Phoebe, who knew just how cruel midlife's invisibility sometimes felt.

The Basses' little dog trotted off to patrol a late-night circuit just like her terriers did, lifting his back leg at regular spots. Phoebe got out her phone to check for messages while she waited, relieved to see that Felix had kept his promise and was on the last train. He'd be here in half an hour.

I'll meet you at the station, she replied, not eager to hurry back to Juno's noisy, rowdy party now it had been rugby-tackled. She didn't really want to go back there at all, but guessed Juno would be disappointed if Felix didn't show his face. And he was a late-night party animal, the nocturnal fox to her daytime hound.

She heard a yap from the cricket outfield and peered into

the darkness in time to see a small, low shape racing across it on the wrong side of the fence, disco collar flashing.

'Come back here!'

The dachshund had escaped.

It was *just* like her ruddy terriers.

When calling and whistling brought no joy, Phoebe tried to find a gateway to the field, but the Basses' high fence was impenetrable to all but a small sausage dog with a secret escape tunnel.

She'd have to go around the long way.

Hurrying back out to the Green, Phoebe jogged towards the cricket field's main gate on Godlington Lane, already questioning her thinking. She was sure the dog would have found his way home by the time she arrived.

Almost at the field entrance, she was forced flat against the hedgerow as a car thundered towards her not dipping its lights, its engine old-fashioned and throaty.

The Inkbury cricket club gates were locked. She climbed over them and ran onto the outfield. It appeared deserted.

Then Phoebe heard yapping beyond the slips.

She hurried in its direction, realising the barking was coming from in front of the pavilion, the building in silhouette with its bell tower pointing towards the moon.

The dog was underneath the decked seating area, growling furiously, light-up collar flashing in the gloom.

Accustomed to terrier-bribing, Phoebe was relieved to find she had treats in her pocket. She laid a trail and waited.

She could hear the throaty engine roaring back along the lane in the opposite direction. Was it the same car? As it faded, she heard feet moving at speed in its wake, a late-night runner perhaps.

At last, the little dog snuffled its way along her bait trail and emerged from beneath the decking. She grabbed his disco collar, relieved to find he wasn't snappy. Instead he seemed delighted to gobble up more bribes as she lifted him into her arms to carry home because she had no lead. He smelled strongly of Debra's perfume.

Phoebe was sure she'd left the utility door to the Bass's house on the latch when she let the dog out. But when she returned, she found she couldn't get back in. The front door was securely bolted too, an all-seeing doorbell camera winking at her. She rang it and rattled the golf caddy novelty door knocker, but the house remained silent. Debra was clearly out for the count.

'Want to go to a party?' she asked the little dog in her arms.

He looked up at her, limpid-eyed.

'Me neither.'

She rang Felix as she started back across the village green.

'Love of my life!' He greeted her with a yawn. Sleepily monosyllabic, he told her Inkbury was the next stop. He'd obviously been napping; another yawn trapped in the back of his throat. He sounded done in, asking hopefully, 'Has Juno's party ended?'

Even from the Green, Phoebe could hear the music thudding from Wheeler's Yard, along with laughter and chatter. A chorus of loud baritone whoops, rowdily cheery, suggested the testosterone count amongst late guests remained raised by quite some margin.

Ahead of her, a solitary figure in a Wexshire Warriors shirt was crossing into Church End with a purposeful bounce to their stride, backpack slung over one shoulder. Another late party guest, no doubt.

Phoebe changed her mind about Juno needing Felix to make an appearance. Tetchy stand-in cricket captain Cosmo wanted his best seam bowler on good form tomorrow, after all. 'They won't miss us, and you should rest.'

'I'm not going to argue.' He laughed softly, yawning again.

'I hope you don't mind, but I'm bringing somebody home with me.' She scratched the little dog's head then read the name on the tag on his collar. 'He's called Bullet.'

Felix's low, sleepy laugh was at its most seductive now. 'Is this when I give you my best 007 line?'

'Please don't,' she smiled into the phone. 'I just met a pissed Pussy Galore who I'm pretty certain puts her ageing Bond in bondage.' She didn't want to think about Debra desperately fulfilling Rich's sexual fantasies, or to wonder where he'd got to after he left the party, and with whom.

Bullet let out an excited bark in the crook of her arm.

Turning to see what had caught his attention, Phoebe spotted the shadowy shapes of a couple on the far side of the Green, walking hand in hand past the duck pond. They paused beneath one of the big horse chestnuts to kiss against its trunk. It was too dark to make out more than the blurriest shapes.

Barking again, Bullet started wriggling and tail-waggling furiously.

'Please don't be Rich,' Phoebe breathed, hurrying away across the lane to the High Street.

Still on the line, Felix let out another gruff laugh. 'I promise you I'm not that.'

7

JUNO

Fuelled by more sparkling wine and raucous company, Juno was determined to cast her melancholy and paranoia aside. She had the karaoke microphone in her hand and Alanis Morissette's final refrain on her lips, along with a smile she couldn't wipe. She sang 'Thank U' with all her heart, repeating the last yeah-yeahs and oh-ohs with gusto, followed by air-punching as her guests applauded and hollered, the deep and full-blooded whoops of Wexshire Warriors loudest of all.

A last, she had men! Mil had come to her party straight from calling 'Time' at The Barton Arms, and he'd brought a host of burly friends. Half his old rugby squad was at her housewarming, the manpower levels in orbit.

'Village cricketers might be on their best behaviour tonight, but we're county warriors!' was Mil's battle cry.

And goodness, could they drink. Mil had brought fresh supplies, but Juno's iced beer buckets were already empty again and the last prosecco bottle had been emptied, although she worried that she'd consumed rather a lot of that herself. Her head was spinning again, and some. They were down to the cheap plonk and canned cocktails.

Most of the over-sixties had already called it a night, but the younger revellers were digging in alongside the post-pub crowd. The rugby players had started on Jägerbombs.

This was how Juno remembered parties, she realised woozily. Her BBBs had often lasted all night, the drinks got progressively worse, and she inevitably sang.

'Thank you all so much for coming!' she told her guests as she took a bow and waved away shouts of 'Encore!'

They were also utterly exhausting. But she needed the buzz of performing to top up her oblivion with adrenaline.

The sadness wouldn't quite shift, that shadow of grief, its dark empty space where Jay had been. Juno knew he'd have hated tonight. He'd have endured it with long-suffering good humour for her sake, but he was never one for parties. Those had always been her thing. Except now they suddenly weren't.

'Mind if we have another singsong after you, darlin'?' One of the rugby players came to claim the karaoke mic.

'Please, do!' Juno gratefully made way, and moments later, they were bursting into a close harmony rendition of Boyz II Men's 'I'll Make Love to You', which wasn't what she expected at all.

Juno covered her mouth in surprise, instantly triggered. It was one of the songs she and Jay had danced to at her wedding. She'd grumbled it was a bit naff, but he loved it; he'd always had unashamedly sentimental taste in music.

Refusing to cry, Juno went in search of a drink, even though she knew she'd already had far too much. Anything to blot out the grief which refused to lie low tonight.

Mil appeared alongside her at the drinks table. 'You were fantastic singing that Morrissey number!'

'I love Alanis Morissette,' she corrected kindly, 'and thanks. That means a lot. You coming here means a lot.'

'Anything for you.' His big smile creased one way then the other. 'I'm your dream man, remember?'

She laughed, feeling happily light-headed again. 'If only you were ten years older.'

He smiled wider, creasing his eyes into sleepy crescents. 'If you're still single when I *am* ten years older, will you marry me?'

'Of course.' She played along with the joke.

'Sweet.' He turned back to the drinks table. 'Any chance of some 6X in the meantime?'

It took a moment for Juno to realise she wasn't being propositioned. She gave him a bottle from the crate of Wadworth 6X ale he'd brought along. 'It's the last one, I'm afraid.'

Opposite them, rumpled blonde Bethany was picking clumsily through the last few cans of ready-mixed cocktails, looking a far cry from her high-kicking Clubbercise persona. 'This is all rank. Isn't Rich Bass fetching more champagne? Been gone ages.'

'You invited the Basses?' Mil asked Juno, surprised.

'She invited everyone,' Bethany told him, 'although pretty much nobody under forty came. Debra Bass got rat-arsed and locked herself in the bog. Hilarious.'

'Phoebe took her home; she must still be over at their place,' Juno realised, checking her phone for messages. There was nothing from Phoebe, but a Dapper and Discreet notification told her Green Man had left her another message.

'Go you!' breathed Bethany, reading it over her shoulder. 'I *knew* Cheryl must have signed you up. And you have a millionaire match!'

Sensing Mil's eyes on her, Juno hastily pocketed her phone.

'You're right!' Bethany whispered with a giggle, pressing a finger to her big red lips. 'Shh!'

Juno glanced at Mil, who was swaying to the music, pretending not to listen in.

Still pouting, Bethany was making eyes at him. 'You're way lovelier than any millionaire I've ever met, Maxi-million.'

Good line, thought Juno jealously, noticing Mil flush.

She hurried to her little bathroom to open the message:

> Another time.

Disappointingly abrupt, but then again, he was being charged by the word. And perhaps Green Man was simply a man of few words, these two conveying with minimalist perfection that he was disappointed she'd been unavailable this evening and would love to rearrange.

She messaged back:

> Absolutely!

Then regretted the exclamation mark. Then she regretted messaging him back after midnight. Or at all.

'Jägerbomb, Juno!' shouted Mil when she came back out.

Mil is too young for me, Juno reminded herself firmly as she shook her head with a cheery smile, grabbing one of the cocktail cans and stepping outside to cool off and check her phone again. She knew it was stupid to imagine Green Man replying at this late hour, but at least it kept her mind busy, not thinking about Jay.

There was a message from Phoebe at last, apologising that she was taking a shattered Felix straight home, adding:

> Do you have Debra Bass's number? I've got Bullet here but her house is locked. I don't want her to panic when she finds he's gone.

> I'll text her, don't worry.

She typed a reply between swigs from the can, pleasantly surprised to find it was a tequila sunrise, and still cold.

'The sun always rises,' she reminded herself. 'What doesn't tequila will make you stronger.'

It had been Jay's favourite spirit.

To cheer herself up, Juno typed:

> Don't panic, Debra! Phoebe's taken the Bullet for you. He's enjoying a night of luxury at Hartridge. (And your bathroom secret's safe with us). Xxx

Then she added her friend's number.

Feeling deliciously squiffy again, she checked her Dapper and Discreet notifications, letting out an excited squeal to find that Green Man had just replied:

> I'll give you more notice next time

Juno reread the words, liking them. *Next time.* She'd been right! And he'd splashed out on a winking emoji!

She swigged some more tequila sunrise. What the hell! She was old skool partying tonight.

Eyes not quite focusing, she thumb-tapped a reply too quickly, mistyping *I lick forward tit*, which made her giggle so much she had to do a wiggly dance to stop herself weeing. She really was ridiculously drunk.

'You are hilarious, Juno!' Bethany was on the step with a roll-up, holding her phone up for another selfie. Juno waved, correcting her message to *I look forward to it (winking emoji)* before hurrying inside to the loo again.

After that, the party got very raucous, although Juno had little memory of it once she'd downed her first Jägerbomb. She certainly had no recollection of checking Dapper and Discreet again, let alone exchanging several long, flirtatious and badly mistyped messages with Green Man. By the early hours, they'd even qualified to view each other's private galleries, although she remained oblivious and, by then, unconscious.

Juno was also blissfully unaware that her wiggly giggle dance – uploaded to Insta, TikTok, YouTube shorts and X in the early hours – was getting a surprising number of views.

The only thing she was certain about, in one of her few lucid moments as she stumbled into the bathroom to gulp water from the basin tap, was that her detective itch hadn't gone away.

She stole a look at her creased reflection in the mirror above the sink, cast in daybreak's harsh, steely light. She could almost hear Jay's voice, his New York drawl husky and amused: 'Gotta bad head, aintcha, angel?'

A crash from further inside the flat made her jump.

Kevin Bacon the cat – who had spent the entire party lying low under Juno's bed – had taken advantage of the open door to go and investigate what mayhem had taken place in his domain. Finding the furniture moved and half-filled black big bags lurking ominously in the shadows, he'd panicked and sprung onto the desk before careering from it along the mantelpiece and bookcase, sending boxes, pictures, and ornaments flying.

He was now puffy tailed and unrepentant on the sofa, clawing frantically at a branded Village Detectives cushion.

Picking up a framed photograph of herself and Jay, Juno ran her finger along his lovely familiar face before sinking down beside Kevin for mutual comfort.

It wasn't her head that hurt.

It was her heart.

8

PHOEBE

Phoebe's phone rang obscenely early, the voice at the other end a hoarse hiss.

'Where is our baby boy? Bring Bullet back!'

Whoever it was rang off before she could respond.

Across the room, Felix stirred sleepily in bed. 'Who was that?'

'One of the Basses, not sure which.' She checked the time. It wasn't yet seven.

Phoebe was already dressed and sitting at the table in front of her computer. She had been up for over an hour, awake for longer, her mind full of the latest Dorothy De'Ath mystery, the first draft of which she'd started rereading to make edit notes. While her laptop screen glowed in front of her, her temporary lapdog glowed beneath.

Unlike the two terriers still snoring on the bed with Felix, Bullet was a commando-trained companion, as alert to her every move as a bodyguard, constantly Velcro-ed to her side – and knees.

'How did the Basses get your number?' Felix asked between yawns.

'Juno must have passed it on.' Phoebe closed the computer lid. 'I'd better take their dog back.'

'I'll come too.' He tumbled from bed, yawning croakily. 'Need a run to limber up for cricket later.'

'I'm not sure Bullet runs.'

The terriers were already racing towards the door, anticipating a rabbit hunt.

Bullet gave them both a withering glance, professional companion to amateur ones.

When Felix told Phoebe not to bother with the slip lead – 'Little dogs like this are bred to stay close' – Bullet cast them an even haughtier look.

For a small dog, he moved astonishingly fast, outstripping the terriers through Hartridge Woods.

'Come back here!' Felix thundered after him, early sunlight streaking through his silvery blond hair, t-shirt flapping, no match for a small canine intent on getting home.

The woods were still in high summer greens, the leaves glossily enamelled, moss lush as velvet, lichen phosphorescently bright. The dense canopy shadowed and camouflaged the speeding Bullet until he burst out through the park gates and onto the bridleway that led into the village.

'Oh, God, he'll get run over if we don't catch up!' Phoebe lamented as they crossed the canal and river bridges, Bullet a speck in the distance. She put on a burst of speed to overtake her husband and catch up before the dog reached Church End.

Thankfully, Bullet had stopped to cock his leg on the lychgate, lingering to check out a scent counter of dog markers left there. Phoebe swooped to grab his collar until Felix arrived with the slip lead.

'Blimey.' He whistled as he passed it to her. 'Those are *massive* bras.'

Phoebe straightened up in shock.

In the churchyard, at least ten headstones were decked in party gear and lingerie.

The Graveyard Ravers had struck again.

Felix unlatched the gate to take a closer look.

Shooting through first, the Sylvians' terriers were soon sniffing round the scene eagerly, tails whirring. Yapping jealously, Bullet strained and squirmed, wriggling free before the slip lead was secure. Racing across the graveyard after the others, the dachshund inadvertently hooked a bra strap over his head. Two giant padded red cups trailed behind him as he bounded off along Church End towards home.

Sprinting in pursuit, Phoebe and Felix passed Wheeler's Yard where the curtains were drawn across the windows of Juno's flat, the pop-up gazebo sheltering a large, lumpy crowd of black bin bags.

Crossing the road, Bullet dodged an Amazon van and narrowly avoided a red hatchback whose driver yelled out of its window.

On the far side of the village green, the Basses' tall wrought-iron gates were closed, and for the first time, Phoebe registered the name of the house picked out in the black metalwork golf clubs: 'GREENSIDE' on one gate and 'MANOR' in the other, with a discreet plaque beneath it, fashioned to look like a golf course tee sign, on which was etched 'Nineteenth Hole'. Beneath that an engraved metal warning read 'No Junk Mail, No Cold Callers'. Below that, and largest of all, was 'Beware of the Dog'.

Meanwhile Bullet, the dog to beware of, had vanished.

Low-profile LED cameras eyed them discreetly from both gateposts.

'That's some architectural soup.' Felix admired the house's mock Regency façade and oak-framed extensions. 'No wonder the villagers call it Flatpack Mansion.'

'How petty minded of them.' Phoebe, who had read the village history pages on the parish website and knew it had been a bungalow called Greenside up until the noughties, thought it an admirable glow-up, especially now she'd seen inside. Felix's architectural snobbery was one of the many reasons they were living in the kitchen of a vast Georgian pile, when they could be renting a far more practical small modern house. Their perpetual cash crisis was another.

He reached for the keypad intercom.

They rang the bell for a long time. There was no answer.

'Can you see where the dog went?' asked Felix.

They strained for sight or sound of Bullet.

'I'll call them.' Phoebe tried the number that had called her earlier, but it rang without answer.

'Just message them saying we dropped him back,' Felix told her.

'That's not very responsible. What if he's run off again? He went to the cricket field last night. I'll check there. You stay here and keep trying the bell in case they answer.'

Retracing her steps from the previous night, Phoebe ran round to Inkbury cricket club, its neatly mown expanse bathed in morning sunlight now, a string of puffy clouds chugging through the sky from which Cassiopeia had watched her search the same spots a few hours earlier.

There was no sign of Bullet near the pavilion, nor under its decked veranda. Phoebe hurried up its steps to get a better view across the outfield. On the Basses' perimeter fence, a wood pigeon eyed her back, then took off as something startled it from behind. Out of sight, a dog barked from the garden. Was it Bullet? As she stepped back to try to see it, she trod on something that cracked underfoot. A pair of sunglasses.

About to pick them up, Phoebe noticed that the padlock on the pavilion door was unlocked, hooked loosely through the hasp.

Surely Debra wasn't here to prepare her cricket teas already?

'Hello?' She unhooked the padlock and opened the door.

Ahead of her, the clubroom's trestle tables were already erected and arranged for the match tea, a slice of early-morning sun stabbing down at it from the fanlight, dust motes dancing. On one table was an open bottle of champagne, a flute and a smaller bottle, along with a tray of curling sandwiches.

To the left, the door to the Away team dressing room was closed, but the Home team room was open. Phoebe could see the row of hooks along one wall above the benches.

Too many coats were all hanging from one.

Then she realised it wasn't coats at all. It was a body.

Hurrying inside, she could see it was dressed in just a feather-trimmed flowered silk kimono and frilly underwear, and strung up by a ligature around the neck.

It was Rich Bass.

And he was dead.

9

JUNO

'This is *not* funny, Juno. Wake up!'

Juno was groggily aware of somebody telling her to sit up and drink her tea. Opening one eye with effort, she was relieved to see that it was just Phoebe before closing it quickly again, but not before registering that the curtains were open and late-morning sunshine was pouring in.

After a long sequence of groans, grunts and single-syllable words, Juno succeeded in stringing a sentence together. 'How did you get in?'

'You gave me a set of keys,' Phoebe reminded her. 'I was worried about you.'

Juno tried to reassure her that she was fine, but it came out as a strangled, nauseous gulp.

'Drink that tea,' Phoebe ordered. She was moving around the room; Juno heard the rustle of a bin bag. 'You were not answering your phone. When I came round here and couldn't get a response knocking on the door, I started to think there might have been two deaths last night, so I let myself in. You do realise you're still fully dressed?'

'What do you mean, there have been two – Argh!' Juno sat up too fast, the room spinning round her like a centrifuge, her stomach whizzing in the opposite direction. Groaning, she flopped back again. For a moment she thought she'd black out. Eventually, she managed to croak, 'What did you just say?'

'You do realise you're still fully dressed?'

'No – something about... death.' Juno touched her forehead tentatively. Cold, clammy and throbbing. 'What time is it?'

'Coming up to midday.'

'It can't be.' Feeling around her, Juno registered that she was not in bed as she'd first thought, but on one of her sofas. She was sure she'd been in bed at some point.

'Did you just say there's been a *death*...?' She sat up again and regretted it, eyes screwed tightly shut, bile rising.

'That's right. Drink some tea. I'll mix you a Berocca too. Then I'll tell you. After which I'm helping you clear up. This place is a bombsite.'

Even through the clanging cacophony of the worst hangover in the world, Juno heard the tightness in Phoebe's voice. Shock always made her very brusque. This was bad.

'Just give me one moment,' Juno asked faintly, still trying to remember how she'd got on the sofa. Why, oh why had she drunk so much last night? She'd been deluded to imagine she could still party like it was 1999.

After she'd managed a few gulps of tea – albeit still with her eyes shut – Juno tried to hold down a still-fizzing Berocca chaser and listened in horror as Phoebe broke the news of what she'd found earlier that morning.

Phoebe had to repeat it several times in her clipped, dry voice. 'Rich Bass, in the cricket pavilion changing room, suspended from a coat hook, wearing nothing but a flowered silk dressing gown and French knickers.'

To Juno, it sounded like a surreal Cluedo solution.

'There was no way I could revive him,' Phoebe went on. 'He was already stiffening up.'

Juno covered her mouth, bile and tears rising.

'I called 999, then I called Felix, who was with Debra Bass mixing Bloody Marys. She'd just let him in full of gratitude, because we'd brought her dog back. It was Bullet I was looking for on the cricket field.'

Juno took a few more deep breaths, eyes tight closed again. Confusion and nausea swamped her. 'Debra must be distraught.'

Phoebe was back on the prowl with her bin bag rustling. 'Felix stayed with her while I waited by the pavilion for the police. She called her brother, who sent Felix packing when he got there. The police had finished with me by that point, so Felix and I went home and drank a lot of tea and talked it through. Then I tried to call you. Now I'm here.'

'Have you told Mil?'

'Felix is at The Barton Arms now.' Phoebe started audibly gathering glasses, her voice trailing away towards the kitchen. 'I said I'd get you dressed and wheel you over there for a hangover cure lunch.'

Embarrassed by her hangover, her excess, her hopeless hostess skills and, above all, her dead party guest, Juno felt the hot lava of shame cover her. She'd predicted this, sensed it coming, had the itch. Then she'd failed to act on it, letting everyone down. 'And you, Freddy – you must be so traumatised, finding Rich like that. Are you sure you're up to talking about it with us all so soon?'

'I'm fine.' The voice softened, the pause longer. 'I'm more worried about you.'

Juno squeezed an eye open, appalled to be such an attention hog. 'I'm fine! This is entirely self-inflicted!' Far better to focus on those more deserving of sympathy, she felt. 'Poor, poor Debra.' She sagged back on the sofa. 'Rich is *dead*.' Then an illogical worry struck her. 'And what about the dog? What happened to Bullet?'

'He's fine. Turned out he was in the Greenside Manor garden with our two.' Phoebe's voice moved closer again, more glasses clinking as she gathered them up. 'But that's an odd thing. The dog tried to lead me to the cricket pavilion last night, just before midnight. Right outside.'

Juno let this sink in, wishing her head would clear. 'Did you see anything suspicious?'

'Not really. There were no lights on, the place looked locked to me.'

Juno heard her scratching the back of her neck.

'But you think it might be murder, don't you?' she breathed, her own detective itch tingling hotly once again. It was that or alcohol poisoning.

'Doubtful,' Phoebe said matter-of-factly as she unloaded yet more glasses noisily from the dishwasher back into the Majestic boxes. 'Looked like a classic case of auto-erotic asphyxiation.'

Each clank made Juno's head pound. She opened her eyes briefly again, but it was still too bright out there. 'Is auto-asterisk... I mean erotic-apex, I mean that thing you just said – is that when somebody, that is a man, accidentally strangles himself whilst having a wa—'

'It's a pretty undignified way to go,' Phoebe interrupted quickly. 'The belt from Rich's kimono was around his neck like macrame, strung up to the hooks. There was champagne and poppers and a tray of sandwiches laid out.'

'Blimey.' Juno sank back onto a sofa again, feeling

extremely nauseous now, the sun hot against her eyelids. She groped around for her bag. Where were her sunglasses when she needed them? 'And Rich was wearing ladies' underwear, you say? What *was* he thinking of?'

'Do you really need to ask?'

Still Juno struggled to make sense of it. 'You really think Rich tied *himself* to the changing room hooks in the cricket pavilion to enhance his self-pleasure?'

'It's a surprisingly common cause of death. Several thousand a year in the western world.'

'That many?'

Phoebe was full of strangely macabre trivia, which Juno supposed must come from being a crime writer.

'Debra must be in bits. Her brother's there with her now, you say?'

'Yes, he's a strange fish, according to Felix.'

'Who's the police officer in charge?' Juno asked. 'Is our friend DI Mason going round the houses, so to speak, in a nutshell?'

Detective Inspector Mason, who had investigated the recent death of the village postman, was a youthful procrastinator.

'I don't think CID are involved,' Phoebe told her. 'Doubt they will be.'

'But surely they'll investigate?'

'That depends on the coroner's verdict. There'll be a post-mortem first, so the funeral directors have whizzed Rich's body straight to the hospital morgue.'

'Wasn't there an ambulance? Forensics? Witness statements?'

'He was very dead, Juno.'

'And the crime scene? Is that preserved?'

'The police took lots of photographs and removed a couple

of bottles and a plate of sandwiches, but it's not taped up with an incident tent alongside, no.'

'Has the cricket match been cancelled, at least?'

'Yes.'

'Thank heaven for that!' Juno rubbed her eyes, forcing them to stay open and squint at her friend. 'I felt this coming, Freddy; I knew something was wrong when I heard about Wayne Baxendale dying so suddenly. Then Autumn told me about her stepmother's crash. Now this; Rich Bass, dead! There's a connection, I'm certain there must be.'

'Juno, I'm sure there isn't. None of them were murdered.'

'But what if they were?' Her brain was freezing and glitching like a laggy computer as she forced it to think. 'It must be to do with the cricket club, don't you think?'

'Let's focus on something else for a bit, shall we?' Phoebe sounded tired.

'Of course. You must still be in shock,' Juno realised guiltily.

'The Graveyard Ravers struck again last night.' Phoebe changed the subject. 'Four headstones were draped up in huge bras.'

Juno's first reaction was that this might be no coincidence if a kinky, cricket-obsessed serial killer was on the loose – and hadn't Phoebe said Rich died wearing French knickers and a flowered robe? – but she knew better than to suggest it. 'What time did they strike?'

'No idea. There were quite a few headstones dressed up this morning. Felix shared photos to the group chat.'

Juno was feeling well enough to start searching around for her phone in her pockets and beneath cushions. When she eventually located it – miraculously on its charger – she groaned at the number of messages. Most were to thank her for the party, along with a stack of photographs shared in messages and social posts. With a pang of sympathy, she spotted a snapshot of Debra singing karaoke with the Clubbercise ladies before her world had fallen apart.

Pity churned her morning-after stomach yet more, and she asked Phoebe: 'Should I send my condolences to Debra Bass, do you think? Ask if she needs moral support?'

Phoebe shook her head. 'Too soon.'

'People always say that, but I needed friends with me from the moment I heard Jay—' She found she couldn't say it.

Something made her look around in a panic, a memory of last night stirring, a momentary flashback of coming in here from the bedroom, barely awake and far from sober, searching for something, pulling out drawers and books. But the recollection faded away faster than a match struck in a storm. She stood up then groaned as the room started to spin. 'I am *never* drinking Jägerbombs again.'

'You need more tea, then a huge pub lunch,' Phoebe prescribed.

Juno made it into the kitchen, where she was faced with tray upon tray of uneaten deli food. 'Don't tell me I forgot to put all this out?'

'You over-catered.' Phoebe followed her.

'But there were lots of people here last night with the munchies. Some were rugby players!'

'You still over-catered. As did your mother.'

'Maybe we could package up some of it to take over to Greenside.'

'I hardly think Debra's going to want party snacks, Juno.'

'People always need food in a crisis, and I don't have time to throw together a lasagne.'

'I don't think you should go round there.'

'Who else in the village will be there for poor Debra? They

all avoid her. She needs a friend, especially if there is something suspicious about her husband's—' Catching sight of Phoebe's sage expression, she stopped herself.

'The police have specially trained liaison officers. Her brother is with her. I'm sure she has all the support she needs. Felix and Mil are waiting for us.'

'I'll message her, at least.' Juno went in search of her phone again, buzzing busily to itself on the sofa.

'Far too soon,' Phoebe repeated firmly.

'Perhaps you're right.' She chewed her lower lip doubtfully, overwhelmed by the number of new messages arriving, worried she'd be more burden than support to Debra right now with her delirium tremens and vibrating phone notifications.

She clicked on another shared WhatsApp link.

Then her jaw dropped as a video loaded.

'No! No! *No!*'

10

PHOEBE

Phoebe rarely gave emergency eyes to her husband, but as she steered Juno to the table he'd commandeered in a far corner of the pub beer garden, she locked straight on target.

Felix gave a ghost of a nod, jumping up to envelope Juno in a big hug. 'Darling one, what an awful village tragedy after your party triumph!'

Taking one look at Juno's grey face, he insisted she needed The Barton Arms' legendary mixed grill, a hangover cure he swore by.

'It's a heart attack on a plate, but what a way to go,' he warned.

'Unfortunate way of putting it.' Juno smiled weakly, sliding as far beneath the shade of the parasol as possible, eyes wincing. 'Must we sit outside? Bit of a sore head, sorry. All my own fault.'

Summer was toasting them with a Mediterranean-hot day, the sky a flawless blue flag, the air dancing with a confetti of butterflies and dandelion puffs. On the canal, narrowboat engines puttered and rowers' oars swished while wildfowl took splashy, quacky flight.

The Sylvians and Juno were occupying the furthest of The Barton Arms' picnic tables dotted along the bank of the River Dunnett, where they wouldn't be overheard. The terriers panted beneath it.

'It's a glorious day,' Felix insisted, basking in full sunlight, his pale hair woven with gold light, eyes at their bluest. He was surrounded by the day's papers, a throwback Sunday indulgence he insisted on maintaining. 'Refuel on Vitamin D, Juno. We need your delicious humour and brilliant intuition.'

Phoebe appreciated his capacity for largesse. Bringing Juno here in this state worried her. Yet after this morning's shock discovery, it had surprised Phoebe how urgently she'd wanted to talk to her friend about Rich Bass's death. Felix was right; for all Juno's wilder Miss Marple imaginings, she had a sixth sense for ill-deeds. And for all Phoebe's pragmatic logic, she knew something about the scene in the pavilion felt very off indeed.

Juno also badly needed a distraction.

Letting herself into the flat above Mr Benn's Favourite Emporium today, Phoebe had been quietly shocked. It made little sense why finding Juno asleep on her sofa, in her party best, affected Phoebe far more than finding Rich Bass dangling dead from a cricket pavilion hook had, but it did.

Before waking Juno, she'd carefully put all the scattered pictures of Jay back in their photo albums and frames, closed and shelved the old diaries, and binned the crumpled, tear-soaked tissues. She'd tidied away the ripped-up photographs too, all of Juno herself.

Finally, Phoebe had slid the smartphone from her friend's hand and put it on charge, quietly deleting the unsent message she was sure she'd regret when sober.

Hiding all the evidence had come instinctively to her, certain that Juno shouldn't face the morning after until her night before had been purged. The afternoon to follow was all about returning Juno to her usual cheery equilibrium, even if that meant playing along with her wilder detective imaginings.

At Phoebe's insistence, Juno had switched off her phone. The video of her dancing in Wheeler's Yard appeared to be minor collateral damage from what had clearly been a self-destructive night, but it did her no good to keep rewatching it.

Right now, she was leafing listlessly through the papers.

'Mil will be here soon,' Felix was telling her as he waved for a waitress's attention. 'Still in bed when I got here.'

'That's unlike Mil.' Juno looked up, bloodshot eyes worried. 'He must be feeling even worse than I do. He was *such* a legend last night.'

'He's not working today.' Felix caught Phoebe's eye with his own emergency signal, but she couldn't read it. 'He was expecting to play cricket all afternoon, so he got extra cover in.'

As Juno returned to leafing through *The Sunday Times*, Felix held Phoebe's eye and she widened hers back, still not understanding.

Amongst today's casual staff was Mil's sulkiest occasional waitress and another Welch, the pouting, sleepy-eyed teenage temptress Courtney who trailed up now, order pad open like a flip phone. 'You eating?'

The mixed grill was off the menu, Courtney told them. 'Everything's pretty much off apart from the roasts,' she announced in a bored Wexshire caw. 'There's some specials, but you'll have to look at the board for those. I think one's soup.'

'I might just manage soup,' Juno ventured weakly, glugging back some of her pint of Diet Coke before adding, 'followed by the roast beef with extra tatties and cauliflower cheese on the side. And please tell me the sticky toffee pudding is still on?'

'You'll be lucky.' Courtney scribbled down the order.

'Tell me, Courtney, what you know about Rich Bass?' Juno asked her in an undertone.

'That a fish special?' The waitress wrinkled her nose, glancing round at the sound of her boss coming out onto the pub's decking.

Juno's eyes brightened at Mil's familiar boom hailing his Sunday regulars with its loud bonhomie. Then she explained breathlessly to Courtney, 'Richard Bass lived at Greenside Manor. He died last night. Surely word's out?'

'First I heard.' Courtney shrugged. 'Everyone here's talking about Mil and my Aunt Beth, far as I can tell.' She glanced over her shoulder again.

They all watched as Mil sauntered towards them, wreathed in smiles, hair wet from the shower. He didn't look remotely hungover.

'Yo! Folks!' There was a new exuberance to his big-shouldered swagger.

Behind him came a familiar blonde, her dreadlocks also wet from the shower.

'I said Bethany can join us if that's okay?' Mil straddled the bench seat, patting a small space beside him.

Phoebe glanced at Juno, who had turned several shades greyer.

But ever the welcoming tour de force, Juno was already raising her Coke glass. 'Of course! Hi, Bethany.'

Too polite to point out that this was an unofficial Village Detectives gathering, Phoebe and Felix smiled stiffly as Bethany perched beside Mil. Close-to, she looked less hot, Phoebe noticed, her eyes sleep-filled and skin blotchy as mortadella, the duck lip pout in need of Chapstick. She was also wearing last night's dress.

'Shocking news about Rich.' Mil inclined his head sadly, looking up.

'May he rest in peace,' Bethany sighed, briefly making prayer hands before she turned to Courtney to order roast pork. 'No potatoes, yorkies, crackling or parsnips.'

'Make that two roast porks, and I'll have her crackling and carbs,' Mil said cheerfully.

'Gotta keep your strength up, big boy.' Bethany shared a growling laugh with him.

Courtney made a long 'ew' noise under her breath which she hastily turned into '*Two*... pork,' when her boss looked up sharply.

Phoebe observed that Juno was trying very hard to hold on to her smile.

Although she always claimed Mil was far too young for her, Juno's crush had been transparent for a while. And the feeling was, Phoebe had been almost certain, mutual. But love and grief were still too closely connected for Juno to trust. Phoebe sensed the reason she wasted so much time and energy on dating apps and websites was self-protective. Fantasist Juno built castles in the sky and dungeons beneath. It was the same reason she was obsessed with murder. She was as much a catastrophist as a dreamer.

And as Phoebe had predicted, Juno was already straight on the case of Rich's shocking and unexpected death, asking, 'Did either of you see anything odd last night, by chance?'

'He saw plenty last night!' Bethany chuckled.

There was another 'ew' behind Phoebe, where Courtney was still hovering, order pad poised.

'What time did you leave the party?' asked Juno.

'Not long after you told everyone to bugger off because you wanted to go to bed,' said Bethany.

This was obviously news to Juno. 'I did?'

'You were hilarious.' Mil chuckled.

'Mil walked me home, thank goodness' – Bethany eye-batted at him – 'or God knows what might have come of me, after what I was faced with.'

'What was that?' Juno was agog.

The damp dreadlocks swished, dark-rimmed eyes flashing. 'Never seen behaviour like it! And I went on my sister's hen weekend in Prague.'

Juno's expectant face quivered. 'What happened?'

Bethany pointed a finger at their waitress. 'Ask my niece.'

'Unfair.' Courtney's jaw cocked, an oath slipping out.

'What have I told you about swearing in front of the customers?' Mil cleared his throat, explaining, 'Bethany's place was full of stoned teenagers tinkering with the dark web. Turned out her lad had invited some mates round. So I said she could kip here.'

'We were watching *Squid Game* on Netflix!' Courtney protested.

'There were *drugs!*' Bethany growled at Courtney.

'Shrooms, Aunt Beth. Least that's what your Seph said they were, but everyone reckoned they were just enokis from that posh hotel where he works.'

'My Joseph – his friends call him Seph – is easily led,' Bethany told the others, then smirked at Mil. 'Like me.'

Mil beamed back, slowly rolled his neck to loosen it. 'Good job I'm not playing cricket. Think I pulled something last night.'

At this, Courtney let slip another 'eww', louder and longer. 'Can you all just please order?'

'Back in a mo!' Juno leapt up, belting off in the direction of the ladies' loo.

'Rein it in, Mil,' muttered Phoebe, who had credited him with more tact.

'What did I say?' He seemed baffled.

'Let's look at the specials, Felix,' she suggested pointedly. Waving aside his protest that he wanted roast beef, she towed him inside, whispering, 'Did you know about this?'

'About what?'

'Mil and that Welch...'

'Bethany.'

'Bethany, yes. Is it a casual thing, do you think?'

'The man's allowed a sex life.'

'Juno is invested.'

'Hardly Mil's problem.'

'You ready to order, yeah?'

They both jumped, realising that Courtney had followed them and was standing close behind with her pad.

'One moment.' Phoebe gazed up at the board, irritated with herself for betraying Juno.

'FYI, they're FWB, I reckon,' Courtney revealed in a stage whisper. 'It's your generation that's up for all that if you ask me. We just watch existential horror and eat exotic fungi, which reminds me' – she pointed her pen up at the Specials Board – 'swerve the wild mushrooms on sourdough. Cat sick on a doormat.'

Having been about to order it, Phoebe's appetite stalled. '*Did* you see anything odd last night, by chance?'

'Nah, same old. We were all supposed to go round to River's cos he's got decent games and gear, and Auntie Cheryl's away, but he and Xanthe were simping *as usual*, so Seph said to go to his place *as usual* and it was crap and boring *as usual*. Mum always said Richard Bass was a dirty old perv and to steer clear.'

Phoebe remembered Zadie saying much the same to her last night. The scene she'd stumbled across this morning had done nothing to dispel that theory.

'You made up your minds cos I ain't got all day?'

As soon as Courtney had gone into the kitchen with their order, Felix drew Phoebe aside, whispering, 'You seriously think a killer might have been at loose in the village last night?'

'Let's humour Juno here.'

'Why? You were only saying last week that she needs to forget all this Miss Marpling and focus more on getting work, and on Eric and her unborn grandchild.'

'This has a lot to do with the unborn grandchild, I think,' Phoebe whispered, silently adding *and its much-missed grandfather*. 'Trust me, she needs this. It's her way of coping.'

Felix nodded. He understood that the way Juno had lost Jay meant she would be forever seeking answers. Believed killed in a bombing raid after being taken captive in Syria, the war photographer's death remained so swathed in mystery it was no wonder his widow constantly sought to solve those around her, even ones she'd imagined.

They could see Juno emerging from the corridor that led to the ladies'. She'd reapplied her lipstick and fluffed up her hair, a determinedly cheery smile glued on, but her eyes were puffy and she looked greyer than ever.

'So the Graveyard Ravers struck again, Juno!' Felix launched into action, striding off to put an arm round her. 'What's your take? Could it be more sinister than we thought? You have a far better detective nose than me.'

Within a few steps, Juno was bouncing on her trainers again, tapping her small, upturned nose with one finger. 'We must gather facts, Felix, and *fast*. In fact, I spotted something earlier I need you all to see.'

'I won't blink until it's in front of my eyes.'

Immensely grateful for him, Phoebe followed them back outside, where Bethany was giving Mil a neck massage.

He had the grace to duck away when they all sat back down. 'What did you see when you discovered Rich dead in the pavilion, Phoebe?'

'Can we not talk about death, guys?' asked Bethany brightly.

'We're Village Detectives,' Mil told her proudly.

'Yeah, and I'm Veronica Mars.' Flashing a dismissive smile, Bethany crossed her arms. 'Go on then. This should be a laugh.'

Instinct told Phoebe not to reveal too much in front of Bethany, so she gave them a nominal summary of finding Rich trussed up to the changing room coat hooks, glossing over the more salacious details. Nor did she share her concerns that all was not quite as it seemed. That could wait.

Showing no such restraint, Juno took over to explain. 'We think Rich's death may be connected with up to two more suspicious deaths locally.'

'We do?' Mil looked nonplussed.

'*Two* more deaths, you say?' asked Felix, looking at Phoebe, who widened her eyes to remind him to humour her.

'It's a theory,' she said carefully.

'That's right,' Juno clarified. 'Three deaths in total.'

'We can summarise those later,' Phoebe said quickly. 'It's all still very nebulous.'

'What happened to investigating the lacy ladies' lingerie on the church headstones?' asked Mil, looking disappointed.

'Oh, that's still ongoing,' Juno assured him. 'In fact, the Graveyard Ravers may well be connected too.'

'Right-ho.' Mil nodded, smiling. 'Now we're getting somewhere.'

'What are you even talking about?' asked Bethany, looking around them all in alarm.

Mil explained about the naughty plus-sized lingerie that had been appearing on the village church headstones. 'Mary the churchwarden reckons it's village kids.'

'They're all way too busy on their screens to bother with old-fashioned vandalism,' said Felix.

'You're right, oldies would be my guess,' said Bethany, eyeing Juno, who had started leafing through the Sunday papers again. 'Reckon it's a drunken prank, something like that, so look out for the boozers. One of the am dram lot after too many clarets in the Golden Balloon, or the allotment grannies fresh from downing dandelion gin in their sheds.'

'Do you think we need to stake out the scene at all?' suggested Mil.

'Good idea!' Juno pushed several sections of newsprint aside to unearth more, clearly searching for something.

'Two of us could lie low in a car all night on Church End,' Mil went on, 'snacks, tea, banter.'

'I'm up for that,' Bethany offered.

'Here!' Juno stabbed a finger at a photograph in the obituary section. 'Wayne Baxendale! Mega-wealthy Wexshire entrepreneur. Made his fortune in ready meals and fast-food delivery apps. Friend and business associate of Rich Bass. Village cricket captain. Died a couple of weeks ago. Freddy was there!'

There was an expectant silence.

'Who is Freddy?' Bethany asked eventually.

'I am,' said Phoebe reluctantly.

'Are you suggesting Phoebe is a suspect?' Felix ventured.

'Of course not,' Phoebe dismissed. 'Wayne had a heart attack.'

'Ready meals and fast food says it all,' Mil sighed.

'He was in a Michelin-starred restaurant.' Juno folded the paper and started scrutinising the piece more closely.

'You seen how much butter they use on Great British Menu?' Mil chortled.

'I wouldn't say no to a meal in The Priory if someone else is paying.' Bethany flicked her dreadlocks from left to right shoulder impatiently.

'What makes you think Rich's and Wayne's deaths are connected?' Mil asked Juno.

'The cricket club is an obvious one,' Felix pointed out.

'Exactly!' Juno agreed. 'Plus they were old friends, did a lot of business together, played golf.' She held up a finger as she read. '*Wayne Baxendale was one of the original members of the Wexshire Enterprise Startup Investment Network, spearheaded by long-term business partner Richard Bass.* Debra mentioned it at Clubbercise after Wayne died, said one particular deal made them a fortune. Were you there when she was talking about it, Bethany?'

'I teach a lot of classes.' She rolled her eyes in exasperation, clearly eager for a change of subject. 'Tell me, how is the online dating going, Juno?'

Mil's smile faded.

Juno looked strained, big grey eyes averted. 'I might knock all that on the head.'

'I feel you.' Bethany nodded. 'It's hard when you get older, isn't it? The algorithms are against you.'

'I am actually very popular,' Juno clarified crossly, 'but I'll still probably step off the digital love path. Far too crowded.'

'Sounds like a wise plan!' Mil encouraged.

'Don't do anything just yet,' Phoebe insisted, thinking back to last night's conversation just before Debra Bass swanned drunkenly upstairs. 'I think Rich might have been invested in... that sector.' She eyed Bethany warily, wondering if she knew more than she was letting on. The change of subject felt almost deliberate.

'The millionaire app!' Bethany duh-ed. Then she pulled a selfie-surprised face, feigning ignorance. 'Just a wild guess.'

'Is she right?' Juno said in a small voice, turning to Phoebe.

'Possibly,' Phoebe hedged, eyeing Bethany, convinced she knew a lot more.

'Not a clue,' Mil shrugged.

'What even is it?' Felix looked blank.

'Kind of like Raya if Waitrose designed it?' Bethany explained. 'It started out local but it went global, and your mate's right.' She leaned closer to Juno. 'Don't delete it. If you have a VIP match, bite his hand off, I say! You do realise a man has to be worth a million minimum to be on that app? No offence, Juno queen, but that's a big result for a woman in her fifties living over a shop.'

'I'm sorry but I'm definitely deleting it.' Juno gulped, looking pale.

'Don't,' Phoebe repeated more forcefully.

'Why not?' asked Mil.

'If Rich Bass put up the venture capital for Dapper and Discreet, it could be relevant. We know Wayne dated online. Useful to have a foot in the door.'

'You *do* think we have a case!' Juno gasped.

'I think we need to keep an open mind, but something isn't right,' she said, glancing at Felix, thinking again about this morning's grim discovery in the cricket pavilion. Could it have been murder?

He held her gaze, reading her uncertainty.

'A man is dead, Freddy.' Juno's voice trembled with emotion. 'What's right about that? A woman in this village has just been widowed.' For a moment, her big grey eyes were fixed, clouded by the grief.

'How do the Graveyard Ravers fit in?' Mil asked again.

'And what was the other death you mentioned, Juno?' queried Felix.

'Just meet your millionaire match!' Bethany's cry was louder than any of them.

Juno covered her ears. 'Can you all please stop!'

There was an awkward silence, broken by the clanking of Courtney arriving with a tray. 'Two chicken popcorn, one soup.' She set it down on the table, saying, 'Loving the meme of you grooving, Juno. It's all over TikTok.'

'Thanks,' she muttered, hands still over her ears.

'What meme?' asked Mil.

'It's nothing,' Phoebe said quickly.

'I'll show you,' offered Courtney. A moment later she was holding up her phone. 'It's everywhere!'

'Was this last night?' asked Felix. 'Are you doing some sort of dance?'

Phoebe, who had already seen it, watched their faces change from confusion to hilarity as they took it in.

It was a video of Juno in front of the pop-up gazebo in Wheeler's Yard, gyrating on the spot, giggling uncontrollably, waving and holding on to her crotch before crab-walking quickly out of shot.

'I took that!' Bethany recognised it. 'I just sent it to the family WhatsApp. Did you share it, Courtney?' The rebuke sounded half-hearted.

'Is that a Michael Jackson move you're busting, Juno love?' asked Mil.

Juno stood up, accidentally upending the soup bowl. 'I'm really not hungry, sorry.'

Half falling out of the picnic table, she hurried away across the pub's beer garden.

Phoebe leapt up to follow. 'I'll go after her.'

But Felix reached for her hand before she could climb out, whispering, 'Give her some space.'

She lowered her voice so that only he could hear. 'You know what today is. It's why she drank too much last night, why she's so hyped and caught up in conspiracy theories...'

Nodding, Felix sucked his lip. 'It's her wedding anniversary.'

Phoebe looked at him in surprise. She'd only realised herself because of the photographs and diaries she'd found earlier.

'It's Juno's four-digit code for everything,' Felix explained. 'All the padlocks on the barns full of Jay's bikes and their clutter at our place. Same code.'

Phoebe sometimes forgot how astute his mind was.

'She and Jay got married twenty five years ago today,' She nodded.

Today would have been their silver wedding anniversary.

11

JUNO

Mother Loves Mother's Ruin
The Party Postscript

So every time I get a sore head, I swear I'll never drink again. This oath never lasted longer than twenty-four hours when I was in my twenties, but it can stretch for weeks and months now I'm Mother Love. Go me, with my midlife self-control. Dry Januarys and 'No'-vembers are welcome fire-breaks in a year of occasional excess.

Full disclosure: last night, not only did I get a bit – okay, way too – fried at my housewarming, but I managed to get the entire village blotto. That takes some doing. Bad Juno. And now, deep breath…

One guest is dead.

Gotta stress the sauce didn't kill him, and he wasn't at my party when he died, but I still feel kinda guilty about it.

So I'm not going to drink for a while. Not for a long time.

And I'm not throwing a party again. Not ever. You heard it here first.

> But I *am* investigating another murder. Possibly more. Because there's something not right...
>
> The Village Detectives are back!
>
> BLOG SPONSORED BY WHEELER'S YARD FLOWERS:
> BLOOMING WITH HAPPINESS!

Juno looked at what she'd written, highlighted it, then pressed the backspace to delete the lot.

Her Mother Love subscribers deserved better, and her sponsors wanted her to spread happiness, not doom and gloom, she decided. Hungover penitence didn't sit well with her brand. She'd write up the party when she could see the funny side.

And much as her readers had loved the unexpected true crime developments in her posts since moving to Britain, Juno knew she needed to hold fire until the others were convinced there was anything to investigate. It didn't do to bulldoze in, especially with grieving widows to think about. She of all people should know that.

Walking to her flat's kitchen, the sight of the high-rise stacks of uneaten food platters in their clingfilm shrouds made Juno's stomach heave. Perhaps she would take some of it to Debra after all?

In her heart, Juno knew it was too soon, but she was filled with such overwhelming obligation and compassion, she felt she had no choice but to call on Greenside Manor, no matter how briefly. And Juno never went anywhere empty handed.

* * *

Although she had met the Basses multiple times, Juno had been to their house just once, and then only for a quick cup of tea with Debra after a fitness class, when she'd been persuaded to donate to the Dunford Golf Club Annual Fundraiser. The Basses weren't big on hosting at home to her knowledge, one of the reasons they had a reputation in the village for being mean as well as overbearing.

When she slipped through the open gates, she spotted a police car parked alongside the Basses' glossy fleet on the turning circle and almost turned back, hearing Phoebe lecturing her in her head: 'Far too soon.'

But Juno hadn't accounted for the Basses' CCTVs alerting those in the house to a new arrival, and the door was already opening, a scowling figure framed in it, gesturing her to hurry up.

She didn't recognise the small, bearded wolverine of a man in a Chelsea strip, Metallica cap and pool sliders, Bullet yapping upside down in his arms. He didn't look like a plainclothes detective, but it was best not to pre-judge these days.

'I'm Juno!' She hurried closer. 'Debra's friend. I am so desperately sorr—'

'I know who you are. You'd better come in.' He beckoned her in with a jerk of the head, sounding more Surrey Street Market than Wexshire Constabulary. 'I'm Grant.'

'Of course!' This was Debra's brother, she realised as she followed him through to the open-plan kitchen.

He was younger than she'd expected, and far smaller. Bow-legged and round-shouldered, he was nothing like the old-fashioned Danny Dyer diamond geezer Debra had tried to sell to her. He wasn't much taller than her, and twice as narrow, like a jockey. Not that this mattered, because Juno had already decided to ditch all her romantic aspirations and live like a nun.

A sleuthing, Sister Boniface type of a nun. Who never threw parties.

'Is Debra around?'

'She'll be finished soon. Good of you to come over. That stuff for us?'

'Yes, sorry – just some bits and bobs because I know how stressful it is to remember to eat, let alone cook. I'll put it in the fridge, shall I?'

Juno loved the Basses' kitchen, a glitzy nod to *TOWIE* and *Dallas* with its sparkly granite, mood lights and multitude of high-tech German appliances. One wall was entirely devoted to ovens, all showroom immaculate. The huge American cooler was as big as a double wardrobe.

Despite its size, she found it already crammed with uneaten sandwiches, quiches and pies.

'Today's cricket tea,' Grant explained, sidling to a window to peer out across the drive towards the village green like a sniper, possibly on the lookout for more casual callers. 'Shame to waste it, we thought, so I fetched it back here.'

Juno was surprised. 'And the police were okay with that?'

'Why wouldn't they be?'

'No reason. Stupid of me.' Closing the fridge door, Juno put her platters on the island.

Phoebe was right, she realised. The police must think Rich's death was self-inflicted if they weren't treating the cricket pavilion as a crime scene.

'Debs hates waste,' Grant went on with a sniff, coming to investigate. 'Some of it might even do for the wake if we're lucky, she says. This too.' He prised open a lid to peer in one tub. 'She told me you like your grub.' Looking up, he smiled in the rictus way that didn't reach his eyes, as though pulling a face in the mirror checking his teeth for spinach.

It was impossible not to stare at those teeth, ultra bleached white with the longest canines she'd ever seen, like a hippo. His hair was a strange shape and texture too, as though he had a fluffy seventies loo mat glued to his head.

Juno heard a mournful wail from further in the house. 'Is Debra still with the...?'

'Police, yeah. They want her to go with them to identify the body.' He helped himself to a beignet. 'Just routine, but Debs has a thing about hospitals.'

'She must be so upset,' Juno sympathised. 'It's such a tragedy.'

'Mmm.' He spoke with his mouth full, crumbs dropping into his beard. 'You make these cheese puffs?'

'Beignets. They're from the village deli.'

'Bit dry.' He squeaked round on his sliders to spit it out in the sink. 'Won't last for a funeral buffet if there's a hold-up.'

'Might there be a delay?'

'Hope not.' He shrugged. 'I've said I'll organise everything. I'm an old hand. Buried both parents in recent years.'

'I'm so sorry to hear that.' Juno found she couldn't shake the image of Grant in a JCB, digging a massive hole. Debra had told her enough times last night that he was a builder, after all. She'd also insisted Juno and Grant would be a perfect match.

Her perfect match was eyeing her closely now. Feeling distinctly uneasy, Juno wished she hadn't come.

'Debs told me all about you.' Grant stepped closer, licking his lips. 'She tells me you're looking for a new—'

'Such an enormous loss!' she interrupted, terrified he was about to say a new man. Her eyes darted along the photographs propped on the sideboard, noticing several missing. Amongst those remaining was one of Debra and Rich grinning alongside a younger, clean-shaven likeness of this man, with less hair and duller hippo teeth.

'We're all in shock,' she rattled on. 'Rich was full of life last night – they both were. They're always a fiery duo, aren't they?'

'Yeah, but Debs says you're in the market for a—'

'It was my friend Phoebe who found his body! She's a very clever crime writer. Brilliant detective too, on the down low. Just in case there are any unanswered questions.'

'Oh, yes?' He helped himself to a whipped feta filo basket.

'Although Phoebe told me Rich's death looked like a terrible accident,' she hurried on reassuringly, not wanting to cause alarm.

'Yeah, whatever,' he said as he chomped the filo basket, cheeks bulging. He stepped closer, voice teasing and intimate. 'Thing is, Debs let me in on your little secret.'

'Yes?' There was no avoiding it, she realised. His timing was awful.

The teeth were out again, gleaming and filo-flecked. 'That you want a thatch!'

It was such an unexpected thing to say, Juno was struck dumb for a moment.

'I have a super little development near Dunford,' Grant went on. 'Heritage-inspired, with some choice three-beds available off-plan. There's a deal to be made if you're quick.'

Still Juno stared at him in shock. His brother-in-law had just died horrifically; his sister was sobbing close by, and...

'Are you trying to sell me a house?'

'Debs says you're in the market for one?'

Astonished, Juno felt her detective itch take hold once more. There had to be more to this. Fascinated where this would go, she urged him to continue.

As Grant set about pitching the artisan, water-reed-roofed

eco-credentials of his latest development in an intense south London monotone, sliders squeaking on the tiled floor, Juno realised he just wanted to sell her a house.

Looking around the immaculate kitchen, she felt another great wave of compassion for Debra. Her eyes crept back to the pictures lined up along the side beam, searching for clues. It didn't take long to light upon a familiar face amongst a group of men in suits, with Rich at its centre. One was a former PM, hair wild, shirt hanging out and thumbs up. Another was the face – and peppery mullet – she'd seen in an obituary in the paper earlier and ripped out for safekeeping. It was currently burning a hole in her pocket. Bingo!

Wayne Baxendale. And who was the man beside them with the squished nose and gummy grin?

Grant was still droning on with his sales spiel. 'A Newbuild Heritage Eco Thatch isn't just a house, it's a way of life, offering a unique blend of timeless design and cutting-edge technology...'

Juno edged towards the photo to examine it more closely, tempted to try to sneak a phone camera shot of the balding man with the flat nose and cold smile standing alongside Rich, Wayne and the ex-PM. Her shameful hangover was kicking in again, her mouth parched, belly foaming. She was desperately dehydrated, but didn't feel she could ask for a cup of tea, nor did it seem possible to interrupt Grant's droning sales spiel, not even to make her excuses and leave. Phoebe was right, it was far too soon to have come here, foolish even.

Then she started as Grant snatched the framed picture she was studying from the shelf.

'Rich and his bent little syndicate made a bomb from lockdown PPE,' he sneered at it. 'Always flashing his cash, throwing money at madcap schemes, but not so much for an honest craftsman like me, his own brother-in-law. Never got a penny from his little cabal.'

'That must be hard when it's family,' sympathised Juno, who knew Debra boasted to anyone willing to listen that her husband had been a key player in Wexshire's own *Dragons' Den*, and Wayne Baxendale's obituary had named the investment syndicate. Bethany even claimed it had funded Dapper and Discreet. She asked casually, 'What madcap schemes were those?'

'Debs and Rich have been very generous to me, don't get me wrong.' Grant flashed his strange teeth, perhaps sensing he'd been too snappy given the tragedy they were facing. He put the photograph back carefully and patted the top of the frame, his eyes lingering on the four men. 'Never been a fan of suits. Only wear one at funerals.'

He looked up as a shrill call echoed along a corridor beyond the hallway.

'Grant? Grant! Who are you talking to?'

Bullet skittered off to greet his mistress, who came through the doorway clinging onto the arm of a uniformed WPC.

Seeing Juno, Debra burst into noisy racks of tears. 'Juno, babes! You're here! Ohmygod, can you believe what's happened, can you? My Rich. Dead! Oh, oh, oh!' She threw herself into Juno's arms and sobbed against her shoulder. 'I'm so glad you came. And you've met Grant! You will both come with me, won't you?'

'Where to?'

'To identify the body. I need a friend, Joo. You can do that, can't you, Juno babes? You'll come? Please say yes.'

Stomach churning yet more and mouth full of ashes, Juno had no choice.

'It would be an honour.'

12

PHOEBE

Having anticipated spending the afternoon playing cricket, Felix and Mil were only too happy to swap the crease for the riverside, where their pub garden partnership was an enduring one, batting trivia and opinions back and forth, over huge plates of roast meat, washed down with craft ale.

Loud, robust female laughter punctuated the meal as Bethany swished her blonde dreadlocks from side to side and showed her appreciation.

Out of loyalty to Juno, Phoebe wanted to find a host of reasons that Bethany was all wrong for Mil, but she liked her outspoken, brash sparkiness. A typical Welch siren, Bethany was a younger, hipper version of her sister Zadie and cousin Cheryl.

She clearly loved nothing more than to chat.

'There's a lot of folk round here bad-mouth us Welches,' she told Phoebe, ''specially the outsiders, but you won't find a closer family. We look out for each other, and know who our friends are, you feel me? Take the Winterbourne boys.' She nodded in Mil's direction. 'We all grew up together, were part of the same crew.'

It was clear she adored Mil. Having witnessed Juno's emotional exit, Bethany had obviously decided she needed an ally, annexing Phoebe to confide, 'Mil went out with my big sister Zadie in secondary school, and they both had my back. I was a few years below and a bit of a weirdo if I'm honest. Got picked on something rotten on the school bus. Never had a big brother of my own, and Dad had pushed off by then, so Mil was the next best thing. He looks after folk. I'm bringing up my boy Joseph – Seph – to be like that. I'm proud he looks out for his friends, and for me. You need that when you're a single mum, you get me?'

Nodding, Phoebe only wished Juno had somebody looking out for her. Her son Eric, so like his father, was a bit of a nomad.

'I had Seph when I was seventeen,' Bethany told her. 'Me and my ex married when Seph was two, but we was too young. He wasn't a great dad, I'll be honest. He only stuck around so long for a roof over his head and food in his belly.

'He walked out when Seph was nine, again when he was twelve and for good when he was fifteen,' Bethany went on, lifting her blonde dreadlocks to rub the other hand over the three stars tattooed on the back of her neck. 'Cheryl was the one who said I'd be better off divorced. We'd been living apart a few years by then, so it was easy. Easier than Cheryl, that's for sure. Her, Zadie and me all got divorced last year. We call ourselves the Three Decrees. Cheryl kept her nice house, Zadie kept her looks, I just about kept my head, and we've all changed our names back to Welch. It's tough on the kids, though. Ours are about the same age and they've always stuck up for each other, thank Christ. Stinky Inks unite! Isn't that right, Mil?' she called across.

Breaking off from laughing about something with Felix, Mil leant in. 'That's what the other school kids called us. Still do. "Stinkbury". Bloody cheek! This village has been in *The Times Best Places to Live* every year for a decade.'

'But ink rhymes with stink,' Felix pointed out.

'Fair point.'

They were soon engaged in a placename-rhyming duel.

Phoebe rolled her eyes. Bethany smiled at her.

'Same old bus, same old bullies. You grow up round here?'

'Not far away.'

'Where d'you go to school? Not Marlbury High?'

'It wasn't local.' Phoebe stifled a yawn, all the drama catching up with her.

'You board?' she scoffed.

'Not bored at all. I want to hear more about the Three Decrees.' She was hoping to steer Bethany onto the subject of the dating app Rich had invested in.

Bethany prodded her teasingly. 'I *meant* did you go to boarding school?'

'I hated it.'

'Like Autumn from the deli. She was at the same year at village primary as Seph and his cousin River. Lovely kid but lost the plot when she went to that posh ladies' college. They's all mates again now, mind you.'

'Yes, I met River and his friend with Autumn at the deli. He's Cheryl's son, isn't he?'

'It's River's fault my place got taken over last night.' She sniffed. 'Seph says his cousin's too loved up to party now he's with Xanthe. They got it together at uni.'

'Not on an app like his mum?'

'As if!' Bethany sneered. 'We all thought Cheryl was mad at first, but she's got her head screwed on. She gets a commission from introducing new female members, more if they meet up with a date. Now she signs everyone up – we're all on it.'

So that's how it worked, Phoebe realised. 'You use it?'

'On and off. Zadie can't be doing with it, but I've made a few matches on it for jokes; bit of flirting, posh night out. They were all ROMs. Rich, old, married. Most of the men on Dapper and Discreet are. The clue's in the name.'

Phoebe felt a fool for not guessing sooner that it was a hook-up app for extra-marital affairs. Hence the anonymising avatars, selective membership and monetised messages.

'Cheryl's new bloke, Rodney, has a wife and three kids near Cirencester,' Bethany told her. 'We looked her up on Facebook. She's big into horses. Looks like one too!'

'A veritable ROM-com,' Phoebe muttered darkly. And she could think of one rich, old married man whose name chimed all too closely. 'How does Rich Bass fit in?'

Bethany's smile vanished. 'He and his local business mob bunged the developer some dosh to launch it. When it took off, they all made a packet selling it to big tech. Dirty work, but someone's gotta do it. Married men will always want affairs. The app helps us girls find the wealthy ones and set the pace.'

The flinty side-eye Bethany was giving Phoebe was a sharp reminder that her trust in the opposite sex had been swiped aside long before she advertised herself in a three-line bio. She came from the school of hard knocks.

'I like a man who spoils and pampers me,' she revealed now, 'makes me feel special.'

Phoebe glanced instinctively at Mil, who was whooping with Felix about something.

Catching her, Bethany laughed. 'Way too soft. I told you Mil's like a big brother.' She smirked, leaning forward to whisper. 'FYI, I slept on the couch last night.'

'NOMB,' Phoebe dismissed quietly.

'Mil's practically family,' she pressed the point. 'Besides, he's into someone else and I'm not looking for commitment right now. Situationships suit me fine. My latest has a band, and I'm not talking music.'

'As in he's married?' Phoebe guessed flatly.

Bethany shrugged, lower lip pouting.

'Don't you feel guilty?' Phoebe asked, appalled.

'They're generous, they're grateful, and I can hand them back. That's the beauty of digital dating. The wife never needs to know, not like the crap that's gone down in this village when affairs come to light. Take Autumn's dad.'

'Cosmo Lovat?' Phoebe leant closer, remembering Cosmo's heated argument with Rich at Juno's party. She also now recalled, 'You said last night that there was a story to be told there.'

'And there is. Nasty bastard, Cosmo. Like I said, our kids were close at primary. Then he told Autumn she couldn't have anything to do with Seph and his cousins, although we all reckoned it had more to do with Holly.'

'Holly?' Phoebe wished Juno was still here, her knowledge of Inkbury's rollcall far better. And Juno loved nothing more than a good gossip. She might even like Bethany.

'Holly Lovat-Dixon was Cosmo's second wife,' Bethany explained, 'although she wasn't back then. She was Holly Dixon, whose daughter was in the year below Seph. She and Cosmo met on the PTA and started having an affair. It was my Seph who found out their secret cos he saw them practically shagging in the kitchens at the Halloween disco when he was in Year 6. Cosmo was dressed as Dracula and the poor lad thought he was trying to kill her. Autumn's mum's a mate of Cheryl's, so we told her what he'd seen. Cosmo had moved out of the marital home by the Nativity play, and she'd filed for divorce by spring term. Her solicitors took him to the cleaners.'

'The fourth decree?'

'Nice one! But this was a few years before us lot, although Cheryl used the same divorce lawyer and made a killing. First decree murder!' She laughed heartily at her own joke. 'Cosmo's hated my Seph ever since. Blames him for bringing the affair out in the open.'

'But Cosmo and Holly must have got together afterwards if they married?'

'They never should have, if you ask me,' Bethany scorned. 'Holly was a piece of work. She and her first hubby tried for a reconciliation at first, but the affair never stopped. He had enough in the end, and she and Cosmo went public after that. It was all very nasty and messy. Those poor kids.'

'How long was this before Holly died?'

'You know about that?' Bethany looked disappointed, lower lip pouting out, as though Phoebe had given away the punchline. 'Six, seven years maybe? She and Cosmo had been wed a while by then. They had one of those beach ceremonies, Tahiti or somewhere. Then they built that swanky cottage of theirs. It happened the day after they threw a big party there for her fortieth. No surprise I wasn't invited. Big shock when she crashed her new sportscar like that. I'd just been teaching a class in the Coronation Hall and heard it from the car park. Everyone thought her brakes must have failed, speed she was going, but she was on the phone, they say. Cosmo was at home, heard the noise too and came out and found her. Imagine that.' She shuddered.

Phoebe wished she couldn't, but the devastating picture was stuck in her head. She also knew Juno was convinced there was more to it, that Holly's death was somehow connected to both Wayne's and now Rich's too.

'Suicide, I reckon,' Bethany announced.

Phoebe reeled back in surprise. 'Why would she want to kill herself?'

'Remember what they say.' She pulled a knowing face. 'When a man marries his mistress, there's a vacancy.'

'Do you think Cosmo was having another affair?'

Bethany said nothing, but the knowing face had bedded in.

'Any idea who the applicants might have been?'

'Well, it wasn't me.' There was a defiant tilt to her chin.

'You're seeing a married man you met on Dapper and Discreet.' Phoebe knew she sounded censorious. 'How do you know Cosmo's not on the app too?'

'Holly always used to take the piss out of how bad he was with tech. Besides, the millionaire app's for jokes, nothing serious.' Bethany was defensive. 'I haven't even *met* this latest fella yet, not in person. The first match I had on there was a bastard, granted, but I learnt a lot. He told me he liked the app so much he bought the company. Seemed to think that was really funny.'

Phoebe sat up in shock, wondering why she'd said nothing sooner. 'He was an *investor*?'

'They're all on there, he told me. The Daddies.'

'Daddies?'

'The men who put the money up for Dapper and Discreet. "Daddies".'

'Was Rich Bass a Daddy? He put money in.'

Bethany laughed coldly, eyes flashing wider, as though this was a rhetorical question.

'*Was* it Rich?'

'Ew! Credit me with some bloody taste.' She looked angry now, draining her bottle of cider.

'What was he called, your first match?'

'Golden Pheasant,' she said stubbornly, crossing her arms. 'That was his avatar name, Golden Pheasant.'

'His real name?'

'I called him Golden Pheasant.' She thrust her chin out further, and Phoebe realised she'd get nothing more, annoyed with herself for it. Her political interviewer abrasiveness invariably put backs up, unlike Juno's boundless charm.

Nevertheless, she tried: 'And the one you're seeing now? Is he another... Daddy?'

'Who knows?' Bethany shrugged evasively, but she couldn't resist boasting. '*Seriously* loaded. My sister reckons it's that Peter Jones off the telly. Only I've not *seen* him, remember? We've cyber-sexed a few times, all waist down, no faces. He wanted to hook up IRL last night, but it's my shark week, so I got wasted at the junk shop party while he explored other options.' One eyebrow shot up, challenging Phoebe to judge. 'You feel me?'

Phoebe wasn't sure what she felt. Shocked, disappointed, mildly despairing and quite irritated sprang to mind, none of which were sentiments she sensed Bethany shared. 'What's his avatar name?'

'Why d'you want to know?'

'Because I'm incurably nosy,' she said honestly, resisting an urge to scratch an itch that had started crawling its way up her arms and legs.

'It's Green Man.'

13

JUNO

'Yes, that's him – that's my Rich,' Debra whispered tearfully, clutching onto Juno's hand.

When she'd agreed to accompany Rich Bass's grieving widow to Wexshire Royal Infirmary to formally identify her husband's body, Juno hadn't appreciated she would be standing alongside Debra *with* the body.

Surely this was a role for close family?

But as soon as they'd arrived, Grant had sloped off to get teas from the hospital canteen, and Debra's vice-like grip had tugged Juno with her as they followed the WPC down to the morgue.

So here she was, staring at Rich Bass's cold, grey face, trying not to think of what he'd been up to as he died.

The female police officer nodded at the morgue technician to cover Rich's face again with the sheet.

'No, leave it off a second,' Debra urged. 'He looks so peaceful.'

Juno watched as she stooped over her husband to bestow a kiss on his lifeless lips. 'Night-night, Big Spoon.'

Tears prickling, Juno caught the eye of the WPC, whose specialist family liaison training was matched with the perfect round-faced, bright-eyed sympathetic expression.

Then Debra slapped her dead husband across his face. 'You *bastard*! Why did you have to *die* like that? You selfish, rotten *pig*!' She grabbed the sheet over his chest with both fists and started shaking him through it. 'What were you *thinking*, making a fool of us both like that? You *bloody idiot*!'

* * *

'These things happen,' Juno assured Debra as she took great gulping hiccups of air.

'I c-can't-t b-believe I j-j-just p-p-pushed Rich off the—' She covered her face, unable to go on.

'Yes, that was a bit unfortunate,' the family liaison officer said tightly.

'But completely understandable,' Juno soothed. 'In fact, it probably happens surprisingly often.'

The WPC gave her a doubtful look but said nothing, glancing up at the wall clock as Debra burst into fresh sobs.

'I c-c-can't *leave him* in this p-p-place! He should b-b-be home! We c-c-can hold a vigil. An open c-c-casket.'

'There needs to be a postmortem before we can release the body, Mrs Bass,' the officer reminded her gently.

'He's not a body, he's *my husband*!' Debra sobbed into the last shredded corner of a wet tissue. 'And these are very thin p-p-ply!'

Juno went to fetch a fresh packet.

They were in the relatives' waiting room while Debra recovered her composure. They'd been here quite some time. The morgue technician, who clearly wanted to go to lunch, had put

Rich back in his refrigerated drawer and was loitering awkwardly. Grant had yet to appear with the much-needed tea.

Still Debra wept, telling them in sobbing fits and starts that she would never forgive herself for what she'd done. 'You sh-should arrest me and b-bang me up forever...!'

Juno and the WPC exchanged a startled look, wondering for a moment what exactly she was confessing to.

'...p-p-pushing him off the s-s-slab like that!' She collapsed into Juno's arms, shoulders heaving.

'Grief isn't a crime,' Juno reminded her, patting her back gently.

It had come as a shock to them all when Rich's body tumbled off the trolley, not least because he'd landed on the WPC's feet. Her sturdy black lace-ups provided inadequate protection against a toe-crunching sixteen-stone corpse, just as her specialist training hadn't stopped her swearing like a trooper.

'Are you sure you don't want to go to A and E?' Juno checked with her again.

'No, I really have to get back to the station,' she said. 'Do you want a lift home, Mrs Bass?'

'We'll get a cab,' Juno assured her.

It took another half packet of tissues before Debra was ready to leave the morgue.

'Can I see him again?' she pleaded with the technician, who apologised that the pathologist had already arrived.

'How long until the police get the report?' Juno asked as he saw them to the exit.

'The preliminary postmortem should be with them tomorrow – I've popped our Next Steps Bereavement Booklet in with these.' He held out a jiffy bag to Debra as he pressed the door release button. 'His personal effects.'

'You take them, Juno!' She backed away. 'I'm not ready, babes!'

Juno squished it in her handbag, spotting her phone in there, still switched off. She hadn't checked on her giggling, need-a-wee dancing meme going viral for hours, she realised proudly. Nor had she thought about Green Man's invitation to view his Dapper and Discreet picture gallery. Helping people in need was a good thing; it pushed all one's self-absorption aside.

'I need to find a loo,' Debra announced urgently, gripping Juno's hand again as they left.

'I'll find it,' she winced back kindly through the pain, feeling very Sister Boniface.

In the nearest ladies', Juno stared at her reflection in horror. Not so bonny faced, after all. Eyes still bloodshot and puffy, propped up by big dark bags, she looked like she should be back in the morgue, only on her own slab. She reapplied her lipstick, self-absorption crowding back in.

In the main hospital, they tracked Grant down to the café, where he was reading the *Sunday Mirror* sports pages, an empty sandwich wrapper, Minstrels packet and two cups of cold tea on the table beside him. The hippo teeth flashed. 'You took your sweet time.'

Debra seemed all wept-out, sinking into a chair, staring blankly out in front of her. 'He's gone, Grant.'

'Better get this funeral organised then.'

Juno was taken aback by the lack of sympathy.

But to her surprise Debra exclaimed, 'You're right, baby bro!' and patted her hands against her filler-smoothed cheeks to galvanise herself. 'Can't hang about, lots to sort out. Call an Uber, Grant. We need to get home. That jobsworth cop pushed off smartish, bloody part-timer.'

Juno knew the WPC had been with Debra since early that morning.

She stole a look at her watch. It was past three. She wondered if Phoebe and the others were still in The Barton Arms beer garden. She had much to report.

Grant was tapping the taxi app, telling Debra, 'I called the golf club while you were busy down there. They bellyached about letting us have the function room for free, but I pointed out Rich was a shareholder and life member like you told me to, and they said we can have two hours in The Above Par Bar on a Monday or Tuesday morning.'

'Good.' Debra stood up. 'Juno's helping, aren't you, babes?'

'I am?' Juno stared at her in alarm.

'She's brilliant at organising parties!'

'Actually I've decided not to host any more of—'

'You two can work on it together,' Debra told them, starting off across the café towards the hospital exit and beckoning them to follow. 'I want you to sing one of your medleys at the wake, Juno babes. Rich was a big Dire Straits fan, so we'll need lots of that, plus some The Who and maybe a bit of Madness.'

'Madness,' Juno repeated, sensing this was just that, especially when Debra told her Grant used to play guitar in a band and would accompany her.

'You'll be like the Eurythmics. Grant has a look of a young Dave Stewart, I've always thought.'

'Dave who?' demanded Grant, following.

In the back of the Uber, Juno discreetly turned on her phone, swiping down past the mountains of notifications from friends and followers who had been sharing her giggling weewee dance, plus several new Green Man messages, to the Village Detectives WhatsApp group where she hurriedly posted:

> Are you still at the pub? Need urgent debrief.

A reply pinged back within seconds. Unusually, it was from Phoebe, who rarely looked at her phone.

> Come ASAP. Also need debrief. Be warned Felix and Mil are wellied.

There was a PS sent as a direct message:

> FYI Bethany has pushed off. She slept on Mil's sofa.

Juno pressed her phone to her chest, suddenly feeling much better, positively warm and fuzzy in fact. Then she turned to find Grant flashing his white hippo teeth beside her.

'You had any more thoughts about my thatch?'

'Your thatch?' She caught herself staring at his strange loo mat hair.

'My heritage newbuild development. I can open the show home for a personal tour anytime.' He made it sound both suggestive and strangely threatening.

Hippos are the world's deadliest land mammals, Juno remembered, the warm fuzz turning icy.

Blowing her nose loudly in the front seat, Debra turned back to tick off her brother. 'Juno doesn't want to be bothered with that at a time like this, Grant!'

'Okay,' he snapped.

They all fell silent.

In the front seat, Debra pressed her hands to her face, tears sliding over her fingers as she stared out at the passing roadside. Beside Juno, Grant glowered out of his side at the traffic cones lined up along the central reservation.

In her lap, her phone vibrated with a loud 'I say!'

'Sorry!' She quickly muted it, hurriedly swiping away a Dapper and Discreet notification reminding her that Green Man was waiting for her response, and that his gallery was now open.

Beneath it, her phone was offering her a memory from its own gallery from ten years ago. She clicked on it mindlessly.

It was a selfie of her and Jay raising two crystal champagne flutes with labels still on the bases, grinning like loons, on their fifteenth wedding anniversary.

Quietly switching off her phone, Juno covered her mouth tightly with her hand and turned to gaze out at the same blurred roadside Debra was looking at.

14

PHOEBE

'And then poor Rich fell off the gurney onto the floor,' Juno reported, swigging back another half pint of lime soda in one.

'Hilarious!'

'Actually, it wasn't at all funny, Mil.'

'Ha! No. Course not. Still, can't have hurt him. Need a pee. Excuse me. Shout if you want another drink.'

'I want another drink!' Felix called out sleepily.

Phoebe's sun-boiled headache was pounding. She caught Juno's eye, sensing the tired irritation there matched her own.

'Maybe some coffee?' she suggested hopefully, but Mil had already lurched out of earshot.

The four of them had all retreated to the cool privacy of The Barton Arms' private dining room, where Juno had just described identifying Rich's body with Debra, and was now starting on her third packet of crisps. 'It was awful. Rich landed on the family liaison officer.'

'You could say he was off his trolley,' murmured Felix. He was stretched out on a padded bench seat with his eyes closed, languidly Holmes-like.

He and Mil had consumed too much beer to take anything seriously, not even the fact that Rich Bass's strange, self-inflicted death seemed increasingly suspicious. They had both already solved the case, they claimed. If it was murder, Felix and Mil agreed they need look no further than his beleaguered widow.

'Isn't it obvious Debra Bass was trying to ensure the pathologist won't pick up on signs of foul play?' Felix went on, sounding more logical now. 'Must have caused some posthumous damage, his body falling like that.'

'I hadn't thought of that.' Juno nodded earnestly. 'I just assumed she was grief-stricken. She seemed truly unhinged by it all, going from tearful mania to catatonic to hardnosed in a heartbeat.' She looked away, drawing breath. 'I was the same. Entirely different circumstances, but the rapid cycling emotions were the same.'

'Grief does strange things to people,' said Phoebe, watching Juno closely.

'Debra was a very strange woman to start with,' Felix pointed out.

'Her brother's even worse,' said Juno.

'Grief-stricken?' He sat up, rolling his shoulders to unclick them.

'The opposite, like Rich's death is a minor inconvenience. On the way back from the hospital, he had another go at selling me an executive thatched eco-home on his new development. Debra kept telling him off, then she suggested we talk about it over a dinner date. It was surreal.'

'Could they be in it together, brother and sister?' Felix asked, raking back his hair and blinking over-exaggeratedly as he tried to concentrate.

'For the money, maybe?' Juno tilted her head uncertainly, weighing up the idea. 'Rich is – was – very rich.'

'And very unfaithful, according to his wife,' Felix added.

'Who was absolutely blotto last night,' Phoebe pointed out. 'I was there. There's no way Debra had the clarity of mind or physical control to pull off a murder and disguise it as auto-erotica.'

'Unless she has her brother as accomplice.' Felix warmed to his theme. 'Grant did it for his sister to avenge her honour and get some of his brother-in-law's lolly. Case closed!'

Juno shook her head. 'I just can't see Debra sanctioning something like that,' she said, 'not even by proxy. She loved Rich. And the way he died has completely humiliated her.'

'I agree.' Phoebe caught her eye again and Juno held it gratefully.

'C'mon, it's bloody obvious Debra's hiding something.' Felix rubbed his brow with the heels of his palms, his voice languid, like a prosecuting barrister summing up after a boozy lunch. 'This morning, when we took the Basses' dog back to Flatpack Mansion, there was no answer, yet the moment Phoebe went to check if it had run off to the cricket field, Debra Bass threw open the door to me as though she'd been watching.'

'They have CCTV everywhere,' Juno pointed out. 'Grant did the same to me.'

'She couldn't wait to mix a jug of Bloody Mary and tell me how well she'd slept,' Felix went on. 'No mention of where Rich was. But when Phoebe called to say there'd been an accident, Debra was immediately full-scale hysterical. She called her brother within seconds, sobbing at him to come straight away.'

'That *is* a bit shifty-sounding.' Juno ate another mouthful of crisps.

'Entirely in character, I'd say,' Phoebe disagreed, all too familiar with middle-aged mood swings.

'For a murderer, certainly,' Felix pressed his point. 'We now know that Grant went round to the cricket pavilion later that morning to clear all the food the Basses had stored there for the match tea. The police had left the scene by then, so he had the place to himself. What else did he tidy up? I can't believe there wasn't even a strand of incident tape warning him to stay away.'

'There's no proof of foul play,' Phoebe reminded him. 'The postmortem might reveal something, but until it does, there's no crime.'

'Assuming shoving him off the trolley didn't cover up the evil deed,' Felix reminded her.

'I really *do* think that was an accident,' Juno insisted.

'And Rich Bass was disliked by plenty of other people around here,' Phoebe contested. 'Juno and I witnessed him having a stand-up row with Cosmo Lovat last night, for a start.'

'About cricket!' Juno scoffed. 'That's hardly grounds for murder, Freddy.'

'You don't know Inkbury CC,' Felix mused. 'We've all felt like killing Rich occasionally, and Cosmo too come to that.'

Phoebe said nothing. She'd decided not to mention what Bethany had told her about Cosmo Lovat's complicated love life just yet, or about anything else. Scurrilous gossip like that needed carefully fact-checking first, especially given Juno was already juggling wild conspiracy theories, doubtless now poised to once again bring up Holly Lovat-Dixon's fatal crash, along with the death of the village's most recent cricket captain, Wayne Baxendale.

But to her surprise Juno didn't mention them. Was she starting to believe Felix's first guess Cluedo solution rather than trust her original detective itch, Phoebe wondered?

To test this, she asked her, 'What about the two other deaths you think might be connected?'

'I got carried away,' Juno dismissed wearily. 'This is just about Rich.'

'And the Graveyard Ravers, don't forget.' Mil reappeared with a tray of beers, crisp packets, a bowl of sticky toffee pudding and a pint of lime soda. 'I promised Mary we'd investigate.' He delivered the soda and pudding to Juno. 'They struck again last night.'

'You are my hero!' She fell on the sticky toffee, speaking with her mouth full to ask Phoebe, 'So what happens next, will there be a police investigation?'

'That depends on the pathologist's report,' she explained. 'If the coroner reads it and suspects foul play, they'll call for a full police investigation ahead of an inquest.'

'Will that delay the funeral?' Juno asked, spooning up more toffee sauce.

'Almost certainly. It can take weeks.'

'Good.' She looked relieved. 'In that case, what can we do to help prove if it was foul play?'

'Nothing at all would be the official line,' Phoebe said firmly. 'Do not interfere.'

'Unofficially?'

She chewed her lip. 'The more I think about it, the more I'm convinced Rich might not have been alone in the pavilion last night.'

'Go on,' Felix urged.

'It was all too theatrical; it felt staged. The way he was hanging in my sightline, the bright colour of his costume, the strange final feast laid out like a Mad Hatter's Tea Party. There was an open bottle of champagne, but no glass, and a little bottle of amyl nitrate next to the tray of sandwiches, like a condiment.'

Juno gave an 'ah-ha!' of recognition. 'Surely he'd have the poppers in his hand or pocket if he was sniffing it whilst...' She started to mime, then quickly stopped.

'Self-pleasuring?' Phoebe helped her out. 'Exactly. And I found some sunglasses dropped outside. I pointed them out to the police, who must have picked them up.'

'Rich was wearing sunglasses at the party,' Juno remembered eagerly. 'Oh, I have his personal possessions here!' She started fishing in her bag. 'We can check.'

'Nice work.' Mil looked impressed.

Holding up a jiffy bag, Juno chewed her lip guiltily, eyes wide. 'Debra asked me to take this because it upset her, then I was in such a hurry to get away from all the talk of link-detached garages and Dire Straits, I forgot to give it back.' As she turned it around, her face fell, and she realised, 'It's security sealed.'

'Let me feel,' Mil offered, taking it and pressing his big, square fingertips into the papery padding expertly, as though searching for shot in a game bird. 'Mostly jewellery, I'd say – a watch, those big chunky gold rings he wore, a bracelet and... these might be glasses of some sort.'

'Don't suppose you can feel a phone?' asked Felix.

'I doubt that went to the morgue with him,' said Phoebe.

'Rich was shouting into his last night,' Juno remembered. 'Could he have been arranging to meet somebody at the pavilion? The police will check call records, won't they?'

'Only if they investigate,' Phoebe reminded her.

'And only the stuff that isn't end-to-end encrypted,' Mil pointed out.

'I can get Eric to deep-dive Rich's digital footprint,' Juno offered, polishing off the sticky toffee pudding. 'He can track social media, clubs, forums as well as social and professional stuff like public records, the kitchen business that Rich made his fortune from before he sold it, and this local business investment syndicate of his.'

'Do no harm.' Mil handed her back the jiffy bag and took her empty bowl with a woozy smile. 'You are *so* good at all this, Juno love.'

'Well, Eric *is* a secret weapon.' Juno beamed back at him, turning pink.

'Maybe get him to check out the Dapper and Discreet app too?' Phoebe suggested.

'I don't need my son to police my dating apps!' Juno said crossly.

Phoebe didn't want to risk upsetting Juno more by revealing that Green Man had also matched with Bethany Welch, but the coincidence was too close to home to ignore. And Dapper and Discreet's connection with 'Daddy' Rich Bass worried her.

'I think it merits closer scrutiny,' she persisted.

'Let's just not bother Eric with it, shall we?' Juno gave her a meaningful look before glancing at Mil again. 'I told you I'm knocking all that on the head.'

'And I said please don't.'

'Tell you what, Freddy, you are welcome to use my log-in to check it out yourself,' Juno huffed. 'It's not as if Curvy Kitten is really me, it's just an avatar.'

'Curvy Kitten?' Felix raised an eyebrow.

'That's Phoebe now,' Juno said hotly, quickly moving on. 'I'll keep scoping out Debra and Grant for more background,' she volunteered. 'As they're our chief suspects.'

'Is that safe?' Mil asked, battered brow creasing.

'It is while I show interest in thatched newbuilds and funerals,' she told him. 'You can gather village intel on the Basses, Mil. Felix can get the cricket club lowdown and try to re-examine the scene. And Phoebe can get—'

'Some sleep.' Phoebe stifled a yawn. 'I need to think.'

'That's not really in the spirit of the Village Detectives, Freddy,' Juno reproved.

Phoebe's headache was reaching peak frequency. 'Let's all please just remember that there may be no crime here. The coroner decides that, not us. Rich Bass may have accidentally asphyxiated himself on a champagne, poppers and cricket sex high. Weirder things have happened in this village.'

The others looked at her disbelievingly. Phoebe stared them out.

She needed to rest. She needed to read and edit.

And she needed to quietly set about finding out more about Wayne Baxendale and Holly Lovat-Dixon, and what linked them both to Rich Bass. Her overwhelming suspicion was that it must be Cosmo Lovat.

Phoebe still trusted Juno's detective itch instinct, even if Juno herself no longer did.

15

JUNO

The following morning, Juno went to the village deli and bought a selection of comfort treats to take to Greenside Manor: her favourite pastries, some locally made fudge, organic coffee beans and kombucha.

'Awful news about Rich Bass, isn't it?' she asked Autumn as the blue-haired student started ringing them up on the till.

'He was a regular' – she nodded – 'said his wife had made them quit caffeine and sugar, so he'd come in for a sneaky caramel latte when he walked the dog. Quite the character.' Her ironic voice underlined the underwhelming eulogy, and Juno now remembered she'd called him 'cringe'.

Juno switched the coffee for a packet of Inner Calm herbal tea but held on to the pastries and fudge for personal use.

'He was old school.' She also recalled Rich leering at Autumn at her party.

'Along with a lot of men in this village.'

'Big shock to the cricket club, I should think?'

'Certainly knocked Dad for six.'

'Were they close?' Juno asked casually. As far as she knew

Autumn hadn't witnessed the argument between Cosmo and Rich at the party, nor did she know that Juno had.

'Friendly rivals, I think.' She shrugged, looking for a price on the teabags.

The argument had struck Juno as more than friendly rivalry, but she didn't want to arouse Autumn's suspicions. 'Village cricket can be like that.'

'Yeah, the Basses kind of took over there, you'll have no doubt heard. But it wasn't long after Holly died, so I think Dad was relieved he didn't have to be here to play every weekend.'

Juno felt a wave of empathy, thinking wistfully of handsome Cosmo with his twinkly blue eyes. 'Is your dad still around?'

'Back in London.'

'Will he be in Inkbury again soon?'

Autumn gave an upside-down smile. 'Funny, your writer friend asked me that question when she was in here earlier.'

'Phoebe was here?'

'My first customer. She was out running. Bought a bottle of water.'

Juno frowned. Phoebe never came into the deli. And certainly not for overpriced Icelandic Glacial.

Autumn held out the contactless payment console, looking up, dark-rimmed eyes scrutinous. 'She asked me to pass on her number to Dad.'

Juno held her phone over it, indignation mounting, wondering what Phoebe was up to. 'I think they have mutual friends she wants to reconnect with.'

'So she said.' Autumn waited for the payment approval, sucking in one cheek. 'It's just, I don't want him getting hurt again. What happened to Holly shattered him. That's why I thought you two would get on. I know what happened to your husband. I read about it, sorry.'

'It's fine, it's a matter of record.' Juno fought a familiar bobbing tide of emotion, so much more manageable these days than it once was, but still ever-present, requiring sea walls, locks, weirs, a safe harbour.

Autumn looked relieved. 'And I appreciate what you went through is *way* more intense than Dad's tragedy, but I still thought you'd understand each other a little. And you're *so* lovely.'

Juno flushed, positivity bouncing back.

'And I know your friend is great too,' Autumn went on, 'but after Holly died there were a lot of women who suddenly popped up from Dad's work or the village or gym, calling in with a homemade casserole or a book recommendation, handing over their number and saying they were always there to listen. More than one was married.'

'Phoebe definitely isn't after your dad,' Juno assured her.

At least she hoped not.

* * *

At Flatpack Mansion, Debra opened the door dressed in a leopard-print sweatshirt and joggers, Bullet yapping furiously underfoot. Dire Straits' 'Brothers in Arms' was playing loudly over the Sonos system. The pillowy smile wobbled red-lipped in the waxy Mrs Potato Head face. Her eyes were puffy from crying.

'Babes! Am I glad you're here. Grant's had to rush off first thing to deal with a crisis on one of his construction sites, and I'm packing up Rich's clothes.' Turning away, she was halfway up the stairs by the time she called back, 'You can help me!'

Juno abandoned her treats on the hall table to follow. She

wasn't sure which stage of grief this was, but she was certain it wasn't a healthy one.

'You don't want to break off for a cup of tea?'

'No, I need to get it all done.'

The music was even louder upstairs.

Rich Bass had possessed a *lot* of clothes. An entire dressing room was devoted to them, one wall of fitted louvre-door wardrobes full of neatly folded designer casualwear in pale creams and yellows, another housing brightly checked golfing and sporting attire, a third made-to-measure suits.

'He looked so lovely in a suit!' Debra shouted over Mark Knopfler's guitar riffs, pulling them off padded hangers, breathing in the lapels before stuffing them into a bin bag.

'Are you sure it's not a bit soon to be doing this?' Juno asked anxiously, alarmed by the speed with which Debra was cramming clothes into refuse sacks.

'He's not going to wear them again, babes! Grant is going to sell it all on Vinted! He's always selling stuff!'

'How enterprising.'

'Pardon?'

'Enterprising!'

'Yes, Grant's quite the entrepreneur! I always said that to Rich! Grant should be in your syndicate, I told him, but he just laughed.'

'Could we turn the music down a bit, d'you think?'

'What?'

'I can't hear everything you're saying!'

'There's no time to talk, babes. Let's bag!'

They took just one short break for tea and fudge, during which Juno's ears still rang from the drumbeat as she asked if there had been any news from the coroner.

'Not yet.' Debra sniffed her herbal tea and grimaced. 'I don't want to think about it, babes.' Pushing her mug away, she complained tearfully, 'D'you know they won't issue a death certificate until the coroner says so? I'm in shreds, babes. Grant was going to take me to register the death in Newborough especially this afternoon. We thought we'd do a shop at Costco while we're there and drop Rich's smalls in the clothes recycling bank in the car park there. I need closure. Have they no heart? I have a funeral to organise. The food won't last, although I've frozen what I can.' She lifted her mug again then put it down. 'This tea's a bit ethnic for me, babes, I'll be honest. Shall we open some champagne?'

'It's kind of early for me.' At least a month, thought Juno, who planned to detox through at least one new series of *White Lotus* and several named storms.

'Buck's Fizz, then. We're celebrating Rich, you understand.' The tears started again. 'It keeps him alive to me.' Plucking tissues from a box to press to her face, Debra waved at the big glass-doored wine fridge. 'Over there, babes. Not the vintage stuff. The oranges are in a bowl by the electric squeezer on the island. This kitchen has everything. Luxury appliances were my husband's life work.' The sobs restarted in earnest.

Hurrying to fix the drinks, Juno reluctantly rejoined her to raise a brimming flute. 'To Rich, a captain of industry!'

'My big Black Horse.' Debra drained her glass in one.

'*Was* he a dark horse then?' Juno leaned in sympathetically.

'No, that was Rich's angel name.'

'His angel name?' Juno braced herself for some spiritual schtick Debs had picked up involving celestial ascendance.

'In the syndicate he joined after he sold the kitchen company.' Debra helped herself to more champagne and topped it up with juice. 'I told you about it, babes, they were like a Wexshire *Dragons' Den*. That's him and Wayne with Bojo back when they started out.' She pointed at the picture of Rich giving the camera a thumbs up alongside the former PM. 'They'd both sold successful businesses they'd built from scratch, so then they helped new ones get off the ground.'

'It was PPE first, wasn't it?' Juno remembered Grant telling her so.

'That's right. It grew from that, became the Wexshire Enterprise Startup Investment Network. They'd brought in a London hotshot to run it all, although Rich was always the driving force, getting other investors to join. They were his business angels, backing the little people, helping local companies launch their ideas. Practically a charity.'

Juno also recalled Grant calling it Rich's 'cabal'. 'Who else was in Wexshire Enterprise Startup um—'

'Just call it "WE SIN", babes. We did, it was Rich's little joke, because it's the initials and because they were angel investors. And there've been quite a lot. They pick and choose their projects. Hospitality, manufacturing, retail, tech, you name it. Rich knew a lot of movers and shakers.'

'Well, he loved his music, so they'd have to be able to move and shake to keep up.' Juno tilted her head as Dire Straits' 'Twisting by the Pool' thudded through the Sonos.

'Never a truer word!' Debra reached for the bottle with a wobbly smile.

'Who's the other guy in the photograph?' Juno pointed to the balding man with the flat nose standing alongside the other three.

'You'd have to ask—' Debra stopped, clearly about to say 'Rich'. Her face crumpled for a moment before she splashed more champagne in her glass, not bothering with the orange juice. 'I never paid his work much attention, if I'm honest. We didn't entertain business associates here. I find all the shop talk boring and can never remember names.'

'What about angel names?'

'That was just another of Rich's little jokes.' She glanced tearfully across at the photograph of him, raising her glass to it. 'He was fed up always being called the Kitchen King whereas Black Horse sounded like a mythical knight superhero.'

'So did the We Sinners all have angel names?'

'I don't think so.' Debra drained the glass in one. 'I only heard him mention a few. There was a White Dove or maybe a swan, and a lion. Purple Pussycat was another. I think there might have been a Phoenix too – no, not a phoenix, but some golden bird or other. Goose, p'raps? And wasn't there a Huntsman? No, that's not right, and it wasn't Robin Hood either. What was it? It'll come to me.'

Debra was right, Juno realised. She really couldn't remember names. 'Who were they all really?'

'Just businesspeople. Like I say, I never took much interest in it. I just told him not to spend too much.' Tears were welling behind the false eyelashes. 'He was too generous, my Rich. He wanted to help everyone. He could never say no.'

Juno, who remembered Bethany's wild suggestion that that Rich had invested in Dapper and Discreet, knew she should ask more. If Phoebe was here, she wouldn't hesitate, but Juno worried it would be insensitive, especially given Debra was crying again and topping up their glasses, pouring more outside than in.

'Did you bring his personal items, babes?' she demanded.

'His...? Oh, yes. They're in my tote.' Juno fetched the hospital morgue jiffy bag and Debra ripped hurriedly into it, sorting through the gold jewellery to clasp in one hand, feeling its weight before pressing it to her trembling lips, then picking up the smart watch.

'Fat lot of good all those daily steps did him!' She cast it aside angrily. 'Let's bag some more clothes, Juno babe.'

Dire Straits were singing about Romeo and Juliet's dice being loaded from the start as they filled tens more black bin liners with Fred Perry polo shorts and Pringle jacquard sweaters, all reeking of Febreze and sandalwood drawer liners. The music was far too loud for more talk.

It was a relief when Grant arrived in his Chelsea strip, hippo teeth bared, to take his sister to Newborough. 'We can still do non-perishables at Costco. Gets you out of the house.'

'Will you come with us, Juno babes?' Debra shouted over 'Sultans of Swing' on its fourth repeat.

'I can't, I promised I'd visit my mother,' she lied.

'But you'll you come back here tomorrow?'

'Of course.' Juno wanted to know more about Rich's business dealings and the mysterious WE SIN group.

Seeing her off at the door with a hiccup, Debra made her promise to arrive no later than ten. 'And wear black next time, will you?'

Looking down, Juno realised her bright pink vest top and flower shorts were probably horribly disrespectful.

'Yes, of course!' she squeaked, feeling ashamed.

Groggy from daytime drinking, she went home to have a brief lie-down, her favourite Britpop chill-out list playing as she updated the Village Detectives WhatsApp group. A strange sense of widow solidarity made her gloss over the fact Debra was bagging up Rich's clothes posthaste, but she told them about Rich initiating the WE SIN syndicate, adding that Boris Johnson might be implicated.

Felix's pithy reaction was:

> Highly suspicious.

Mil gave that a thumbs up. Phoebe stayed on one grey tick.

Juno asked what the others had found.

Felix messaged another pithy line that he was working in London and had no time to investigate the cricket club; Mil left a voice note apologising that he was finishing lunch service and nobody had much to say about Rich Bass; Phoebe stayed on one grey tick.

Irritated, Juno messaged her directly:

> Has Cosmo Lovat called you yet?!

Then she video-called Eric.

'Whassup, Mom?' Her golden cocker spaniel of a son was a bearded, strawberry blond, more laid-back facsimile of his father, beaming out from his high-tech houseboat.

Stifling yawns, she asked him to deep dive Richard Bass's digital footprint, then asked, 'Any news of the baby?'

'You'll be the first to know.' He looked distracted, continually glancing at another screen. 'It's at least a fortnight away.'

'*You* arrived ten days early.'

'Well, this baby can't. I gotta move the boat to a new mooring first. This one's only temp...' He was too distracted by whatever was happening on his other screen to finish the sentence.

'Are you gaming?'

'No, I'm on a webinar.'

'For work?' Juno asked excitedly, hoping GCHQ had finally lowered the drawbridge on his suspension.

'It's about support for noncustodial fathers,' he said awkwardly. 'You were the one who sent me the link.'

'Keep watching – do not blink! I'll call another time,' she urged, waving him away with kisses, proud that he was taking steps at last. It was huge progress.

Awash with maternal love, Juno felt a sudden longing to see her own mother for wise words and comfort. But when she called her to suggest she pop over to Godlington Hall, Judy turned out to be poking around an antiques fair with Dennis on the other side of Marlbury. 'He's convinced he's unearthed a Barbara Hepworth, Pusscat. Drive over and join us!'

'I've no car right now,' Juno reminded her.

'Whose fault is that?' Judy huffed, ringing off. She was very touchy on the subject.

Juno had been hampered by recent car troubles. Both the sexy Mini with a Union Jack roof that she'd bought when she'd first arrived from the States, and her mother's redundant runaround, were currently languishing with her young friends at village mechanics Drum n' Brakes. Juno had resorted to temporary pedal power, impulse-buying an electric bike online. It was still in the shipping box.

Probably no bad thing her mother was out, Juno reflected hazily. She didn't trust herself to cycle to Godlington after so much Buck's Fizz. Even unboxing it might be a challenge.

Instead, she refocused her attention on looking for work. First, she checked her LinkedIn profile on her phone, then scrolled all the job sites she was signed up to, in case something new had come up to match her limited skill base and limitless desire for job fulfilment. It hadn't. Nobody was looking for an unqualified private detective, one-time stand-up comic and lapsed blogger.

Juno googled the Wexshire Enterprise Startup Investment Network and landed on a website featuring a stylish corporate logo and a sliding gallery of local vistas. Its soundbites looked impressively corporate, but told her nothing, and the About Us page was pure AI spiel with no names. The social feeds were just as oblique. Frustrated, she swiped them all away.

Her thumb hovered over the Dapper and Discreet app, which she still hadn't deleted. Juno had yet to click on Green Man's last message granting her access to his gallery. Whilst she liked to think this was noble self-control, doing so would also automatically grant him access to her gallery, and the only thing she'd uploaded to Curvy Kitten's private showcase so far was a photograph of Kevin Bacon the cat.

At least it wasn't her giggling need-a-wee dance, she thought darkly as she spotted yet more shares of the viral video on all her feeds. The clip's view count was up to ten thousand on Courtney Welch's TikTok alone.

Juno pulled a cushion over her face and groaned.

She'd rewrite that scintillatingly witty Mother Love blog all about it to cheer herself up and entertain her followers later today, she decided. They had been grumbling rather a lot about all her sponsored content recently.

She'd just close her eyes for two minutes first.

* * *

Juno dreamed that she was dancing with the Jolly Green Giant from the tinned vegetables ads, booming 'ho, ho, ho!' as they jived and vibed together to EMF's 'Unbelievable'. It was unexpectedly sensual.

Then she realised it was Mil in green body paint and an off-the-shoulder leafy tunic, which was even nicer.

The music changed to the Stone Roses' 'I Wanna Be Adored' and they moved closer together. Lovely. Other couples were dancing around them in exotic costumes: a man dressed as a swan was entwined with a human lioness; a golden goose and a Siamese cat the colour of amethysts were kissing; and a black knight embraced a turtledove ballerina. Shapely and elegant, the ballerina turned to Juno and winked. It was Bethany Welch.

When Juno woke, it was dark outside and Kevin Bacon was asleep on her chest, claws deep in her t-shirt.

She groped groggily for her phone. It was just before ten.

Phoebe had replied to her direct message.

> No word from Cosmo Lovat. Need to find out his connection to Rich and why they argued. Are you okay?

Juno called her.

'Yes?' She sounded sleepy.

'Sorry, Freddy, I woke you, didn't I?'

'It's fine. I was napping, Felix still isn't back. His train's not due until quarter to. Scratch your itch.'

'I think you're right. We need to look beyond Debra and Grant. Rich's syndicate, The Wexshire Enterprise something or other. Have you read my WhatsApp notes?' She didn't need to wait for an answer; Phoebe mostly muted everything. 'They were business "angels". Wayne Baxendale was one of them, and there was some hotshot from London who ran it. I'm not sure who else was involved because Debra says there were lots, and Rich gave some of them nicknames. I don't think she shared much of his business life with her, and she wasn't interested. Eric is on the case. There must be an official record of it somewhere. The website's useless, but Eric's deep dive should bring it up.'

'What were the nicknames?'

Juno recounted them. 'If we can find out the real investors' identities and match them, it might tell us something.' She confided that she'd identified the dove as Bethany Welch in her weird sofa dream, although she didn't mention Mil guest-starring in his leafy tunic. 'Probably nothing.'

'Never underestimate the power of the nap,' Phoebe reassured her. 'That's how I think up my best plot twists. Embrace middle-age siestas.'

'Never.'

'So you've spoken to Eric?'

'Briefly. He was a bit distracted.' She remembered the fatherhood webinar with a smile. Then she recalled, 'He said something about having to move his boat. He only gets fourteen days' mooring.' Eric's permanent Oxford spot had been sold off a few weeks earlier, scattering his little community of houseboats throughout the local waterways.

'Any idea where's he going next?' Phoebe sounded uncharacteristically cheery.

'Eric never plans ahead, and even if he did, I'd be the last to know,' she sighed. 'I just hope he finds somewhere before the baby comes.'

'Of course he will!' Again, Phoebe's gung-ho positivity was unexpected. 'And we will find out what exactly happened to Rich Bass, Juno, never fear. That's Felix on call waiting. I must go. Take more naps. They're obviously good for you.'

Ringing off, Juno thought about her subconscious slow dance with the Jolly Green Giant and worried she was drinking too much.

Feeling guilty that she'd left Mil and Felix out of the loop, she long-windedly thumb-typed another update to the group WhatsApp including more detail of her conversation with Debra about the WE SIN syndicate's 'angels', finishing:

> I think we need to spread the net wider.

She was tempted to drop in Bethany's name but stopped herself in time.

Mil left a voice note shortly afterwards amid the hubbub of the pub's last orders. 'I'd still lay down money Debra Bass and her brother did it, and Felix here agrees, doncha, mate?'

'Absolutely!' Felix said in the background, having clearly stepped off the train straight into the nearby pub for a nightcap.

Phoebe stayed on a grey tick, but Juno already knew she was onside. And if Phoebe said they would find out what had happened to Rich Bass, she had no doubt they would.

* * *

The next morning, Juno was back in the deli, buying a small fudge selection, baked root crisps and some hand-pressed local apple juice.

Autumn's beautiful friend couple were in there, draped decoratively over the counter, sharing a single cold brew coffee with two paper straws.

'Nice drip.' One admired Juno's black playsuit, matched with a floppy sunhat and cross-laced espadrilles.

Juno recognised him as Cheryl's son River, who was house-sitting for his mum while she was away. 'Thanks.' She felt cheered. She was a bright colours person, and this was the only black thing she could find in her wardrobe. She just hoped Debra would deem it respectful enough.

'Have you heard from your mum?' she asked River, eager for the distraction of knowing how Cheryl was faring with Hot Rod and the seismic tremors in Santorini.

'She's cool.'

'How's the house-sitting going for you?'

'It's cool.'

'I used to love house-sitting when my parents were away,' she confided. 'Sleeping 'til lunchtime, raiding the freezer, watching junk TV all day.'

He gave her a blank look. Beside him, his friend had shaven eyebrows and yet somehow cocked their absence with devastating irony.

'Streaming, gaming, hanging,' Juno floundered on, earning a brace of tight half-smiles, streetwise savants to ageing hipster.

'How about you, Autumn?' Juno turned her attention hopefully. 'Are you living in your dad's place on your own while you're down here?' She vaguely recalled Autumn was at university somewhere miles away like Newcastle or Durham.

'No, I'm with my mum in Dunford. Dad's cottage on Woodridge Lane is kind of a shrine.' She shared a look with River and the pixie-haired friend, who was chewing on a hoody cuff, eyes rolling. 'Full-on thatched Tiggywinkle cottagecore.'

River gave a cartoon reaction shudder.

'Sounds lovely,' Juno sighed, making a mental note to cycle past once she'd unpacked her e-bike.

'Bad memories.' Autumn wrinkled her nose, glancing at her friends again. 'I hope he'll make better ones there soon.' She tilted her head to beam at Juno. 'He's so ready to love again.'

It was hard to tell if the ironic voice was genuine, but Juno gave her the benefit of the doubt. She empathised with handsome widower Cosmo holding on to all his wife's things in their homespun shrine.

Then she thought about Debra and her frantic bin bag filling and wondered whether it was perhaps wiser to relinquish all the material things straight after bereavement rather than attaching so much significance to them that they formed part of a memorial. Hers had been shipped over in almost its entirety from the States: Jay's motorcycle leathers, old jeans, vinyl, helmets and even the bikes themselves, currently taking up space in Phoebe and Felix's barns at Hartridge.

Juno would help Debra in whichever way she could, she decided. While her widow's weeds might be overgrown, it didn't mean she couldn't prune others'.

But when Juno got to Greenside Manor, Debra was waiting outside wearing a full-length clingy black dress with a hint of leopard print, a hat with a veil and a pair of familiar, oversized Jackie O sunglasses. Beside her, Wayne was in a tight single-breasted black suit and bootlace tie. Even Bullet was wearing a black waistcoat.

Debra threw up her arms with a wail. 'You're late, babes, get in the car! Thank God you dressed up; I don't think you'd fit in anything of mine. Is that a beach outfit? You should have fake tanned. Never mind.'

'Where are we going?'

'The funeral, of course! Didn't I say?'

Juno's jaw dropped and her heartbeat spiked. 'You're having Rich's funeral already? I thought they hadn't released the bod—'

'Not *Rich*!' Debra fished in her black Balenciaga City for a tissue. '*Wayne*. We're going to Wayne Baxendale's funeral. This is the worst week of my life. Hold my hand, babes, and don't let go.'

16

PHOEBE

Up before dawn to edit, Phoebe turned on her phone to message her daughters in their faraway afternoon time-zones as usual, and spotted a mistyped update from Juno on the Village Detectives WhatsApp group left late the night before:

> I cqnt feel my right hand. Am typing this with my left, plus nose. Sorry about thw typos. Wld call but is very late. Gives me an idew...

Beneath it was a voice note.

Juno spoke in her usual fast, breathless jumble, clearly tight again: 'Hello? Is this recording? Thank goodness. Now I know why you do this, Mil. Genius! Hi, all! 'Scuse the late hour. I've been at a wake. It was Wayne Baxendale! Remember, Freddy? One minute, he was on the phone to Rich, telling him he'd found love again, the next – "boof" – heart attack in his amuse bouche. Anyway, Wayne Baxendale's funeral was today. I was there, and kind of attached to Debra's hand throughout. Bones may have broken.

'I don't think she should have attended, if I'm honest. She's no longer crying non-stop, but she's become *seriously* controlling and a bit scary, and her drinking is out of control. She kept the after-party going until last orders and introduced me to everyone as her "bestie". My hand is *crushed* from her holding it.

'Anyway, Wayne Baxendale was a local fast-food tech big hitter who ran corporations and sponsored all sorts. The funeral was weirdly corporate. The tributes felt more like a sales conference award ceremony. Hardly any family, just one grown-up daughter who looked suitably miserable. Debra told me that this daughter hasn't spoken to Wayne since the noughties when he went off with the au pair. He remarried at least twice afterwards, although no wives past or present were there. No sign of any new girlfriend either – Wayne was meant to be meeting her at The Priory when he died, but she was a no-show and nobody had a clue who she might be. Doesn't that strike you as weird? According to Debra, Wayne confided to Rich that night that he was besotted with her, but she thinks they'd only ever communicated online.

'After the funeral, the mourners went to Wayne's favourite pub for a buffet lunch, the Pheasant Inn or something like that. *Lots* of suits. Debra's paranoid word's out about Rich being found hanged in ladies' undies, but as far as I could tell most of them didn't even know he's dead.

'I couldn't get anything more out of her because she got quite drunk, and Grant was with us the whole time trying to flog me this house on his development again. He's offering me a big discount for early completion. I confess I'm quite tempted. It sounds lovely, although I think he might be having some cashflow problems, so maybe not.

'But Grant did let slip something *very* interesting when Debs was in the loo and I had my hand in a jug of iced water. I asked him what he knew about the WE SIN syndicate – he called it a "cabal" the first time he mentioned it, you'll recall – and he said that when it was just Wayne and Rich, it had been all about boys-only golf breaks in Thailand and ski weekends in Latvia, but all went dark and digital when they became the Wexshire Enterprise Startup Investment Network. Grant calls them "Sin Dickheads" and says some of the investors were anonymous, for which you can read tax dodger according to him. So that could be why they all had codenames, maybe? Also, Debra thinks Wayne Baxendale's nickname was Golden something, but she couldn't remember what. Gun, maybe? Balls?

'I'm seeing her again tomorrow so I'll keep digging. She's determined to take part in Clubbercise as usual, although I really don't think she should while she's in the denial stage of grief. Or it might be the bargaining stage. Possibly acceptance. Then again, she was super angry when she saw her bar tab at the Fox and Pheasant, or whatever it was called. And depressed when I said I couldn't sleep over at Greenside Manor tonight. I'll come to The Barton Arms after the class and hope to see you guys there.

'If Debra is holding my hand, please use all means possible to detach her.'

After sending a quick thumbs up, Phoebe tapped the edge of the phone's case against her lower lip, thinking back to her conversation with Bethany Welch in The Barton Arms beer garden. A mistrustful niggle told her not to believe everything Bethany had said. And yet too much of it rang true to simply dismiss. Phoebe's mind kept circling back to the 'Daddies'. At Juno's party, she was almost certain she could remember Bethany calling Rich 'Daddy'.

Phoebe put down her phone then picked it up again.

Saying a quiet apology, she downloaded the Dapper and Discreet app. It was Juno herself who had told her to do this, she justified.

Phoebe signed in using Juno's email, guessing the password in just two tries – 'Juno' followed by her anniversary. To her relief, it didn't request a verification code.

She landed on Curvy Kitten's account page. It told her it had been two days since her last log-in and that she had messages waiting, all from the same VIP member.

Green Man.

The app reminded her that his picture gallery was open.

Phoebe clicked on it.

What she saw made her smile in surprised delight.

17

JUNO

'It's eight forty-five and you're listening to Smiley Face Radio, for happy people who love happy tunes, and heeeeeeeeeeere's Supergrass!'

'Be happy!' Juno told her reflection in the Bacardi Breezer mirror in the shop beneath her flat. 'You have successfully unboxed an electric bicycle.'

It had taken over half an hour, a surprisingly strenuous activity, the endorphin kick so welcome Juno decided to shelve trying the bike out until after her first deli coffee and LinkedIn scroll. It probably needed charging first anyway.

As soon as she checked her phone, Juno's sunny mood clouded over again.

She felt last night's lengthy recorded message to the Village Detectives group WhatsApp merited more than a single belated thumbs up emoji from Phoebe, especially given the voice note that Mil left this morning had already received two shocked face emojis from the Sylvians and the *Seriously?* she was typing now.

But it was the voice note itself which pained her.

'Rich Bass's death is not being treated as suspicious so there won't be a police investigation,' Mil had just told their WhatsApp group surprisingly cheerfully.

Mil's cousin, who was a constable at Dunford Police Station, had passed on the news that the police were not treating Rich's death as a criminal investigation and the coroner had concluded no more than routine enquiries would be needed ahead of the inquest. The autopsy had confirmed death by asphyxiation. No other parties were thought to be involved.

Yet Juno couldn't help feeling her party had been very much involved.

Mil's voice note went on: 'Word from pathology is that Rich had consumed a pervy old cocktail on top of all the champagne to get himself revved up, and then he choked in the act so to speak.'

> What pervy cocktail?

She resisted adding the shocked emoji to her reply.

Three days of hand holding Debra, her high grief and excessive daytime drinking at Greenside Manor had left Juno unsurprised Rich had needed recreational drugs. That and Dire Straits piping through every room on repeat was enough to drive anybody to Class A.

Mil's voice note reply had already landed: 'Viagra, GHB – that's liquid ecstasy – and poppers. Insiders call it a Chemsex on the Beach, my cousin says.'

Juno hoped he wasn't planning to add it to the cocktail board for Happy Hour at The Barton Arms. She'd be sticking to a soft drink after Clubbercise.

* * *

'Your largest glass of white wine!' Juno demanded that evening, sweat still glistening on her brow. 'Or better still, just hand me the bottle and a straw.'

'Bethany put you ladies through your paces tonight, did she?' Mil reached for the Pinot Grigio, grinning widely.

'I didn't get there. It ended ages ago.' She checked her watch. 'Debra was all dressed up in her leopard-print leotard when I called round, but insisted we do an Arlene Phillips DVD class in her lounge instead. She made Grant join in in his Chelsea strip. I was *trapped* there for *hours*. Haven't any of the class been in?' She looked round expectantly.

'A couple of them popped across for a quick drink a while back now you mention it,' Mil said, placing her wine in front of her, 'but I've been too busy to chat. Courtney didn't turn up for her shift tonight.' The creases in his handsomely craggy face deepened.

He was looking almost as harassed as her, Juno realised. 'Is she okay?'

'Got a job at The Priory at Dunford that pays more, she says. It even sends a minibus around to collect staff. I've got an eightieth birthday in the dining room, twenty covers in the restaurant, the darts league in the snug and no waitress!'

'I'll help,' Juno offered.

'Mate, you're a life saver!' He made to hug her then stopped, pulling his chin back to examine her face more closely. 'You look done in. I can't ask you to help.'

'Flatterer,' Juno scoffed, worrying that he thought looking 'done in' would put off the customers. 'Trust me, after the day I've had, it would be the perfect distraction. Hand over an apron.'

'If you're sure?'

'I'll enjoy it!' she promised, grateful to be needed. She had plenty of waitressing experience from her early stand-up years supplementing lean patches, and loved the sociable side, serving smiles and laughter with great food, adding to the fun.

As a bonus, on the terrace outside overlooking the Dunnett, she discovered two of the Clubbercise ladies polishing off a bottle of house white. They hailed her excitedly.

'We missed you at class! We were all talking about you tonight. Bethany says you're a legend.'

'Oh, yes?' Juno perked up. Like Oscar Wilde, she found the only thing worse than being talked about was not being talked about.

She wondered if rumours of her investigation into Rich's death had spread. Or was news of her sudden and intense friendship with Debra Bass causing a stir?

'That video she took of you needing the loo at your party has reached a quarter of a million TikTok views, Bethany says.'

Which just about capped Juno's bad day.

When at last the dining room had emptied, the darts team packed up and the pub crowd thinned to a few regulars, Mil presented Juno with an enormous glass of his best rosé at the bar in thanks, helping himself to a bottle of lager. She didn't have the heart to tell him she'd far rather have a cup of tea, preferably intravenously.

Walking round from behind the bar, Mil sagged on a stool beside her, rubbing his craggy face with a forearm. 'It's been like this all day. Thank God my brother is back off holiday tomorrow is all I'll say.'

'Does that mean you've not got much village intel yet?'

"Fraid not.'

'I have lots, don't worry. First, the big news is Rich's funeral is next Tuesday. Now the coroner's ruled out a suspicious death, Debra has applied for an interim death certificate so that she can arrange a burial asap. She doesn't hang about. It's the first morning slot in the crematorium, with a buffet brunch at the golf club afterwards. She wants me to drum up mourners and' – she took a bolstering breath – 'sing.'

It had been a testing few days, overshadowed by Debra, whose manic neediness had already become such a guilty drain. Thankfully, Debra didn't do messaging or voice notes, but this morning, the first phone calls had come in just before eight with: 'Oh, God, babes, a song Scott Mills is playing's just set me off! Listen to this! Can you put that on your list?' The calls and song requests had then continued every few minutes until: 'Are you watching *This Morning*, babes? They're interviewing that Real Housewife of Cheshire who won *Dancing on Ice* after her husband died. I can't stop crying. When are you coming round?'

'We're meeting up for Clubbercise this evening,' Juno had reminded her brightly.

'But you'll come here first, yeah? I've written a guest list for the funeral, only we'll need to add to it so Rich has more mourners than Wayne did. I owe him that. You and I can have a drinkie before class. Shall we say five? Or come to lunch! In fact, we can have a Bloody Mary now. Come straight round.'

Juno had quickly apologised that she was visiting mum Judy, followed by, 'Then running errands for her.' Then, just to be sure, she'd added, 'All day.'

'I exaggerated a bit,' she told Mil in The Barton Arms now, 'but I couldn't face her, and I've been neglecting Mum.'

'That woman is taking advantage of you, Juno,' Mil warned her. 'She's an unhinged boozer.'

'Yes, but she's my mother,' Juno joked, pushing her wine away.

After the call with Debra that morning, she'd strapped on

her helmet and hurriedly ridden the e-bike to Godlington Hall, where Judy was having coffee with best friend Pam, both agog to know how the latest crime investigation was going.

When Juno had explained that it looked like Rich Bass's death was misadventure, they'd both huffed in exasperation.

'We're not referring to that unfortunate man's demise!' Judy had dismissed.

'We're talking about the pervert who keeps dressing up graves!' Pam had clarified, then confided, 'We have information.'

Slugging back wine now, Juno told Mil, 'Pam is good chums with Mary the churchwarden, who first spoke to you about the Graveyard Ravers. You promised her you'd investigate it and set up a surveillance operation, remember?'

'And I will! I'll go and see her again tomorrow.'

'No need, I already have.'

Mil's battered face softened. 'No word of a lie, Juno, you are a saint.' He gazed at her with such misty-eyed admiration, she felt the woes of the day melting away. 'The way you're supporting Debra is bloody lovely. Helping me out tonight, and now this too. All from the kindness of your heart. We don't deserve you.'

Juno flushed. She decided not to mention the old-fashioned ticking off that ex-games mistress Pam had given her earlier: 'Mary is banking on you all! Go round there and reassure them you and your friends are doing what you can! She's seventy-eight, her mother is a hundred. What's more – and this is strictly confidential, given Judy is a something of a local celebrity – Mary tells us that—'

'She's started knitting your grandchild a cardigan!' Judy had interrupted, which confused Juno, who sensed Pam had been going to say something different.

Nor did Juno confide to Mil that her mother had hectored her about the imminent family addition: 'This baby needs you to be the strong one, Pusscat'; 'A grandchild will stop you obsessing about your love life'; 'You *must* stand up for Eric through this'; 'It might be the only chance you get to be a granny.'

And she certainly wasn't about to share the uncharacteristically testy way her mother had reacted when Juno explained that she couldn't go and see Eric until her car was mended. Face darkening thunderously, she'd bellowed, 'What about my car?'

Although she no longer drove, Judy was sentimentally attached to her bright orange Honda Jazz – the boot of which she used to stash her many sartorial impulse purchases – and she remained furious with Juno for treating it so badly.

Nor did Juno tell Mil that while she was at Godlington Hall, Debra had rung so incessantly she'd eventually had to put her mobile on silent. But this just made things worse when Debra then called Judy's landline in tears. Juno deeply regretted sharing the number.

Coming off the phone, Judy's eyes had bulged. 'You of all people should know how much that poor widow needs friends at a time like this, Pusscat!'

'Too right!' Pam had echoed, unfairly, Juno felt, given she'd sailed off on a six-week European river cruise shortly after Judy had been widowed.

That's when both older women had cranked up their sermonising 'for your own good', lecturing Juno to sort out her priorities, get a job, and find somewhere decent to live with space for her son, who clearly needed her support.

'Put your family first!' Pam had summarised afterwards.

'Don't become a selfish party animal like your brother,

Pusscat,' Judy had scolded. 'How I could give birth to two such hedonistic children is beyond me. Now you're going to have to push off because Dennis will be back any minute and the Campbells are coming round for hot tub drinks in half an hour. You're cramping my style.'

Pam had walked Juno down to the grand Godlington entrance. 'Your mother's being firm because she's worried about you. I'll wave you off.'

It was only as she was about to set off on the electric bike to visit Mary the churchwarden that Juno had finally discovered the truth.

'Keep this to yourself,' Pam had muttered, 'but a lot of the lingerie the "Graveyard Ravers" have been adorning headstones with once belonged to your mother. She's furious about it. Most of it had only been worn once.'

This, it transpired, was the 'information' they'd promised. And it shocked Juno deeply. Her mother, inveterate impulse-purchaser of flamboyant clothing, had lately donated unwanted items to the church jumble. Some of it had been used by the Graveyard Ravers to make their mark.

Not that Juno was going to tell Mil that either.

Talking to him, she was determinedly positive. 'I cycled to Mary's. Exhausting! I'll be as fit as you soon!'

'Isn't yours an electric bike?'

'Turns out you have to charge it longer.'

The bike had run out of charge halfway there.

Thighs on fire, she'd located a brick and flint cottage behind the Coronation Hall, which elderly churchwarden Mary shared with her even more elderly mother, along with one of Kevin Bacon's ginger sisters called Shirley MacLaine, whose eyes didn't once leave the dancing ball of yellow wool as Mary resumed her knitting whilst divulging valuable information.

'She told me what she'd told Mum and Pam,' she recounted to Mil now. 'Mary recently collected a lot of unwanted clothes from Godlington residents for the church jumble sale. It was then stored in boxes under the church hall stage – you know, where I do Clubbercise. She'd made a start on sorting it, so she knew there was a lot of high quality but outré stuff amongst it that she set aside.'

'Outré?'

'It means risky – sexy negligees and the like. In unusually large sizes.' Juno cleared her throat awkwardly, now familiar with her mother's high turnover of niche impulse purchases. 'Mary recognised certain items of these on the headstones after the night of my party.'

'Did she see who bought the stuff from the jumble sale?'

'There hasn't been a jumble sale yet, that's the point. Somebody must have taken them from the church hall.'

'Who?'

'No idea, but that's not all. Listen to this: Mary says that amongst the stuff she remembered sorting through was a particularly beautiful floral silk kimono with a marabou trim.'

Mil nodded eagerly. 'Sounds great.'

'Just like the one Rich was wearing when he died?' Juno nudged his memory.

'Why would someone as well off as Rich buy jumble sale stuff?'

'It went missing at the same time as the other stuff. But it wasn't part of the Graveyard Ravers' latest fashion show. It was part of Rich's death scene.'

His mouth fell open in surprise. 'You mean…'

She nodded.

'*Rich Bass* was the Graveyard Raver?'

'What? No!' This hadn't occurred to Juno, whose wild imagination had already cast the Graveyard Ravers as a depraved village sex cult that had ritualistically murdered its most unpopular self-styled squire. 'At least, I doubt it. Then again, maybe you have a point? God, I'm rubbish at this. There's more.'

After reassuring churchwarden Mary that the case was in hand, Juno had cycled on to funky village mechanics Drum n' Brakes to check progress on the car repairs, delighted that the Mini was almost ready, less so that her mother's Jazz was far from it. The young couple had fast-charged the e-bike and made her a cup of tea while she waited. That's when they'd told her more about Wayne Baxendale's classic eighties car collection, most of them soft tops, and how he'd boasted about taking lady friends out in them.

'Wayne had a Lotus, a TVR, a Morgan and more Spiders than your cellars,' she told Mil. 'The Drum n' Brakes guys serviced them all. Turns out they got their original startup funding from the Wexshire Enterprise Investment whatnot – WE SIN – and that's how they got to know Wayne. They'd often see him gunning one along the Old London Road, giving it serious *Miami Vice* vibes. Apparently, a couple of times recently they spotted a woman in the passenger seat, her blonde hair flying around. Or rather, her *blonde dreadlocks*...' She waited for a reaction.

Mil was nodding, his brow creased. 'Morgans are nice beasts, don't get me wrong, but I've always thought your Caterham has the edge, more of a driving thrill.'

'*Dreadlocks*, Mil. It had to be Bethany Welch!'

'You sure?'

'Drum n' Brakes swore they saw Wayne Baxendale driving Bethany through this village in a BMW cabriolet more than once.'

'What's that got to do with the Graveyard Ravers?'

'Don't you see, Mil? It's all connected. Wayne Baxendale died just a week before his old friend and business ally, Rich. He was waiting for a date with his new girlfriend. Could she have been Bethany?'

'Bit of a shot in the dark.'

'Or, more likely, a Chemsex on the Beach slipped in his aperitif!'

'I don't follow.'

'Do you remember at lunch when I mentioned Wayne's sudden death, Bethany said "I wouldn't say no to a meal in The Priory"? How did she know that was the restaurant he died in?'

'Her son Seph washes pots there. He's the one who got Courtney – his cousin – a job. Half the village kids work there. Minibus, remember.' He looked peeved.

Juno felt deflated, her brilliant deduction flawed. 'Okay, so it might be common knowledge where Wayne died, but it doesn't take away from the fact that Bethany was spotted *in a car with him*, or – and this is a key point – that the clothes Rich was wearing when *he* died were stolen from beneath a stage on which Bethany *teaches a fitness class*.' Even as she said it, Juno realised how feeble this sounded.

'I think you're clutching at straws here, Juno.' Mil scratched his head.

'Maybe you're right.' She slumped on her bar stool. 'The trouble is, nobody in this village has anything much to say about Rich Bass, except that he wasn't liked. I went round to see Oscar in the antiques shop this afternoon, and he had no idea who Rich Bass even was. I had to google him on my phone and show him a photograph. Lots of villagers still call the Basses newcomers, yet Rich and Debra moved here over a decade ago. They might have muscled their way onto every committee, but they were never a part of day-to-day village life. In fact, they were surprisingly insular.'

To Juno's frustration, village gossip was uncomfortably muted about Rich Bass's death. The more salacious details hadn't got out, so the story being circulated was that the unpopular retired kitchen tycoon had committed suicide, driven to hanging himself by who knew what demons, although Debra's nagging was a popular guess. An awkward, collective embarrassment permeated.

'Meanwhile, poor Debra is grief-stricken,' she told Mil. 'And Grant is obsessing about heavy metal and heritage thatch. I thought I'd never get away this evening. I had to bring out the big guns.'

'What's that?'

'*Clarkson's Farm* box set on Amazon. They both love him. I said I was going to pop home to feed the cat.' She looked at her watch. 'I'd better go back and check on her.'

'Him, don't you mean?' asked Mil. 'Kevin's a boy, isn't he?'

'I mean Debra,' Juno explained, touched he remembered her cat's name, even if Kevin's pronouns were his own business.

'Debra will be in bed by now,' Mil dismissed. 'Give yourself a night off.'

A tall figure sat down on the bar stool beside Juno. 'We're going nowhere.'

It was Phoebe.

She laid a Moleskine notebook down on the bar and placed her phone on top of it.

'The app holds the secret,' she told them. 'Dapper and Discreet is the connection between the deaths, I'm certain of it. I think some, if not all, of the original WE SIN investment angels are on it. And somebody wants them dead.'

18

PHOEBE

Phoebe opened her notebook.

On the first page, she'd written three lines:

Rich Bass – auto-erotic asphyxiation this week
Wayne Baxendale – heart attack three weeks ago
Holly Lovat-Dixon – car crash over a year ago

'I have been thinking about these three deaths all day, which is frankly maddening given my workload, but I confess they're fascinating me. None of them died the same way' – she studied the list – 'and none of the deaths was deemed suspicious by the police, so they don't seem to merit investigation individually, let alone as a group. And yet...'

On the next page she'd written:

WE SIN: Wexshire Enterprise Startup Investment Network
(Local Business Angels)
Dapper & Discreet 'Daddies'
Black Horse – Rich Bass

Golden Pheasant – Wayne Baxendale
Purple Pussycat – ?
White Swan or Dove – ?
(Red?) Lion – ?
Huntsman/Robin Hood… Green Man – ?

Beside her, Juno gasped. 'Green Man?'

'He may not be in the syndicate,' Phoebe explained, 'but I think it's the name Debra was trying to remember when she told you about them.'

'There's a Green Man in Great Dunton,' Mil pointed out. 'Are these all the names of pubs, then?'

'That or online dating avatars.' Phoebe tapped the list with her pen. 'Possibly both. WE SIN invested in several award-winning Wexshire gastro-pubs. Did you notice the name of the one Wayne's funeral breakfast was held in?' she asked Juno.

'The Golden Pheasant.' Juno looked down at the list again. 'That's genius, Freddy!'

'I don't know any boozer round here called the Purple Pussycat.' Mil frowned.

'Wasn't it a bar in the Austin Powers movies?' asked Juno.

'No, that's the Electric Psychedelic Pussycat Swingers Club,' Mil corrected without thinking, then looked embarrassed.

'I agree it doesn't fit in' – Phoebe pinched the bridge of her nose in frustration – 'but two people on this list are nonetheless dead.' She glanced around to make sure none of the pub's other customers were listening in. 'We need to know the real names of the others on here, and whether Holly Lovat-Dixon can be linked to any of them.'

'I am happy to investigate local pubs if it helps,' Mil volunteered nobly. 'Albie's back tomorrow and he owes me some time off for working my butt off while he sunned his.'

'Mil, we're dying of thirst here!' called a voice further along the bar.

'Talking of which... don't go away, I'll be right back.' Mil reluctantly peeled away to serve them.

Phoebe leaned closer to Juno. 'Green Man is our key, I'm certain,' she told her in an undertone. 'He messaged you that he was going to be in this area on the night Rich died. He contacted Bethany Welch on the app too.'

'*Bethany's* on the app?'

'Cheryl gets an introduction fee, so lots of her family and friends are on it. Bethany is certain that all the original investors – the "Daddies" – got VIP membership as a perk when they sold out. I've a shrewd suspicion Wayne was her first match on there. She couldn't deny Green Man might be a Daddy too. I thought he had to be Rich, but she insists not.'

'She *must* have met Wayne through it, she was seen in his car more than once.' Juno's eyes were saucers, her voice trembling. 'Tell me Bethany's top of your suspect list? It surely can't be a coincidence that she's already hooked up with two – what did you call them? – Daddies. She's obviously picking them off!'

'It's one theory, although the app uses geolocation, so it stands to reason Inkbury women have a higher chance of being matched with one of a local syndicate. You were.' Phoebe told Juno about the Welches making a pact after their divorces. 'They called themselves the Three Decrees. Bethany, her big sister Zadie and their cousin Cheryl all signed up to Dapper and Discreet, knowing full well that most of its members were rich married men. And they vowed to treat cheating husbands as badly as their cheating husbands had treated them.'

'By murdering them?'

'Again, it's possible, although according to Bethany, they are in it for the fine dining, gifts, attention, the holidays even, then they walk away before it gets messy. That doesn't suggest murder on the menu.'

'She's hardly going to tell you if she Chemsexes her dates to death.'

'Maybe, but my guess would be it's a syndicate insider. One of the Daddies. If the original investors had special VIP privileges, could one of them be using these to kill the others?'

'You really think so?' Juno's eyes were now like dinner plates.

Phoebe picked up her notebook, flicking back a page. 'We can't categorically say that any of these three were murdered, can we? So this is pure speculation, but there are plenty of examples out there where matchmaking apps have been exploited by insiders for blackmail and coercion as well as personal pleasure, especially those offering anonymous affairs like Dapper and Discreet does.'

'It doesn't implicitly offer that, though, does it?'

'That's the whole point of it, Juno! Or rather the point of it is to make money out of people who want to have an affair. And it's made a lot of money, which is another very strong motive for murder, both for those who stand to gain and for those who may have lost out. The app maximises value out of its members by persuading them to buy credits to pay for messages.'

'Only the men pay, so you must think our murderer is a man?'

'Men outnumber women on dating apps four to one, and even more on illicit ones. The majority of Dapper and Discreet's female members will almost certainly be fake, either AI bots or remote workers paid by the company, generating income from all those paid-for messages their unsuspecting matches send. It's horribly cynical, but it's nothing new.'

'Have you been talking to Eric?' Juno asked beadily.

Staying poker-faced, Phoebe said, 'I remember covering the Ashley Madison scandal when I was still in journalism, but if you were to ask Eric about it, I promise he'd back me up here.'

Juno had a mother's laser insight. 'Because you've already asked Eric about it.'

'Okay, so I asked Eric about it. Just a very quick call. Lucky to catch him.'

'Freddy, how *could* you?' Juno squeaked. 'Did you tell him I'm on Dapper and Discreet? I am deleting it straight away.'

'You are not! We need to find out who this Green Man character is.'

Phoebe turned the page. Under 'Suspects', she had written just one name.

Green Man.

'Have you any idea who he might be?' Juno asked in a small voice.

'My first guess was Rich.'

'But Rich was known as Black Horse in the syndicate.'

'He could have used two aliases. Greenside Manor is an obvious clue.'

'Also he's dead, Freddy.'

'That's actually another thing that initially led me to think it was him. You see, Green Man stopped messaging you straight after Rich died, which had to be sometime between two and five in the morning. You and Green Man messaged a lot in those early hours.'

'You think Rich was indulging in Chemsex on the Beach and pleasuring himself whilst messaging *me*?' Juno looked horrified.

'Not any more.' Phoebe was quick to reassure her. 'Green

Man isn't dead, Juno. I logged into your Dapper and Discreet account today.'

'You hacked into the app as me?'

'You gave me express permission,' Phoebe reminded her. 'All I did was look at his gallery.'

'That means you must know who he is!'

'No, but I do know he's still alive. Check the app and you'll see.'

Juno picked up her phone and opened it.

There was a new message from Green Man.

> Caught you peeking.

Juno yelped again, hurriedly navigating away from the screen. 'I'm definitely deleting this thing.'

'Absolutely not!' Phoebe ordered, quickly taking the phone from her. 'We need to unmask Green Man.'

'You just said you've looked at his gallery, so you must know what he looks like.'

'There are no pictures of his face on here, Juno.' Phoebe held the phone up.

'I don't want to see!' Juno covered her eyes.

'You've seen plenty of these before,' Phoebe told her, amused.

'Are they of his *private parts*?' Juno asked in trepidation from behind her hands.

'It's one of the nicest ones I've seen,' she reassured her.

Juno peeked out between her fingers and Phoebe watched her face cycling from dread to confusion to relief.

A smiling black Labrador beamed from her screen, his teeth even whiter and canines even sharper than Grant's.

'They're all of his dog!' Juno squealed with relief as Phoebe flipped through the gallery. 'But that's not Bullet the dachshund.'

'Because Green Man isn't Rich,' Phoebe repeated, 'and he's obviously trying to conceal his identity, although if you look in the background you can see some artily blurred bits of a man's foot, his hand and even a bit of his ear here, see?'

'I really don't want to message him any more.'

'He's our only decent lead.'

'You're the writer, Freddy. *You* message him. You can flirt with him far better than me, lure him in.'

'So you want a Cyrano de Bergerac?' Phoebe asked.

'Only got an Australian Chardonnay, I'm afraid.' Mil reappeared with the wine bottle and topped up their glasses.

'Cyrano de Bergerac was a person.' Juno picked hers up then put it straight down again.

'Cyrano penned love letters to the beautiful Roxane on behalf of his inarticulate friend Christian,' Phoebe explained, 'but ended up falling in love with her and vice versa.'

'Do *not* fall in love with Green Man, Freddy,' Juno warned as her phone started to ring. 'I must take this.' She turned away to answer it. 'Debra! How are you bearing up? ...Oh, poor you... That's okay, take your time... Oh, do you have a tissue?'

'What's this about?' Mil asked Phoebe, who outlined her plan to flush out Green Man by arranging for Juno to meet him on a date.

Watching Juno talking animatedly into the phone, Mil said in an undertone, 'You'd really put her through that?'

'It's a honeytrap, Mil.' Phoebe fished out her own phone, logged onto the app and sent Green Man a wink. 'And I'm the one doing the flirting.'

Mil's handsomely furrowed face frowned from Thor to

Thanos. 'Well, I don't like the sound of it. Nor will Felix, I reckon, you sexting a stranger.'

'He wouldn't even notice,' she deadpanned.

'Movie still taking up all his time?'

'He thinks all this is pointless, that there's been no murder.' She pushed aside the Moleskine notebook, half inclined to agree.

'But you reckon this Green Man might be connected to Rich's death?' Mil put his big hand on the book and pushed it back.

'He's of interest,' she said, watching Mil flip to the list on the next page, 'as are that lot.'

Overleaf, she had written:

<u>Other suspects:</u>
Debra Bass
Grant Roberts (brother)
Other syndicate members
Cosmo Lovat
The Three Decrees

'Who are the Three Decrees?' asked Mil.

'Bethany, Zadie and Cheryl Welch.'

'As if!' He looked personally affronted. 'They never killed Rich. Cheryl's abroad, Bethany kipped over here that night, and as for Zadie, well, why would she?'

He had a point, Phoebe conceded, although she was tempted to ask whether he could vouch for Bethany's exact whereabouts in the small hours given she'd slept on his sofa.

'And why Cosmo?' Mil asked.

'They argued the night Rich died. And I've heard Cosmo bears grudges.' She'd called mutual friend Saskia Seaton, head of an old family dynasty of chartered surveyors. She'd told Phoebe that Cosmo, who specialised in land banking and property development, was a very prickly customer indeed. Her pithy summary had been *gorgeous but bloodless*. 'Where's his house in the village?'

'He's never there,' Mil told her. 'Think he stays in a hotel out Marlbury way when he's here nowadays. Can't say I blame him, seeing what he found that day.'

'Holly crashed her car right outside their place, didn't she?'

Wincing, Mil nodded. 'It's out Woodridge way,' he told her, 'on the dogleg bend. There's a gated estate where the sawmill used to be. Pretty spot. All the new houses there are made to look old, but they only got built a few years back. Cosmo bought up the site to develop, and his place is by far the biggest, set apart from the others with its own driveway. Thatched, it is. Has a straw cat on its roof ridge and a big brick and flint wall out front.'

'Is that the wall his wife...'

'Yeah.' He nodded. 'Holly must have been going some speed, poor woman. Always did drive like a maniac.'

'What was she like?'

'Part of the yummy mummy set. Her ex used to drink in here before they split. That was around the time me and Albie took over the licence. Nice bloke, but a bit of a doormat. Worked in pharmaceuticals over Oxford way. He moved there after the divorce, although I heard he's now in Northumberland doing some off-grid eco thing. His mates used to call him Doc Green, but I never knew why cos his name was Dixon and he wasn't a doctor.'

'*Dixon of Dock Green* was a television show years ago,' Phoebe enlightened him, quietly irritated that Mil had defined Holly by her ex-husband. 'What was Holly's line of work?'

'I heard she gave up some high-flying career when kiddies came along, but I don't know of anything else 'til Cosmo bought her the village deli to give her something to do. Their kids must have been quite grown up by then, off to college sort of thing. Reckon Holly was a bit too fond of her shopping, tennis and ladies' lunches for Cosmo's liking.'

'So he doesn't stay in their cottage when he's here?'

'Shame to see a beautiful place like that lying empty.' He looked up as Juno came bustling back from her call. She was wiping a tear.

'Debra's in a bit of a state,' she reported breathlessly.

'Tell me you're not going round there again?' Phoebe could see how tired she was.

'No, she's in bed, but she's booked us a spa day tomorrow, which is perfect. She has lots of treat day vouchers stored up, she says, because Rich always gave her them for birthdays and Christmas, so this is in his honour. She just needed somebody to listen. She's been sending out emails to everyone in Rich's contacts about the funeral. It's set her off.'

'Debra's lucky to have a friend like you,' Mil told her admiringly.

'Debra has Rich's contacts?' Phoebe sat up. 'Can you find a way to look at them, do you think? Take a copy?'

'I can't do that to her. She needs me to have her back right now,' Juno said, confiding, 'and I don't trust Grant. He's hiding something.'

'All the more reason to be our spy on the inside,' Phoebe reassured her.

'I'll see what I can do,' Juno promised. 'But my first priority is to look out for Debra.'

'I've said it before,' Mil beamed at her admiringly, 'you are a saint, Juno.' He reached for her glass to refill it, then realised it was still full.

'Would you mind terribly if I had a peppermint tea?' Juno asked. 'I think the most dangerous thing about being at Greenside Manor so much is the threat to my liver.'

Phoebe looked down as her phone vibrated.

Green Man had sent an aubergine.

'Operation Cyrano has engaged the target,' she told the others.

19

JUNO

'The spa day was quite boozy,' Juno updated the Village Detectives WhatsApp group in a sleepy voice note the following evening. 'One bottle per facial, body wrap and sauna. Debs fell asleep during the massage. I had to pay the drinks bill. No useful intel. Any developments with you guys? How's Cyrano getting on?'

> Still communicating in fruit and vegetables. P x

'I've brought a few Warriors to check out The White Swan in Nether Bassett,' Mil's voice note reported, a rowdy male chorus in the background. 'We're on the case.'

> Green Man just sent hotdog and cherry. I'm on the case too. Have sent winking emoji and thumbs up. P x

'Now at The Blue Lion in Upper Wallop. Still on the case!'

> Green Man has sent a screwdriver and smiley cat. Not sure what that means. Have you heard anything more from Eric, Juno? I know he's on the move, but it would be useful. P x

'Sorry, slow reply! Been asleep power napping on the sofa... Get off, Kevin... I've messaged Eric again about that deep dive, and left messages... I said, get *off*, Kevin! It's not like him to be this lax, although he's probably got an eSport tournament. You don't think the baby could have come? I'll call him again now.'

'Black Horse in Rushbury! Go the lads! Go Warriors!'

> Green Man has sent a taco and water drops. Even more confused. P x

'Send back a fire and lips, Freddy. Still no word from Eric.'

> Late to this. On train home. Rushbury is my next stop. Might join you guys at the Black Horse. Felix.

'Reporting in from the Green Man in Great Dunton! Felix is here – say hello, Felix. Go Warriors! All together now, lads: Swing looooow, sweeet chaaariooot...'

> Green Man (human, not pub) says he might be in the area next week if I/we want to meet. Have sent Yeats quote. Curvy Kitten is all out of emojis and Cyrano's in charge. P x

'Hey, guys, Eric has messaged! It's just a gif of Popeye flying along in a rowing boat, but I'm sure that means he's on the case!'

* * *

Eric was proving frustratingly uncommunicative, and Juno started to worry even more. In the past four days, all he'd shared was one Popeye gif and a screenshot of a map with a pin dropped near Oxford.

Aware that asking him anything about the baby would inevitably be met with silence, Juno sent him multiple messages repeating her request for any information he could dredge up about Rich Bass, Wayne Baxendale and Holly Lovat-Dixon, along with the Wexshire Enterprise Startup Investment Network and its members. Bracing herself, she also reminded him to try to identify the developers of the app called Dapper and Discreet that the syndicate had backed.

'I know you spoke to Freddy about it already, honey, and I know you're busy, but googling's getting me nowhere and we think there may be a very serious crime involved,' she told her son in a voice note, which was fast becoming her favourite way of communicating. 'The Village Detectives need as much insider information as possible before—' An incoming call interrupted her recording.

Debra was already sobbing so hard it was difficult to make out what she was saying. 'Juno, babes... funeral directors need something to dress... Gave all Rich's clothes away... Just looked in his drawers... Can't be happening to me!'

'I'll come straight round,' she promised, certain Debra must have found Rich's kinky clothes stash, and hoping this had to be a vital clue.

But it turned out that the funeral directors had requested an outfit to dress Rich in as they prepared him for his final exit. And there wasn't so much as a Pringle sock left in the house.

'He's being cremated,' Debra explained, 'but he can hardly be put in there wearing a lady's kimono and frilly knickers, can he? All his clothes have gone!' The sobs intensified.

'Can you ask Grant to bring back a favourite suit?'

'He's already sold them all!'

'He doesn't hang about.'

'You must help me find something, Juno babes!'

'Do you want to go shopping? We can do it online if you're not up to going out.'

'I don't want to *buy* anything.' She blew her nose. 'It's only going up in flames. That's why I chose the budget coffin. And even the charity shops in Marlbury charge a mint for a double-breasted M&S Autograph range.'

'I suppose there's always the village jumble,' Juno suggested reluctantly, uncomfortably aware that the 'lady's kimono' Debra had just mentioned may have come from it. Should she say something?

'You're a life saver!' Debra seemed delighted at the suggestion. 'The God squad always have tons of stuff donated, don't they? Can you ask one of the old busybodies if they can spare me some men's clothes?'

Juno couldn't bear it if she found out another way, and she blurted the truth. 'It's possible the clothes Rich was found in when he – that they were – from there!'

Debra's voice trembled with fresh tears. 'You are such a sweetheart to tell me, Juno. But it's okay, babes. The police said it was designer. I'm sure we'll find something.'

When Juno got special permission from churchwarden Mary to take Debra to raid the jumble stored beneath the church hall stage, she was alarmed to find several more designer shopping bags containing her mother's cast-offs, including the lacy Boohoo emerald-green cupcake sleepwear set Juno had bought her for Christmas. With them were also a clutch of Dennis's over-bright hand-tailored linen suits, one of which Debra selected for Rich, along with a sapphire-blue shirt and matching silk tie.

'Lovely shade of yellow!' she sobbed into the suit appreciatively. 'What would I do without you, Juno babes?'

As Debra's funeral planning kicked into overdrive, she kept Juno on an open line, constantly demanding attention. Grief-stricken in her floodlit gin palace, Debra needed a shoulder to cry on, a drinking buddy and a PA.

Grant slithered in and out, the sight of his snarly pick-up parked outside Flatpack Mansion always filling Juno with dread.

'He's supposed to be organising this thing,' she told the WhatsApp group chat, 'but he just eats, loafs around and plays loud music. He's like a spoiled kid. Debra needs more support.'

There were half-finished lists scattered throughout Greenside Manor: guests, food, tributes, service sheet proofs and a draft obituary. When the celebrant arrived to ask about Rich's life and many achievements, Debra was too upset to speak and sent her away again.

'She got me to type it all in an email instead,' Juno reported to the WhatsApp group in another voice note afterwards, now completely addicted to the short, breathless recordings she could make from the Basses' downstairs loo. 'She was very vague on the details. I think she made quite a lot of it up. She's seriously unstable.'

And yet Debra was also completely controlling; she let no decision pass without her say-so, especially those involving money.

'The golf club's letting her have a function room gratis, as long as everyone's out of it by midday,' Juno told the group in a hasty recording from the loo. 'Debra's going to feed guests everything she made for the cricket tea that she could freeze and some of my leftover party snacks. The bar has a one-drink limit before guests pay, and even the celebrant is a trainee doing this as a freebee. It's no wonder she and Rich are loaded. Deep pockets, short arms, as Jay used to say.'

Seeing Debra so distraught reminded Juno perpetually of Jay and of the unfathomable pain of losing him. It made her long to talk to Eric all the more, a soul so like his father.

But when she sent an urgent 'call me' text, he just shared another map with a pin drop near Abingdon.

To Juno's horror, Debra also insisted on overseeing rehearsals of the Dire Straits medley she'd asked her to perform, and was still demanding that Grant accompany everything with his guitar.

'Nobody will hear me,' she told Phoebe after one particularly painful run through of 'Walk of Life'. 'Grant was in a heavy metal thrash band in the noughties and will only play with his amp at eleven.'

She'd escaped Debra for an hour by offering to take Bullet for a walk, joining forces with Phoebe and the terriers to do so. They were all crossing the Green together, eyes narrowed against a lowering sun. It was such a relief to get away from Flatpack Mansion that Juno was bouncing on springs while she towed the dachshund along to hand-deliver invitations around the village to Rich's wake, grateful for Phoebe's wise counsel. 'Debra wants a big crowd. It even says "music and nibbles" on these.' She thrust one at Phoebe. 'I persuaded her to ditch "bring a bottle", because the golf club doesn't offer corkage.'

'Is "Walk of Life" quite fitting for a funeral?' Phoebe asked, studying the invitation.

'"Kicks for Free" is worse. Wait till you hear the riff. And don't even get me started on the Madness track which we're doing in the style of Metallica. There's something seriously dodgy about Grant.'

Throughout the week, Juno's suspicions had slowly transferred from Bethany to Grant, whose big blue pick-up truck with *G. M. Roberts Newbuild Heritage Eco Thatch* emblazoned in its sides was now constantly parked outside Flatpack Mansion. He remained in situ at Greenside Manor almost round the clock, guarding his sister vigilantly from all comers, the siblings apparently existing on a diet of ageing cricket sandwiches and deli snacks that couldn't be frozen. Up to her eyeballs on Valium and mojitos, Debra was barely eating at all, the frantic self-absorption frequently giving way to catatonia.

'I think Grant might be drugging her,' Juno reported in an undertone. 'The more I'm there, the more I'm convinced he's the one up to no good. And he's *still* trying to sell me a house. It's no wonder his wife walked out on him if you ask me. Debra says she was a flighty little trollop who met someone else online, so his music and his work is all he's got.'

When not deafening Juno with reverb, Grant droned on in his monotone about thatched newbuilds for so long that Juno strongly suspected this was a deliberate ploy to stop her asking awkward questions. Despite the flotilla of paperwork everywhere – much of which Juno had guiltily and secretly photographed to send to the group chat – she had found out nothing more about the WE SIN syndicate, and nobody to match to the list of angel codenames. When she'd snapped the face of the flat-nosed man in the framed picture with Rich and fed it through Google Image Search, it had suggested he was Jeff Bezos.

'Felix and Mil are devoting themselves to investigating

pubs,' Phoebe told Juno. 'Have you still not been able to get sight of Rich's contacts?'

Juno shook her head. 'Debra keeps his phone and laptop in the safe, and she's been cramming more files and stuff in there each day. I'm worried she's struggling with the legal side. There've been a lot of shouty phone calls behind closed doors that make her cry, but she won't talk about it. She's increasingly reluctant to leave the house, not even to walk Bullet round the garden. She wouldn't come out with me to do this today even though the weather's glorious. I've suggested she try again to come with me to Clubbercise class this week, but it was a hard no.'

'That would be too much, surely?'

'You're probably right. And Cheryl will be back by then. All that loved-up happiness to a trippy techno beat could finish Debra off.'

'Especially given Cheryl met her married lover on Dapper and Discreet,' Phoebe reminded her.

'Shh, that's supposed to be a secret.' Juno looked round warily. 'Debra doesn't know that.'

'She probably knows more than she's letting on. She told me just how much she hated the app the night of your party, remember? She knows Rich invested in its startup.'

'But do you really think he was *using* it?'

'Have you asked her outright?'

'I couldn't do that in her state of mind! Her husband's just *died*, Freddy. She hasn't got the emotional bandwidth.'

'Okay, but let's say there *is* a killer – and that's by no means certain – and let's say they were one of the initial investors in as well as a user of Dapper and Discreet, it would really help to know if Rich was on it too.'

'I'll do my best,' Juno promised, not for the first time.

'Meanwhile, let's focus on Green Man,' Phoebe said firmly. 'He's really into you right now. The vegetable emojis are ripe for harvest. If he's one of them, he's our key to it all.'

Juno wished she could be so sure. She was secretly more than a bit annoyed with her friend for pimping her, and very anxious about the prospect of going undercover.

She was grateful at least to be leaving all the communication to Phoebe, who briefed her now.

'Mil is going to borrow a wire for you to wear when you meet him next week. We'll be close by and listening in at all times.'

'What do you mean, *meet next week*?'

'Green Man wants to get together for drinks next Monday evening. I told you that!' She looked seriously put out. 'I've worked bloody hard to set it up.'

Juno had a vague memory of reading something about it on the WhatsApp group chat, but she had a lot on her mind.

'That's the night before the funeral!' she pointed out with relief. 'I can't possibly do it. Debra needs me there. She's going to book a visiting aromatherapist or reflexologist or something, using another one of the vouchers Rich gave her. You can be me instead, Freddy. Green Man has no idea what I look like anyway.'

'You described yourself in your bio as a short, curvaceous blonde,' Phoebe pointed out, striding out ahead.

'Can we find a stand-in? Felix knows lots of actors. Stunt doubles, even. Anybody but me.'

'Too late. I got Felix to put pics of you up on Curvy Kitten's gallery.'

'You did *what*? What pictures?'

'From your blog. They're very arty and vague, like Green Man's.'

'His are of a dog! What do mine reveal? Please say it's Kevin Bacon,' she panted, hurrying to catch up with Phoebe, who was marching past the tennis courts. 'And where are we going now?'

'To look at Cosmo Lovat's cottage. One of those invitations is for him, surely?'

'I think Debra emailed him, but she's not expecting him to attend.'

'Did you ask her what the deal was between them?'

'No,' Juno admitted feebly.

'Let's pop an invite through his door just to be sure,' Phoebe said brusquely, and Juno guessed she just wanted to have a good snoop at the place.

And no wonder, Juno realised a moment later.

'Cosmo lives *here*?' she gasped in awe at one of the prettiest thatched Wexshire houses she'd seen, discreetly set back from the lane behind a honeysuckle-festooned brick and flint wall. Too big to be categorised as a cottage, yet homely and sweet faced, it had a neatly bobbed blond straw roof and fat red-brick chimneys like owl ears, its multitude of casement windows glittering like filigree.

'He's not lived here much recently.' Phoebe let them in through a pedestrian gate, glancing up. 'Look out for CCTV.'

'Could that be hiding a camera?' Juno pointed at a life-sized cat on the decorative thatched roof ridge, modelled in straw. 'What even is it? Is it some sort of witchcraft thing?'

'Traditional thatchers often put an animal motif on their work,' Phoebe explained. 'It's like a signature. This house – and the little gated development in the old sawmill over there – are all newbuilds made to look old, using materials and techniques from—'

'Please stop!' Juno held up her hand. 'You sound just like Grant.'

They turned to look at one another, the same thought clearly occurring to them.

'Could Grant have been involved in building all this?' Juno asked, sensing the web tightening.

'Worth finding out.'

'You know I *do* feel like we're being watched.' Juno pointed to a clay wall-plaque built into the porch gable brickwork, featuring an old man's face with its beard made of oak leaves.

She stopped and stared at it, remembering her father pointing out similar ones years ago on holiday in Devon.

'You realise what that is, don't you?' she asked Phoebe, who looked up at it and tilted her head.

'It's a Green Man.'

Juno felt a quiver of excitement, her mission suddenly far more thrilling. 'You don't think *Cosmo Lovat* could be Green Man?'

'Lots of houses have those plaques around here, Juno,' Phoebe dismissed.

'But Cosmo oversaw this one's construction; he must have made the decision to put it there.'

'Lovat *is* a shade of green,' Phoebe conceded.

'Is it? There you go!' Juno cheered her friend's wealth of trivia. She was feeling alive now, the detective itch raging, along with a hefty dose of property lust. 'What if Cosmo was in the syndicate? Or what if' – she covered her mouth with both hands for a moment, almost too excited to let this fresh idea out – 'what if Cosmo is secretly undercover like us?'

Phoebe nodded slowly, absorbing this idea, her forehead creased. 'What are you even talking about, Juno?'

'Cosmo's wife Holly was the first to die,' Juno went on, turning to point towards the road. 'Right there. And Cosmo was right here. I wouldn't be surprised if he—'

'Killed her.' Phoebe's head nodded faster.

'No! I was going to say that I wouldn't be surprised if he was investigating her death too. Autumn hinted at it, I'm sure. She knows all about our detective work and said he still wanted answers. We'll need to talk to her, Freddy. Giving nothing away, of course. If Cosmo's joined the app to flush out the syndicate like we have, we must respect that.'

'I think it's *very* unlikely, Juno.' Phoebe gave a tight smile, clearly trying to contain her impatience. 'We have it on record that Cosmo's terrible with tech and not even on social media. Green Man's bilingual in emojis.'

'Well, who do you think he is if it's not Cosmo?'

'Grant?'

'Ew! No, you're wrong. I think Cosmo might be Green Man. And when I meet him, I'll need all the facts at my fingertips.'

'So you no longer want Felix to look for an actor to be your stand-in?'

'That depends on Debra.' Juno waited a beat. 'And whether she'll rumble a stand-in.'

It took Phoebe a moment to register the joke, one eyebrow angling above her high-boned face before the smile curled up one side, down the other.

'But seriously, I can't leave her that night if she's in a state,' Juno fretted. 'Although Debra's usually shipped so much hooch by the evening, she wouldn't notice if Mil stood in for me wearing a wig and colourful separates.'

'Let's not risk it.'

* * *

There was something different about the atmosphere at Greenside Manor when Juno returned with Bullet. As she tapped the novelty golf knocker, there was no music pounding through the Sonos system, and Grant's V-shaped Jackson guitar was eerily silent. Bullet sat beside her on the step whimpering anxiously.

Opening the door at last, Debra looked haggard, her face make-up free. She was starting to really look her age despite her skin's artificial tightness, a corolla of silver already threaded along her hairline, the Mrs Potato Head lips puckered.

'Come through, babes. You pass on all those invites?'

Eating a vol-au-vent in the kitchen, Grant's cold hippo smile gleamed between swallows.

'All invitations delivered!' Juno reported. 'And I gather word's spreading fast through the village email trees and WhatsApp groups, so I'm sure you'll have a good turn-out.'

'They do know it's not a free bar?' Debra checked.

'But the music and nibbles are gratis,' Juno confirmed.

'You're too good to me, Juno babes,' Debra said shakily. 'Which makes me feel even worse about what I'm about to say.'

Juno started to panic that she'd been rumbled, that they knew her kindness came with a devious sideline in nosiness and suspicion.

'Me and Grant are meeting a... a friend on Monday night,' Debra told her now, her voice tight and strained. 'I know we were going to have our special pamper evening here, babes. I'm just as disappointed we can't have it.'

Butterflies flapping in her belly, Juno felt fate take charge, casting her centre stage in her own hot date detective action role after all. Undercover, wearing a wire, meeting a man who might or might not be another undercover operative, AKA Green Man, AKA...

'It's the only time we can both do,' Debra went on, 'and it's got to be before the funeral. Clear up a bit of family business, you understand. In Rich's memory. You don't mind, do you, babe?'

'Of course not! It's great you're meeting up with a friend!' Juno enthused.

'Hardly a friend,' Grant sneered.

Seeing Debra starting to quiver, Juno waited for more.

'Acquaintance,' Debra corrected, but her taut-skinned face was already dissolving into the inevitable tears. 'I can't believe Rich would let this happen to me!'

Juno's own eyes prickled as they so often did when faced with this raw grief. 'I know how hard it is, Debra. Believe me, I know.'

'No, you don't, babes. Forgive me, but you don't understand at all. It's obvious that you and your friends think Rich was murdered, along with Wayne.'

'Well, we're just—'

'And you're right to be suspicious, Juno babes. I didn't want to believe it, but I know for certain today. I don't care what the coroner says. My Rich wouldn't do this to me. Not on top of everything else.'

'You also think he was murdered?' Juno gasped, looking from Debra to teeth-baring Grant and back.

'At first, I thought maybe... maybe he sacrificed himself, the silly fool. But not in ladies' undies. Never in those!' She turned away to compose herself.

'Why would he sacrifice himself?' asked Juno.

'There's something I haven't told you.' Too upset to go on, Debra shook her head, mopping her eyes.

Grant cleared his throat pointedly, then helped himself to another vol-au-vent.

It was a long time before Debra could speak for sobbing. Juno held her comfortingly.

Eventually, she pulled away, blinking back more tears. 'I know I'm asking a lot when you're doing so much already, babes. But whatever it takes, you must find who killed my husband, Juno!'

'Of course we will.'

She fished a tissue from her pocket and blew her noise. 'I only wish I could pay you.' Her voice shook, another tearful onslaught threatening.

'You mustn't worry about that.'

'Only I do. It's *all* I think about.' She mopped her eyes. 'Well, there's poor Rich's death now too, obviously, but I've been worrying myself sick about this for months. About our secret...' She covered her face with her hands.

'This is the thing you've not been telling me?'

'Yes, babes. You see... Oh, God, it's so awful... I'm so ashamed... Sometimes I think I should just end it all... Rich and me... we've been *living a lie*!'

Sobbing uncontrollably again now, Debra bolted upstairs and locked herself in the bathroom.

Juno hurried after her.

No amount of gentle knocking and cajoling could lure her out. Locking herself in bathrooms was clearly a motif. At Juno's feet, Bullet whined and scrabbled helpfully, but his mistress stayed put.

Eventually Grant appeared, now eating a bag of crisps, and shouted at the bathroom door. 'You coming out, Debs?'

There was a muffled, 'Go away, I'm having a bath.'

'You heard her.' He waved Juno back towards the stairs.

'What did she mean, "living a lie"?' Juno whispered, glancing over her shoulder, fearing the stage of grief Debra had reached might be critical, bathroom wrecking and possibly life threatening even. 'What lie? How can I help?'

'Buy a nice newbuild eco-thatch off me?' he hummed hopefully.

'Not that again! I can't believe you're trying to do a deal at a time like this.'

He turned to face her halfway down the stairs, his small eyes hard, and Juno felt a prickle of fear.

'I'm not trying to do a deal for me,' he told her in a low voice. 'It's for Debs. This place belongs to the bank and they're about to foreclose. I've been helping Debs out, but I'm going under too. Without a cash injection, we sink. It's why she's so upset.'

'You mean this is about *money*?'

'Isn't everything?' Grant shrugged and flashed his white hippo teeth. Then, to Juno's astonishment, he suggested running through Madness's 'One Step Beyond' again. 'The thrash riff we added in the middle section needs work. I'll tell you everything while we rehearse. Debs really will be taking a bath. She spends hours in one, always did. Only thing that slows her drinking these days, the soak having a soak.' His small eyes blinked sadly. 'And playing music is the only thing that stops me eating. Warp-speed metabolism before you ask.' He patted his skinny torso. 'Runs in the family. We burn through food and money, the Robertses. Makes us dangerous to be around. Let's play.'

Grant dialled his amp volume down from max for once so that he could still be heard. In between thumbing through the familiar ska bassline, with an added lick of screaming Metallica strings, he broke the news. 'Rich was not rich at all.'

'Who exactly was he then?' Juno asked without thinking.

Grant didn't find this funny. 'I'm saying he was skint, all out of muller. Broke, not rich. Dead broke now, I guess.'

'But I thought he made a fortune in kitchens?'

'Many years ago, Rich might have made a swift million when he sold his company...' He struck a chord on his guitar. 'More than he'd seen in a hard-grafting lifetime...' He struck another one, minor this time. 'But that all went on bad investments, holidays and house extensions. There's nothing left in the pot. He's been blagging for years, trousering a little bit here, a little bit there, but never enough. Debs had no idea how bad it really was. Rich always had to keep up the pretence, put on the show. Turns out the bank will take the keys to this place if Debs can't bung them a five-figure sum by the end of the month.' He played a diminished seventh, with a screech of feedback.

'That's just awful!' Juno sympathised. 'Poor Debra.'

'Rich had a fat life insurance policy,' Grant went on with a minor arpeggio, 'but today, she found out that it won't pay out.'

'Oh, no! Why not?'

'Auto-erotic asphyxia counts as a self-inflicted injury, they say.' He shredded the frets briefly, fingertips sliding noisily. 'It was her last hope. Shall we take it from the top?' He silenced his humming strings. Then he struck the opening chord to cue her in.

Juno didn't sing.

Was money really the primary reason Debra was so upset, she wondered? Could that even be a motive for murdering her husband, she reasoned, banking on his big insurance policy paying out? Rich had built the dream house, swept Debra off on exotic holidays, funded her tweakments and lavished jewels on her like Burton on Taylor, but he'd blown their savings doing so.

And then there was his other dark side. The Black Horse.

Had Rich been lavishing money on his mistresses too?

'Did the WE SIN syndicate have anything to do with him

losing all his money?' she asked Grant, forced to shout over a fresh assault of guitar riffs.

'Rich liked to show off that he was a big blue-chip player' – Grant shredded more chords faster as he spoke – 'but being an angel investor stretched him way too far, and truthfully most of their investments were losses. The only thing that made a decent return was that bent dating app, but it brought a whole heap of crap.'

'Was Rich secretly on Dapper and Discreet?'

'They all were. Shareholders' perk. Not so much angel investors as devils in disguise. Debs hates it for a reason.'

'Daddies.'

'You what?'

'It's what they called themselves, as well as codenames like Black Horse, White Swan. Do you know who any of them were?'

He turned away to play a loud, angry minor chord. 'Sound like pubs.'

'Are you on it?'

'As if!' The hippo teeth gleamed over his shoulder. 'I hated everything about it.'

'Not even when you were married?'

'Especially then.' He silenced the strings again, the teeth vanishing as he stopped smiling. 'And I still am married to Tiff. Separated, but still married.'

'Sorry. My bad.'

'Debra set us up. My sister likes playing Cupid, as you can probably tell.'

They shared a long-suffering smile.

'Tiff was Rich's PA,' Grant sighed, plucking an open D string. 'Big metal fan.' He slid his finger to play an F. 'Has a Slayer tattoo on one shoulder' – he played an A – 'Megadeath on the other' – he pulled his Whammy bar to distort it. 'Just beautiful.' He smashed out a loud, angry G Minor, shouting, 'Rich made her wear long sleeves!'

Juno would have liked to ask what had happened to make the marriage go wrong, but Grant was running the 'One Step Beyond' riff again, his guitar making too much noise for more talk even with the amp volume lowered, and he looked like he might be about to cry.

But then, to her surprise, Grant switched chord sequences, picking out a much quieter air and saying in a choked voice, 'Believe it or not, I'm an old-fashioned romantic. I prefer this Madness track...'

Juno recognised the song straight away. She preferred it too. His rendition was more thrash metal than two-tone ska, but it was by far her favourite Madness track.

Closing her eyes, she sang to Jay. She had to sing very loudly to be heard as she reminded her great love in G major that she never thought she'd miss him half as much as she did, never thought she'd feel the way she did.

Grant stopped playing, one snaggy tooth pressing into his lower lip. His small eyes were gleaming. 'Let's play "It Must Be Love" for Rich next week, shall we? Because Debs did love him, you know. She really bloody loved him.'

Juno nodded, too choked to speak.

There was a shriek of feedback from Grant's amp.

Grimacing, he turned to look at it, saying quietly, 'I'm still in love with my wife too. She's not even bloody dead.'

Juno breathed deeply and admitted, 'I still love my husband far too much to love anybody new. And he is dead.'

'Soppy buggers, aren't we?' Grant rubbed one t-shirt arm across his eyes then swung back to launch into a frenzy of thrash metal, skinny fingers shredding up and down his guitar frets.

Leaving him to it, Juno went back upstairs to check on Debra, relieved to find she'd left the bathroom and was sitting at her dressing table, rubbing in face cream. Her rings had gone, Juno realised.

'My last pot of Crème de la Mer,' she said shakily, holding it up.

'I swear by Nivea. I'm so sorry things are so tough on top of everything else.'

'Grant told you about the life insurance not paying out, I take it?'

'If somebody really did do this to Rich, Debra, we *will* find them.'

'Thank you, babes, that would be kind.' She made it sound like Juno had reassured her she'd find a lost scarf.

By contrast, when Juno suggested that perhaps she could lend Debra some money to tide her over – 'I have cash on deposit' – she exploded into laughter and sobs combined, jumping up to hug her.

'You have no idea how much that means to me, babes! There might be no need. Don't want to jinx it. If Monday works out, Rich might just go out with a smile on his face the next morning.'

'This is the acquaintance you're meeting?'

Debra tapped her nose, hurrying to the door to listen to Grant's guitar riffs. 'You have cheered him up! I knew you and my little brother would hit it off! I'll admit I was giving up hope for you two, this Cupid's been looking into other options, but it's not too late! Let's all have some champagne, babes, then I'm going to put you two in the cinema room with all three *Fifty Shades* movies while I order a take-out. No excuses.'

As she danced out, Juno looked in the dressing table mirror and caught her own panic-stricken eye.

Then she saw it light up as her phone chirped with the high pitched 'mee-mee-mee' of Beaker from The Muppets, a message notification sound dedicated to her favourite person.

Eric asked if she was free to video call later.

He'd broken her out of jail. She hurried after Debra to explain that she must get back home to talk to her son on an urgent soon-to-be-grandmotherly matter.

* * *

'Mom, you don't need a rookie spook to tell you this Rich Bass dude was busted.' Eric's familiar bearded face was a welcome sight on Juno's phone screen later that evening.

'Actually, I do – *did*,' she corrected herself. 'It would have been incredibly helpful to know that Rich was in financial difficulty. I asked for your help days ago. I know you're busy with your video games—'

'I'm a professional eSports player, Mom, but that's not—'

'And I'm very proud of you. I am! It's just I don't understand these maps you keep sending.'

'I'm relocating, Mom. You know I had to move mooring. It's a long schlep. I've been on the water seven hours every day and there's been lousy data signal everywhere I've tied up overnight.'

'Where are you taking the boat, the Panama Canal?'

'Not that far, but she only moves at four miles an hour. Got a tip-off about a permanent mooring. Not seen it yet, but I guess it's gonna be okay. Thing is, Mom, with the baby almost here I need some permanence, somewhere a bit less fly-by-night.'

'Of course! That's wonderful! And I'm being wholly selfish. Don't give it another thought, darling. Go where you're going and put down that anchor. Get yourself sorted.'

'It's cool, I have a 5G signal tonight. That's why I'm calling.'

'You're the bee's knees! What have you got for me?'

'It's all base-level data grabbing, Mom. This syndicate, the Wexshire Enterprise Startup Investment Network, is legit.' He yawned tiredly, typing in the background. 'There were a bunch of investors signed up, and they could pick and choose projects according to interest and experience, way too many of them to pick through, although I'm guessing it's this dating app you need to know about, yeah?'

'Yes.' Juno hoped Curvy Kitten's membership was still unknown to him.

'Dapper and Discreet had anonymous backers. The syndicate ran a few of those, mostly high-risk low-stake projects: events, niche products, entertainment, tech. It was a side hustle if you like. The real angels stay hidden behind nominated directors or offshore shell companies – you can pretty much click-to-buy financial anonymity nowadays – so on the rare occasion one of these little gambles makes it big, the tax break is huge. Dapper and Discreet made it big.'

'So why was Rich broke?'

'My guess would be blackmail.'

'Of course!' Juno gasped. She had been reading up about something Phoebe had mentioned, the Ashley Madison scandal, and it had opened her eyes to the potential extortion involved in illicit dating sites. That service, also for married people seeking affairs, had suffered a catastrophic data breach in which hackers had threatened to make public the names of all the people who had signed up. When their demands weren't met, they had published thirty-six million of them online, ruining countless lives.

She told Eric about it now, proud of her research. 'If you ask me, the Dapper and Discreet developers booby trapped this one from the start. Like Ashley Madison, its database is one hell of a bargaining chip for a hacker. Those hackers – they called themselves The Impact Team – claimed it was a moral crusade; they wanted the site to shut down, and everything pointed to an inside job. My bet is that money is replacing moral imperative here. I bet they demanded money from Rich, didn't they? That would explain why he was broke. It could even point at suicide after all. *Have* they leaked any names from the database, Eric? What have you found online?'

Please don't let Curvy Kitten's real identity be there, she prayed.

There was a long pause. Juno dreaded what was coming next.

'Nothing, Mom. When I suggested someone was blackmailing Rich, I just meant that they knew *he* was on there and he didn't want his wife to find out.'

'Because his name is on a database that's about to be published in full?'

'No, Mom, just because somebody knows he's in there. Somebody else using the site, maybe? Someone he met on it? Or one of the original investors.'

'So not a hacker?'

'Why would they blackmail Rich Bass? His syndicate sold the app, remember? Any hacker is the problem of the big tech that owns it now, not the venture capitalist that first backed it and made a fat profit. I guess it's always possible the developer could still access the database; most devs leave themselves a secret door in the coding fabric, but why would they?'

'Could you find that door?' Juno asked.

'Not without the coding files, and not while I'm moving the boat, no.'

'Understood. How about the original WE SIN syndicate that backed it – the Daddies. Have you found out who their real identities are?'

'Only Rich Bass self-declared and flexed some local PR. Not even this Wayne Baxendale dude is listed by name, so it reeks of tax avoidance. I can look up anyone you want me to check out to see if they were a part of the wider syndicate. Maybe invested in other startup projects.'

'What about Cosmo Lovat?'

'Cosmo, you say?'

'Property developer. Cricketer. His second wife died in a car crash.'

'Let me run another search.'

Juno, who had googled Cosmo extensively and guiltily since guessing he must be Green Man, waited patiently, certain her son wouldn't dig up anything she hadn't. Hers had been a slow excavation with few finds. Corporate website, no picture. Companies House, several retired directorships, mostly in property and hospitality. Facebook feed not updated in three years, with a broody profile pic and privacy settings at max. No mutual friends. Plentiful mentions in village cricket league write-ups on Inkbury.org.

'Got him,' Eric said within seconds. 'Born South Africa, educated at Lancing, scraped a 2:2 from UEL then dropped out of officer training corps before becoming an estate agent, later a property consultant and developer. Married at twenty-nine, again at forty-four. One three-month driving ban, several court judgments, two insolvencies and a tranche of repossessions. No obvious connection to him being a WE SIN member, but there's a lot of data to check out here.'

'How do you find all that?' she marvelled.

'Easy. And... hang on, this is interesting...'

'What?'

'His wife died, you say? Violet Lovat? Only she's showing up all over this with a big digital pulse. Okay, no, I get it, Violet is his first wife, his second wife passed away. Looks like Violet used to run an online lingerie site called Purple Pussycat.'

'Send me the links!'

20

PHOEBE

Phoebe broke off from editing to let the dogs out for a stretch. Taking her vape and phone into the garden with her, she navigated to the last corner of lowering evening sunlight to soak in its glow and listen to yet another group chat voice note from Juno:

'Hey, guys, major scoop! Rich was boracic, all out of muller, and Debra has just been told his life insurance won't pay out if it's self-inflicted. Grant confided that Rich and Debra lived way beyond their means. The drinks bill must be bigger than the national debt for a start. Poor Debra's in bits and wants to help us prove it was murder in whatever way she can, so I'm going to ask her to share Rich's contacts as soon as I find a suitable moment. When she's more sober and not in a bath, basically.

'Then I spoke to Eric, and he suggested Rich could have been being blackmailed over Dapper and Discreet. I thought he meant like Ashley Madison – look it up if you don't know about it – but he pointed out that makes no real sense given the app's been sold, especially as Rich made a stash from that and clearly lost it all. Most likely, he's being extorted by someone like the Welches who found out he was using the app, or by another Daddy. Eric couldn't find out any of those other WE SIN angel investor names, although to be honest I don't think he tried very hard. What he did tell me was that it's possible the original developers have left a back door in the coding so they manipulate Dapper and Discreet to harvest data or manipulate matches, so that's something to think about.

'Also, *major* scoop part two: I think Purple Pussycat might be Cosmo's first wife Violet! It was the name of her e-commerce site and it *sold lingerie*, although it's no longer trading and she upcycles old festival tents into waterproof dungarees now. Bit of a sideways step. She lives in Dunford. I get my Mini back tomorrow and might drive over there, but I'll have a google first to see what I can find out and maybe suss out things with Autumn who lives with her mum. I don't want to upset things. What do you think? Also, tell me your latest. More soon!'

When the voice note finished playing, Phoebe found a reply from Mil already queued on the group chat:

'Evening all. Me and a few old Warriors have checked out the White Lion in Wootton Hill, the Red Lion in Marlbury, the Golden Lion in Marsh and the Dun Cow in West Woodridge – that's not a name on the list, but a mate runs it – and nobody at any of them knows anything about a secret syndicate. Violet Lovat is a lovely lady though. I'll be honest, I can't see her murdering nobody, and certainly not the way Rich ended up in that changing room.'

Phoebe could see *Felix is typing...* beside his picture on WhatsApp, and she edged into the shrinking patch of sunlight to wait for it to land, listening to the wood pigeons roosting noisily in the coppice beyond the park railing.

> On the train thinking this over. We still don't know where Rich got to between leaving Juno's party and going to the cricket pavilion. We know he said something about fetching more champagne. Maybe he met up with whoever he was overheard shouting at on his phone? We do know he wasn't at Flatpack Mansion when Phoebe brought Debra home, although it's possible he could have been and gone. And he wasn't at the cricket pavilion when Bullet escaped there. So where exactly was Rich in the hours leading up to his death, and who was he with? Let's try to find out who was on that call. Can you get a look at his phone now Debra's onside, Juno? Felix.

Another alert made Phoebe switch apps, scrolling past a greengrocer's worth of fruit and veg emojis to read the short message. She sent back a thumbs up and swiped quickly back to WhatsApp.

The sun had dropped behind the woods now, into which the terriers had escaped to let out excited rabbiting yelps. Starting to feel cold, Phoebe typed as she walked to the fence to call for them:

> I agree with Felix about needing to know where Rich was. Also who stole the clothes from under the church hall stage. P x

> P.S. Green Man wants to meet at The Priory at Dunford on Monday night. Let's not overthink that.

Juno's reply arrived at the same time as the terriers came bounding back, both wearing big smiles and earthy noses.

'Ohmygod, The Priory is where Wayne Baxendale died!

Okay, so I'm quite scared now. Oof, I need to calm down. What am I going to *wear*?'

Mil was first to answer, just seconds later:

'A wire, Juno love. You're going to wear a wire.'

The voice notes between Mil and Juno on the group chat pinged back and forth at speed for the next hour while Phoebe dashed off more small manuscript changes, awaiting Felix's return from London. She quickly turned her phone to silent. While grateful that they had such a good rapport, she couldn't understand why they didn't simply have a private phone conversation.

'You're Jurassic, my darling one,' Felix teased when she complained about it later. 'You still think an online hook-up is something a switchboard operator does.'

'I'm on Dapper and Discreet,' she reminded him. 'Curvy Kitten has a date.'

* * *

The following morning, dressed for her run, Phoebe first walked the dogs with Felix to the station, worried by his jaw-dislocating yawns. Despite trailing home on a late train yesterday, he was once again catching the first London one this morning, great bags propping up his handsome blue eyes.

'You should have stayed up in town,' she told him. 'All this commuting is exhausting you.'

'You hate it when I stay in town.'

'I hate it more when you're this beaten up with tiredness.' Any cynics who accused Felix of dilettantism – and many had – just needed to see how hard he pushed himself to give each movie the best chance and earn his stakeholders' money back.

His team were devoted to him, even though he drove them almost as hard as he drove himself.

'It's not for much longer,' he promised, stifling another yawn. 'And I want to be here with you to add my detective genius.' He grinned sideways. They both knew he'd fallen asleep last night while Phoebe was talking about the case.

But Felix also realised how the trauma ripple effect of finding Rich's body in the pavilion had yet to leave her, and that curling up tight against him every night was a great comfort, even if he had no energy left for detection, that intuitive insight recharging. Phoebe was grateful for his intense loyalty.

She thought back to Debra's tearful Norma Desmond moment on the stairs the night of Juno's party, when she'd shared the village rumours that Felix was a player like Rich. Phoebe's faith in her marriage often said more about her self-belief than her trust in her charming, magnetic husband, and she had to guiltily admit that Green Man's increasingly amorous attention had given her ego a boost, even if they did largely communicate in small digital icons.

She also had a sneaking suspicion Felix was making it home each night because he wanted to keep close tabs on her while she was playing Cyrano de Bergerac for Juno. He'd been conspicuously silent about his wife's flirtation with Green Man, which Phoebe could tell was because he disliked the idea intensely.

'You never send me suggestive fruit and vegetable emojis,' he grumbled as they waited on the eastbound platform together.

'Would you like me to?'

'I'd prefer a carefully chosen Yeats quote.'

'"Whenever green is worn... a terrible beauty is born",' she paraphrased.

'Not what I had in mind.'

'"Surely some Revelation is at hand",' she quoted from 'Second Coming'.

Chewing thoughtfully on his lower lip, Felix was keen to provide that revelation. 'So we think Green Man was in the area the night Rich died, yes? He'd suggested meeting up with both Bethany and Juno.'

'That's right.' Phoebe nodded. 'It's one of the reasons Juno's convinced herself it might be Cosmo Lovat, who was down here from London for the village cricket match.'

'Makes sense. As captain, he'd have keys to the pavilion. And we don't yet know Cosmo's whereabouts after he left the party either.'

'I just don't think Green Man is Cosmo Lovat,' she said decisively. 'Cosmo's testy, cocky and old-school alpha. Green Man's introverted, geeky even.'

'You can tell that from exchanging vegetable emojis?'

'Also Cosmo's apparently very bad at tech.'

'As are you,' Felix pointed out. He bit on his lip again, grimacing. 'I'm worried this "date" could be dangerous. We've no idea who Juno's meeting, and I'm not sure having you and Mil loitering about with earpieces is any guarantee of her safety.'

'What do you suggest?'

'I should be there too.' Felix squinted down the track, his train approaching in the distance. 'Someone can cover for me in London.'

'They can't and you won't.' Monday night was the make-or-break first test screening of the film's new edit. 'Juno will be fine. I'll make sure of it. Just be sure you get back for Rich's funeral the next morning.'

He raised his voice over the incoming train hissing and rattling in. 'I barely knew the man!'

'Juno wants us both there.'

'To be eyes and ears, I know.'

'To make up numbers, I think,' she downgraded kindly, kissing him.

As soon as Felix's train had trundled east towards London, Phoebe set off on her run, crossing the village's famous picture-perfect bridge, passing The Barton Arms, then along the High Street and across the village green. The terriers bounded behind.

The Basses' big, garish house still had most of its curtains drawn and blinds lowered, Grant's snarly Chelsea-blue pick-up truck not yet parked up outside.

Phoebe paused by the duck pond to catch her breath, thinking back to the night Rich had died.

When she'd run round to the cricket field to fetch Bullet, she'd heard a car engine, she remembered, distinctive and throaty, a blast from the past. But that must have been two or three hours before Rich died in the pavilion.

Soon afterwards, there'd been a couple kissing here amongst the trees on the Green, and she'd seen somebody with a rucksack heading to Juno's party wearing a Wexshire Warriors shirt. Or had they been going elsewhere? The Graveyard Ravers had struck that night, after all.

A car door bang made Phoebe turn. There was a taxi outside the house next door to Greenside Manor, with an athletically tanned blonde woman climbing out carrying a clutch of duty-free bags, while the driver took a suitcase from the boot. Phoebe recognised her as one of the Welch family sirens – it had to be Cheryl, she realised – who heaved the case to the front door to ring the bell, then hammer the knocker, then ring the bell again.

Eventually, it opened and she pushed her way past her sleepy-looking son, whose tumbling blond Lord Fauntleroy curls Phoebe knew belonged to Autumn's friend River.

Phoebe set off again, running around the far perimeter of the village green and back past the war memorial to cross into Church End.

As she passed the deli, she glanced in and spotted a familiar short blonde figure at the counter.

Phoebe stopped and backed up. The figure at the counter turned and waved excitedly, hurrying to the door to poke out her head.

'Freddy!' Juno's cheeks were bulging, her mouth full of pastry. 'I'm having breakfast. Can I treat you?'

Phoebe hadn't eaten breakfast since the early nineties, but she could see the imploring look in Juno's eyes, an unmistakeable call for back-up.

'I'd love to.'

With the dogs tied up outside, she admired Autumn grinding, clicking and steaming her way to create the perfect flat white.

'Autumn was just telling me about her mum, Violet,' Juno told Phoebe pointedly.

'Oh, yes?'

'How she was a fashion student too.'

'It's what I study,' Autumn said in her amused, ironic voice. 'Mum tried to talk me out of it, pointed out the career prospects are lousy. She wanted me to study a STEM subject, but this is my passion, and Mum forgets what a success she made of it.'

'She had her own range straight out of college, apparently.

Corsets as outerwear, inspired by Westwood. Phoebe has lots of vintage Westwood,' Juno told Autumn.

'You don't!' The blue-haired student swung round eagerly, milk jug in hand. 'I'd love to see it sometime.'

'Of course.' Phoebe smiled. 'I bet I'd have loved your mum's label. What was it called?'

'Purple Pussycat,' she groaned, turning back to the coffee machine. 'That was Dad's pet name for her when they first got together. He was at UEL and she was at the London School of Fashion. They were so cool.'

'What brought them to Inkbury?' Juno sounded like a bad chat show host reading off an autocue, but Autumn didn't seem to notice.

'Mum's from Marlbury originally; she didn't want to raise a kid in London. Dad loved village life, threw himself into the whole cricket, tennis, am dram thing. Then the PTA.' She twisted her mouth to one side briefly, looking away. 'You probably know the rest. They have long memories round here.'

'It must have been tough.'

'It was a horrible split. Mum went through a seriously shitty time; the divorce was awful. I lived between them at first, but then Holly's marriage ended and she and Dad moved in together, and that was less of a blended family, more nuclear fusion.'

The doorbell clattered as River rushed in, less suave than usual in the same hoody and shorts Phoebe had just seen him wearing when opening the front door to Cheryl, and which he looked as though he'd slept in. 'Need to sort Mum out with a sugar high, Autumn. Me and Xanthe forgot she was coming back today. She's big mad.'

'Here.' Autumn took her tongs and filled a box with a pastry selection. 'How much of a tip is your place?'

'Supersized.'

Autumn added two more pains au chocolat before handing him the box. 'On the house.'

'I owe you!' He hurried back out again, not acknowledging Juno and Phoebe.

'River and Xanthe went through it too,' Autumn told them after he'd gone. 'There were a gang of us in the village who were all at the primary school together and stayed close. All our parents' marriages split. We became chosen family. It's how I really clicked with my step-sibs, not all those crap "family bonding days"' – she air-quoted – 'that Dad and Holly took us on.'

'Are you still close?' asked Phoebe.

'They moved away with their dad after Holly died, went completely off grid for a bit, made some big changes, but we've all found each other again. We're cool now. Our group's always been borderline incestuous.' Seeing Phoebe's eyebrow shoot up, Autumn laughed. 'Our Discord is called The Fiancés because whoever's still single at thirty will marry each other, polygamously or monogamously. Looks like that's just me and Seph at the moment, which is way too vanilla.'

'I have a pact like that,' Juno sighed.

Phoebe glanced at her in surprise, wondering who she meant.

'Will you honour it, do you think?' asked Autumn.

'Only if we're still single in ten years.' Juno caught Phoebe's eye, then looked away pinkly.

'Dad's single right now.' Autumn's ironic voice drew this out. 'He's always much more fun when he has a girlfriend.'

'I'm sure he won't be single for long.' Juno looked to Phoebe again, now even pinker. It was obvious she was thinking about her upcoming assignation at The Priory.

'Does he do online dating at all?' Phoebe asked casually.

Autumn laughed. 'That's so cheugy, but Dad's always a decade behind, and he's 100 per cent swiped right a few times because he's had some meets lately. I think there might even be someone round here.'

Glancing at Phoebe again, Juno was on full alert. 'Tell me more.'

'He said he was coming back to take a friend out last time we spoke.'

'When?' Juno demanded.

Autumn looked surprised. 'I'm not copied into his diary.'

'By coincidence, I have a date next week,' Juno bragged, clearly fishing in the hope it was with Cosmo, or just not wanting to lose face. 'All *very* top secret.'

Phoebe cleared her throat noisily to warn her to say nothing more.

Autumn was leaning eagerly over the counter. 'Is this your latest case? Has it got anything to do with Rich Bass's death? I heard he was found dressed as a Playboy bunny with an orange in his mouth.'

Juno tapped her nose. 'It might be. Sex, wealth and business angels. We're looking into a syndicate of anony— Ow!'

Phoebe kicked her on the ankle to shut her up.

Juno glanced at Phoebe, looking hurt and guilty.

'And does your father ever stay in his lovely cottage when he's here?' she asked instead.

'No,' Autumn said flatly.

'But it's a beautiful place!' Juno enthused. 'I'm surprised you don't take advantage with it lying empty, especially working here in the village.'

'I'm happy living in Dunford with Mum.'

'Of course' – Juno stepped closer to the counter – 'the house here must have such tragic associations, all those unanswered questions, the need to know what really made Holly crash her car. The mystery must still torture your poor dad.'

Realising Juno was about to hint at her theory that Cosmo was secretly investigating the death of his second wife, Phoebe hurriedly asked, 'And has your mum met anyone new, Autumn? Violet, isn't it?'

'Yeah, Mum and Louise are slippers and lap-trays together forever.' She grinned. 'Best four years of their lives, they say. They're super cute together. I want that, only way less beige. When I got home after your party, they were having a Scrabble marathon with the neighbours.'

'What time was that?' Juno asked.

'I caught the last train, so midnight maybe, but they kept going half the night. I had to go down twice to tell them to turn down the Bach.'

'My kind of party,' Phoebe said, earning a hurt look from Juno, who asked Autumn:

'And what about your dad, where did he get to? I was sorry he didn't stay longer.'

'Yeah, sorry about that.' Autumn sounded disapprovingly amused. 'They had some old nineties muso playing the bar piano at The Priory at Dunford, and Dad loves that pseudo Soho Farmhouse vibe.' She looked up as the door pinged. 'Hello!'

It was Ree and Bernard Cole, bustling in to demand how Phoebe and Juno were getting on investigating Graveyard Ravers: 'We have it on good authority that Zadie Welch's boy and his hooligan friends were spotted drinking cider in the bus shelter the last time they struck! Now tell us that's not a coincidence!'

'Apart from the fact they do that every night,' Autumn

pointed out with a wry smile, turning away to make the Coles two cappuccinos, leaving Juno making excited 'told you so' eyes at Phoebe.

* * *

Juno accompanied Phoebe as far as the grassy canal bridge, chattering all the way.

'I knew it! Cosmo has to be Green Man, doesn't he? It's so obvious. That's why he wants to meet at The Priory, which Autumn says he loves. It's where he was the night Rich died, possibly with another Dapper and Discreet match – if he's only just started using dating apps it's no wonder he's a bit polyamorous – and no doubt with countless witnesses, so it can't have been Cosmo. The same goes for Violet Lovat even if she is Purple Pussycat, because she was playing Scrabble all night. And I doubt Rich joined them during the time he was unaccounted for, although I suppose it *is* possible he went to The Priory too, but unlikely given he and Cosmo had rowed. But we still have no idea what Rich *did* do. I'm starting to wonder if maybe Mil's theory is right and Rich was the Graveyard Raver. He can be quite brilliant sometimes, can't he? Mil, I mean.'

Juno had finally run out of breath. Sighing wistfully, she turned to stare out across the old Hartridge lock island, past the old fishery towards the village's famous bridge and The Barton Arms.

'Have you talked to the Hartridge Estate people about the lock keeper's cottage again, Freddy?' she panted, admiring it.

'What?' Following her gaze, Phoebe's eyes lingered on the derelict little roofless ruin that Juno still had dreamily earmarked as her 'doer upper'.

Sensing Juno was about to hijack the conversation with a body-swerve change of subject, and to a subject she was trying to avoid, Phoebe asked, 'What time exactly did Rich leave the party?'

'I lost track of time after my fifth or sixth glass.'

'Cosmo had already stormed off – to mingle with the London crowd in The Priory we're told, although that's yet to be proven – but did you notice anyone else leaving around then?'

'You're better at remembering these things, Freddy.'

'You took some pictures, didn't you?'

'Did I?' She looked nonplussed for a moment, then, 'You're right! For the Mother Loves Housewarming Parties blog I still haven't written.'

She fished out her phone and unlocked its screen.

'This is why I need to go on a proper detective course.' Juno started scrolling through the gallery, its recent activity taken up with pages of stealthily snapped photographs of Debra's lists. 'The police would have been all over details like this days ago. I looked courses up online and they're surprisingly reasonable – here we go!'

Phoebe moved closer and shaded the screen with her hand as Juno flicked through the few random, drunken shots she'd taken the night of her party. 'That's my nose – so's that. That's the cobbles. Here's Rich! It's time stamped just after ten-thirty. I must have taken this not long before he strode out onto the lane, never to return. That's so sad.' She held the phone to her chest for a moment, gazing out at the cottage. 'Imagine how peaceful it would be living here? It's such a beautiful spot.'

'Draughty, with no roof.' Refusing to be deflected, Phoebe asked to look at the photograph again.

'It's just so awful seeing him alive and well like this, knowing what's going to happen to him.' Juno lowered her arm, flicking hurriedly on. 'Now he's shouting in his phone again, and here he is leaving – there's Bethany Welch hanging about the gateway. I don't trust her.'

'Go back to that first one of Rich,' Phoebe urged.

Juno found it.

Rich was smiling, posing for the camera, hands thrown wide, one of them glowing brightly like Michael Jackson's luminous glove.

'Zoom in on that, will you?' asked Phoebe.

She watched as Juno used her finger and thumb to enlarge the picture, focusing tightly in on the glowing rectangle of light. Bingo!

'That's his phone screen lighting up with the incoming call,' she pointed out. 'Can you read the contact name or a number on it?'

Phoebe lowered her reading glasses from her head, and Juno extracted hers from a pocket. Both women peered at it closely for a long time.

The incoming call announcement on Rich's phone was too faint and blurry to make out.

'Eric bought me this cell,' said Juno, holding her own phone at arm's length. 'It does everything from taking my blood pressure to scanning satellites, he tells me. There's bound to be a zoom enhance tool somewhere, hang on.' Tapping at the screen, she turned the picture sepia then black and white, fishbowl distorted it, spun it 180 degrees and added sparkles before finding the right tool. Instantly, the image of the phone sharpened into focus.

Now they could make out a coloured circle with the initials GM in it.

Beneath that was *Green Man*.

21

JUNO

'Debra's forgotten the safe code,' Juno told the WhatsApp group in a voice note. 'It was written on a piece of paper that's gone missing. We've looked everywhere. There are a *lot* of pieces of paper. Rich's phone is locked in there, so I can't look at it before... Hang on... No, it's okay, I just thought somebody was listening outside the door. I'm in her downstairs loo. Are all of you going to be at The Priory tonight? I'm having a mini-makeover first. How many wires do we have?'

Each time a reply came, she hurried back to the loo to read it or listen:

> Got a screening tonight, sorry. I'll head straight back to Wexshire afterwards. Felix.

'Me and Phoebe will be there, Juno love. I've borrowed three radio sets and earpieces off Bernard. Don't wear anything too revealing or tight, Juno.'

Now on her third trip to the loo in an hour, Juno whispered into her phone mic, 'I appreciate your concern, Mil, but it's not really your place to dictate the demureness of my undercover date outfit.'

On her fourth visit, she was mollified by his reply: 'Sorry, I meant so the two-way radio pack doesn't show.' But then Mil's voice note went on to admit, 'I'll be honest, they're a bit bigger than I remembered.'

This made Juno start to panic even more: 'I wasn't very good with a wire last time. What if Cosmo realises and we blow everything?'

At which point Phoebe intervened with a firm text:

> You'll be fine. Mil and I will have a drink in the bar at The Priory and keep you in sight at all times. Also, Green Man is not Cosmo, I'm certain of it. P x

After which Debra offered Juno some Imodium, and she pocketed her phone to avoid suspicion, throwing herself into a final run-through of the funeral musical tribute with Grant.

Debra grew predictably tearful when Juno took her leave to go to her beautician appointment, gripping her hands in the doorway. 'I'm sorry we can't have our girls' pamper session this evening, babes. We gotta meet this... acquaintance, you understand. Need to do everything right by my Rich. He deserves that honour. Big day tomorrow.'

* * *

'It's no good, it just looks like a hearing aid.' Juno pulled the radio receiver out of her ear and unplugged it from the little box hidden beneath her bra.

'It's better if you can hear us too, Juno,' Phoebe explained.

'So I can hear you apologise when it is Cosmo Lovat who

turns up after all? No, thanks, Freddy. This is honestly fine. I'm just going to be asking him a lot of questions.'

'So here's how this evening's undercover operation works.' Mil ran back through the plan, sounding reassuring. 'We will all enter the establishment separately. You will position yourself at the cloisters bar, Juno. Phoebe and I will position ourselves at a table ensuring good sight lines and no obstacles to radio signal. We will be able to hear everything you say in our earpieces, although not record it because this equipment is practically bloody antique. You must try to lead the suspect into a confession, Juno.'

'In a bar on a date? Can't I just flirt a bit?'

'I really think Juno should wear an earpiece, Mil.'

'Not one the size of a Bluetooth headset,' Juno insisted.

She, Phoebe and Mil were sitting in the Mini in the car park of The Priory trying to sort out an elderly two-way radio. It was horribly cramped and hot. Juno was secretly terrified, which made her tetchy and wisecracking: 'People always tell me I don't listen. At least, it's something like that. I probably wasn't—'

'Listening,' Phoebe finished the joke drily.

'Perhaps if you pulled your hair down at the sides it would cover it?' suggested Mil, who was crammed in the back seat.

'I paid good money to have this blow dry!'

'And you look gorgeous, Juno love. Honestly, you're cracking.'

'Thank you, Mil.' Juno smiled gratefully over her shoulder, desperate for the boost. Combined with her Mini Midlife Makeover, she sensed the look was more ageing cable TV news anchor than Emma Peel, but vanity was playing second fiddle to pure terror right now. 'Wish me luck.'

The Priory at Dunford was a gourmet mecca on the banks

of the River Dunnett, just outside historic Marlbury. A small luxury hotel fashioned from a former Augustinian monastery, its restaurant boasted a hotshot young celebrity chef, two Michelin stars and eye-watering London prices. Juno – who had longed to see inside, since a Blur band member got married there – was thrilled to be waiting in its bar fashioned from the old stone cloisters, admiring the glamour of moneyed media-types enjoying an aperitif.

Amongst them was an alluringly stylish couple, the woman model slim in vintage Vivienne Westwood, the man as broad as a Marvel action hero, and nobly craggy.

'Nod if you can hear me,' Juno muttered.

The man nodded. His companion nodded alongside, shooting Juno a discreet wink.

Juno was certain she'd been right not to wear an earpiece herself. It had been too obvious and too distracting. Her nervous habit of tucking her hair behind her ears drew attention to it, and she didn't want Cosmo Lovat to think she was going deaf in old age.

Even though she was undercover, Juno still thought of this as a 'date', and she was quietly excited, thinking back to how attractive she'd found Cosmo at her party. Detective work had never felt so glamorous, or high stakes. His cool blue eyes and apple-slice smile had haunted her dreams an alarming amount in recent nights – along with green-painted Mil in a leafy tunic, but she didn't want to dwell on that one – a thrillingly dangerous mini-crush. Now she had to outwit him.

Juno shifted nervously on her high stool, trying not to catch her own eye in the mirror behind the bar, her pink-cheeked middle-aged reflection nothing like the foxy undercover agent she envisaged herself right now.

She cast her gaze around the long, vaulted room, studying

the occupants of its luxurious sofas and leather wingback chairs, a pampered sub-species she rarely ever rubbed shoulders with in the wild. Had any of them travelled here for Rich Bass's funeral tomorrow, she wondered? This was the most expensive hotel in the area, and while the dead kitchen magnate wasn't as loaded as he'd made out, he'd nonetheless moved in some impressive circles.

She must stay alert.

'Can I get you anything else, madam?' offered the barman, taking her glass.

Juno realised she'd not only gulped back her fiendishly expensive gin and tonic far too quickly, she'd crunched all the leftover ice and nibbled the flesh off the lemon slice.

'Another one of those would be great!' Again, she was grateful she'd removed her earpiece so she couldn't hear Phoebe muttering to slow down.

Hurry up, Green Man! she willed anxiously.

She checked her phone, but the only notification was from her plant care app reminding her to water her peace lily.

A waitress appeared with a tray to take the drinks for a couple sitting beside Juno who were moving through to the restaurant. She caught Juno's eye as she passed.

It was Courtney Welch – Mil's former employee at The Barton Arms, and daughter of Zadie – her dip-dyed hair scraped back into a French braid, piercings removed. Beaming nervously back, Juno was grateful for a familiar face. Nothing got past Courtney's wise, side-sliding eyes.

The next time Courtney passed, Juno asked for a menu. 'I heard you worked here now.'

'Half the Zoomers from the village do – all my old schoolmates are here,' Courtney told her. 'It pays better than the pub and I don't have to put up with Mil's dumb pranks.'

Not wanting to draw her attention to the fact Mil was currently sitting at a nearby table, his bulk only part shielded by a potted fig, Juno didn't dare look across at him.

'The uni lot temp here through summer too,' Courtney went on as she collected a drinks order onto her tray, 'so there's a party vibe. Seph and Xanthe are also on tonight's rota. You got a date?'

'What makes you think that?'

'There's always loads of hooks-ups here; besides, I heard Auntie Cheryl telling Mum you're now on the millionaire app.'

'Shhh,' she breathed, glancing round.

'It's cool. Half my family's on it. Auntie Cheryl gets a big cash ker-ching every time she signs someone up and treats us to— Oh, sorry, Mr Lovat, didn't see you there...' She moved aside as a figure stepped between them. 'Autumn never said you was back.'

It was Cosmo, simmering suavely in a perfectly cut linen suit. 'Good evening, Courtney. Change of plan. My usual, please.' He cast his sexy, creasy-eyed smile in Juno's direction. 'Hi there.'

'Well, hello,' Juno beamed back, heart instantly hammering. She *knew* it!

'Your name is on the tip of my tongue.' His blue eyes twinkled playfully.

Juno still didn't dare risk looking at Phoebe and Mil, but the told-you-so thrill coursed through her. She'd always known she was right. Cosmo was Green Man, here to meet his...

'Curvy Kitten.' She lifted an eyebrow with her best Mae West chutzpah.

The smile became fixed, his eyes no longer quite so creasy. 'I'm sorry?'

Wondering if she might have misjudged this, Juno felt a

body-splash of embarrassment. 'It's what all my friends call me, but Juno's fine.'

'Cosmo Lovat,' he reminded her unnecessarily.

'Small world!'

'Hardly,' he tsked. 'Only one decent restaurant within fifteen minutes' drive of Inkbury, for a start.'

'So you're a regular here?'

'I know the owner.' Cosmo smiled to himself as two large lime and mint spritzes appeared in front of him, followed by a bowl of olives. He picked up the drinks. 'If you'll excuse me.'

'Lovely to see you again!' Juno waved him off, waiting for him to be out of earshot before muttering into her lapel, 'False alarm, Cosmo isn't Green Man.'

He'd left his olives behind, she realised, eating one and finally glancing at Mil, who was eyeing a light fitting, and Phoebe, who was staring fixedly at a nearby painting, both looking as though they were trying not to laugh.

Then an awful thought struck Juno. She wondered if Cosmo *was* Green Man and had been messaging her but hadn't realised that Juno was Curvy Kitten until tonight. She'd assumed he'd guessed who was behind the avatar and the arty gallery pics Felix had uploaded, but what if the opposite were true? Had he changed his mind as soon as he recognised her? Perhaps it was all over already and time to bail.

She ate another olive. They were delicious. She stuffed in three at once, watching as a short, broad-shouldered figure approached the bar.

He nodded politely, ordering a large Johnnie Walker.

Then, just as Juno was looking around to pull a comedy face at Phoebe and Mil, he leaned forwards to whisper, 'You must be Curvy Kitten. I'm Green Man.'

Juno turned to him in surprise, mouth full of olives.

Stout, bald and wet-lipped in a too-tight fitted shirt and shiny grey suit trousers, her date had pale, goaty eyes, big hockey-guard teeth and a distinctively flat nose, as though he was pressing it up against a window.

Juno knew without hesitation that she'd seen this face before. It was the man captured in the photograph with Rich Bass, Wayne Baxendale and Boris Johnson.

'Don Greenwood.' He held out a hand to shake, the Trumpian vigour of his double grip almost yanking her off the bar stool.

'I'm Juno.' She spoke out of the side of her mouth to avoid gunning him down with olive stones.

'Good to meet you, Juno.' He flashed his big mouthguard teeth and settled in the bar stool beside her, nodding in thanks as a bartender in a waistcoat placed a large Scotch on a napkin in front of him.

Juno took her own drink napkin and hurriedly dabbed her lips so she could discreetly lose the olive stones into it.

As Don 'Green Man' Greenwood reached for his drink, Juno couldn't help checking out his ring finger. The pale stripe was a giveaway.

You are undercover, she reminded herself. *There have been three deaths which might be connected by this app. The night Rich Bass died, a 'Green Man' called him. The Green Man in front of you wanted to meet up that evening.* His marital status was less important than his whereabouts that night.

'Do you travel around the country a lot, Don?' Get information, then leave was her plan, her fantasies of a steamy Bond-style flirtation with Cosmo – laden with innuendo and detective gameplay – gone.

'Yes.' Don took a sip of his Scotch, his strange goat eyes doing a swift, perfunctory tour of her body.

She did the same in return, concluding that she'd made a lot more effort. Squeezed into her strongest shapewear beneath plunging black crepe, glowing from her Midlife Mini Makeover, Juno's sassy show of late-blooming body positivity had got Mil gratifyingly red-cheeked. Don Greenwood by contrast had a coffee stain on his shirt and dog hair on his trousers. His over-pumped shoulders might boast many hours in hotel gyms, but the pot belly hinted at equal periods of time spent in its bar, and his pallid complexion screamed 'online life'.

Their conversation had already stalled.

Juno slid the bowl of olives closer to him. 'These are jolly good.'

He lobbed one behind the big teeth.

'Do you often use Dapper and Discreet to meet women on your travels?' she asked, slipping into chat show host mode.

He made her wait until he'd moved the olive around his mouth at length, stripping every shred of flesh from its stone and spitting it out into the pits saucer before he answered. 'Sometimes.'

Juno glanced across at Phoebe and Mil, both of whom were busy on their phones, no doubt frantically googling the name Don Greenwood. She glanced around to see where Cosmo had got to, but he must have moved through to another room.

Realising Don was speaking, she turned back.

'You're not what I was expecting,' he repeated.

'In what way?'

'Well, you're hardly a kitten, although "curvy" passes quality assurance.'

'Nor are you green,' she bristled.

'I drive a Tesla.' One eyebrow lifted. 'And I'm all man.'

'Good for you,' Juno humoured him uncomfortably. 'Have you had many matches on Dapper and Discreet?'

Sighing deeply, he looked away. 'Let's not body count.'

'Of course.'

Juno waited politely for him to move the conversation on. When he didn't, she asked what work field he was in.

'Finance,' he said with a superior tone that implied she wouldn't understand.

'Tell me more,' she urged, determined to prove him wrong.

Winkling details out of Don Greenwood was an effort, and most of what he said about corporate finance did truthfully go over her head, but Juno established that he'd started by working in mergers and acquisitions, then moved on to finding ventures for those owners and shareholders who had released capital. 'Startups, mostly. Angel investments.'

'Angels?' Her ears pricked up. 'Any local names?'

'Discretion is an essential part of venture capital.'

Juno's quizzing got her no closer to the other Daddies' identities. Instead, Don explained how the arrangement worked and what percentage return his clients could expect. This went straight over Juno's head too, but she hoped Mil and Phoebe were taking notes.

He was hard going. He talked about deal-making, money and travel in deliberately vague abbreviated soundbites, and asked Juno nothing about herself. Had this been a real date, she would already be planning her escape. Don's monotone short sentences were deadly dull; he barely registered her wisecracks and one-liners; the goat eyes only held hers for brief moments, although they lingered longer at her cleavage as his Scotch went down. He also hoovered up all the olives in record time.

Juno couldn't decide if he was supremely arrogant or

acutely shy. Either way, Don Greenwood seemed an unlikely killer unless it was by boring people to death.

'Let me get you another drink.' He beckoned for the waistcoated bartender.

While he ordered, she looked across at Phoebe and Mil, eking out a pint and a mineral water at their table.

Mil gave her a discreet double thumbs up while Phoebe curled a withering lip and widened her eyes. Juno knew she wanted more undercover detective inquisition.

A waistcoated server had whisked up with a tray to replace the empty olive bowl with a full one, which Don was already plundering. Juno competitively ate three, stomach rumbling.

To her relief, the second drink loosened Don up remarkably swiftly. He became positively animated, naming his top three hotels in each of Europe's biggest capitals. He certainly travelled in style, Juno reflected as she fed him more questions about his business interests, munching olives and swigging her gin and tonic too fast while he spoke, occasionally glancing across at Mil and Phoebe, who made increasingly pointed eye signals to find a connection to the Daddies.

'Here's a thing, Don—' As Juno lowered her voice and leant forward confidentially, she was forced to cling onto the bar, to stop herself falling off the stool. She was already feeling unexpectedly tight, she realised. 'I heard somebody dropped dead in the restaurant here recently.'

'Probably saw the bill.'

She laughed, pleasantly surprised he had a little wit after all. 'He was called Wayne Baxendale. Friend of a friend.'

Juno watched his face for reaction. He was looking at her cleavage again. He and Rich had that in common; it was her job to find out what else.

'I went to his funeral last week, actually,' she told him, still gripping onto the countertop to stop a sudden, unexpected onset of bar stool vertigo.

'So did I,' he said, holding firmly onto the bar top too, she noticed. 'Wayne was a client.'

'I don't remember seeing you there.' Juno thought back to the corporate grey sea of men in suits and realised why.

'I'm pretty sure I remember you, now I think about it.' He tilted his head. 'You were wearing a sundress and strappy sandals. Lovely smile. Breath of fresh air.'

Juno flushed, the lovely smile briefly unstoppable. 'You should have said hello.'

'I didn't stay for the reception.' He checked his phone, a message briefly lighting up on lockscreen. 'I had a prior engagement. A date.' He cleared his throat, putting his phone down. 'But she just wanted to talk about dogs. I get that a lot.'

Did he arrange his Dapper and Discreet liaisons around funerals? Juno wondered nervously.

'I'm going to another funeral service tomorrow,' she said, testing this theory.

'That's a coincidence.' He looked up, the caprine eyes briefly holding hers before sliding away, straight to Mil and Phoebe. Then they snapped back to her.

Juno felt a twinge of panic, wondering if Don had rumbled their stakeout. Instinct told her to be nervous. Was he also perhaps responsible for the funerals happening in the first place? If so, she needed to get away.

But Don was talking again: 'How did you know Rich Bass?'

Panic rising, Juno decided honesty was best, and she was feeling far too jumpy – and squiffy – to improvise. 'I do a Clubbercise class with his wife.'

For the first time, Don laughed. A big, bass Father

Christmas belly laugh, it took her by surprise and lit up his face, the goat eyes softening from satyr to big softie.

It was strangely catching. 'Why's that so funny?'

'Forgive me, it's just you don't look like you exercise much.'

Juno stopped laughing. 'Excuse me. Just popping to the loo.' She hurried there.

Phoebe was right behind her with team talk: 'You must be more direct! Ask him about Rich and the syndicate, and who the other investors were – White Swan, whatever colour the Lion is, Purple Pussycat. Ask about them using the app, about the "Daddies". And stop drinking so much. You need to focus.'

'You're right.' Juno took a pee, watching the cubicle shift in and out of focus around her, like the walls were closing in. 'They mix them very strong here.'

She cannoned back out of the cubicle to wash her hands, staring at her reflection alongside Phoebe's. 'Thing is, it's hard to be a seductive honeytrap spy when there's zero chemistry and the man's fat-shamed me twice.'

'I think he's just socially inept,' Phoebe told her. 'His body language says the complete opposite. He can't stop looking at you, leaning in, mirroring you, fidgeting, and he's been flexing his muscles and sucking in his belly non-stop. He's putty in your hands.'

'Seriously?' Juno perked up, feeling like Mata Hari once more. She splashed cold water on her man-puttying hands and held them to her neck, trying to stop the room swaying. 'How do I pretend to fancy him?'

'Imagine he's somebody you secretly lust after,' Phoebe advised.

She briefly pictured Cosmo Lovat, then dismissed the idea as too intimidating.

'I'm going to pretend he's Mil,' she decided, whispering,

'You know I've been having *the weirdest* erotic dreams about him lately? What are you doing, Freddy?'

Phoebe had reached beneath Juno's dress to cover the wire on her bra strap, breathing: 'Mil can still hear everything coming from your mic, Juno.'

'Everything I just said?' Juno bleated.

'And did.' Phoebe's gaze switched to the loo cubicle.

For a moment Juno felt faint, her head spinning. Then she seemed to burst through the surface into sunshine, relieved to find she didn't much care, found it funny in fact. 'What the hell! I have a recurring dream that Mil's dressed as the Jolly Green Giant,' she confided, snorting with laughter. 'We slow dance to sexy nineties trance music. How *weird* is that?'

Phoebe looked at her curiously, then smiled. 'He's probably taken his earpiece out,' she reassured her, removing her hand from the mic. 'Now get out there and get Green Man talking. And slow down with the drinking, remember.'

Unable to look at Mil as she passed, Juno hurried back to Don, who was still holding on to the bar looking faintly stunned to see her back. 'Thought you'd done a runner.'

'Why would I?' She gave him her loveliest smile and noticed him pulling in his stomach encouragingly. Maybe Phoebe *was* right.

Climbing back onto her stool took several attempts, her dress twisting so the skirt split was at the front. 'Tell me, Don, how do *you* know Rich Bass?'

Don was gazing at her legs, her stocking tops now on display. 'I sold his kitchen company for him.'

He must be the London hotshot! Juno realised.

'Then I helped him reinvest the money,' he went on. 'Rich fancied himself a bit of a venture capitalist. He introduced me to Wayne Baxendale and they asked me to oversee a local business initiative they wanted to set up, the Wexshire Enterprise Start—'

'WE SIN, I know. So you turned Rich into an angel investor?'

'If you like.'

'And by an ironic twist of fate, he's now up in heaven.'

'I doubt that very much.' He laughed once again, even more heartily, his gaze still on her thighs.

'What makes you say that?' Juno tried to shift her dress back over them. Then she leant forwards to whisper, 'Is he going to *the other place*?' The move meant she could release the skirt bunched up beneath her, stocking tops demurely curtained once more.

The laugh stopped as quickly as it had started. 'Rich was an old-fashioned conman.'

'In what way?'

'In the way he did business.'

'Like the app we met through, you mean, Dapper and Discreet?'

'That was one of his pet projects, yes.' He took a big swig of Scotch. 'An IT guy Rich knew asked his advice how to get funding for some software he was developing, called it Tinder for married Boomers. Rich identified it as a startup and brought his own anonymous investors in, using the Wexshire enterprise initiative to legitimise it all.'

Juno felt her focus returning. Now they were getting somewhere! 'How did that work?'

'The developer retained the biggest share; I took a stake in exchange for facilitating it and no doubt Wayne was on board from the get-go.' Don drained his glass, becoming voluble now. 'He and Rich were wingmen in business and pleasure. They found a couple of local angels, although I never met them, or the developer come to that. Rich claimed to know them all through the village cricket club, but I think that was a joke.'

'Go on,' Juno urged, worrying it wasn't.

'We all stayed anonymous apart from Rich, who liked to boast he was the new Zuckerberg, not that he knew a thing about tech. Nobody was more shocked than he was when it made money. I don't think that had even occurred to him.'

'Why not?'

'It was all a ruse to find' – he cleared his throat – 'booty calls near home. Rich basically just wanted to use the app himself.' He picked up his empty glass and put it down again.

Juno found his sanctimony hypocritical.

'You use it too,' she pointed out. 'So did Wayne. What about the others?' She only just stopped herself from adding 'the Daddies'.

'Rich insisted all the angels had VIP membership.' Don was happy to spill all now, polishing off the olives as he did so. 'One of his conditions of sale was we retained them indefinitely. I only started using mine recently, but I don't regret it. I've just met you, after all.' He stared dreamily into her face then down at her cleavage. 'Curvy Kitten.'

This made Juno felt weirdly excited and a bit light-headed. She glanced across at Phoebe, who nudged her on with her eyes. Juno still couldn't look at Mil.

'Dapper and Discreet has been a huge success, hasn't it?' she asked Don, trying to stay on task.

'It was a fluke that it took off. But tech can be like that. It's shady as hell, but it's a money-making phenomenon. Within six months it was global, and just a year after that, we sold it for big bucks.'

'Did you make much?' she asked lightly.

'We all did.'

Juno eyed the pale stripe on his ring finger as he picked up his empty glass once again and put it down again. 'Why do you use it to meet women?'

'Do you need to ask?'

'Your wife doesn't understand you?'

He grimaced, looking up from his glass. 'We divorced last year.'

Juno smiled sympathetically. Then, without thinking, she confided, 'My husband died.'

He nodded as though she'd just said 'same'.

It's all about him, Juno realised. She'd been so intent on getting to the facts about WE SIN and Rich, she hadn't noticed that Don had still asked her absolutely nothing about herself. His focus was entirely upon himself.

Although in fact, now she looked, his focus was on her cleavage again, the pupils large and black in his goat eyes, his body language mirroring hers just as Phoebe had described.

'It was a while before I tried the app,' he was saying. 'But I find dating again tough, all the instant judgement, the emphasis on looks. Dapper and Discreet feels more cerebral, and I like the avatars. I know it's got a reputation for married sharks, but it's not bad for shy guys too.'

Juno looked at him with growing understanding. He was one of the awkward mob. Jay had also been a strong, silent type, not given to small talk, and had often been judged arrogant when the truth was far more self-critical and complicated.

'I'm lucky that I get a free pass to a VIP service which means I don't get strung along by bots or fake dates,' he went on. 'Although that's one odd thing; I get matched with Inkbury women all the time.'

Juno remembered Eric warning her that the software could potentially be manipulated from the inside.

'And most of you don't match my WLTM range at all,' he sighed.

'Which is?'

'Twenty-five to thirty-five, petite, slim, exotic.'

'Good luck with that.' Juno gave him a pitying look, one over-fifty, overweight, pasty lowlander to another.

'Still, let's make the most of this.' He smiled woozily. 'You look like you enjoy your grub too. And you already have a menu.' He picked up the one resting next to Juno on the bar. 'Let's eat.'

Juno's stomach let out a treacherous rumble. The olives were all finished.

He's socially inept, she reminded herself. *You are on a mission. His candour is strangely endearing. I do like my grub.*

'You were staying locally the night Rich died, weren't you?' she asked while he was studying the menu. 'You wanted to get together.'

'That's right. We were supposed to meet here, but Rich was at some party, told me he'd drunk too much to drive.'

It took Juno a moment to realise what he was saying. He thought she'd meant he wanted to get together with Rich. Her leading questioning skills must be better than she realised. They'd leap-frogged right to the shouty conversation Rich had conducted on her front step, the phone lighting up in his hand saying Green Man just before his unaccountable two-hour disappearance.

'*Did* you manage to see him that night?' she pressed the advantage.

'I drove to Inkbury and picked him up.'

'Why did you want to meet?' she asked beguilingly, leaning towards him and tilting her head. 'What was so urgent it couldn't wait?'

He looked up from the menu, leaning forwards and tilting his head too, voice low. 'The new owners of Dapper and Discreet think we planted a bug in the coding. They've found evidence of someone poking around in the backend. That's the developer interface.'

'It's been *hacked*?' Remembering her son dismissing the notion, Juno experienced another I-told-you-so moment. Well, ya-boo to you, Eric!

'Not hacked' – Don put out her maternal fire – 'but there are discrepancies that point to someone unauthorised still using a back door. They're threatening to sue, but Rich wouldn't take it seriously. I thought I could talk some sense into him, but it was hopeless. First he laughed, then he got angry, even accused me of blackmailing him. Told me to drive him back to Inkbury.'

'Had you brought him here to The Priory?' She tilted her head the other way.

He shook his head then tilted it to match. 'Rich said he wouldn't cross the threshold; he'd fallen out with the owner, so we went to an after-hours bar he knew near Newborough.'

'The Black Horse?' She took a wild guess.

'Thirst Trap, I think it's called. There were' – he cleared his throat, looking at her body hungrily – 'dancers.'

'How long were you there?'

'Not long. I dropped him back in the village. He had a new match lined up on the app. Hungarian, I think he said, claimed to be a yoga teacher but sounded like a pro. There are plenty on there, along with the bots and fakes. They were meeting up. Rich was hyped. He loved his risky encounters.'

'And do you love them too?'

They were almost nose to nose again, Juno realised, wondering how that had happened. The only thing separating them was the menu. She took it, knowing she needed food to counterbalance the killer drinks. Her Mata Hari alter ego was getting dangerously out of control. 'Let's eat.'

'Choose anything you like, as long as I'm what you have for dessert.' Don was emboldened now and strangely sexier for it, his gaze greedier, his laugh deeper. He turned to order himself another drink and one for Juno, telling the waistcoated bartender, 'Have them brought through to the restaurant, will you?'

Then he slid off his stool and held out a hand to Juno, the goat eyes gleaming.

Almost falling off her own stool, Juno realised that – despite some serious cocktail tolerance training with Debra of late – she was seriously wasted.

Don was leering at her chest again. 'Pretty necklace. Unusual.'

Juno looked down and realised her neckline had plunged yet more, revealing the transparent cable of her wire.

She'd completely forgotten about Phoebe and Mil listening in.

Juno looked across at them, lurching slightly, suddenly finding herself fighting giggles. Mil was glaring furiously at Don while Phoebe made throat-cutting 'stop' gestures.

Shooting them a wink and a barely discernible shrug, laughter still bursting like champagne bubbles in her throat, Juno turned to follow Don into the restaurant.

Like Bethany Welch, she wasn't about to turn down a free meal at The Priory.

She was on an undercover mission.

And, now thoroughly in her cups, she was starting to enjoy herself.

22

PHOEBE

'We should get her out of there,' said Mil, watching Juno sashaying beneath the vast stone arch that marked the entrance to The Priory's celebrated restaurant.

'I'm not so sure.' Phoebe watched too. 'She's doing brilliantly, and she's quite safe while there are people all around.'

'You heard Don say he was the one with Rich the night he died!' Mil whispered.

'Exactly. He was probably the last person to see Rich alive apart from the killer.'

'What if *he's* the killer?'

The thought had crossed Phoebe's mind. Don Greenwood was angry with Rich for not taking seriously the threat of legal action from the app's new owners, but she found it hard to believe he would go on to string him up in the cricket village pavilion dressed in stolen jumble for it. Don was an outsider; it made no sense.

Mil was less circumspect. 'He's a creep if you ask me. It was probably his idea to take Rich to a strip club. And he could have made all that stuff up about Rich meeting a Hungarian yoga instruct—' He fell silent as Courtney swept over with a cocktail menu.

'Can I get you guys another drink?' she demanded, eyeing the inch of lager and water left in Mil and Phoebe's glasses.

'We're good, thanks,' Phoebe dismissed, angling her chair so she could see into the restaurant, where Don had just rejected the table he'd been offered, and a waitress was hurriedly preparing one by a big gothic window overlooking the river.

'The restaurant manager will do his nut,' Courtney sighed, following her gaze. 'Xanthe's not supposed to do that. The students are always too eager to please. Are you sure you don't want something? This month's feature cocktail from our in-house mixologist is Dill Martini with Icelandic Vodka and Mustard Pickle Brine.'

'Not at these prices,' Mil muttered, handing the menu back, still sulking about Courtney abandoning The Barton Arms to work here.

'Honestly, we're fine,' Phoebe assured her, eager to listen in on Juno who now seemed to be riffing one of her old stand-up routines about an incendiary candlelit dinner. Don was laughing immoderately.

'I offered Courtney time and a half for a shift in The Barton Arms tonight,' Mil told Phoebe after she had gone.

Phoebe shushed him, listening in on the wire as Juno and Don took their seats, giggling flirtatiously and agreeing the view was gorgeous, then snickering even more conspiratorially, as though the view they were talking about wasn't outside but right in front of them.

'I can't believe she's letting him hit on her like that,' Mil grumbled.

Phoebe shushed him again. They both listened in. Don was

now telling Juno how sexy he found funny women; she told him she had a weakness for strong, silent types.

'Juno is a consummate actress,' Phoebe reassured Mil, but he looked ever more despondent.

In their ears, Don asked Juno if she'd ever had a one-night stand.

Apparently unable to sit and listen any more, Mil stood up, loosening his earpiece. 'I'll just have a scout round to check if Cosmo's still here.'

While he was gone, Phoebe squinted short-sightedly at Don and Juno's silhouettes leaning close together, their table framed by the vast mullioned window. A cascade of weeping willows glittered beyond it, spun gold in the evening sunlight.

It was warm enough for diners to be sitting outside on the terrace overlooking the river. Phoebe's eye was caught by three figures, one in bright pink leopard print. She craned to try to get a better look. Eventually, she picked up her phone and used the camera zoom as a telescope to check she wasn't imagining things.

'Put the phone away, Phoebe,' Mil muttered, glancing round like a bodyguard as he slipped his earpiece back in and sat back down. 'Far too obvious, mate. Have you never watched *Line of Duty*?' He lowered his voice even more. 'Can't see Cosmo anywhere.'

'Well, Debra Bass and Grant are right outside,' Phoebe hissed, showing him the photograph she'd taken on her mobile of the brother and sister.

Mil peered at it. 'Bloody hell, so they are.'

With them was a woman, her back to the window, one tanned shoulder poking from a slipping gypsy top, a few strands of blonde hair visible beneath a denim baker boy cap. 'Recognise her?'

He peered closer. 'Not a hope. Too low res and she's facing the wrong way.'

'Where's the photo-enhance on this?' She fiddled with it, remembering Juno using the one on hers.

Mil took it to have a look before scoffing and handing it back. 'How old is this thing?'

'It's perfectly serviceable.' She studied the screen. The figure was just a grainy blur.

She and Mil looked through to the restaurant again, but their view both of Juno's dinner date and out to the terrace was now obscured by a group of diners settling around a table in the foreground.

'Typical,' Mil muttered, touching a finger to his earpiece and listening in to Juno and Don agreeing that a dozen oysters would be fun to kick off with. 'Has Juno noticed Debra and Grant outside, d'you think?'

Craning her neck to see past the other diners, Phoebe watched as their waitress delivered their drinks, and Juno moved her face closer to Don's to blearily suggest asparagus as a second starter, their noses practically touching.

'I think she's preoccupied.' Phoebe craned the other way to get a better view of Don who was leaning further across the table to speak into Juno's ear, murmuring in a slurred voice that he loved nothing more than sinking his tongue into a roasted fig with prosciutto.

'Is that off menu?' asked Mil gruffly, listening in too.

'Shh! I think we just missed Don say something about an attack.'

To Phoebe's relief, she heard Juno demand, 'Repeat that again.'

Good old Juno. She hadn't lost it after all. This had to be important.

Then, in Phoebe's ear, she heard Don murmur woozily, 'Has anyone told you you're a dead ringer for Emily Atack?'

'Practically daily.' Juno's tipsy, kittenish giggle became a leopardess growl. 'Has anyone told you you're a dead ringer for Jason Statham?'

Mil let out his own panther snarl. 'She said that to me!'

'Why isn't she asking him more about the syndicate? The other codenames?' Phoebe muttered. 'They both sound totally wrecked.'

By the time the starters arrived, Juno had gone seriously off topic, laughing and flirting throatily as she quizzed Don about his favourite cities for naughty weekends and top five seduction tracks.

What was happening? Phoebe wondered in alarm as Don asked Juno again if she'd ever had a one-night stand. 'Because you're about to, beautiful lady.'

Soon they were feeding one another oysters and enjoying a Tom Jones feast of aphrodisiacs, loaded with erotic anticipation.

Beside Phoebe, Mil was looking increasingly combustible. It was almost a blessing when his brother phoned to report an oven crisis. As he headed outside to take the call, Phoebe listened in to Juno and Don flirting lustily over asparagus.

'You have *such* sexy lips.'

'Yours are sexier – oh, do that again.'

'To the asparagus or to something else?'

'You're exciting the hell out of me. Let me feed you.'

The slurpy eating sounds made Phoebe almost wish they were still talking in seventies porn dialogue.

Her own phone lit up with a call from Felix.

She pulled out her earpiece with relief to take it.

He was still in London, he explained, about to go into the

screening. His voice was hoarse from a long day of publicity planning. 'How's it going?'

She told him about the Cosmo Lovat mix-up, finance man Don Greenwood's surprise entrance as Green Man, and Juno's even more unexpected flirtation. 'They're mooning over each other like horny teenagers. Juno's banjaxed.'

'Rich was full of Chemsex on the Beach, don't forget,' Felix said in an urgent undertone. 'It removes all inhibitions. Is it possible her drink's been spiked?'

'Oh, God, why didn't I think of that?'

Then Phoebe looked round and realised the table by the window was now empty.

'Call you back.'

She pushed the earpiece back in. She could hear frantic panting.

The feed was crackly and breaking up, suggesting Juno had moved almost out of range.

'I've never done anything like this,' her slurred voice crackled breathlessly.

'You'll like it, trust me.'

Realising things were progressing fast, Phoebe jumped up, hurrying to the restaurant entrance to scan it for Juno and Don, but there was no sign of them. Nor were they at the bar.

She dashed outside to find Mil. He was talking loudly into his phone. 'Then spark up the burners again, only with half gas and—'

Phoebe grabbed his arm. 'Put your earpiece back in!'

She covered her own ear to blot out the background noise.

Sounds of frantic kissing greeted them.

Mil pulled his straight back out. 'That is none of our business.'

'This is *not* like Juno. Felix thinks she's been roofied. We must rescue her.'

23

JUNO

Juno wasn't sure if they kissed all the way up in the lift or if she imagined it. She wasn't sure if there even *was* a lift. Either way, it was nice to be kissed again. Especially by Jason Statham.

No, that wasn't right.

Especially by Mil.

No, that wasn't right either.

She knew there was definitely a room with a huge bed because she was lying in it gazing up at the chandelier above her spinning around. She didn't appear to be able to move.

Don! His name was Don. She was a sexy Emma Peel undercover spy.

Her mission appeared to have gone a bit wrong…

Don was in the bathroom. He'd said he needed to freshen up. He'd been in there a long time. He would be very fresh indeed.

Eminem was rapping loudly nearby about once-in-a-lifetime opportunities.

How did he get in the room? Eminem lived in America, didn't he?

The chandelier was spinning seriously fast now.

She might just close her eyes.

'If you can hear this, Freddy and Mil,' Juno mumbled woozily, 'I think I've been poisoned. Or it might be the oysters. Either way... help.'

24

PHOEBE

'We're detectives!' Mil flashed his cash and carry card at the hotel manager. 'We need to be let into Don Greenwood's room. Possible homicide!'

'Don't say that,' Phoebe hissed aside to him as the manager hurried out from behind the reception desk to usher them to the stairs.

'It worked, didn't it?' he whispered back, tapping at his earpiece.

There had been no sound from Juno for several minutes.

They hurried after the manager up the grand staircase, slamming through a succession of fire doors along endless corridors before arriving at a door.

There was nobody inside the small, neat room, a hotel bathrobe still folded in its cardboard sleeve on the immaculately made double bed. The room appeared unoccupied, with no evidence of luggage, nor of anyone having been in it at all since housekeeping prepared it.

'Are you sure this is Don Greenwood's room?' Mil asked the manager as he looked around it.

'I wasn't on shift when he checked in. I suppose it's possible he asked for a different room and the change hasn't been logged correctly. Shall I go down and check on the computer while you wait here in case Mr Greenwood's on his way up?'

'How long will that take?' Phoebe demanded, tapping her earpiece. It still made no sound.

'You can come too, if you prefer?'

'They were pretty slewed,' Mil pointed out. 'It might just be taking them a while to find his room.'

'Let's wait,' Phoebe said firmly, a decision she would soon regret.

It was almost twenty minutes before the manager reappeared, apologising that a large party had just arrived and needed checking in. 'Mr Greenwood did change rooms. He was upgraded. Quite an upgrade, in fact. Follow me.'

Back they went along endless corridors and through fire doors, down the grand staircase again, navigating what felt like miles of tapestried cloisters – was that Debra Bass coming out of the ladies', Phoebe wondered as they raced past – into a vaulted inner vestibule, along another long hallway before climbing back up a smaller, twisting staircase.

At last, they arrived at the arched door to a room housed in one of The Priory's medieval turrets. A plaque on it read *The Red Priest Suite*.

Phoebe's earpiece had come to life again, a terrible gurgling death rattle sounding in it. 'Do you hear that, Mil?'

He held his hand over his ear to listen, turning pale.

'Open the door!' he demanded as the manageress waved the master key uselessly in front of the sensor.

'This suite can be temperamental.' She breathed on it, rubbed it against her sleeve and tried again.

'Oh, for God's sake!' Mil ran at the door with his shoulder. It didn't budge, and he let out a wail of pain.

'Please don't do that, sir, it's sixteenth century.'

'Juno!' Phoebe shouted at the door. 'Are you in there? Can you hear me?' In her ear, the death rattle continued unabated. 'Is there another way in?'

'There's a fire escape, but that's authorised personnel only. I'll fetch another keycard.' She started off towards the turret stairs, calling back, 'I'll be as quick as I can.'

'I'll go too to make sure,' Mil told Phoebe, turning to follow, 'you keep shouting at the door.'

Ten more agonising minutes passed during which the death knell in Phoebe's ear quickened and deepened, and she shouted herself hoarse, before Mil returned with the breathless manager.

'The door code had been updated with the guest change. Happens all the time.'

This time the keycard lock made the mechanism buzz obligingly, the light turning green.

Inside the room, Juno was spreadeagled on a vast four-poster bed, still fully dressed.

She was snoring loudly. It was the same rattling, gurgling sound that had been coming through their earpieces.

Phoebe hurried to her, overwhelmed with relief. 'Juno, we're here!' She shook her. 'Juno!'

Juno groaned, not opening her eyes.

'Juno, you're going to be okay. Can you hear me? Can you speak?'

'Get off, Mum,' Juno mumbled, muttering something inaudible about being allowed to lie in. Then she started snoring again.

'She's going to be fine,' Phoebe told the manager, who was hovering anxiously.

'One of our best undercover operatives,' Mil added, trying the bathroom door. It was locked. He hammered on it.

The manager swallowed nervously. 'You need to get into there?'

'I'm sure it's nothing to be alarmed about,' Phoebe reassured her, imagining Don cowering in there in his underpants, his professional reputation about to be shattered.

Mill hammered on the door again. 'Can you open it from this side?'

'I'll need a screwdriver.'

'Do it!'

'Less of the *Sweeney* act,' Phoebe warned him after she'd hurried out, shaking Juno again. 'Wake up, sunshine. Juno. *Juno!* We need to know what happened. Where's Don?'

But Juno snored on.

'Do you think we should call the real police?' asked Mil, who was searching round the room now. 'What if the manager asks for my ID again? I almost got rumbled when I went back down with her and saw Cosmo coming the other way. Had to duck behind a tapestry.'

'We have no evidence of any crime apart from you impersonating a police officer,' Phoebe pointed out, putting a pillow under Juno's head.

'I said I'm a detective, which I am.' He opened the wardrobe to look inside. 'And it's obvious Juno's been drugged!'

'We don't know that for certain.' Phoebe patted Juno's pink cheeks. 'Juno! Hello?'

'No kinky clothes in here.' Mil closed the wardrobe doors and started looking through the chest of drawers, a pair of socks flying up in alarm as the manager burst back into the room bearing a screwdriver like Doctor Who.

She quickly dismantled the bathroom's locking door handle. 'You'd be surprised how many guests lock themselves in bathrooms.'

When she tried to push the door open, it met resistance. Mil went to help, shouldering it.

'There's something stuck on the other side of this door,' he complained as he shoved.

It was Don Greenwood.

He was hanging lifelessly from the robe hook, his feet dangling on the ground.

Still warm, but no longer breathing, he was wearing stockings, suspenders and an emerald-green lacy negligee, covered with cupcakes.

25

JUNO

'What do you mean, you can't come!' Debra shrieked down the phone at Juno. 'I need you here. The funeral sedan will be here any minute. You're singing the Dire Straits medley!'

'I'm with the police. There's been a... sudden death.'

'Where?'

'At The Priory in Dunford.'

Debra sounded close to hysterical. 'You're at The Priory? What are you doing there?'

'I'm at Hartridge with Phoebe and Felix now. I'm fine.'

There was a pause before Debra asked in a tight, high voice, 'So you're okay?'

'Yes.' Tears welled up, but Juno held them in check.

She could hear a muffled sob at the other end. Then, 'I *cannot* do this alone, Juno. Grant cannot do this alone!'

'Did you hear me, Debra? Someone's died.'

'Yes, yes, you said. But you're okay, yes?'

'It's someone we were investigating. He and Rich did business together.'

'Rich had a lot of professional associates.'

'This man was staying down here for the funeral.'

'Oh, God, that means one less guest for the buffet, and the golf club's already kicking off about serving staff given the low numbers and—'

'He died the exact same way as Rich!'

There was another pause, and what sounded like a familiar stifled, tearful hiccup at the other end. Or it could have been a hysterical half laugh.

Clutching her pounding head, Juno ploughed on. 'It was in a hotel bathroom, and he was asphyxiated whilst dressed up in—'

'Don't say it, babes!'

'He was wearing my mother's lingerie!' Juno broke into sobs first. Matching sobs greeted her at the other end.

Beside her, Phoebe gently prised the phone from Juno's grip, putting it on speaker. 'Debra, it's Phoebe Fredericks here. I appreciate what an incredibly difficult day this is for you, and this tragic news must just add to the trauma.'

'On the contrary!' Debra sounded triumphant, her voice high and shaking with emotion. 'Don't you see this changes everything? I *knew* my Rich wouldn't do that despicable act to himself! There's a murderer on the loose! This proves it. Will the police need Rich's body back, do you think, or can we go ahead? Only the food won't freeze again.'

Phoebe took a moment to compose herself to tell her: 'You'd have to ask them, but I'm pretty sure you can go ahead.'

'Tell Juno we'll postpone Dire Straits until after the buffet brunch if she needs a little longer to pull herself together.'

'Juno is *not* up to it,' Phoebe said firmly.

'I'll see what I can do, Debra!' Juno told the phone.

'Oh, who died by the way?' Debra asked, remarkably cheery now.

'Don Greenw—'

'Never heard of him,' she confirmed before Phoebe had even finished saying his name.

* * *

Juno had barely slept all night. It had been after midnight by the time she left the hotel. She'd been given an all-clear from the paramedics – 'any dizziness or repeated vomiting, go into A and E' – and at Phoebe's insistence she had gone back to Hartridge with her, where Felix had been waiting up with a mountain of tea and toast.

Felix always made tea and toast in a crisis. It was one of the few domestic things about him, and strangely endearing, like a lion purring.

He was making more now for DI Mason and his deputy DS Alsop, daylight streaming through the high windows, a rolling news BBC feed muted on the television in case the story broke of a suspicious death in one of Wexshire's favourite celebrity haunts.

'We're not releasing it yet,' DI Mason was saying, 'although there's always a danger somebody will leak it on social media – I won't have tea, thank you, Mr Sylvian, I brought my own thermos – so time is of the essence so to speak, to establish whether, to coin a phrase, we have grounds for suspicion here.'

'There are several stadiums for suspicion, surely?' Phoebe huffed. 'Two deaths in the same hotel in less than a month looks highly suspicious to me, add in a third nearby, all three victims connected to one another, with two of those three dying as the result of auto-erotic asphyxia, and there must be an investigation?'

DI Mason smiled good-naturedly, revealing his braces. He

was absurdly young for a detective inspector, probably still in his twenties, a judicious graduate with a roundabout way of talking but an endearingly kind and direct gaze.

The Village Detectives had dealt with both Mason and his thuggishly cheery deputy before. They knew the DI was a man who refused to be rushed.

'I can assure you correct steps are being taken with regards to the death of Mr Greenwood. We are a small force with limited resources. The coroner will guide us how best to proceed.'

'But that could take days!'

'Meanwhile, we are sensitive to the fact there's a funeral taking place today,' he explained, 'so we are quietly fact-gathering, until Mr Bass's widow, family and friends have bid him farewell with the dignity they all deserve.'

'I need to get to that funeral to sing a thrash metal Dire Straits medley,' Juno yelped, jumping up, then holding her head as it took a moment to catch up. 'What's the time? Debra said the funeral cortege was coming any minute!'

'The funeral isn't until nine-thirty,' Phoebe reassured her. 'You've over an hour. We'll get you there.'

'Before then, it would help if we could ask you a few question, Mrs Mulligan,' said DI Mason. 'You might prefer to do so in private.'

'I want Freddy to stay,' Juno insisted.

'Mrs Sylvian is a separate witness.'

'Am I under suspicion for something?' Juno bleated, panicking now, her memory in pieces. Last night was a dark shadow which her imagination kept trying to fill with scenes from Hitchcock movies and bleak TV dramas.

'Just routine questions.'

'I want Freddy to stay.'

Sitting on one of the capacious Hartridge kitchen sofas, still wearing her crumpled plunge-neck date dress, she listened gratefully as Phoebe lectured the police officers.

'She's been through hell. She needs a friend here with her.'

Juno wasn't sure there was anything more she could usefully tell the police. She still had a haze of blank spots surrounding the events of the previous evening, although Phoebe had helpfully filled many of them when briefing Felix late last night. 'Juno and Don were like two pissed sex tourists' was a description that had stuck and was haunting her.

DI Mason waited for Felix to tactfully take the dogs out before explaining that the police had run blood tests overnight.

'You and Mr Greenwood both had significant traces of the same substances in your blood,' he told Juno, consulting his phone.

'I knew it!' Juno groaned.

'Chemsex on the Beach?' asked Phoebe.

'I believe that might be the colloquial term for it, yes.' He reeled off a list of pharmaceutical names that she didn't take in, then described what the hotel CCTV footage had revealed.

It seemed she and Don had barely made it through their starters before horny urges had overwhelmed them. They'd then stolen through the hotel, kissing up against walls, tapestries and staircases until they moved beyond the camera coverage to the oldest part of the building where his tower suite was located. Once there, he must have slipped into the bathroom, never to return. It was, as Phoebe had said several times last night – with a macabre writer's relish, Juno felt – a proper locked-room mystery.

'Do you remember any more of what happened after you entered the room?' asked the inspector. 'You told the attending officer last night that Mr Greenwood had excused himself to the bathroom while you waited in the room and you must have nodded off on the bed.'

'I did?' She rubbed her face. 'I did!' She had no memory of either Don excusing himself, or of relating the tale to an attending officer later, but it was a relief to realise she couldn't have ranted too much about her wilder Hitchcock imaginings.

DI Mason consulted his notes again. 'Then you told the constable that Don must have slipped out of his tight shirt and shiny suit trousers into a green negligee recently pilfered from the jumble sale stash beneath Inkbury Church Hall's stage, and had knotted the cord, looping one end around his neck and the other over the hook on the back of the door, after which he must have, and I quote, "pleased himself to death".'

'I think you'll find I said pleasured,' Juno said in a small voice, realising she must have ranted quite a lot.

'Can I ask how you knew this if the bathroom door was locked throughout?'

'That would be guesswork,' she said firmly. 'I was out cold when it happened.'

'May I remind you that this is a very serious matter indeed, Mrs Mulligan?'

'I know. And call me Juno.'

'Can you remember hearing anything from the bathroom?' Mason asked.

'He'd put music on in the room. He had one of those Bluetooth speakers. It was very loud. Eminem, I think, "Lose Yourself", or I might have imagined that.'

'Oh, I like that one,' said DS Alsop, earning a reproving look from her boss.

'It was Eminem,' Phoebe confirmed. 'We heard Don telling you it was his favourite seduction track.'

'You were already at the door to overhear this?' Mason asked her.

'No, we were in the bar downstairs. They were both still in the restaurant at that point.'

'I was wearing a wire,' Juno explained to the police detectives. 'They heard everything.'

'Not everything,' Phoebe corrected. 'It was intermittent.'

'Do you have a recording?' asked Mason.

'It's not that sophisticated,' Phoebe said apologetically. 'Mil Winterbourne borrowed it from one of his regulars who uses it for cricket umpiring.'

'Can I inquire *why* exactly you were wearing a wire, Mrs Mulligan?'

'Internet dating can be a very dangerous undertaking these days,' Juno said. 'I wanted to make sure I was safe.'

'Didn't stop you getting your drink spiked and ending up in a hotel room with a dead man in the bathroom, did it?' DS Alsop pointed out cheerfully.

'That's uncalled for, Detective Sergeant,' DI Mason reproved gently.

Juno pressed her hands to her mouth, last night's shadows darkening again, *Psycho* violins striking in her head.

'So Don spiked my drink?' she asked.

'You and Mr Greenwood both had your drinks spiked, Juno,' DI Mason clarified.

'By whom?'

'That's what we're trying to establish.'

'It makes no sense.' She rubbed her face tiredly. 'Whoever heard of *both* people on a date being roofied?'

'Did Don and Juno have the same cocktail of drugs in their systems as Rich Bass?' Phoebe asked Mason.

'There are strong similarities.'

'You must think this is murder, surely?'

'It happened in a locked bathroom. But we're looking into all possibilities.'

'Just not terribly fast,' Phoebe muttered, clearly convinced her fictional 1920s detectives would be chasing the culprit down in a Model T by now, silk neck scarves flapping.

DI Mason ran his tongue over his braces with an awkward smile, looking from Phoebe to Juno, benign eyes sympathetic. 'I've already explained, as a small force with limited resources, we must await official channels to sanction formal criminal investigations. The moment those investigations are underway, we strongly discourage members of the public from engaging in their own inquiries.'

'And before then?' Phoebe asked wryly. 'If you were, say, stuck on hold for a couple of days before getting the go-ahead?'

'That's not for me to say.' His braces gleamed.

* * *

As soon as Mason and Alsop had left, Juno insisted she needed to get back to her flat to shower and change into something funereal.

'You can't go to Rich's funeral, Juno,' Phoebe told her. 'You had a toxic cocktail of date rape drugs a few hours ago. A man was murdered in the next room just feet away. You haven't slept. You're in shock.'

'I must be there, Freddy!' Juno was adamant. 'I will not let Chemsex on the Beach ruin this investigation or my duty of care. Debra needs me there. And she needs me to sing the medley. They danced to "Sultans of Swing" at their wedding.'

Phoebe came to sit down beside her.

'Juno, Debra was at The Priory last night,' she told her.

'Don't be silly.'

'She and Grant were eating outside. There was a woman with them. We didn't get a good look at her.'

'Of course! Debra told me they were meeting someone. She didn't mention it was at The Priory.'

'Only one decent restaurant within fifteen minutes' drive of Inkbury.'

'Don't be so snobbish, Freddy. The Damselfly has a Michelin star. And what about The Barton Arms?'

'That's what Cosmo Lovat said to you last night,' Phoebe explained. 'You can't have forgotten he was there too?'

'He was?' She shook her head to try to loosen the memory and then started to feel dizzy. Last night's shadows were shifting again. 'I remember Courtney Welch waitressing, along with that other girl from the village who helped us move tables. And I remember Don's strange flat nose, and how shy he was, but funny, and weirdly sexy. I can't believe he's dead, can you?' For a moment tears rose like floodwater, sadness overwhelming her.

She covered her head with her arms, trying to picture him. But it was Jay's face she saw, that familiar sideways smile, the intense gaze looking straight into her soul, the endless ache of grief from missing him.

'What am I *thinking*?' She jumped up. 'I met Don for a couple of hours. Debra was married to Rich almost thirty-five years. I must get to this funeral!'

Phoebe was already walking alongside her. 'Well, if you insist on going, Felix and I are taking you there. We'll be your ears and eyes. And mates,' she added, glancing sideways, clever green gaze bright with kindness.

Juno felt overwhelmed with relief. 'You will?'

'Absolutely. We've got your back.'

Which made Juno stupidly feel tearful again, but in a good way. The image of Jay she had in her head refused to fade. He was striding along with them.

Felix drove Juno's newly repaired Mini to Newborough Crematorium, Juno lolling beside him, feeling spacy and car sick. Phoebe was in the back leaning between their seats. She and Felix were talking animatedly via Bluetooth to Mil, who was stuck at the pub taking deliveries and on an open line.

'So the police are definitely treating Don Greenwood's death as murder?' he asked.

'It's not yet a formal investigation,' Felix explained, 'but DI Mason thinks it might soon be.'

'Which gives us a couple of days max,' said Phoebe.

'In the meantime, Mason more or less told us to go for it,' Felix interpreted, 'as long as we're law abiding and discreet.'

'We can't tread on their toes once they're on it,' Mil agreed. 'I'll ask my cousin for the heads up.'

Phoebe began laying out some probabilities: 'The roofies that Juno and Don ingested were either in the olives, the drinks or the starters. My guess is the olives, and Cosmo Lovat left those behind when he ordered drinks. Was that deliberate, knowing Juno and Don would consume them?'

'Or were they meant for Cosmo all along?' asked Felix.

'Unlikely, given the pre-planning that must have gone into getting into Don's bathroom to kill him,' Phoebe pointed out. 'He was always the intended victim if you ask me.'

'Actually, we had two bowls of olives,' Juno remembered illogically. But they had all already moved on.

'The manager took us to the wrong hotel bedroom first,'

Phoebe was saying, 'which bought the killer valuable time to despatch Don. She said he'd had a room upgrade which hadn't been logged in the system properly, and a whopping one. The Red Priest Suite is pretty much as far out of earshot of any room in The Priory; Johnny Depp always requests it apparently. The key code had been changed, which is common practice with a new guest, but again it delayed us, otherwise we might have got there in time to save him. My guess is whoever planned this had a passkey and let themselves in after Don and Juno, knowing they'd be way too out of it to notice. They'd already made sure Eminem was playing at max – that could have been done from outside the room if they'd paired with the room's Bluetooth beforehand – and bundled Don into the bathroom to do the deed.'

'But how did the killer get out of the bathroom?' asked Mil on the stereo.

'The bathroom windows to all the tower rooms on the side of the hotel are adjacent to the external fire escape,' Phoebe explained, 'but they all have restrictors which means they can only be open a few inches. Mil and I got a quick glance at the one in Don's bathroom when we found his body and spotted something odd, didn't we?'

'We did?' Mil's disjointed voice sounded impressed.

'The obscured glass was at the top.'

'You noticed that?' He sounded even more amazed.

'Meaning?' asked Felix.

'It's a sash window, and the obscured glass should have been on the bottom frame where it protects guests' modesty, not at the top. Somebody had closed it the wrong way round in a hurry.'

'Escaping via the emergency balcony after killing him, you think?' Felix followed her logic.

'Those restrictors can only be removed from the inside, so they couldn't have got in that way – unless they'd gone in earlier to remove them – but they could get out, especially if they heard me banging and shouting at the suite's door.'

'You're bloody brilliant, Phoebe!' Mil cheered on Bluetooth.

'And do you know who it was?' asked Felix.

'Not yet,' she admitted, 'but I have some thoughts.'

Lolling in the passenger seat listening to all this, Juno would have liked to contribute, but almost all her focus was taken up debating whether to ask Felix to stop so she could get out and be sick. A tiny reserve supply of focus and adrenaline was running through the lyrics to 'Walk of Life'. What little was left listened in, as Phoebe switched back to what appeared to be her current top suspect: 'Cosmo told Juno that he knows the hotel owner and was having a drink with them. If that's true, Cosmo could have access to areas others didn't.'

'Who is the owner of The Priory?' Juno managed to blurt before motion sickness swept her away again.

'I'll google it,' offered Mil, making loud humming and hawing noises as he did so before reporting, 'It's a bloody WE SIN business!'

'Debra and Grant were there last night too,' Felix reminded them all.

'I don't trust Grant,' Juno managed to declare between nausea swells.

'And there was the woman with them we didn't recognise,' said Phoebe.

'Here we go, mourning faces on,' Felix said as the Mini swung into the crematorium car park.

Just before Felix cut the engine, Mil admitted gruffly, 'I wasn't sure at the time, but I think I might have recognised the woman with Debra and Wayne. At least, not exactly who, but...

she was a Welch, I reckon. One of the three, what did you call them, Phoebe?'

'The Three Decrees? Cheryl, Zadie or Bethany.'

'Yeah. Very beautiful necks, the Welches. I'd know one anywhere. They've all got three stars tattooed on them. Forgive me, Phoebe, but your phone's crap so there's no way of knowing for sure. But I'd lay down money she was a Welch. Beautiful necks,' he sighed again.

'I'm terribly sorry.' Vision swimming, Juno closed her eyes. Dire Straits' 'Romeo and Juliet' was playing through her head. 'But I might just need to be sick before we go in?'

26

PHOEBE

As 'Rockin' All Over the World' faded, the trainee celebrant stepped forward to the lectern mic to tell the mourners in a trembling voice: 'Richard Bass was a much-loved and respected pillar of the Inkbury community.'

Beside Phoebe, Felix sucked his teeth with a quietly cynical pop of his lips. They both knew few in the room would agree with the statement.

Phoebe turned away to study the mourners. It was a big crowd; Juno had spread the word well.

She was now sitting up front with Debra, who was sporting a huge black veiled hat with a brim so wide that Juno was also beneath it, looking like she was sharing an umbrella. Also beneath it, on Debra's other side, Grant resembled a skinny schoolboy in a fitted black suit, his hair slicked down by gel.

The celebrant was reading too fast from a shaking piece of paper as she listed the timeline of Rich's upbringing in Blackheath, his early career as a kitchen fitter, his marriage to 'the beautiful Miss England finalist Debra' after a long engagement, through which he started Bass Kitchens and Appliances and made his first million: 'Although he always said he would have achieved that sooner if Debra had let him bet on Last Suspect at 50/1 in the 1985 Grand National!' She left a pause for laughter which didn't come. 'Rich loved his horse racing, along with Formula One, snooker, cricket and, above all, his golf.' She launched into a long list of his minor sporting trophies and amateur tours.

The Inkbury cricket club members were out in force, Phoebe noticed. Its longest-standing member and scorekeeper, Bernard Cole, stepped forward to read Auden in a nasal drone. Acting captain Cosmo was reluctantly perched on the end of the row, discreetly reading an alert on his smart watch.

To Phoebe's mind, Cosmo was a chief suspect for Don's demise, and possibly the others too. He looked unsettled, head constantly darting up and around, classic signs of frayed nerves and a guilty conscience.

Cosmo had been at The Priory last night; he could have been lying in wait for Don in the bathroom of the Red Priest Suite; he was a tough, athletic man, capable of overcoming heavily drugged and distracted Don; he could have got away through the window to the fire escape. It was also feasible he'd been there the night Wayne died and overdone the drug dose in the olives, just as he could have been waiting to accost Rich at the cricket pavilion. The two had already been seen arguing that night.

Cosmo had the opportunity and the means, but what motive?

What she kept coming back to was Holly. Eighteen months ago, Cosmo's second wife had died suddenly and brutally. Had it been deliberate, and if so, why? Could Cosmo be avenging his wife's murder, or just continuing a murder spree that had started there?

The only way to find out was to question him, and Phoebe knew her best opportunity was today. But Cosmo was a chippy, defensive character, and a funeral was hardly the best place to play amateur sleuth. Gaining his trust would be hard at the best of times. And judging from the way he was looking from his smart watch face to the guests sitting around him, he already suspected that a fox was here amongst the hens.

That was when Phoebe realised phone screens were glowing all around the crematorium. Beside her, Felix had discreetly opened a news feed notification on his own smart watch, which he shared with her.

Wexshire: Mystery Death in 5-Star Luxury Hotel. Police Suspect Serial Killer.

'Serial killer?' she mouthed in shock. There was no way DI Mason had thought that earlier, and he certainly wouldn't have sanctioned this.

Voices had started whispering around them as the notification was shared. There was an audible F-bomb from the front row, which made monotone Bernard falter in his Auden recital, a silence that genuinely seemed to stop the clocks.

Phoebe looked up to see the distinctive blonde dreadlocks of Bethany Welch, piled high on her head in a bun pinned in place with black roses, the three tattooed stars clearly visible on the back of her neck. Sitting to one side with her arms around her was older sister Zadie, her short blonde undercut revealing one jewelled ear, its rim glittering with studs and hoops, three stars also stamped on her tanned, slender nape. On Bethany's other side she recognised the mahogany-skinned blonde with sun-bleached hair she'd witnessed being dropped home by taxi. Cheryl Welch back from her Greek adventure, her three ink stars pierced through like lightning by the many gold chains glittering around her neck.

The Three Decrees.

Pulling out her own phone, Phoebe took a discreet photograph of them. Opening the gallery, she swiped it back and forth to compare with the one she'd taken the previous evening of the woman in the baker boy hat sitting outside with Debra and Grant on The Priory's terrace.

Mil was right. Each had the same distinctive square shoulders, long neck and flash of blonde hair.

It could have been any one of them, she realised. But which?

Felix nudged her again, showing her another news feed headline:

Wexshire Celebrity Hotel Serial Killer linked to death of respected local businessman.

* * *

Phoebe used her phone to search for the source of the story as soon as she and Felix were in the Mini driving between the service at the crematorium and the golf club for the reception. Juno was travelling there with Debra, who once again refused to let go of her hand, but Mil was back on the speaker via Bluetooth, booming, 'What bloody serial killer?'

'The full story is here.' Phoebe found it. '*A source close to the luxury five-hundred-pound-a-night hotel, a favourite of A List stars such as...* Blah blah... This is all clickbait. Here we go... *Has revealed that this is the second death at The Priory in Dunford in the past month and local police are involved. Furthermore, a respected local businessman with close connections to the hotel is thought to be a third victim of the killer after dying close by in what was first assumed to be a tragic, self-inflicted accident.* Who wrote this tosh? It's not coming from a legitimate platform; it's just a cut-and-paste fake news stream that drives social media traffic; they don't fact check. Somebody's fed them this.'

'Someone inside the hotel, do you think?' asked Felix.

'Kids is my guess,' Mil suggested. 'A lot of older village ones work at The Priory. Courtney's never off social media and she was waitressing there last night, and her cousin Seph.'

'And the punky one, Xanthe,' Phoebe remembered, 'Autumn's friend.'

'I'll find out what I can from here,' Mil promised.

* * *

Rumours that Rich might have been the victim of a serial killer had spread rapidly around his funeral. No victims had been named, the circumstances yet to be reported, but such a scandal at the renowned local hotel meant the story about The Priory had soon been shared far and wide, becoming the main topic of conversation whispered between the gold club car park and the Above Par function room as the guests arrived for the wake.

'Is there a Below Par in the basement?' Felix asked Phoebe, who had briefed him to chat up the Three Decrees for information while she annexed Cosmo Lovat.

'One of them was at that hotel last night,' she told him. 'Try to find out which. Use your charm.'

'Let's swap and I'll talk to Cosmo instead?' He looked unexpectedly fazed at the prospect of tackling the three village sirens. The trio were first to the bar for their free drink.

'Tie yourself to the mast,' Phoebe advised. When he looked blank, she explained, 'Odysseus?'

'In that case, I'm tucking in to the Lotus Eaters' feast first,' he said, eyeing what was on offer. 'From what Juno said, I thought it was going to be hot and cold listeria, but this is splendid.'

Only Debra shrieked in horror when she saw the luxurious food laid out, three long trestle tables loaded with the finest organic local fork buffet.

'What's happened to my sandwiches?' she squawked, gaping at the mountains of fresh salads, cold meats, cheeses and pastries. 'I'm not paying for all this!'

She and Grant went into an urgent huddle with the club's duty manager.

'An anonymous benefactor stepped forward, apparently,' Juno told Phoebe and Felix as they queued together to load their plates. 'You're spared my old party food.'

'But all this *is* from Inkbury Deli?' Phoebe recognised the same smoked trout croquettes Juno had served at her housewarming a fortnight earlier, along with whipped feta filo baskets.

'Possibly,' Juno said vaguely.

The sight of blue-haired Autumn replenishing supplies from chill boxes confirmed it.

Meanwhile the bar was doing a roaring trade.

'Just one glass each!' ordered Debra.

'And whoever it is that donated the buffet also put a tab behind the bar,' Juno said in an undertone as the drink kept flowing, 'although I am touching nothing stronger than Vimto until Christmas. You have to stop me if I do.'

As soon as Debra realised she wasn't footing the bill, she

secured herself a bottle of champagne, tearfully announcing that she was drinking it in Rich's honour.

'How are you bearing up?' Phoebe asked Juno, worried how pale she looked.

'Not bad.' She put on a brave smile. 'I can't remember a word of "Money for Nothing", Debra's on the edge, and we might have a killer in the room.' She looked around nervously.

'That story's fake,' Felix reassured her.

'What story?' asked Juno, and Phoebe realised she couldn't have heard about it yet. That was when it occurred to her that, even though the story itself was fake, it was exactly what the Village Detectives suspected: there were now as many as four unexplained deaths that they feared were linked. What's more, several of their suspects were in this room.

'As long as nothing here's spiked with Chemsex on the Beach we're fine,' she muttered, putting down her plate. She craved a mug of tea. 'Have those cold boxes of Autumn's been left long enough for someone to tamper with them?'

'Who would do that?' gasped Juno. 'Not at a funeral, surely?'

Watching her hurry back to rejoin Debra, Phoebe spotted Cosmo with Autumn, looking even more agitated. Muttering something urgently to his daughter, he stalked out onto the Above Par balcony to make a phone call.

'Food's amazing,' Felix said, cheeks bulging with salad. 'Try some.'

Phoebe thought back to the bowl of olives Cosmo had left on the bar for Juno and Don to plunder. 'Tell me I'm being paranoid, but what if this really is a Lotus Eaters' feast, and somebody's doctored the food?'

'Like a king's taster, I can assure you that you are being

madly paranoid, but I'll keep checking.' He nodded nobly, wolfing back a brace of chorizo pinwheels. 'The killer is hardly going to drug everyone at a funeral. They might have got all the victims they want.'

Phoebe shook her head. 'There's still a lion, a cat and swan or dove unaccounted for by my reckoning. Purple Pussycat might be right under our noses.' She eyed the Welches warily as they passed round yet more free drinks from the bar.

'Is this another Greek myth?'

'The Dapper and Discreet investors' angel names,' she reminded him, 'which were almost certainly also their usernames on the Dapper and Discreet app.'

'Of course, the pubs!' he remembered. 'Wayne was Golden Pheasant, Rich was Black Horse, Don was Green Man.'

'And they're all dead. From what we can work out, that leaves White Swan or Dove, Purple Pussycat and a lion of unknown colour.'

'Maybe *they* are our killers.'

'That just sounds like a Marvel movie plot.'

Felix laughed. 'Now that's more my field of expertise.' He dropped a pastry-dusted kiss on her cheek, whispering, 'Can't put this off any longer. I'll see if our Wayward Sisters will give anything away.'

Phoebe watched gratefully as he wandered off to charm the Three Decrees, pausing to thank Autumn, who was setting up a fourth trestle table with mountains of cheesecake, profiteroles and miniature trifles.

The sight of so many sweet treats had set off Debra, who was holding court in the centre of the room. 'Rich's favourite desserts! I can feel him looking down on us right now; it's almost as though he's here walking amongst us.'

'That must be who just pinched my backside,' Juno muttered to Phoebe as she hurried past with a fresh bottle of fizz.

Glancing around, Phoebe noticed that Cosmo was still out on the Above Par balcony, staring moodily out across the golf course.

She headed outside with her vape.

'Do you play?'

He reeled around, wide-eyed, then smiled briefly. 'You made me jump.'

'Sorry, I asked if you play golf?'

'I've a decent handicap.'

'So are you a member here?'

'I am.'

'Making business deals on the fairways too, I bet.'

'Sometimes.' He paused to gaze broodily out across the course again. He was clearly on edge, tapping his phone against his chin, the fingers of the other hand drumming on the balcony rail, then a chair back, then his thigh.

Grasping the rail, Phoebe turned to study him. He was such a coiled spring of a man, it seemed unlikely he'd be willing to trust her. She envied Felix psyching out the candid, confessional Welches. Perhaps he'd been right; they should have swapped targets.

Cosmo was eyeing her back now. 'That husband of yours neglecting you?'

With a thud of disappointment, Phoebe realised that – like Felix with the Three Decrees – she might have to flirt. Anything but that.

Wearily, she raised a femme fatale eyebrow. 'Neglect implies I've noticed what he's doing.'

He laughed briefly. 'You noticed what I'm doing enough and came out to talk to me.'

'I came out to vape.' She turned round to lean back against the rail so she could see his face better. 'But tell me, if you and Rich Bass hated each other so much, why are you here at his funeral?'

He chewed a tight, irritated smile. 'Debra wanted me here.'

'I didn't know you were close.'

'We're not.' He laughed coldly. 'I've always felt sorry for her.'

'Generous of you to gift the buffet from your deli,' she said, certain he hadn't. 'Are you paying for the open bar too?'

The tight smile was sucked away. 'I haven't stood Rich Bass a drink in a long time, I'm not about to start now he's dead.'

'Somebody else then.'

'You'll have to ask your friend Juno about that.'

'Ah, mystery solved. Thank you.' Phoebe had already guessed as much. 'Juno is a very generous soul.'

This disarmed Cosmo, who assumed that was all this interrogation was about.

'So my daughter keeps telling me,' he sighed. 'Autumn's trying to set us up. Waste of time.'

'Still too soon?' Phoebe asked sympathetically.

'Not my type.' He held her gaze, unsmiling.

Phoebe's femme fatale eyebrow refused to go up again.

Watching his edgy, phone-tapping, finger-drumming distraction, she had another idea. 'You're not hers either, I'm afraid.' She wrinkled her nose. 'Too vulnerable.'

'Vulnerable?' he scoffed.

Phoebe shrugged. 'Juno thinks someone wants to kill you.'

The tight smile twitched. 'That's ridiculous.'

'I tend to agree, although Wexshire's serial killer might well strike again.'

'Ludicrous story!' he snapped. 'You do realise it's fake news?'

'Perhaps. It's certainly not legitimate... yet... but I think you'll find the police do eventually connect what happened at The Priory last night with Rich's death, and quite probably with Wayne Baxendale's too. We've already been looking into it, and all three men shared the same secret. There's a strong possibility they were killed for it.'

'What secret was that?' He was trying to hide how uptight he was, but his fingers were playing timpani on his phone case and the balcony rails.

'I think you already know.' She watched his face. There was a muscle twitching in his cheek. Was it guilt or fear, she wondered?

Phoebe decided it was time to play the face cards in her poker hand. 'Tell me, are you the White Bird, Purple Pussycat or the Lion?'

He dropped his phone, which landed with a crack at their feet, its screen shattering.

Frightening him into talking was a far more satisfactory and effective solution than flirting, Phoebe concluded happily, stooping to pick it up.

He turned away, raking back his hair. 'Christ, you know about that?'

'We know Rich used his investment syndicate to legitimise a group of anonymous "angels" who backed a dating app. We think somebody is now picking those investors off. Three are dead in as many weeks.'

'*Three?* Of course, Wayne too, you said. Oh, God, I knew it!' He rubbed his face fretfully. 'Oh, God, oh, God, oh, God. I'm in serious danger here, aren't I?'

'Yes.' She handed him back his phone, its screen now shattered and glitching wildly.

Cosmo's expression looked much the same. 'Why should I trust you?'

Sensing his volatility, Phoebe kept her voice low and reassuring. 'I have nothing financial to gain out of this and no skin in the game.' Curvy Kitten didn't count, she decided. 'Besides, I could ask you the same. You were at The Priory last night. You know the owners well, I hear.'

A cackle behind them made him look round, a pair of smokers sparking up in the doorway behind them.

'Shall we go somewhere less overlooked?' Phoebe suggested.

Cosmo hesitated and she worried he was going to tell her to go to hell. But then he nodded, letting her lead him out of sight of the Above Par bar windows, down a flight of steps to a lower terrace set out with café tables overlooking the driving range.

There he settled opposite her at a table, turning his broken phone around in his hands.

'I'm White Swan,' he admitted eventually.

So he *was* a Daddy. Phoebe hid her excitement behind a deadpan face to ask, 'Nether Bassett or Upper Benham?'

'What?'

'The codenames are Wexshire pubs, aren't they? WE SIN invested in several including a White Swan in Nether Bassett and another in Upper Benham.' Mil had been filling up the WhatsApp group feed with his extensive fieldwork.

He shook his head. 'White as in cricket whites and swan because I like paddleboarding on the river.'

They were getting side-tracked, she realised. 'But you *were* an anonymous angel in Rich Bass's Dapper and Discreet syndicate?'

Cosmo explained that he had never formally been a part of WE SIN, although he'd got to know several of its investors when the syndicate had backed The Priory at Dunford. 'I was the one who bought the site and developed it into a hotel.'

'So *you* own it?'

He shook his head. 'WE SIN still owns it. I retained a 25 per cent share when they invested, and a few of the backers like Rich later sold their stakes back to me, so I now have about a third and I'm the biggest single stakeholder, but I was never a WE SIN angel. Mine was the startup project. And I love the place. I lived there briefly after my first marriage ended, and it's where I always stay now, although I'm not sure I will any more.' He raked his hair again. 'It's not safe, is it? Christ, Wayne too?'

Aware he would have unrivalled access to doctor its olives and sneak into its suites, Phoebe's suspicions hardened. And yet, if Cosmo was their killer, why was he so frightened for his own life?

'Tell me about investing in Dapper and Discreet?'

'It was Holly who saw the potential,' he explained. 'She'd not long launched the deli, but running it was never her thing, all the homespun village-core. She wanted something bigger, more exciting.'

When Rich had approached Cosmo and Holly at a village cricket match seeking small investors to back Dapper and Discreet, they'd seen it as an entertaining community gamble. 'A bit of fun, we thought, and Holly loved the idea of being a business angel.'

'So you didn't know who else was involved?'

He shook his head. 'I figured out Wayne was in on it, but the angels never met. We all had stupid codenames. *What* is that noise?'

A loud screeching from above made them turn in surprise. A familiar voice cut through it, wailing that she wanted her

MTV. Then the guitar shrieked and buzzed through an almost-familiar riff, souped up with snarling heavy metal fret slides.

'It's Juno.' Phoebe smiled fondly, then remembered. 'And Grant.'

The Dire Straits tribute medley had started.

'How personally invested in Dapper and Discreet were you?' she asked Cosmo.

'About 40K.'

'No, I mean were you a Daddy?' Phoebe guessed Bethany Welch was wrong when she'd described Cosmo as an old-fashioned village adulterer who preferred his affairs offline. 'Wayne, Rich and Don "Green Man" Greenwood were all prolific users of the app. Did you also enjoy digital booty calls?'

'I wasn't a part of that,' he dismissed. From the way his fingers drummed on the table, Phoebe guessed he was covering.

'But you were given VIP membership.'

He pushed his phone away, turning to look across at the driving range. 'It hadn't even been beta tested when we invested. I had no idea about tech launches or online brand building. That was Holly's field. Ask anyone, I'm a luddite.' He turned to glance up towards the Above Par hubbub and its wailing guitar.

'That's your excuse.'

'My marriage was in trouble. Holly wasn't happy.'

'And you thought buying into an app enabling people to have affairs would help?'

'Holly was the one who wanted us to invest in the app, not me!' Cosmo snarled.

His sudden flash of anger made Phoebe reel back.

She took a beat to absorb its intensity, wondering if she should make her way back to the safety of the Above Par bar, listening to the beat thumping from above as Juno sang about installing microwave ovens and custom kitchen deliveries.

But then Cosmo confided, 'Holly was Purple Pussycat.'

Phoebe was even more taken aback, her poker face slipping as she stared at him incredulously. 'But wasn't that your first wife's pet name?'

'Christ, you know that too?' He glared at the table furiously. 'Holly knew it would trigger me. We were all encouraged to be guinea pigs on the app before it launched. I think she chose it to see if we'd match. She was always insanely jealous of Violet.'

Phoebe guessed he hadn't been exaggerating about their marriage being in a bad place. 'And did you match?'

'I didn't go on it to find out.' He tilted his head back and listened to the music as, up in the bar, Grant put his all into drowning out Juno with the final refrain of 'Money for Nothing'.

It seemed Dire Straits had the same effect on Cosmo as a shot of Chemsex on the Beach, because when he started talking again, it was as though the coiled spring had suddenly come unravelled. 'I'll be honest, when Rich had initially approached me asking if I wanted to back a dating app for extra-marital affairs, I hated the idea. I even wondered if it was an elaborate joke at mine and Holly's expense. Our relationship had been something of a running gag in the village; it kept tongues wagging for years. But when I told Holly about it, she just saw profit where I just saw conspiracy theories. She understood that online world, so I let her run with it. I wanted no part of it.'

Despite her suspicions, Phoebe sensed he was telling the truth about this.

'I was wrapped up in the old sawmill development,' he went on, 'trying to keep my builder's spending under control. Holly had a lot of digital marketing experience – it was her background – and she was happy to help beta test it.'

'So you knew Holly was on the app?'

'The developer desperately needed women to try it out. Rich's PA was co-opted, Holly told me, and his cleaner too, I think. It was all purely hands off – testing out the gallery, the user interface, direct messaging. Holly's feedback was so good, they relied on her expertise. She was working back in product launch and loving it. The deli bored her. I bored her.' He picked up his damaged phone again as though she was somehow still in there.

'Holly threw herself into the launch campaign, found a bunch of like-minded women to sign up through social media campaigns, worked out a commission system for them to recruit friends.' He turned to glare out across the course. 'Turns out she also found a new lover.'

Phoebe found herself thinking back to her conversation with Bethany Welch again, remembering her quoting the old truism: *When a man marries his mistress, he creates a vacancy*.

In Cosmo and Holly's case, however, the roles had been reversed. When Holly had married her man on the side, she'd craved another clandestine affair.

'Who was it?'

'I never found out.' Cosmo fiddled with the chipped screen again, pulling off glass shards. The glitching had stopped, the phone apparently dead. 'It was Holly's daughter who uncovered what was going on.' He looked pained at the memory. 'Astonishing how quickly she guessed.'

Above them, Grant was now incorporating a lot of fast metal chord shredding into 'Sultans of Swing', playing so loudly that Phoebe had to strain to hear.

'She's super-sensitive' – Cosmo was talking about his step-daughter – 'screwed up by her parents' divorce, lives on her phone. Hates me. Probably understandable.'

'But she told you what was happening?'

'It was more of a digital billboard campaign.' He winced at the memory. 'We'd only just moved into the new house, and Holly was so excited to show it off. It was her fortieth birthday weekend and our kids were trying out the high-tech teenager annexe, hanging out there with their friends. The hope was they might spend a bit more time staying with us – things had been strained and we'd neither seen much of them. But then Autumn felt sick and wanted to go home. When I came back from dropping her with Violet, there was an atomic row going on because Holly's phone had somehow found itself sharing its screen with all of our TVs, projecting her Dapper and Discreet secrets round the house.'

'Her phone?'

'It's a smart house. Wasted on me, but the builder was a specialist and Holly desperately wanted to turn the lights on from Italy or talk to the kettle while she was out running. Everything is set up to be accessed remotely. Only Holly sharing her Spotify playlists to it was no match for a teenager with a GCSE grade 9 in IT. A slideshow from her phone was showing on TV in every room, all the Dapper and Discreet messages, the galleries full of Purple Pussycat's intimate selfies. Holly couldn't hide the fact she'd been having an affair.'

'Her daughter exposed it?'

'Who else? They were screaming at each other so hysterically, I might as well not have been there. I stormed out, drove up onto the downs, got drunk, slept in the car. By the time I got home, Holly's daughter had gone back to her dad's and the caterers were there. It was Holly's fortieth that day. We were throwing a big party. Terrible timing. It was too late to cancel;

friends were on their way. I'm not sure how we got through it; I don't remember much except that we both got mullered and slept in separate rooms. The following morning, Holly smashed her car into a wall right outside our house. I was still in bed. I heard the sound and went out.'

'I'm so very sorry.' Phoebe watched his face twist with the effort to not break down.

Eventually, he sat back in his chair, staring up at the spotless blue sky.

'Do you think anyone else could have been involved in Holly's accident?' she asked carefully.

Cosmo let out a cynical half-cough. 'She was on her phone when she crashed, not looking at the road at all. When they cut her out of the car, they found the Dapper and Discreet app still open on it.' He leant forwards, picking up his own broken-screened mobile once more, spinning it around in his hand. 'We kept that detail quiet for obvious reasons. The only people who know that specific detail are me, the fire officers and the police. Now you do too. The inquest simply recorded that she'd been using her mobile phone and lost control of the car.'

Above them the music had changed, the melancholy arpeggio lick of 'Brother in Arms' ringing out, Juno's soft pure voice lifting beneath it, lamenting the displaced suffering of war.

'I never spent another night in that house. It was supposed to be the big, blended family dream home, but it ended up being a mausoleum. I'd sell it, but I'm still in dispute with the builder. The whole development is a pain in the neck and has lost me money thanks to him.' He listened to the music irritably.

Phoebe made another connection she should have seen much sooner, one Juno had already suggested. A craftsman who specialised in traditional thatches with deceptively high-tech mod cons. 'The builder was Grant Roberts, wasn't it?'

'You have been checking up on me. I only accepted the bloody man's tender as a favour for Rich. That was before we fell out.'

'Why did you two fall out?'

'He had me replaced as cricket captain for a start.'

Phoebe recalled being told this had come as a relief to Cosmo after Holly died. 'Was that what you and Rich were arguing about on the night of Juno's party?'

Cosmo looked away furiously. 'Rich was waging a war of attrition. He thought I'd been blackmailing him, threatening to tell Debra that he'd only bought Dapper and Discreet as a personal toy to use indiscriminately.'

'Were you?'

'No!' He slammed his phone back down on the table, its face breaking apart even more.

Phoebe remembered Don Greenwood telling Juno that Rich had accused him of blackmail too. 'Any idea who might have been?'

'None, but whoever it was, Rich had been paying up. It's why he sold me back his share in The Priory. Wiped him out, the stupid fool. Whatever evidence they have, it must have been so bad even Debra wouldn't stand for it. It's not as though she wasn't wise to his ways, or to blackmail, come to that. She's ruthless, that woman. Must run in the family.'

Another screeching guitar chord tore through the bar above them as 'Brothers in Arms' gave way to 'Walk of Life', its tempo feverishly upbeat. Grant's thrash metal spin on the song was like a horror track.

Juno had always suspected Grant.

Phoebe turned the idea around in her head. Could he be

their killer? Grant had also been at The Priory last night. A builder with a knowledge of high-tech systems made for a possible suspect in a locked room killing like Don's. Grant could have feasibly also killed Rich and Wayne too, possibly even Holly if he'd tampered with her car. But all this seemed unlikely to Phoebe, who doubted avenging his sister's honour would stretch to mass murder. More likely, Debra's strange brother was a blackmailer.

Grant had been working on the Lovats' home shortly before Holly's death. He'd blown the budget and was still in financial dispute with Cosmo. From what Grant himself had told Juno about his business going under, he still burned through money. His relationship with his brother-in-law, Rich, had been transactional at best, if not downright hostile. Grant remained angry that Rich's 'cabal' hadn't ever backed any of his building projects. But what about the Dapper and Discreet investment? Could he be a secret insider too? As far as Phoebe knew, there was only one anonymous angel unaccounted for.

'What colour is the lion?' she asked Cosmo.

He looked at her blankly.

'White Swan, Purple Pussycat, Golden Pheasant, Black Horse, Green Man – what about the lion?'

'Red,' he sighed, rubbing his face tiredly. 'Red Lion.'

'Any idea who that might be?'

'None. I just know they're the developer, and they got the biggest equity share.'

'Red Lion designed the app?' Phoebe felt her pulses quicken. A breakthrough at last.

'The evil genius.' He nodded.

'Is he one person?'

'Might be a "she" for all I know.'

'If they designed the app, might they be able to still manipulate it from inside, through a back door in the coding say?'

'You're asking the wrong person. I can't even upload a new avatar. I must go.' He stood up irritably, reaching for his phone.

Phoebe covered it with her hand. She was certain he knew more than he was letting on.

'Are you using Dapper and Discreet?'

'I told you, it was my wife who used it.'

Phoebe doubted herself. Autumn had said her father swiped right, but so did most of the single population these days. 'It might just save your life if you tell me the truth.'

He didn't immediately answer, taking his car key out of his pocket before saying, 'My mobile's dead. How can I use an app?'

'Fair point.' She uncovered his phone.

He stared at it for a long time.

'Autumn keeps telling me to try dating apps. I had a username and login, so it seemed a good place to learn the ropes. I'm a beginner, although there's one match I get along quite well with, Story Weaver, real name Edit, which is ironic. Originally from Budapest, working here in a wellness retreat. We were supposed to meet last night, then I had second thoughts. We're rescheduling.' He reached for the dead phone. 'Or we were.'

'I'd advise against it.' Phoebe gave a weary sigh. 'But if you're found dead in the lotus position clutching a wheatgrass smoothie, I'll know where to look.'

To her surprise, he laughed, the cold eyes appraising. 'And if I'm not, I'll buy you dinner sometime.'

'I'm married.'

'Haven't you heard?' He picked up his phone. 'Just my type.'

After he'd gone, Phoebe remained outside for a few minutes

with her vape, running back through everything Cosmo had just told her. She still didn't trust him, but she believed what he'd told her about Holly getting caught up in her illicit Dapper and Discreet adventure.

Phoebe was more certain than ever that it was the app that was responsible for its angel investors' deaths.

Behind her, the Dire Straits medley was supplanted by a familiar Madness ballad, Juno's voice finally allowed to shine as she told Rich's mourners that it must be love.

Love had very little to do with what had happened to Rich Bass, as far as Phoebe could tell.

* * *

Phoebe returned to the Above Par bar in time to catch the last few bars of The Who's 'Won't Get Fooled Again', Grant windmilling his arm like Pete Townsend. Juno looked pale but elated to have made it through as she thanked everyone and wished Rich a final farewell.

Seeing the Three Decrees clapping and whooping at the bar, Phoebe looked around for Felix, but he wasn't with them. Then she spotted him trapped in a corner with Debra Bass, who was weeping into his shoulder, huge hat brim almost garrotting him. He peered round it and caught Phoebe's eye with an urgent rescue request.

But before Phoebe could make it across the room, Debra had broken free to make her way to the stage.

Straightening her enormous hat, she grabbed a champagne flute and produced a sheaf of notes as she bustled up to the mic, her cheeks wet. She waited for the string hums, feedback and faint smattering of applause to fade before approaching the mic. 'Thank you, Grant! My talented baby brother. So, so talented! Thank you, Grant! Grant Roberts there, accompanied by Juno Munni – Mulli – by Juno. Rich would have loved that.' She blinked hard, fanned her face and cleared her throat before hurrying on. 'Quick bit of housekeeping: you all need to leave in the next five minutes. Please leave charity donations in Rich's golf cap by the exit. Cash only.

'But before you leave, I will read Rich's favourite poem, "Tiger Tiger Burning Bright"...'

Felix stepped in beside Phoebe, rubbing his neck which still bore a mark from Debra's hat brim. There was bronzer on his suit lapels and lipstick on his collar.

'You missed the music,' he said. 'That was a long conversation you had with Cosmo. Please tell me you didn't flirt too much?'

'Barely. You?'

'Brazenly.'

'With Debra too?'

'She ambushed me.' He was watching the stage, smiling like a ventriloquist. 'Is she doing a tiger claw hands mime?'

'Yup.'

'What did you find out?'

'Lots – I'll tell you later. You?'

'Nothing. The Welch women are tight-lipped. Then Debra swooped just as the music started, after which conversation was rendered impossible. Couldn't hear a word Juno sang either over that racket.'

Breaking away from Grant, Juno hurried to join them, whispering anxiously, 'What did you think? Could you hear me over the thrash guitar? Honest critique.'

'Every word.' Phoebe knew she was expected to lie.

'What thrash guitar?' said Felix, who was better at it. 'You were magnificent!'

Juno hugged them. 'I love you both. What did Cosmo say?'

'Yes, what *did* Cosmo say?' asked Felix.

'I'll tell you once we're out of here.'

'I might have to go back to Flatpack Mansion with Debra,' Juno whispered tiredly, glancing across to Debra, who was miming *twist the sinews of thy heart* as though she was wringing out washing. 'She wants a hand taking all the uneaten food home.'

'We're springing you,' Phoebe insisted. 'Let's get out of here before the stars throw down their spears and water heaven with their tears.'

'Yes, please.' Juno's tired, bloodshot eyes looked too burned out to water anything. 'And before there's another murder.'

'Too late for William Blake's poetry,' muttered Felix, putting a hand on each of their backs to quietly steer them away while everyone was preoccupied.

But Grant was minding the donation cap by the door in his school uniform suit and slicked-down hair, like a small, wiry bouncer. Hippo teeth flashing, he barred their way. 'Debra wants a word when she's done.'

It sounded menacing.

Phoebe put her arm around Juno, who had started to shake. The trio waited through Debra completing her recital of 'The Tyger', miming hammer, anvil, chain and furnace before she framed the big cat's fearful symmetry with some Vogue dance moves.

'Was she theatrically trained?' Felix asked, clearly astounded.

'She did a lot of acting classes in the eighties,' Grant told him. 'It was her dream.'

Debra joined them as the remaining guests stampeded

gratefully for the exit. 'Juno babes! And your friends! What did you think of my poem, Felix?' she asked him eagerly.

'Beyond words!' said Felix.

'I was nearly cast in *Eastenders* from the start, did Grant say? I was down to the final five for Kathy Beale, but they decided I was too young. Still, it's never too late, is it, Felix?'

'Absolutely not.'

'In fact, I'd value your advice, babes. Who to talk to, what agent to hire, maybe you know someone? Are you free tomorrow morning? Coffee and leftover profiteroles?'

'I'm not – that is I – er—'

'He's free,' Phoebe reassured her.

'Just bring yourself,' Debra told Felix. 'Thing is' – she lowered her voice – 'I might need a career now poor Rich has gone. It's all over the news that there's a murderer on the loose – have you seen? Serial killer, they say.' She clamped her hand to her mouth, fresh sobs bubbling.

'We're on the case,' Juno promised weakly, looking even paler.

'Oh, you poor babe!' The tears broke their banks. 'You must not give it another thought, do you hear? It's so awful that you were in that room with the man who died last night. Awful! What were you doing there, what were you *thinking*?'

'I was undercover,' Juno said in a small voice. 'But then I was under sedation, and I can't remember anything much.'

'Oh, babes, you *must* rest!' Blinking tears, Debra clamped a gel-clawed hand on Juno's shoulder. 'I can't thank you enough, Juno. You have been my rock, my brick, my sanity these past couple of weeks. Now I know I said to come back to mine, but it's been a very emotional morning. And you need to put everything that happened last night behind you and have some me time!'

'It's fine.' Juno tried to sound bright, but her voice cracked.

'Oh, babes.' Debra drew her to her into her arms and lowered her head so that Juno's head disappeared into the hat like a candle being snuffed. 'You go get some rest. Me and Grant have to make a trip to Newborough this afternoon. You don't mind, do you? We've got a few bits and bobs of Rich's to show a jewellery dealer there.' The hat lifted and she looked from Juno to Phoebe to Felix and back. 'You look after her. Keep her distracted.'

'They will,' Juno promised shakily. 'We all have a killer to catch.'

'That's the spirit, babes.' Patting her shoulder like she would a dog, Debra released Juno.

Clearing her throat, Phoebe stepped closer to Debra. 'Did you see anything suspicious when you were at The Priory last night?' she asked, earning a horrified look from Juno who clearly thought this very bad taste to ask a grieving widow at her husband's wake.

But Debra nodded, more tears brimming. 'Now you mention it, I was very put out by those teenagers from the village. I swear they doctored my strawberry champagne cocktail. I felt very groggy afterwards. And one of them claimed my voucher was out of date.'

'Who were you meeting there?'

But Debra had already turned away to clap her hands above her head and announce, 'You all need to leave *now*! Fast as you can! Thank you for coming. Please take your rubbish with you! And don't forget to leave a charity donation. Grab the hat, Grant!'

* * *

The Little Black Book Killer

The Village Detectives hurriedly shared what they had learned as they drove back to Inkbury in the Mini.

'Say that again?' Mil was once again on Bluetooth, having ducked into The Barton Arms car park at the start of a busy lunch service to take their call.

'Red Lion was the app developer,' Phoebe repeated. 'They and Cosmo are the only two of the original Dapper and Discreet stakeholders still alive, although Red Lion may also be dead for all we know.'

'Or the murderer,' said Felix.

'And Cosmo has no idea who it might be?' asked Juno.

'No, but he's clearly worried he's next on the hit list.'

'He could be right,' said Felix.

'And Holly Lovat-Dixon was Purple Pussycat, you say?' asked Mil.

'That's right,' said Phoebe. 'Holly – aka Purple Pussycat – started having an affair with a match before the app even went live and died in a collision not long afterwards.' She summarised what Cosmo Lovat had told her about Holly beta testing and recruiting members for Dapper and Discreet before her secrets were exposed on her home's TV screens.

'Wayne Baxendale – who was Golden Pheasant – met multiple app matches including Bethany Welch, then died waiting for another on a dinner date. No toxicology test was run, so we'll never know if his drink was spiked and triggered a massive cardiac arrest before the murderer got to play out the full scene. However, the fact it happened in The Priory is a compelling coincidence, particularly given what happened next. Rich "Black Horse" Bass died of auto-erotic asphyxia the night he was supposed to be meeting a match from the app, and he'd definitely ingested the Chemsex cocktail. The fourth death had the same hallmarks; Don "Green Man" Greenwood was a venture capital broker who took a stake in the app in exchange for keeping it all legit whilst hiding it from the taxman.'

'And I got drugged too,' said Juno jadedly. 'Which makes it personal.'

'We'll find whoever did it to you, Juno love!' Mil's voice boomed over the stereo.

'And what about the two who are still alive?' asked Felix.

'White Swan – aka Cosmo Lovat – claims he only invested in the app because his wife wanted to, but he's not as innocent as he makes out and he is now using his Dapper and Discreet VIP membership. His latest match is a wellness guru calling herself Dream Weaver. I've told him he'd be mad to meet her. He's a spiky character and contrary, so I don't trust him to do anything I suggest, and I don't trust him full stop. As the last angel, he's got to be near the top of the list for both our suspect and potential victim.

'Red Lion is our other original stakeholder, who designed the app. It's probable they can still hack into it. Don told Juno that the new owners have found evidence of someone accessing it through a back door.'

'I have absolutely no memory of that conversation.' Juno yawned.

'It makes Red Lion another prime suspect,' Phoebe told her.

'We're also looking for a blackmailer,' said Felix.

'And the Graveyard Ravers, don't forget!' Mil boomed on speaker. 'Mary's still after me to find them.'

'Grant Roberts is another suspect,' Felix suggested. 'And it's highly possible he was blackmailing Rich. He also fell out with Cosmo over the sawmill development, and Grant must have known how their smart home worked given he built it, so let's not dismiss the idea that he remotely broadcast Holly's secrets onto its TVs in front of her teenage daughter.'

'You've lost me,' Juno muttered faintly.

'Getting a bit sci-fi there, darling,' Phoebe warned Felix, telling them, 'I'm going to psych Grant out tomorrow. I've messaged him to say I'm interested in buying one of his heritage thatches and asked for a tour.'

'*We're* going to psych him out tomorrow,' Felix corrected. 'I don't want you alone with him.'

'No, you will be psyching out Debra while I'm distracting Grant. She likes you. Find out if she knows anything about Rich being blackmailed, even if you have to offer her a part in your next film to do so.'

'Shouldn't I be psyching them both out?' Juno demanded faintly. 'Grant's been trying to sell me a heritage eco thatch from the start, and Debra thinks I'm her bestie. But I just can't believe she's a murderer, Freddy. And I'm starting to think Grant is too self-obsessed to waste energy killing anyone.'

'You are going to rest,' Phoebe ordered, 'that's one thing I agree with Debra about. Stay in bed all day tomorrow if you want, or have another midlife makeover. You've been through a total nightmare with Don, and you were utterly brilliant today. So you need to recharge.'

'But you heard DI Mason this morning. We probably only have two days until the police start a formal investigation. We need to find out who Red Lion is.'

'I'm onto that!' Mil cried on speaker. 'I've just googled it, and there's Red Lions in Kintsmere, East Woodbury, Newborough and Old Dunning. Most popular pub name in the UK, unfortunately, but I can check those ones out with the boys to start with.'

'That won't be necessary,' said Phoebe.

'Walk me back here,' he entreated. 'How are the pubs involved?'

'They're not. Turns out they're not pub names.'

'Right. Gutted here. Lot of time went into that.'

'Sorry, Mil,' Juno told the stereo, stifling another yawn, 'I know how hard you worked on it.'

'Never mind, Juno love. Why don't I take you out to a Red Lion for lunch tomorrow anyway if you're free?' Mil suggested. 'You deserve a treat, and Albie still owes me time off.'

But Juno had fallen asleep on the back seat.

27

JUNO

'Folks, the Graveyard Ravers have struck again! One of my regulars spotted it when he was heading home. Sharing the picture here. Definitely kinkier than before. Looks like bondage stuff to me.'

Juno peered at the photograph Mil had posted on the WhatsApp group after his voice note and recoiled in surprise, pressing the little microphone in the reply box:

'Thanks, Mil. Gosh. I just want to say, that's not my mother's jumble donations. Also, they always strike when there's been a murder, don't they? They did it the night Rich died, and now so soon after Don. There was also one not long after Wayne died, am I right? Is that deliberate? It couldn't be a serial killer's calling card, could it?'

Phoebe replied soon afterwards:

> Serial killers generally leave their calling cards *at* the scene of the crime. P x

> Ps. I'd check out those kids that hang out at the deli. The goth students. They might have planted that story about the Wexshire Serial Killer too.

Later that morning, Juno went to the deli to settle her bill for the funeral breakfast, handing Autumn a fat cash tip. 'I'm *so* grateful you could do it.'

'Was Debra grateful to you?' Autumn asked shrewdly.

'Wildly,' Juno insisted, although the truth was Debra didn't know.

'To be honest, it was good to get out of here for a morning,' Autumn confided. 'Trade's so quiet, it's pointless having two of us most days.' She glanced over her shoulder towards the kitchen where the deli's full-timer – a taciturn middle-aged pâtissier who avoided talking to customers – was wiping off surfaces after morning food prep. 'I've told Dad I might get a job at The Priory for the rest of the summer. It's all happening there. But he's against it after what's just happened. I heard what you went through, and I can't believe you just sang at Rich Bass's funeral right after it. That's so rock and roll. You're a ledge.'

'And I only just found out your dad owns the place.' Juno knew she'd been briefed to find out about the Graveyard Ravers and not think about the Wexshire serial killer, but this was too good an opportunity to miss.

'A wing of it, Dad always says. He's terrified the bad publicity will affect bookings, but that viral story is already having the opposite effect. The place is jammed. Real crime tourism had taken over sex tourism, folks.' She raised a cynical pierced eyebrow.

'Your friends work there, don't they?' Juno remembered, getting back on track. 'River and...'

'Xanthe. Not often, and River has a job at the pop-up bar near Valence Lock. They've only been working to save money to travel. They find repetitive tasks triggering.' She grinned sardonically. 'They're wildly clever and destined to brilliant careers, whereas I'm an artisan.'

'Would you call them disrupters, then?'

But Autumn's thoughts were focused on the big drama at the hotel. 'Our friend Seph is in the kitchens at The Priory most days, you could talk to him. He was on a shift. And I think Courtney Welch was working that night.'

'Mil already talked to her.' He'd learned that Courtney had been fired that night for trying to film a real-life crime TikTok sequence on her phone outside Don Greenwood's room after his death.

'Who even was this Don dude?' Autumn handed Juno a coffee. 'On the house.'

'Thanks. He oversaw investment portfolios, including something called the Wexshire Enterprise Startup Investment Network.' When she looked blank, Juno ventured, 'WE SIN.' Autumn just shrugged, so she went all in. 'They backed the Dapper and Discreet dating app.' Mindful of Cosmo's involvement, Juno quickly added, 'Amongst many other local startups.'

'That app's toxic,' Autumn said with feeling. 'It's ended at least one village marriage. I might still think Dad and Holly were shabby having an affair when they were on the primary school PTA, but at least their eyes met across a crowded tombola stall. They didn't cynically sign up to an adultery matchmaking service.'

Juno said nothing, uncertain how to navigate the abrupt and brutal way the dating app had widowed Cosmo. It had been Autumn who had first suggested to Juno that there might be more to her stepmother's death, after all.

But to her surprise, theirs wasn't the marriage Autumn was thinking about at all. 'River's parents split because of it. His dad ran off with a woman he met on there. Cheryl was destroyed afterwards.'

'River's father used Dapper and Discreet?' Juno was shocked, wondering how Cheryl could sign up to and recommend an app that her own husband had joined specifically to have an affair.

'It went on for ages behind Cheryl's back, River says. She had no idea anything was wrong until Russell took off. But get this – top secret – she's now using the app herself. River told me.'

Juno took a beat, wondering how Autumn could not know this was amongst the worst-kept secrets in the village. Cheryl recruited everybody. Even she, Juno, was on it. But it was probably a generational thing, she realised. Genzees now saw dating apps as something for oldies, even those too old to ever feel comfortable with it. 'And River's okay with that?'

'Yeah. He encouraged her. She's great, Cheryl. She says she's reclaiming her power. It's pretty dope if you think about it, the way she's owning it.'

'Hang on, Cheryl *owns* the app?' Alarm bells went off in her head, a Red Lion roaring there.

'Not literally owns. Emotionally, morally, you know. All things being fair, she should get a cut, mind you, after what River's dad did to her.' Autumn's eyes flashed.

'She kind of does,' Juno said, thinking uneasily about the introduction fee Cheryl pocketed each time she signed up an unwitting friend. 'And it sounds like she's better off without her ex.'

'Yeah, Russell's totally cringe. We spy on his socials and he's just had a Turkish Daddy makeover. Ick. He and his girlfriend live somewhere swanky near Reading now, splashing the cash. River won't go there. He's so mad at him it's unreal.'

'These things take a long time to heal.'

'Tell me about it. A load of our parents' marriages fell apart at a fairly similar time. Mine were first, but Mum always was a trendsetter. She should be the First Decree by rights, but there's a pecking order. The Welches own that brand.'

'Cheryl's first decree,' Juno remembered. It was a phrase Phoebe had repeated more than once, because Phoebe listened to people more carefully than Juno did and noticed when something sounded odd. Which meant there was something else pun-loving Phoebe had shared. 'As in first "decree" murder?'

'Yeah, she's hilarious like that. Always was too good for a cheugy little nerd like Russell. Everyone used to say she deserved better when they were together. Even River said it and that's his dad.'

'Remind me, what is it Russell does for a living?' Juno fished.

'I don't think he works now. River says his dad won the lottery or something, which seems really unfair, but Cheryl insists it's all cool because they're the lucky ones now he's gone. I like to think she paid him off from her own big win. Either way, Cheryl's the winner. She's a queen.'

Juno didn't want to suspect Cheryl Welch of misdeeds. The woman was one of her village heroines, a glossy, golden Hannah Waddingham of take-me-as-I-am midlife cool. But as the first person to introduce Dapper and Discreet into Juno's life, she'd planted a bad seed. The app wasn't the perfect way to meet a millionaire she'd promised. According to Autumn, using it was Cheryl's way of taking back control over her unfaithful ex and all the men like him who used it.

But just how far had she taken that revenge?

* * *

Juno hurried around to call on Cheryl Welch, approaching stealthily through the trees by the duck pond because she didn't want to be spotted by Debra or Grant via Greenside Manor's many CCTVs scoping the village green.

Cheryl's cottage was next door to Flatpack Mansion, modest by comparison but still a village jewel. A substantial brick and flint semi with a riotously colourful, hollyhock-filled front garden, it stood testament to a profitable marriage and an excellent divorce lawyer.

The front door was opened by River, sleepy eyed in an Arcane hoodie and surfer shorts. He didn't seem to recognise her.

'Is your mum in?' Juno asked brightly.

He took out his ear-pods and she repeated the question.

He shrugged.

'Can you check?'

'Sure.' He wandered off, leaving the door open.

Inside, one of Cheryl's cats was weaving around a table in the hallway, posing on tiptoes. Juno remembered Cheryl telling her all her cats were close relatives of Kevin Bacon. Like Welches, there were many in the village, all named after redheads, even the black and white ones.

'Hello.' Juno stepped in to stroke it. 'Who are you?'

'Xanthe,' said a voice overhead. 'Oh, you're talking to the cat. He's Prince Harry the whingy ginge.'

River's pixie-haired goth partner was peering through the banisters. They were sitting halfway up the stairs in a stringy spider-knit jumper and checked bondage trousers, phone glowing in one hand. Face painted with fierce tribal make-up, they looked like a Picasso portrait.

'I'm Juno, a friend of Cheryl's. We've met at the deli.'

Xanthe sat back and propped their elbows on the step above. 'You're the one who that man died with at The Priory?'

'That's right.' Juno felt a spike of delayed shock flashback, blowing out through her lips to calm down. 'I was in a different room at the time.'

'Still, that must be *so weird*. Did you see him?' Xanthe's dark-rimmed eyes were huge.

'I was pretty out of it.'

'So what did the drugs feel like?'

'The closest I've come before was gas and air during labour.'

Losing interest, Xanthe looked at their phone again.

But now Juno was back in that room, Eminem rapping, vaguely aware of a dark shadow looming over her – or was it past her – a groaning struggle, or was she thinking about childbirth again?

Casting around for a distraction, she noticed two big backpacks propped against the understairs.

'Are you two going travelling?'

'Yeah, now Cheryl's back, it's our turn for adventure.'

'She's not here,' River reported, coming back. 'She's probably round at her sister's.'

'Showing off her holiday pics, no doubt!'

'Whatever.' He looked disinterested.

Realising River might not share his friend Autumn's approval of his mother 'owning' her ex's favourite dating app, Juno hurriedly deflected. 'I gather you're the ones off travelling now?'

'All packed and ready.' He half-smiled, then added acerbically, 'We've saved up, no freebies or handouts. I work at a pop-up bar on the canal and Xanthe does shifts at—'

'The Priory!' Juno remembered. A nagging memory was plaguing her, of that same shaven-browed face helping them change tables in the restaurant. Oh, God, had Xanthe witnessed Juno sucking on asparagus and slurping oysters like a middle-aged, over-sexed Nell Gwynn?

'I'm done with that now,' said Xanthe, sliding a step lower, smiling at River. 'We want to go to Berlin, see the—'

'Brandenburg Gate and Museum Island.' River began climbing towards his lover, their eyes locked together. 'Then go to—'

'Amsterdam.' Xanthe took his face in their hands. 'Loveland Festival. We both—'

'—love—'

'—festivals.' The couple started laughing together, irresistible in their mutual adoration.

The way they looked at each other and finished one another's sentences reminded Juno just how fierce and precious first love was. Oh, to love like that again.

On the wall straight in front of her was a large canvas photograph, a professional studio portrait featuring a pure white background, an artificially happy family trio lying on their bellies, chins in their hands, as though they'd just tumbled there from a John Lewis advert. River, plump-cheeked, white-blond and utterly gorgeous, looked about six. Cheryl resembled a glossy Boden model mum, and although Juno hated to judge, she was in her opinion several leagues apart from what she guessed must be her ex, a pasty ginger with thick glasses, bad teeth and thinning hair. His eyes were the only ones in the picture not smiling.

Juno felt a fierce burst of pity for Russell being so physically outclassed by his wife. He must be very clever, she reasoned, and no doubt professionally successful to buy a house like this, more still to be able to afford to walk away from it.

Russell was also the one who had signed up to a dating app in search of an affair, she reminded herself. And he was the one who had walked out.

Juno would have liked to study his picture more closely, but River and Xanthe were now kissing quite vigorously on the stairs, so she reversed politely back outside.

Standing in the gaudy, blossoming front garden, Juno still couldn't shake First Decree Murder from her head. It was buzzing in there, like the bees vibrating in the technicolour hollyhocks all around her.

Phoebe was convinced she'd seen one of the Welch sirens at The Priory on the night Don had died. Felix hadn't been able to get a straight answer out of them at the funeral, but the fact all three had been there at all was telling. Hadn't they all called Rich a creep? Yet they were also all on the app he had championed. Cheryl upsold it; Bethany had matched with Wayne and Don on it; Zadie dissed it, but her daughter Courtney had been serving drinks and olives at The Priory the night Don died.

Could they have been laying honeytraps all along?

The Three Decrees had shifted dramatically back up Juno's suspect list. And First Decree was top of the list.

Just how far had Cheryl gone to get revenge, Juno wondered fearfully, and who had helped her?

28

PHOEBE

'What a beautiful thatch!' Phoebe admired.

'Water reed – very lightweight, but with the advantage of added stiffness, durability and longevity,' Grant told her.

'The cat is charming.'

'My thatcher's trademark.'

While Felix was calling on Debra with chocolates, comfort and careers advice, Phoebe was getting a personal guided tour of Number Six Orchard Way, the show home on a modern heritage gated estate on the outskirts of Dunford.

'You worked on the Inkbury sawmill redevelopment, didn't you?' she asked Grant. 'With Cosmo Lovat?'

'*Big* success,' he boasted, hippo teeth gleaming. 'Would've won awards, but Cosmo kept slashing the budget. Wanted to cut corners. You see it a lot in my line. No pride. This place is all my own work, so no expense spared. Top spec.' He beckoned her into the nonpareil of craftsmanship and fine details.

'And it's beautiful.'

'I always say "build the house you wish you'd been raised in".' Grant led the way inside beneath a thatched porch, punching a code into a small smart screen so the thick oak door swung obligingly open. 'It's keyless, climate-controlled and practically carbon neutral.'

'So you grew up somewhere a bit different from this?'

'You could say. But me and my sister escaped all that. Well, she escaped, I followed. These are Jersey cream antique chiselled-edge porcelain slabs with underfloor heating.' He gestured downwards.

'Lovely.' Phoebe stepped on them reverently. 'How old were you when Debra and Rich married?'

'Fourteen. They were engaged a long time. Almost ten years. Debra told him to make a million, which he did. Eventually.' He flashed his fangy teeth again. 'This is the open-plan family space we'll explore later. But let me show you the garden. European oak bifold patio doors here, for the inside-outside fusion with unrivalled thermal efficiency. Mind the step.'

Phoebe followed him into a small freshly turfed square roughly half the size of the open-plan reception inside the house which was boxed in by six-foot wooden fencing. 'So you were, what, four when they met?'

'Rumpelstiltskin, she called him. After the fairytale.'

'The man who wove straw into gold for the miller's daughter in exchange for her first-born child.'

'Yeah, that's the one. Debs used to read it to me. She was brilliant at all the voices. Debs wanted to be an actress. Took classes and found herself an agent. She went to loads of auditions, almost got a part in *Eastenders*. But then she married Rich in the end.'

'You must have missed her?'

'I was almost an adult by then.' Crossing his arms, he turned to look up at the house he wished he'd grown up in.

'Got an apprenticeship as soon as I left school. Rich helped set it up, then my City and Guilds. Gave me a head start in the building trade.'

'He helped you a lot?'

'Yeah, Debs was good at prodding him into it.'

He waved her back inside and showed her upstairs, starting with a bedroom dressed to look like a nursery, with candy-striped walls and a tree mural over the cot. It was so beautifully staged, even Phoebe felt the stirrings of latent maternal yearning, finding herself envying Juno her imminent grandchild she could read bedtime stories to.

'Gotta love this room!' Grant sighed.

Phoebe thought about Rumpelstiltskin's demands in the fairytale that Debra had often told her little brother. What, she wondered, if the miller's daughter had already borne her child and was prepared to marry Rumpelstiltskin to help him out through life?

The hypothesis was probably way too far-fetched, she decided. And even if it was true, Grant was far too chippy and evasive to tell her. She lacked Juno's ability to wheedle truths out of people through chatty kindness.

But, unlike Juno, Phoebe was a cool-headed risk taker.

'When did you find out Debra was your mother?'

Grant's small eyes bulged, and Phoebe prepared herself for an eviscerating denial, followed by a show home expulsion.

Instead, there was an explosion of disbelieving laughter. 'I heard you're a writer! That's bloody brilliant, that is. Priceless! Don't tell Debs you said that. She'll skin you.'

And Phoebe realised her cool-headed calculation had added things up all wrong.

'Debs can't have kids,' Grant told her. 'She already knew that when she met Rich. Told him the truth. Most men would have run a mile, but he hung around. She said she didn't fancy him much, so she challenged him to make a million.'

'To weave straw into gold,' said Phoebe.

'If you like. And he bloody did.' Grant sat down on the linen-upholstered button-back nursing chair, put his head in his hands and let out a deep, half-amused sigh.

Phoebe said nothing, waiting for more.

'She could have had somebody better. They lived together in a shitty Beckenham flat all that time, him wheeler-dealing kitchens, her trying make it in acting, me stuck at home down the road with Mum and Dad, watching the soaps Debs hoped to star in. By the time she and Rich married, she'd given up that dream. Played the role of his loyal wife instead.'

'She's bloody good at it.'

'Isn't she just?' His eyes gleamed. 'Proud of her. Hard man to love, Rich. And Debs has a lotta love. She'd have been a great mum. I promised I'll make her an aunt one day. Left it a bit late, but there's hope.'

Phoebe looked around the pretty room with its Scandi furniture and Annie Sloan paint and realised Grant hadn't just created the house he wished he and Debs had grown up in. This was the house in which he longed to raise his children, her nieces and nephews.

'Debs wanted me to live with them after they married,' he told her, looking up at a ceiling light shaped like a hot-air balloon. 'Had a room decorated specially in that big place Rich bought them in Cheam, but he was having none of it. Rich never wanted kids. He didn't do family, he said. Had a thing for identical twins, but that was different.' He flashed his strange teeth at Phoebe with an audible sigh, making the insinuation clear.

'You knew what he got up to behind Debra's back, I take it?'

Grant laughed angrily.

'Not always behind,' he muttered. 'But yeah, I knew it all. Even the worst stuff. He tried to initiate me into his boys-only club more than once, but I was having none of it. Some of the stuff they got up to was filthy. Debra didn't deserve that sort of disrespect.'

'Were you blackmailing him?' Phoebe asked.

Saying nothing, Grant stared fixedly up at the light. But he didn't deny it.

'Somebody was,' she went on softly. 'It makes sense that it's you, that it was not just about money. You were angry with him for not doing more for you, for caring more about his business buddies than his family.'

He pulled a cuddly lion from a row of plushies on the shelf beside him and clutched it in crossed arms, still stubbornly silent.

'Your one reassurance was that he genuinely seemed to love Debra,' Phoebe went on, starting to worry she might be as wrong about this as she had been about Grant's parentage. 'Or so you thought at first. He'd spun gold out of straw for her after all, or out of fitted kitchens. Rich kept her safe, or so you thought. Until you found out about his dalliances on Dapper and Discreet.'

'He was never off it!'

'What did that drive you to do?'

'I didn't kill him, if that's what you're implying! I could never kill anyone!' He clutched the lion toy even more tightly.

'But you did extort money out of him, didn't you?'

'There's very narrow profit margins in high-tech heritage newbuilds, especially carbon-neutral ones. It's easy to make a loss. Just look at Cosmo Lovat's sawmill project. He wanted his own house so flash, he kept trying to make me cut corners on the development next door, but I told him, "If builders cut corners, the walls won't stand up."'

'Was it through Cosmo that you found out what was happening on Dapper and Discreet? His wife was on it, wasn't she?'

'That's their business.'

'How much did you know?' She thought about Holly's phone's gallery beaming its pictures around the smart home Grant had built.

'I just knew I had to get the job finished. When Holly died, I was working on the last unit in the sawmill development just along from their place. I was up on its roof the morning it happened, working on the thatching myself to try to make up some time.'

'You saw the accident?'

He shook his head. 'There were trees in the way. But I saw how fast she was driving just before, saw her overtaking the other car like a lunatic.'

'Hang on, there was another car involved?'

'Yeah. Always drove too fast, did Holly. Almost had me off that stretch of road more than once.'

'Did you go down to investigate what happened after you heard the crash?'

'Of course I did. Cosmo was already there in a right state, saying she was dead. I couldn't look.'

'And the other car?'

He sucked his lips, looking away. 'A few people had stopped by then. It took me a while to get down off the scaffold and across there. Everyone was in shock. Then the ambulance came, along with the fire brigade, so I went back to roofing.'

Phoebe sensed there was something he wasn't telling her, but he was already talking again. 'Cosmo couldn't give a monkey's about the sawmill development after that, spent most of his time in London. Can't say I blame him, although it cost me dear. Can't blame him for falling out with Rich neither, but I don't know what that was about. Cricket, I heard.' He looked up at the balloon light again, clearly uncomfortable now, whatever it was he was holding back playing on his mind.

'So it wasn't Cosmo who revealed to you what Rich was up to?'

'You mean that Rich told Debra...' For a moment, Phoebe sensed Grant was about to say something else, then he checked himself. 'That Dapper and Discreet was Rich's dirty little secret dressed up as a retirement project, you mean? No. I didn't know about that until later. When the wife started acting oddly.'

'Your wife?'

He stood up angrily. 'Tiff met her new fella on it.'

Phoebe stepped back in surprise as he marched past, still carrying the cuddly lion. 'Let me show you the master bedroom.'

There, by an oak sleigh bed dressed in Pembroke stripe linen, he explained that his wife had worked as Rich's PA.

'That's how we met – Debs introduced us. She loves playing Cupid. Rich only hired the prettiest girls, and Debs wanted to make sure he didn't get too familiar, so it worked out perfectly for everyone, except Rich, who had to fork out for the wedding marquee.'

When Rich invested in Dapper and Discreet, his PA had been co-opted into beta testing like Holly. 'Tiff wasn't supposed to talk about it – she'd signed an NDA – but she couldn't help herself. She was the one who first told me what Rich was up to. She had to keep showing him how to use it because he was rubbish at tech, almost as bad as Cosmo.'

In the en suite by a copper bath, Grant told Phoebe that a

few months after the app launched, Tiff became more distant, withdrew affection and started to act secretly.

'I'd had a lot on my mind, what with losing so much money on the sawmill job,' he told her in the en suite, his story a curious echo of Cosmo's. 'And I'd probably neglected her. But I knew she was up to something and as soon as I found that app on her phone, I guessed.'

As the show home tour gathered pace, Grant revealed a little of the end of his marriage in each room.

'I couldn't get into it on her phone,' he told Phoebe in the guest bedroom, which was decorated in tasteful *eau de nil* with a view across the micro-garden to another heritage thatch. 'I even tried signing up for the app myself, but it wouldn't let me be a VIP. I didn't meet the financial criteria, apparently.'

'Did you confront her?'

'Didn't get a chance.'

Back downstairs, Grant showed off a state-of-the-art utility room where lucky eco heritage householders could set off their spin cycle or no-crease drying from their phones anywhere in the world. 'I came home one day and she'd gone. Left a note saying she'd found herself a sugar daddy. I thought we were doing all right. Cracking four-bed heritage newbuild, talking about starting a family. Then she upped and left, telling me I was just a big kid and she deserved a man.'

Still carrying the cuddly lion, he marched her through the open-plan reception to a small, fitted study designed for the ultimate WFH experience.

'I saw red.' Grant distractedly demonstrated the soft-touch pop-up USB hubs. 'I was convinced it must be Rich. I imagined him setting her up in a little flat somewhere. I set up an email account calling myself Avenging Angel, telling him I knew what he'd been up to on Dapper and Discreet and that I was going to tell Debra.'

'What happened next?' Phoebe followed him back out and into a cosy television room with Cole & Son flock wallpaper and a bioethanol stove.

'I got an OOO reply saying that his PA was on leave. Then Debs came round to look after me and told me Rich was apoplectic about Tiff dumping her job. He had no more idea where she was than I did. Royal Caribbean Ultimate World Cruise with her new fella as it turns out, although they're living near Reading now. The Avenging Angel email went out of my head. Only then it got a reply from Rich himself, so badly typed I knew it had to be him, offering hush money.'

'Just like that?'

'Pretty much.' Grant sat down on a brocade sofa, lion plushie in one hand. 'We did it all by PayPal.'

Phoebe perched on the sofa opposite. 'But he must have paid you thousands. You almost bankrupted him.'

'He had a lot to hide, although Debs already knew most of it if I'm honest. A lot of what Avenging Angel threatened to tell her was stuff she'd confessed to me when she was drunk. Rich had no idea how wise she was to him, or that she'd forgiven him for it and still loved him. Amazing woman, my sister.'

'Let me get this right. You blackmailed your brother-in-law by threatening to expose secrets to his wife that she had told you?'

'Basically. Only even Debs didn't know Rich's biggest secret, which was that he was pretty much stone broke to start with, massively overstretched and over mortgaged, borrowing Peter to pay Paul, and now Grant on top. That's why I feel so bad, and it's why I need to sell a house. Do you want to buy one? I'll do you a good deal.'

'I don't, but I have a friend who might. How big is the garage?'

In a vast double garage, carrying the lion under one arm like a Metallica-loving Sebastian Flyte, Grant asked Phoebe if she was going to tell the police he'd blackmailed Rich.

'It depends if you murdered him too,' she said lightly, watching his face.

He looked stricken at the idea. 'I told you, I couldn't kill anyone.'

'You bled Rich dry a different way, just as fatal for some.'

'Better than him wasting it on cheap tarts and golfing holidays.' He rubbed his mouth nervously. 'So *are* you going to tell the police?'

Phoebe shook her head. 'I'm not sure how it would help Debra. Might she really lose the house?'

'We've got some breathing room. Debs sold some old watches of Rich's yesterday. It means she's safe for a while. Turns out he had an eighties Rolex Daytona worth over fifty grand that he'd given to an acquaintance for safekeeping.'

'Some friend to give it back,' Phoebe whistled.

'Acquaintance,' Grant corrected.

Suddenly Phoebe remembered. 'Hang on, was this the woman who you and Debra met in The Priory last night? I thought it was it one of the Welches?'

The snarling smile was defensive. 'That was just a blind date Debra was setting me up on.'

'The night before her husband's funeral?'

'Debra used a champagne tea gift voucher and there are only limited days you can claim them on. Matchmaking cheers her up.'

'Which of the Welches was it?'

'Didn't catch her name.' The smile stayed put. 'I can't tell them apart, if I'm honest.'

Phoebe was certain he was hiding something. 'Where did all the money you took from Rich really go?'

'On heritage thatch developments like I told you.' He led her back from the garage to the house, standing in the vast open-plan kitchen and turning around to look at the place he wished he'd grown up in. 'And trying to win my wife back. Tiff said I was too immature when she went off with her older fella. Regrets it big time now. I thought if I made her a million, she'd change her mind.'

'I don't think that's how it works.'

'It worked for Rich.'

'Look where that got him.'

'You're probably right.' He sighed ruefully. 'But me and Tiff have been messaging a lot. She wants to get away from him. We've both done a lot of growing up.'

'Good luck, I hope it works out for you.' Phoebe shook his hand. 'Thank you for the house viewing.'

'I can do you a deal with stamp duty paid.'

'I'll tell my friend.'

They went back outside and he locked up the show home.

Awkwardly, having just exposed his shameful blackmail secret, Phoebe had to rely on him for a lift back to Inkbury.

In his big, glossy pick-up – another bonus from Rich's money she had no doubt – she asked him more about his plan to woo back his wife.

'I've told Tiff I'll rescue her!' he shouted over the rock music pounding from the stereo. 'She says she's thinking about it. I love the bones of that girl. This bloke she's with might be loaded, but he's a sneaky bastard. Disappeared the whole of last week not telling her where he was going, came back looking like he'd been in a fight. And, get this, Tiff's not the first woman he's hooked up with from that app. And if you ask me, he's up to his old tricks.' He turned the music volume down. 'I reckon Red Lion's on the prowl for fresh meat again.'

'Hang on.' Phoebe swung round to look at him. 'This is a joke, right?'

'You think everything I said about Tiff leaving was a *joke*?'

'Why didn't you *say* he was Red Lion?'

'Why would I? That's what Tiff calls him. It's not even his real name.' He chewed the inside of one cheek, brows creased. 'That's Loewe. Or lowlife wanker as I like to think of him.'

'Loewe means lion,' Phoebe told him. The protagonist in her gritty eighties crime series was Carrick Lowe. She only wished he was with her now. He wouldn't have forgotten to ask Grant a crucial question like whether any of the Dapper and Discreet angel names meant anything to him. DI Lowe always got answers, and fast.

They drove on.

'They live near Reading, you say?'

'That's right. Winterbottom Wick. Why?'

'I think it's time you rescued your wife.'

* * *

Five minutes later, Phoebe hurried into the kitchen at Hartridge Court, relieved to find Felix there, working at his laptop.

'Debra threw me out so she could drink champagne in the bath when I refused to call Guy Ritchie on her behalf.' He smiled up at her. 'But not before I found out who she and Grant met at The Priory.'

'Great, because he can't remember which Welch it was.' She

grabbed the dogs' leads and tipped closed his laptop lid. 'So you can enlighten us on the way.'

'The way where?'

'Somewhere near Reading called Winterbottom Wick. We're going to see Red Lion.' She headed for the back door again.

'How are we getting there?' Grabbing his laptop under his arm, Felix followed her. 'And what do you mean, enlighten *us*?'

'Grant's driving.' She hurried along the back corridor. 'Red Lion's latest girlfriend is Grant's ex-wife, Tiffany.'

Felix started to laugh. 'No, that's just too ridiculous!'

'I know, that's exactly what I said, although Red Lion is the one who designed the app and might well still be manipulating it as well as picking off its angel investors, so all coincidences are clues here.'

But Felix wasn't listening, still half-laughing disbelievingly as they made their way outside. 'Seriously, Tiffany and Grant? And now we're going in search of a Lion in Winterbottom. You'll be telling me next that Juno's going undercover again to Ride a White Swan with—'

Phoebe swiftly pulled back her right arm to elbow her husband in the ribs and he 'oofed' into silence.

Ahead of them, wearing dark glasses at the wheel of his enormous American pick-up, heavy metal booming, Grant snarled his fanged teeth.

'Are you sure this is wise?' Felix coughed under his breath.

'Possibly not, but it gets us there and I don't think we have time to lose. My hunch is the killer will strike again, and soon, if we don't stop whatever's happening inside that app. If it's Red Lion who's behind it all, the more of us the better.'

29

JUNO

Reading a WhatsApp update from Felix on her phone whilst hurrying along an Inkbury pavement on bin day, Juno had so far walked into several compost caddies, a host of recycling tubs and a lamppost.

> With Phoebe on our way to Winterbottom Wick to find Red Lion. I'll share our location on Google Maps. He's called Loewe and used to live in the village, but we don't know much more than that. He designed Dapper and Discreet and that means he could still be able to access it and manipulate it. We think he's also still using it.

> And we can confirm Grant was the one blackmailing Rich. His marriage was another casualty of the millionaire app. We're with him now. His music taste is diabolical.

> Grant and Debra both say it was one of the Welches they met at The Priory the night Don died, although Grant doesn't know which and Debra claims she's so bad with names, she went from 'Daisy' to 'Chelsea' to 'Hayley' in a single sentence. I'm not buying it. Can you shed light, Mil? Debra insisted she was setting Grant up, but she's obviously hiding something, so best check it out with the Welches, and be careful. They might be more involved in this than we thought. They were all on the app, after all, and matched with at least two of our victims. Felix.

Juno recorded a breathless voice note in reply: 'Already on the way to see the Three Decrees! I think it – oof! Sorry, just fell over a wheelie bin. I think it might have been Cheryl at The Priory. And you're right to suspect them. Don't worry, I'm going to be very – argh! Garden waste grab-bag – very careful and act very dumb. She won't know I'm onto her. I'll tell you everything later, too out of puff now.'

Dodging kerbside collections, Juno dashed along the crescent of thirties semis in Inkbury nicknamed Welch World because so many members of the old village family occupied them.

She'd just called on Zadie at the opposite end and been waylaid by Courtney, who said her mum was out but who felt impelled to drag Juno inside for a blow-by-blow account of every staff member's movements at The Priory on the night of Don's murder 'on account of you being a detective and almost dying and all that'. After listening in open-mouthed horror to the scandalous goings-on in the hotel's kitchens for over half an hour, it finally dawned to Juno that the teenager was making it all up to frame the restaurant manager who had fired her for recording a true crime TikTok that night. 'I prefer working for Mil if I'm honest, cos he's a laugh and lets me eat crisps.'

Making her escape had been challenging.

And now, as Juno finally reached Bethany's gate, pausing to catch her breath by a recycling tub overflowing with Monster cans and Prime bottles, she realised she was being recorded.

'You falling over all that rubbish was *hilarious!*'

Courtney had followed her, brandishing a phone on a gimbal stick.

Juno tried to remember what she'd just said about Cheryl in her voice note.

'So here we are at my second cousin Bethany's house,' Courtney told the camera in a low voice, 'where Village Detective Juno Mulligan is going to accuse my aunt Cheryl of *murder*.'

Well, that had blown it. Perhaps she should leave?

But Courtney was filming her again, and performer Juno could never resist an audience. Besides which, she was hardly going to get bumped off whilst being recorded on a teenager's iPhone.

Juno panted up to Bethany's front door and knocked, hearing music thudding from the other side.

'Only me!' she beamed when Bethany opened it. 'Is Cheryl here?'

Then her smile faltered. Behind her, Courtney let out a cackle of laughter. 'What are you *wearing*?'

Bethany was sporting a lace shrug and a feather boa over her Superdry tracksuit. Taylor Swift's 'Shake It Off' was pumping out in the open-plan lounge behind her, where another familiar blonde in a pink satin robe was holding a sequinned bra top up to a third.

The Three Decrees were all together. With them was a pile of stolen church hall jumble. The same jumble from which the clothes used to dress Rich and Don in their death throes had been carefully selected.

Juno had caught them red-handed.

Her first instinct was to protect herself and Courtney, deciding her only option was to bluff it. 'Are you all dressing up for a big night out?'

'Just having a laugh.' Bethany looked wary.

That's when Juno spotted more women's clothes strewn everywhere. Big, flouncy, naughty clothes.

'Those are my mother's! You took them from under the church hall stage!'

'You'd better come in.' Bethany held the door wider, glancing around outside before ushering her in, along with Courtney, who was holding her phone gimbal out in front of her like the Sword of State. 'Put that away, Courtney!'

Zadie shrugged off the pink satin robe, laughing. 'So, are you going to arrest us?'

'It rather depends how you used them,' Juno said nervously, realising just how outnumbered she was.

Then it occurred to her that Courtney might have directed her here intentionally, following her with the camera to record her final moments. Had they recorded the others too – Rich in his marabou-trimmed kimono, Don in his cupcake sleep-set? They could have her trussed in a velvet basque in a Chemsex on the Beach coma in moments, ready to 'stage' her death. Did women die from auto-erotic asphyxia, she fretted?

'It's just a bit of fun,' said Bethany sulkily.

'What's fun about doing something so terrible?' Juno bleated, now wishing she hadn't come alone.

'This village is so sanctimonious,' Bethany complained. 'Judging us for being single mums, for being Welches.'

'Churchy Mary and her mother are the worst,' Zadie took

over, 'always bad-mouthing this family. Half those headstones belong to our relatives.'

'We figured they wouldn't mind,' said Cheryl. 'Welch women always enjoy the last laugh.'

'And we had a lot of those dressing them up,' chuckled Zadie.

With a cry of relief, Juno realised they weren't confessing to producing a quartet of corpses. 'You're the Graveyard Ravers!'

'What did you think we'd been up to?'

'Murder?' Courtney suggested behind her, still videoing.

'Yes, that was what I thought. My bad.'

To her relief, the Welches just seemed to find this hilarious.

'Juno, you're bloody priceless!' Cheryl howled as all three Decrees fell about, their giggles so infectious, Juno felt a tickle of laughter in her own ribs, the absurdity of it all striking her.

'We took turns dressing up the gravestones,' Bethany explained when she could finally speak again. 'Each trying to out-do the other.'

'Who did last night's?' Juno asked, noticing Courtney zooming in on her face and hoping she wasn't looking too flushed and sweaty. She discreetly reached up to fluff out her hair.

'That was me,' Cheryl admitted. 'My homecoming treat. Used some of my old clubbing gear cos the girls say old Mary's been getting suspicious round the church hall jumble stash.'

'Not as good as my last lot,' boasted Zadie. 'They were particularly fine! I blame all that fizz I drank at your party, Juno.'

'Whatever made you think we could have killed anyone?' asked Cheryl.

'Two men have recently died from asphyxiation whilst

wearing items of clothing taken from the jumble beneath the church hall.' Juno picked up a satin camisole and held it up.

'*Seriously?*' gasped Zadie.

'They were both Dapper and Discreet investors. We think that four of the original six stakeholders are now dead.'

'That *is* a coincidence.' Cheryl looked stunned.

Aware of the camera recording, Juno felt herself clasping her hands together and thrusting her shoulders back as she conjured a funked-up Miss Marple, quizzing intently. 'Bethany, you were in contact with Don – Green Man – on the app, and Wayne – Golden Pheasant – before that. Both of them were in the syndicate.'

'Now I'm starting to think Bethany did it,' admitted Cheryl.

'Oi!' Bethany protested.

'Well, I was in Greece when Rich died, so it can't have been me!'

'But you *were* back in Wexshire the night Don Greenwood died.' Juno turned to Cheryl, casting a knowing glance at Courtney's camera phone as she did so. 'And I put it to you that you were having a champagne tea at The Priory early that evening.'

'Yeah, Cheryl,' Bethany barracked. 'You did it!'

At this, Zadie held up her hand with a loud wolf-whistle. 'Breaking news, it was me in The Priory that night.'

'What were you doing there, Mum?' Courtney lowered her phone. 'I never saw you!'

'I didn't much want to be seen. I had your brother's hat on. And if you must know, I was making my peace with Debra and giving her back something she wanted Rich to be buried with. A gift I should never have accepted.'

'Zadie, were you Rich's mistress?' Juno asked, then corrected herself. 'One of his mistresses?'

'Pull the other one! I used to clean for the Basses over at Greenside. I had a key. Last year I caught Rich and Debra in bed with – well, that's not important. Rich gave me a bunch of designer clobber to buy my silence, pulled it from his dresser drawers and ran after me still in his pants to hand it over as hush money, begging me not to tell anyone.'

'In bed with who? What?' Juno asked.

She remained tight-lipped.

'Wayne? The vicar? A Hungarian yoga instructor?'

'Tell us, Mum!' Courtney's camera phone closed in.

'Let's just say the Basses didn't want it to get out. End of.'

Everyone groaned, except Zadie who visibly crossed herself before hurrying on. 'When I looked through the stuff I'd been given, it was mostly tat – naff old cufflinks, bracelets and a whopping fake Rolex.'

'D'you sell any of it?' asked Bethany jealously.

'I flogged the gold. I kept the fake Rolex and wore it. Rich was always going on those kinky Thai holidays back then, so I figured he must've bought it from a stall over there. My boy Roman reckoned it was the worst fake he'd ever seen.'

'I think it was real,' Juno told her. 'And it wasn't cremated with him; jewellery never is. I think it was sold to a watch dealer later that day.'

'That fake Rolex was *real*?' Bethany started to laugh.

Courtney turned the camera round to tell it, 'My mum is a total numpty. You heard it here first.'

Zadie sucked her teeth and nodded. 'Yeah, I figured it had to be the real deal when Debra said she wanted back. She told me it was the first thing Rich bought when he made a million. The second was their wedding rings.'

'And you still gave it back to her, just like that?' Bethany looked horrified.

'I felt sorry for her. What I saw that day, well, I don't think she was enjoying it. I always felt bad that I didn't say anything, *do* anything.'

Juno could guess enough. She remembered Debra locked in the bathroom on the night of her party, tearfully confessing that she'd tried all sorts of things to spice up her marriage and to stop Rich straying.

'Why did you meet at The Priory at Dunford?' she asked, thinking out loud. 'Why not somewhere less obvious?'

'I wondered that. It was Debra's idea. She said she had a champagne tea gift voucher Rich had given her ages ago and she told me she wanted to use it to treat me as a thank you for keeping the watch safe.'

'She has a lot of luxury experience vouchers stored up.' Juno guessed cash-strapped Debra had been using them while too broke to pay her way. 'It's what Rich gave her every birthday and Christmas.'

'Nice,' sighed Bethany.

'Rich was *not* nice,' Cheryl reminded her. 'Those diamond rings, maybe. Corporate gift vouchers, no.'

'I handed the watch over in the ladies' so her brother didn't see,' said Zadie. 'But then she made me go back and have the champagne tea with Grant while she went home. She said the voucher was only for two people and she wanted to catch up with *Eastenders* on BBC iPlayer. Turned out she was trying to set me up with that drippy brother of hers. Apparently, she'd had someone else in mind, but Grant thought she was too old and mumsy.'

Juno smiled tightly. 'How would you describe her mood?'

'She was lovely, as it goes. A bit teary.'

'Not murderous then?' Courtney chipped in, still videoing. 'Could she have killed in cold blood, do you think, Mum?'

'Don't talk bollocks!' Cheryl snorted. 'The only thing that woman can murder is a song.'

'What about her brother Grant?' asked Juno, suddenly fearing Phoebe and Felix might be at this moment heading into a trap.

'He's just a big, stroppy kid,' said Zadie. 'Bit weird, but quite gentle. Tried to sell me a heritage thatch. Likes his grub. Told me he's still in love with his wife who ran off with some flash harry she met online and she's now fed up with, so he's planning to rescue her. Typical omega male. Mildly repellent. Weird teeth. Rampant BO. Otherwise, harmless.'

Juno nodded in agreement, feeling relieved.

'So where is she, the wife?' asked Bethany. 'Rapunzel's tower? *Love Island*? Baghdad?'

'Winterbottom something,' Juno remembered.

'*Wick!*' snarled Cheryl. 'Which is precisely what that flash-drive harry gets on: my bloody wick! I can't believe he's still at it.'

Before Juno could ask what she meant, they all jumped as a fist banged frantically on the door. Then a craggy face appeared at the window.

It was Mil, breathless from running all the way from The Barton Arms. 'I came as fast as I could!'

The sight of three Welch sirens and a bunch of sexy clothes made him turn a deep, excited shade of red, which Courtney captured on her phone in a slow one-eighty shot around him.

'What's all this about Phoebe and Felix going to the Red Lion in Winterwick Bottom?' he asked Juno hotly.

'Winter*bottom Wick*,' corrected Cheryl. 'That's where Russell lives.'

'Her ex-husband,' Bethany told Juno. 'Russell Loewe. Total tosser.'

'Tosser,' agreed Zadie darkly.

'Tosser,' Cheryl sighed.

'Roger to that,' Courtney told her camera.

'He is a tosser,' Mil agreed.

Juno felt the pieces drop into place like a slot machine payout. The man in the studio portrait in Cheryl's hallway. He hadn't simply met someone on the app. He had *invented* that app in the first place.

'Did the tosser develop Dapper and Discreet, Cheryl?' she asked.

Cheryl sucked her teeth angrily, nodding her head. 'My ex-husband might have spent his days de-bugging payroll software, but by night, in his shed, it seems he was building an app to get his end away, yes.'

'Russell Loewe is Red Lion,' Juno told Mil.

'Do you think he's capable of murder?' Mil asked Cheryl.

She scrunched up her face doubtfully. 'He's pretty bitter, and very petty, but killing someone…?'

'Definitely,' said Bethany. 'I've seen him playing *Grand Theft Auto*.'

'Hundred per cent.' Zadie nodded.

'The net is closing in!' Courtney breathed into her phone camera.

'I'll warn Freddy and Felix.' Juno pulled out her own phone to contact the WhatsApp group.

30

PHOEBE

'Hi, guys, Felix here again. Thanks for the detail, Juno. Grant has just spoken to his wife Tiffany to tell her we're coming – I told you she's the one Russell Loewe got together with, didn't I? – and she's ready to bail out. Apparently, Russell's been behaving very oddly for a while, staying up late, sneaking around with a second phone, going out at funny hours without telling her where, sometimes overnight. He even went to Turkey recently for surgery to change his appearance. We've let DI Mason know our concerns, although fat lot of interest he took. Keep your phones handy.'

* * *

Russell Loewe and his girlfriend Tiffany lived in a newbuild gated executive estate on the leafiest outskirts of Reading, with his-and-hers electric cars sharing a wall charger on its paved driveway.

Grant parked the glossy blue pick-up around the corner

and agreed to wait, thrash metal rocking its axles at low volume.

'We need to gain Russell's trust, you understand?' Felix told him. 'Best he doesn't see you just yet. We'll message as soon as the time is right.'

'Yep, totally, absolutely!' Grant seemed relieved to sit this one out, his Block Blast! app already open on his phone.

Answering the door in joggers and a Pokémon sweatshirt, Russell was a round-shouldered, loose-jowled and unremarkable middle-aged man, apart from the fact he looked as though he'd been beaten up. There were blood bruises beneath his eyes, a bandage around his jaw and a baseball cap riding too high on his head at an odd angle.

'We're private investigators,' Felix said smoothly, assured and confident as a head of international intelligence. 'For your own personal safety, we recommend you talk to us as a priority. The police have been informed that we're here. Perhaps we could step inside?'

Swallowing with an audible gulp and a bob of his Adam's apple, Russell beckoned them in. 'What's going on?' He was pallid yet over-energised, a man who Phoebe guessed spent too much screentime hoovering up content aimed at a younger manosphere. His bruised eyes slid straight past her to Felix. 'Are you special services or something?'

'Independent consultants.' Felix nodded. 'Good of you to make time for us. This is a matter of supreme urgency, so I'll be quick. You developed an app called Dapper and Discreet, am I right?'

'Yes.' He swallowed, clearly torn between pride and high alert.

'And an investor named Rich Bass backed it?' Phoebe interrupted. 'AKA Black Horse.'

'That's right.'

'He's dead.'

'Right. Sorry to hear it.' It was obvious he already knew.

'And a man called Wayne Baxendale backed it? Golden Pheasant.'

'Possibly, I—'

'Also dead. Don "Green Man" Greenwood?'

'Let me guess? He's dead?'

'Holly Lovat-Dixon? AKA Purple—'

'Pussycat. I know she's dead.' He took off his hat, a brief shadow of sadness passing over his face.

The top of his head was dotted with rows of hair implants sewn too far apart.

'Freshly seeded,' he explained with a hangdog smile. 'The other half keeps telling me I look old. She got new Turkey teeth last year, so I figured it was my turn.'

'Is she here?'

'Having a coffee round at a friend's.' He looked even more uncomfortable. 'About the app. I didn't know the startup investors to begin with, apart from Black Horse – Rich, I mean – who I initially approached. He was in a big Wexshire syndicate that had given funding to another company I was involved with. I'd helped develop a payroll software package for them, so I knew he had connections. He introduced me to Don Greenman, I mean Greenwood. Big money wood, I mean man. Big money man.' He stopped there, nerves fraying, sweat beading on his forehead.

Felix nodded. 'Go on.'

'I knew this app could be huge. Rich loved the idea. Every time we were at nets, he'd bring it up, suggest he pitched it to his syndicate. It became a clubroom secret. He said he'd cherry-picked a few anonymous "angels" and they snapped it up. Didn't realise they were all *in* the cricket club, mind you.'

'Apart from Don Greenwood,' Phoebe clarified, asking, 'When did you first come up with the idea?'

'It cooked for a while,' Russell said vaguely, waiting for Felix to speak again.

'You all beta tested it, am I right?' he obliged, casting Phoebe a puzzled look.

'Yes, that bit was a laugh, although there were so few women testers, we almost all got matched with Holly Lovat-Dixon – Purple Pussycat – who was another investor. She and I started messaging a lot. She was from the village; our kids were at school together.'

'What about Tiffany?' Phoebe asked.

'That came later,' Russell told Felix. 'One for the back pocket, shall we say. Holly was very good at the testing stage and bang on the target market. Those pre-launch tests threw up a lot of bugs. The algorithms took a huge amount of tweaking. The initial seed idea had been over forties only, and very local, heavily focused on unhappy marriages. It was called "Cor Rapta", for a start, so that had to change.'

'Corrupter?' Felix checked.

'No, Cor Rapta. Stolen heart in Latin, *cor rapta*.'

'When exactly did you first come up with the idea of Cor Rapta?' Phoebe pressed him.

Russell pulled a smiley grimace. 'It was inspired by a partially developed design I stumbled across, very homespun and incomplete. I took it on, made it commercially viable.'

'So whose idea was it initially?' Felix demanded.

He rubbed his mouth, looking away. 'I'd rather not say. Protecting them, you understand.'

'They might be in danger too,' Felix warned.

'It was my son's!'

'River?' Phoebe asked in surprise.

'Yes. Designing an app was part of River's GCSE Computer Science coursework.'

'You stole your son's school project?'

'River had rejected the dating app concept by then. They all had to come up with several ideas for consideration. His teacher didn't think an infidelity dating app would sit well with the examining board, so River switched to developing a well-being virtual pet friend instead. I found a copy of the Cor Rapta source code files on an external hard drive I was about to reformat, and I had a tinker.'

'How did River feel about you taking his original idea and turning it into a huge commercial success?' asked Felix.

'He didn't know at first. He wasn't very interested in anything I did, and nor was his mother. I just came and went from that house like a shadow. I had a bank of high-speed computers in my home office garden pod, tinkered with the software design every evening. That app was my get-out-of-jail card. I'd built others before, just for fun, quizzes mostly, launched them all with limited success. But this was the first one with decent funding to market and monetise.

'I kept meaning to tell River, but it got harder as time went on, and then the whole project became cloaked in secrecy once the angel investors were on board. When Dapper and Discreet launched, it was there on Google Play and iOS for anyone to find. It started trending incredibly quickly and getting noticed, but it wasn't going to register on my family's radars.'

Dry-mouthed from talking so much, Russell rubbed his lips, turning away to open a glossy black larder fridge and pull out a carton of pineapple juice which he drank straight from the tab before continuing. 'I'd met a few matches on it myself.

Mostly for meaningless sex, but I needed that to make meaning of my sexless marriage. When I finally matched with a woman who wanted to commit, I had the confidence to pack my bags. The divorce from Cheryl was brutal; she hired an assassin; my new relationship was over by the time it was granted, but the app always provided. I never went short.'

'So your family still didn't know you were involved with Dapper and Discreet when you and Cheryl divorced?' Phoebe clarified. 'River didn't know his idea was taking off?'

'The finished app bears very little similarity to his school project,' Russell reminded them tetchily. 'It was only when the syndicate sold it that River got wind of what was going on. And he was completely unreasonable about it.' He slurped more juice from the carton. 'Yes, it came from his little germ of an idea, but it was scaled up, developed and produced by a pro. Still, River was furious about it, vile, unhinged even, but by then I'd made a mint from the sale. I'd also matched with Tiffany, so we took off on a cruise, started a new life.'

'When did you and your son last speak?' Felix asked.

'His birthday.'

'Which one?' Phoebe checked.

Russell had the grace to look abashed.

'Are you still active on the app?' she asked.

The expression on his bruised face grew more furtive. 'Why would I be?'

'We have intelligence that somebody is manipulating it from the inside, through a back door in the coding,' Felix told him, playing his international espionage investigation card again.

This seriously rattled Russell, who swallowed with an audible gulp, followed by a nervous pineapple-scented burp.

'What are you saying? Making fake matches? Luring VIP members into traps?'

'Four of the original investors are dead,' Phoebe reminded him. 'You are one of just two remaining.'

He had gone very pale. 'You think my life is under threat?'

'We don't think you should meet anyone through Dapper and Discreet.'

He picked up his mobile phone and put it down again, leaving a sweaty palm print on it.

'Who are you currently messaging on the app, Russell?' Phoebe asked.

'I'm not going to tell you that!'

'Is it, by any chance, a hot Hungarian yoga instructor called Edit? Her avatar name is Story Weaver.'

He stared at her open-mouthed for so long, his face turning monochrome, that she knew Red Lion was still very much prowling Dapper and Discreet, and it was Story Weaver he had just re-cropped his scalp and tucked his eye-bags for.

Eventually Russell closed his mouth, swallowing dryly.

'Edit's a catfish, as you have no doubt just guessed,' said Felix.

'Oh, God.' Russell dropped his dot-covered head into his hands. 'Please don't tell me that's my son? No!' He rubbed his face and raked a hand over his freshly seeded hair, pulling himself together. 'River could never do that.'

'You think River might be doing this?' Phoebe asked with a cold jolt of foreboding.

'Could he still access the app now?' Felix demanded.

'Not possible,' Russell insisted.

'He's a smart kid,' said Phoebe.

Russell shook his head vehemently. 'I'm a smarter dad, and

no way. I made that thing impenetrable. Besides, River's an out-an-out front door coder, obsessed with UI and UX.'

'Which are?'

'User Interface, User Experience. For that GCSE, he got one of his friends to do all the backroom stuff, genius gamer dev, a savant of stack.'

'Could they still be helping him?'

He shook his head. 'Xanthe moved away. She stopped all contact, went off grid with her dad after her mum died.'

'Xanthe, you say?' asked Felix.

'River's lover?' Phoebe checked.

He laughed unkindly at this. 'River and Xanthe Dixon have been like brother and sister since primary school. They've always hung out in the same gang, but there was nothing romantic.'

'There is now,' Phoebe told him. 'They stayed in touch. They've been living together at your ex-wife's place all summer.'

'Dixon... as in, Lovat-Dixon?' asked Felix, catching up with his wife's thinking. 'She's Holly's daughter?'

Russell nodded. 'Difficult kid. Lots of issues.'

Phoebe turned away and closed her eyes tightly for a moment, furious with herself for not guessing, for none of them coming close to knowing, that Xanthe was Holly's child, the clever tech-savant teenager who had beamed their mother's infidelity across every screen in their new smart home. Hadn't Autumn said that River and Xanthe had recently reconnected at university? They'd all talked about a homecoming.

'This is bad.' Phoebe started pacing, logic cogs whirring. 'Xanthe must blame Dapper and Discreet for Holly's death. Xanthe knew their mother was on the app. They were probably the one who beamed Purple Pussycat's private gallery and messages all over the smart home TVs.'

'We protected the angels' identities with gold-standard cyber security,' Russell protested. 'Nobody knew Holly was Purple Pussycat.'

'You knew it was Holly. You told us earlier.'

'We got close.'

'You two had an affair?'

'Purely cyber and cerebral. We already knew each other through the school, but not socially. Holly liked posers like Cosmo. But when we connected online beta testing the app, the attraction was immediate. We messaged non-stop. It was still very GCSE romancing-by-numbers back then, mind you. Looking back at it, maybe River and Xanthe had set the algorithms to manipulate matches.'

'How do you mean?'

'The app was designed specifically to match single or unhappily married parents in the village. I read all the coursework notes on that USB stick. It was the sort of mad idea that could only come out of teenagers' heads. River and Xanthe sold the idea of their "chosen" family being blended by digital alchemy. The school gates affair between Xanthe's mother Holly and Autumn's father Cosmo Lovat had already transformed Xanthe's friendship with cool girl Autumn Lovat to a big sister one. They wanted more.

'River knew Cheryl and I were heading the same way as Xanthe's parents, Holly and Doc Dixon, and he imagined he could invent an app that would put us both together with the right new peer matches, build his stepsibling master tribe, like Xanthe's had become in real life. In their naivety, they probably fantasised getting me together with Autumn's mother, although

Cheryl would have been a more realistic match for Violet as things turned out. Either way, it was all pure make-believe.'

'Violet was on the app?' Felix asked, confused.

'Nobody was on it. This was a GCSE project, remember, Cor Rapta? It means stolen heart.'

'What's Latin for stolen app?' Phoebe wondered.

Russell glared at her. 'When those kids designed the app, it was specifically coded so that they could stage manage it from the inside to play Cupid; more than that, to play God if you like. That would have been Xanthe's work; River could never have programmed something so complex. No wonder the teacher vetoed it. It wasn't his original design, it was a collaboration with Xanthe. It was also far too clever for GCSE. And too immoral, too open to chance.'

'Until an immoral chancer like you found it,' Felix sighed.

Phoebe followed his logic, addressing Russell: 'You developed it into an app for married people wanting secret affairs.'

He looked unapologetic. 'It was a relatively straightforward adaptation for an experienced software designer. The tricky bit was getting funding, making it commercial, but Rich's enthusiasm lifted it to a whole new level.'

'It would have been huge by the time River and Xanthe found out.' Felix took up the tale. 'They had no idea their little homespun school coursework app was live and monetised until it was attracting the interest of big tech buyers.'

'Not so,' Phoebe realised. 'They discovered it early on. Remember, Xanthe knew all about her mother beta testing it because that's when she revealed the truth to Cosmo. She and River would have found Red Lion's messages and pictures on her account and worked out Russell had stolen the GCSE design.'

'He said nothing,' Russell insisted. 'Literally. My son never spoke to me anyway.'

'Finding you and Holly had been sexting each other was a disaster. He and Xanthe had been madly in love since junior school. They certainly didn't want to find *themselves* as stepsiblings in the big, blended family they'd once dreamed of creating, not to mention Autumn being cast out of the pack. Xanthe wanted your flirtation with Holly to stop, so she exposed the truth to Cosmo, thinking that would put an end to it.'

'Which it did,' Felix said bluntly. 'Because the next day Holly fatally crashed her car.'

Russell looked down, ashen at the memory.

'Holly was messaging you at the time, wasn't she?' Phoebe asked him.

'Not me.' He shook his head. 'Our little micro affair had all but petered out. We'd both found others more fun to play with by then.'

'Who else was Holly playing with?'

'Rich.'

'I knew it!'

'And Wayne.'

'*Both* of them?'

'Don too, although that was just a few topless pics because he was shy and terrified his wife would find out. There were also a couple of agency beta testers Holly got very fruity with in private chats. She knew each account's media and messages could be accessed by the developer pre-launch, but it didn't put her off. I think she enjoyed the thrill. I certainly appreciated it.'

'Not so sure she wanted it all featuring as a slideshow on the family's home entertainment system,' Phoebe pointed out.

'Is that what happened?' Russell whistled.

'Her daughter found everything and shared it. Cosmo would have seen every photo and message on his smart home TVs: Black Horse, Golden Pheasant, Green Man...'

'Red Lion too.' Russell nodded. 'It might never have got physical with Purple Pussycat, but our messages were damned hot.' He looked offensively pleased with himself.

'What happened to Xanthe after Holly died?' asked Felix.

'She moved away with her dad; they cut all contact. River was gutted. He became even more withdrawn, dropped out of sixth form for a bit. By then I'd met someone new and moved out. My son wants nothing to do with me. I had no idea he and Xanthe were back in touch. They're a couple, you say? Good old River. Thought he'd never lose that cherry.'

'They met again at university last year,' Phoebe realised, remembering Autumn describing the shock friends-to-lovers reunion when they'd been kissing in the deli. 'My guess is it's only then Xanthe realised how huge the app's become.' She pictured them together poring over the matchmaking service to check how similar it was to the one they had initially designed. 'And I think they signed up for membership – as a woman, which was free, let's say a Hungarian yoga instructor called Edit – to see if they could still use Xanthe's original back door in the coding to poke around in the user under-face.'

'Interface,' Russell corrected.

'Would that be possible?' Felix asked Russell. 'You said their original GCSE design was made to be manipulated from the inside so that they could decide who matched with whom?'

'I suppose it's feasible they could have coded their version in a way that allowed them to access all areas via a secret door in that UI. But surely there's no way they could have believed a commercial developer would have overlooked such a vulnerability, so they would have left it there. Not fiddled. River's terrified of stuff like that. He won't even download pirated movies and music.'

Phoebe sucked her teeth, picturing a pale face with shaven brows and unblinking eyes. 'I bet Xanthe would.'

'Especially if they found their back door was still unlocked, the way in easy,' Felix finished for her.

Russell looked like he was going to cry. 'What has River done?'

'He broke back into his own app,' Phoebe said, 'to play Cupid. Then I suspect he and Xanthe set up dates for "Edit" at the restaurant where Xanthe works, or in Rich's case the cricket pavilion conveniently just over the fence from River's mother's house. They might just be responsible for three deaths. And your app's to blame.'

Russell put his reseeded head in his hands and groaned. 'It's supposed to be a bit of harmless extra-marital fun! It's just a bloody app! Most of the people on it never get past sexting.'

Beside him, Felix raked back his own hair and turned to Phoebe despairingly. 'Why can't people be satisfied with old-fashioned, real-life, skin-on-skin infidelity any more?'

Phoebe would have liked to take issue with him on this, but her phone was ringing; it was Juno. She stepped outside to take it.

Juno was panting breathlessly as though she'd been running. 'I'm sorry to interrupt, Freddy, but I wanted to check you're still alive, because you've taken no notice of our voice notes and it really is quite urgent. I don't think Cosmo took your advice. He's still meeting his date.'

'You're sure?'

'I was just in my flat and saw him coming out of the florist with a massive bunch of roses. By the time I got down to the courtyard, he'd gone. Gemma the florist says he asked for something for a special lady he was meeting.'

'The total prat!' Phoebe groaned, then asked urgently, 'Juno, have you seen River and Xanthe today?'

'At Cheryl's earlier, yes. They're about to set off travelling. So loved up! They're not involved, are they?'

'Very, I'm afraid. Xanthe is Holly Lovat-Dixon's daughter.'

'I think they'd prefer "offspring", Fre—' She let out cry of alarm as she realised what she'd just heard. 'Hang on, they're *what*? Why didn't we *know* this?'

'Because people in British villages always assume you know absolutely everybody or nobody at all,' Phoebe told her.

She hurriedly explained that the millionaire app had originally been River's school project, and he could still access it using his and Xanthe's old coding. 'We're pretty sure that Edit the Hungarian yoga instructor is their invention. If that's who Cosmo thinks he's meeting, he's walking into a trap. You must find them and stop them. No, forget that, find *Cosmo* and stop *him*. They're too dangerous. They've already drugged you once.'

'*They* drugged me?'

'Yes! I think they killed Don, Rich and probably Wayne too.'

'But Cosmo could be meeting his date anywhere, Freddy. Can't Russell hack into the app to find out where and when?'

'He hasn't a clue how River and Xanthe did it.'

'*You* hacked into my account, Freddy.'

'Because your password is easier to work out than most Wordles. With Xanthe's help, River coded that app in labyrinthine detail; his dad merely finessed the edges.'

'I've just hurried across to the pub to see Mil,' Juno panted. 'We'll put a plan together, don't worry. Now I need you to do something for me, okay? It relies on my darling boy Eric, which I appreciate is a high-risk gamble at the best of times, but I have complete faith he can do this. Except, oh God, I don't know exactly where Eric *is* right now.'

'I do,' Phoebe told her. 'Keep talking.'

'Okay, go straight back in there to get what we need from Russell "Red Lion" Loewe and don't take no for an answer...'

* * *

When the call ended a minute later, Phoebe raced back inside.

'Do you still have the original files you found on that thumb drive,' she asked Russell urgently, 'the one River designed for his GCSE?'

'It's backed up on the cloud, but the coding has changed wholesale since then.'

'Still, could we have a copy?'

'No way. I had to submit every bit of development coding when we sold the app and sign all sorts of NDAs and DSAs that mean I can never share them again. I probably shouldn't have anything still backed up.'

'But you kept those source files to yourself because you didn't want the new owners knowing it wasn't your idea at all, that your son had designed it when he was fifteen.'

'You mustn't tell them. They'll sue me to the moon.'

'Let me have the original source code files and I won't breathe a word.'

'What are you going to do with them?'

'Show them to someone at MI5.' She gave Felix the ghost of a wink.

Russell looked like he was going to faint.

'It's all right, our spook is on a break,' Felix assured him.

'Paternity leave,' Phoebe explained, crossing her fingers hopefully.

'Congratulations,' Russell said to Felix, who caught Phoebe's eye with a smirk.

He still thinks Felix is a government agent, Phoebe realised.

Unamused, she snapped at Russell to get a bloody move on.

Racing outside as soon as they had the thumb drive, Phoebe wailed. 'We completely forgot about Grant!'

Felix, who was on his mobile trying to get through to DI Mason again, waved at her to be quiet, barking into the mouthpiece, 'No, it's not about a stolen lawnmower, Constable, it's about a murder!'

They found Grant's blue pick-up still mercifully parked further along the road, rocking on its suspension with the thud of thrash metal.

A small, round blonde woman was slouching down in the passenger seat wearing dark glasses and Grant's Metallica hat. She had *Slayer* tattooed on one arm and *Megadeath* on the other.

'This is Tiffany,' Grant introduced them proudly. 'She's coming back with us.' They were holding hands over the gear shift.

'I should never have left!' she half-laughed, half-sobbed.

'Hello, Tiffany, that's wonderful news.' Phoebe jumped on the back alongside Felix. 'Now I know it's a big ask, but would you mind terribly driving extremely fast to Newborough, Grant? We need to find a man called Eric on the North Wessex Canal. He's in a narrowboat called *Atlantis*. He must look at this.' She held up the thumb drive. 'Cosmo Lovat's life depends on – agh!'

She and Felix were instantly slammed back into the leather seats with G-force as Grant accelerated out of the estate. 'Always wanted to do this!'

'My hero!' cried Tiffany, pulling off her hat and shaking out her hair. She was still holding Grant's hand.

'Perhaps slow down while we're in a thirty zone and keep both hands on the wheel?' Phoebe suggested over the thrash metal. 'Other lives depend on that, including ours.' She realised her own hand was in Felix's. There was an alarmed chorus of yaps from the back of the truck. 'And our dogs' lives too.'

31

JUNO

'Keep me on an open line, Freddy!' Juno demanded, leaving in one AirPod and hurrying to the Mini which was parked in The Barton Arms car park. 'I'm driving straight to Cosmo's cottage,' she told Phoebe, who had her on speakerphone at the other end. 'He's not at The Priory, I've checked with them and he left yesterday, and I know it's a long shot but I thought he might have gone there. Mil's already on his way to the village green to try and catch River and Xanthe at Cheryl's place.'

'I said *not* to do that!' Phoebe's crackly voice warned, barely audible over a roaring engine. 'Those kids are dangerous.'

'What did the police say?' Juno asked.

'That DI Mason will call us back,' Felix's voice told her through a cacophony of noise.

'Where are you both? What's that awful sound?'

'Anthrax. We're on the M4.'

'What are you doing there?' she bleated, climbing into her car. 'Eric's boat was in Abingdon last time he messaged me.'

'That was days ago, Juno,' Phoebe said at the other end. 'He's not there now, although we don't yet have an exact location. He's not answering his phone, but we'll keep trying. Meanwhile, we know he's left the Thames and is on the canal near Newborough.'

'How do you know that?' Juno demanded, then she squeaked as she realised how close that put him to her. She'd be able to take the electric bike along the towpath to visit him.

'Because I know where his next mooring is,' Phoebe told her. 'And—'

The line dropped for a moment as Juno buckled herself in and fired up the engine, her call transferring from her AirPod to handsfree. 'You must hurry, Freddy!'

Through the car speakers came a flurry of beeping at Phoebe's end, then her voice became distorted, as though she was holding her phone's microphone close to her mouth, entreating, 'Please don't say "hurry" again, Juno. Grant's driving and he's easily triggered.'

'Understood.' Juno pressed her own accelerator and belted out of the pub car park towards the sawmill development.

There was a beep on the line. Her Mini Connected screen told her she had a call waiting.

'Be right back, Freddy.' She switched to it.

'I'm outside Cheryl and River's place and it's locked up.' It was Mil. 'River and Xanthe aren't here.'

'Are there two backpacks in the hallway?'

'Hang on, I'll look through the window. Yup, roger that.'

'Then they haven't left yet. They're probably still in the village. Go and see if you can find Cheryl. She might be in Ash Tree Crescent with her sisters. I'm almost at Cosmo's. Call you back.'

She switched the call back to Phoebe again. 'River and Xanthe are still at large, but we don't know exactly where.'

'Calm down, Juno. It's early. We have the advantage of foresight. Cosmo could well be checking over his old place, so that's good thinking. We've just arrived in Newborough. Grant's dropping us on the bridge now.'

'That was fast!' Juno hadn't yet made it out of Three Bridge Lane, stuck behind a driver carefully parallel parking a Nissan Leaf, a solid line of traffic in the opposite lane waiting for the railway crossing to reopen. 'Is Grant rally trained?'

'No, just a rally bad driver,' Phoebe joked faintly, the sound of thrash metal fading.

At last, Juno made it out onto the High Street, then left into Woodridge Lane. 'Don't hang up, Freddy.'

Two minutes later, she was standing outside Cosmo's locked cottage.

'He's not here!' she wailed, looking up at the Green Man hanging over the porch gable. She felt stupid for imagining he might be, stupider still that she'd envisaged herself rushing in to find Cosmo preparing for his date with the fake Hungarian honeytrap – in Juno's imagination the date would be taking place here, candles already lit, Cosmo fresh from the bath in nothing but a towel – and she would drive him away to safety in the nick of time. 'Where can he be?'

'He probably hasn't got his date literally right now this minute.' Phoebe was blowing hard.

'What if it's a lunch date? He had *flowers*, Freddy. Ohmygod, I've just had a thought!' she squealed. 'You know one of my first theories was that Cosmo might be investigating Holly's death?'

'Juno, I don't think—'

'Yes, but what if he's worked out what Xanthe and River have been up to? Why else would he go on this date when you expressly warned him that it was unsafe, unless it's to flush them out? He probably still blames Xanthe for Holly's death, sharing all her secrets like that. Like us, Cosmo has figured out they're now picking off all the original angels in some sort of personal revenge, using the app as bait. That's why he was in The Priory on the night Don died. He'd guessed Don was their next target!'

'Hang on, Cosmo told me he'd arranged a date with Edit "Story Weaver" that night.' Phoebe spoke in breathless bursts. 'If anyone was being targeted, Cosmo was. *You* were Don's date. Why would Xanthe and River suddenly decide to kill Don, not Cosmo?'

'Because we ate Cosmo's olives!'

'It still makes no sense,' Phoebe panted. 'We know Don's murder was carefully pre-meditated.'

'Either way, Cosmo's in danger, Freddy! We can't have another death on our consciences!'

But Phoebe was characteristically unruffled, albeit very out of breath.

'I'm sure there's no need to panic,' she puffed, muttered a few 'oops!' and shouted an apology.

'What are you doing now?'

'Running along a canal towpath. It's busy.'

'Now is not the time for jogging, Freddy,' Juno said distractedly, still looking up at Cosmo's windows. 'I have a bad feeling about all this.'

'So do I. Eric's boat's not here! The mooring's empty. He must have moved on.'

'Where to?' Juno's visions of towpath cycling with her grandchild in a baby trailer faded.

Phoebe was panting harder now. 'He'll be heading to Inkbury. Narrowboats move so slowly, he won't have got far. Felix and I are going to keep running.'

'Eric is coming to Inkbury?' Juno shrieked.

'I wasn't going to tell you this yet – it's supposed to be a surprise – but I've persuaded the Hartridge Estate to let him use the old lock mooring for a while.'

'Ohmygod, Eric's going to live in Inkbury!' Juno realised ecstatically. 'He's coming here! I love you, Freddy. I'm going to the deli.'

'Now is not the time for pastries, Juno,' Phoebe joked breathlessly, but she sounded pleased.

Juno was already jumping back in her car. 'I'm going to see if Autumn knows where her father is. If I hurry, it'll still be open!'

* * *

'Where's your dad? We must find him!' Juno burst into the deli.

'My dad is dead.'

'No!' Juno wailed, then realised the deli's ageing full-timer looked at her calmly over the counter. 'Sorry. I mean, that's terribly sad for you.'

'It was twenty years ago. If you're looking for Autumn, she's just left. She'll be at the train station.'

Juno remembered she commuted from Dunford where her mother lived. 'Thanks. I might need a pastry to take with me. Bit of a sugar low.'

The deli worker handed her a cinnamon swirl.

'And if you're looking for her dad, Cosmo, just follow the smell of aftershave. He was in here earlier helping himself to the best Charbonnel et Walker gift box.'

'Thanks for the tip!'

Wolfing the pastry for energy, Juno dashed out onto Church End to find the Mini was now blocked in by a delivery van. She ran into Wheeler's Yard to grab her electric bike from the shop.

Next door, her florist neighbour was outside marking down a bucket of gladioli.

'Cosmo didn't say where he was meeting his "special lady", did he?'

The florist shook her head. 'He was wearing board shorts and had a towel round his neck though, if that helps?'

The call with Phoebe had disconnected, so Juno rang back as she climbed on her bike, quickly updating her. 'Was he off paddleboarding, maybe?'

'Again... no need... to panic.' Phoebe was breathless from running. 'Try and catch Autumn. Felix got hold of Eric and he's at the next lock, so we're meeting him there.'

Juno cycled along Witch's Broom to the station, where Autumn was sitting on a bench on the westbound platform, earbuds in, blue hair bobbing.

Flopping down beside her, breathing heavily, Juno tapped urgently on one.

Autumn removed it. 'You just skipped three tracks!'

'Where might your dad arrange to meet a date round here?'

Autumn drew back her chin in mock horror. 'I've told you you're too late. That boat sailed.'

'It's important. Where, Autumn? The Priory? The Damselfly? A picnic by the river?'

'Swipe right date or introduced by a mutual friend date?'

'The first one.'

'Her place.'

'Second one?'

'The swimming pontoon at Valence Lock, maybe? There's a pop-up champagne bar and glamping pods in summer.'

'Oh, that's so romantic.'

'Yeah, that's where River works. It's bougie.'

Juno gulped. 'We have to get there now!'

'Is Dad in danger?' Autumn suddenly looked frightened.

Juno covered her hand gently but urgently. 'I know this is going to come as a shock...'

The usually sanguine, sardonic Autumn looked horrified when Juno broke it to her that her father's date might be a lethal honeytrap, more devastated still to learn that her close village friends could be behind it and had been targeting a local business syndicate.

'What's more,' Juno finished breathlessly, 'I think your dad has been playing vigilante detective. I think he knows exactly who he's meeting.'

'I did tell him you were investigating some sort of syndicate sex scandal revenge crime,' Autumn admitted.

'Who told you that?'

'You did. You told me you were going on a date. Dad was fascinated.'

Before Juno could answer, Phoebe's voice crackled through the AirPod in Juno's ear. 'We're with Eric! He's almost reached Inkbury. He says Valence Lock is a few minutes away by narrowboat, but it's faster if we run. We're all headed there now.'

'Has Eric looked at the app's software codes?'

'He's navigating a narrowboat, Juno. He also says to tell you that you probably overestimated his powers of geekery there, but when he profiled Cosmo for you, his Map My Fitness showed activity by the swimming pontoon more than once over the past month, so it's a regular haunt.'

'Oh, my son is good! Heading there now.'

'I'm coming too.' Autumn sprang up. 'We'll run there.'

'I have an electric bike!' Juno remembered with relief.

'In that case, you can give me a backie.'

* * *

'Folks, it's Mil. Quick update. Cheryl says River has one more work shift before he and Xanthe leave. We're heading there now. She and Bethany are coming too. They're a bit wound up, I'm afr—'

'Give that thing here, Mil Winterbourne! My River wouldn't hurt anyone, do you hear? Anyone who says otherwise will see my—'

The voice note ended abruptly.

* * *

Juno and Autumn rattled along the towpath, the electric bike almost wobbling off the bank and into the water multiple times on the dash to Valence Lock. Halfway there, the battery indicator flashed red, the bike slowed and the pedals became heavy and resistant. Juno had forgotten to charge it again. Her leg muscles screamed with the effort. The next few hundred yards almost finished her off.

'I'll pedal,' Autumn shouted in her ear. 'I'm my uni's top *Descenders* cross-country mountain-biking champ.'

'You saviour!' Juno panted, shaking gratefully to a halt with the aid of the hedgerow before remembering *Descenders* was a video game. But Autumn had younger legs.

After they'd swapped places, they were almost back to battery-powered speed.

Even though it was midweek, the champagne bar was doing a brisk lunchtime trade, its pontoon pool hosting a small shoal of freshwater bathers cooling off from the heat. The pretty riverside spot was a mecca for day trippers and holidaymakers in high season, tens of pleasure boats and narrowboats moored alongside nearby Valence Lock. Cars were double parked to either side of the little road bridge that crossed the canal here. But there was no sign of Cosmo. Nor was there any sign of River.

Juno got Autumn to show the bar's owner a photo of Cosmo on her phone.

'Oh, yes, he was here earlier,' the owner told them. 'I think he was waiting for someone, but they never showed. He looked like he'd had a skinful. Left maybe twenty minutes ago? My bar assistant had to help him, worried he'd fall in the water. If you'll excuse me, he's not back yet and I need to serve customers.'

Juno and Autumn looked at each other in alarm.

'If River's slipped your father a roofie, I can tell you from experience that he's going to be out of it.'

'Dad's army trained.'

'I'm nightclub trained.'

'Where could they have gone?' asked Autumn.

'They can't be heading back towards Inkbury because we'd have passed them coming the other way,' Juno pointed out, 'so they must be going towards Newborough. Why would they go that way?'

'I think I know!' Autumn grabbed the bike.

Clambering back on, they started out along the bank, Autumn standing up and pedalling, Juno on the seat clinging to the rear rack, talking to Phoebe again: 'We're between Valence and Holt locks. How far away are you?'

'We're running in your direction and we haven't seen them yet; Eric's boat's not far behind us.'

'And Mil and the Welches must be behind us,' Juno realised. 'Nobody's seen a glimpse of them. Where can they *be*?'

There were far fewer towpath users this far from the village, but it was still a popular right of way, walkers and cyclists passing every few minutes along with river and canal users.

None of them had seen River and Cosmo when asked, nor had they seen anyone young and punky looking with cropped hair and shaven eyebrows. Kayakers, paddleboarders and narrowboats passed regularly.

It was hardly an ideal spot to stage auto-erotic asphyxia.

'Do you think we should have checked the glamping pods?' Juno fretted. 'There's been no sign of Xanthe either, so she must be waiting somewhere for – argh!' She almost fell off the bike as Autumn slammed on the brakes.

'The Chill Pillbox!' Autumn cried. 'They'll be at the Chill Pillbox.'

* * *

The banks of the River Dunnett and the towpath of its neighbouring canal were punctuated with old concrete pillboxes, strategically placed there during the Second World War. Offering cover for gun emplacements and soldiers, these fortified little outposts had been constructed to impede a potential Nazi invasion. Many still survived, some almost reabsorbed into the landscape, overgrown with moss and brambles. Local teenagers had long annexed the driest and remotest as hangouts. The hidden entrances tucked round the back and arrow-slit windows offered ultimate privacy.

'The Chill Pillbox is on the far bank,' Autumn told Juno, pedalling furiously now. 'It's under the willows, totally private. We used to hang out there all the time in the school holidays.'

Clinging on to the bike's rear rack, Juno relayed this information down the line to Phoebe, then told Siri to call Mil. As soon as he answered, she asked: 'Where are you now?'

'Passing the champagne bar,' he rasped, totally out of breath. 'Just stopped for a sec. Need a drink.'

'Don't celebrate just yet. I hope to God we're in time.'

'Water, Juno love, I'm drinking water.'

No sooner had he rung off than Siri announced an incoming call from Eric: 'Big news! I just got a call, Mum! It's a—'

Juno's AirPod flew out of her ear as Autumn slammed on the brakes again.

'Over there!' She pointed across the water.

'Eric?' Juno slid off to search through the towpath for her earphone. 'Eric?'

'Shh!' In front of her, Autumn was pointing across at a group of three willows on the far bank, whispering. 'You can't see it from here, but it's in there. The Chill Pillbox.'

There was no sign of a pillbox, the only sounds water, birds and rustling leaves.

'How do we get across there?' asked Juno, eyeing a rickety construction about fifty yards further ahead, most of which appeared to have collapsed into the water. A big 'DANGER' placard was pinned to it, along with several 'Private – Keep Out' signs and a poster for Marlbury Folk Festival.

'The wooden footbridge just up there.' Autumn pointed at the poster and what little remaining structure it was attached to.

'I was hoping you weren't going to say that.'

Juno somehow made it across. She was astonished a long, elegantly spindly youth like River could manhandle a drugged chunk like Cosmo across, even with Xanthe's help.

But somehow, it seemed they had.

'He's stronger than he looks, River,' Autumn breathed. She

was looking very pale, increasingly anxious and clearly conflicted. 'You don't think he really wants to hurt Dad?'

Creeping round the pillbox behind Autumn, Juno heard low voices coming from inside, then a stifled giggle. She couched down to peer through one of the open slit windows, just able to make out a gloomy stone room like a dungeon. The smell of damp and dank hit her nostrils. Followed by top notes of expensive aftershave.

Propped up against one wall, Cosmo appeared to be unconscious.

Standing over him, River was tugging off his trousers while Xanthe was dressing him in a padded bra and a leopard-print wrap. Both were snickering and giggling.

Juno turned silently to Autumn. But before she could whisper very quietly that they must call 999 and wait for the others, Autumn cannoned her aside and charged round the pillbox to its doorway. 'Dad! *Dad!* Christ, what have you *done* to him?'

Groaning, Juno rushed to follow in case she needed to defend her.

Inside, Autumn had gathered her father into her arms, screaming furiously at the others. 'How could you do this to him? To me? We're family.'

'He was one of them! They're the reason Mum's dead.' Xanthe's eyes were wild and unblinking. 'Him and River's dad and Rich Bass-tard and the rest, with their creepy infidelity app, but Cosmo most of all! He as good as killed her!'

Dodging brambles, Juno made her way in. 'Murdering them all isn't the answer!'

'Who said anything about *murdering* him!' River objected, flicking back his blond curls and looking offended.

'We're just going to video him.' Xanthe waved their phone to demonstrate. 'For our rogues' gallery.'

Juno held up her hands, struggling to understand. 'You want to film a man dying for some sort of sick TikTok channel?'

'Not *dying*,' River protested. 'Dressed up and spaced out.'

'Then all his friends and colleagues can see what a kinky old sad act he is,' Xanthe snarled.

'We're going to shame him online,' River explained.

'Tell me if I've got this right,' Juno humoured them, playing for time while she worked out how she was going to call for help. 'You found your way into Dapper and Discreet through some sort of back door in the coding, because it was built on an app you designed yourself at school.'

'That's right.' River looked grudgingly impressed. 'Cor Rapta.'

'It was your father who had stolen that design and turned it into a huge commercial success. You knew that, just like him, the "angel" investors who originally backed the enterprise had all used it to meet women and still did. So you created a fake profile, Dream Weaver, and used her as a honeytrap, manipulating the app from the inside to match all those original angels. Then you made sure they arranged to meet Dream Weaver somewhere you could spike their drink or food unobserved while they waited. How am I doing?'

'Close enough.'

'And you're trying to tell me the original plan was then to dress them up in church jumble and take photos?' Juno asked incredulously.

'Videos,' River corrected.

'We're going to use lots of post effects, make memes,' said Xanthe. 'We haven't decided exactly yet. Cosmo's will be our first.'

'Even so, three men are...' Juno ran this back. 'What do you mean, your *first*?'

River flicked back his hair defiantly. 'We didn't do anything with footage we took of Rich Bass because then he went and killed himself after we'd left, and obviously that was problematic.'

'Obviously!' Juno cried. 'You killed him!'

'We did *not* kill him!' He looked even more offended, rolling his eyes. 'How many *times*? We just dressed him up.'

'Like you dressed up Don Greenwood?'

'Am I expected to know who Don Greenwood is?' he asked sulkily.

'Green Man,' Xanthe reminded him. 'That dude who got stiffed at the hotel. He managed the WE SIN venture capital.' Turning to Juno, Xanthe shook their head vigorously. 'His death was nothing to do with us.'

'Nothing to do with us!' echoed River, shaking his head too, curls swinging.

'And Wayne "Golden Pheasant" Baxendale, I suppose *his* death was nothing to do with you either?'

'He had a heart attack,' Xanthe said quickly.

'After you got the dose wrong when you spiked his drink at The Priory,' River reminded her.

'I knew it!' Juno sighed victoriously, as much to herself as them.

'So?' Xanthe was challenging River. 'We both agreed he would have died anyway! He was super unfit and seriously old – at least sixty – and he said in his messages to Edit that he had a pacemaker which is why he liked his ladies on top. My mum was just forty when she died. It was their fault, *his* fault.' They jabbed a finger towards Cosmo who was still semi-conscious on the ground, being supported by Autumn who had been frantically trying to pull his clothes back on him.

'You know how much Dad loved Holly!' she cried.

'You never heard what Rich Bass said when he was out of it in the cricket pavilion.'

'What did Rich say?' asked Juno.

'It's like a truth drug, that stuff,' said River, looking down at Cosmo. 'He might start up in a minute then he can tell you himself what he did to Holly.'

'What did Rich tell you?' Juno asked again.

'He kept going on that he knew a dirty secret about the cricket captain,' River started.

'That when he'd found out his wife had been cheating on him with all these men online,' Xanthe took over, 'he'd stepped out in front of her car and—' Their face crumpled into a sob.

'She swerved to avoid him and hit a wall instead,' River finished, putting his arms around Xanthe.

'You're lying!' Autumn raged. 'Dad was still in bed when it happened.'

'He was in the road.' River rocked the sobbing Xanthe in his arms. 'Rich Bass told us Holly had just overtaken his wife in her car. Debra was right behind when it happened and saw the lot, but she was too shaken to tell anyone at the time. Her brother drove her home. Later she confided in Rich, who told her to keep it quiet.'

'And used it to his advantage ever since,' Juno realised. 'No wonder you killed him.'

'How many times?' howled River. 'We didn't kill Rich Bass! The man was alive when we left the pavilion! We have the video to prove it!'

To Juno's relief, she heard footsteps pounding through the undergrowth outside, Phoebe's voice saying, 'This must be it!'

'We didn't *kill* any of them!' River was shouting as Felix hurried inside.

He paused to take in the scene, putting a quick comforting hand on Juno's shoulder before stooping to check Cosmo, who was starting to make audible groaning noises now. 'The police and air ambulance are on their way,' he told a terrified Autumn. 'He's going to be fine.'

'Of course he's going to be fine!' howled River. 'He's just had some roofies, blues and happy pills. He's having a ball.'

'Just like Rich Bass was when we left him sleeping it off in that pavilion,' said Xanthe, mopping her face.

'It's not our fault the man woke up with his flag still flying,' River pleaded. 'What he did to himself next was nothing to do with us.'

'The same goes for Wayne's lifestyle choices!' Xanthe said defiantly.

'And what happened to Green Man was definitely nothing to do with us.' River laughed hollowly. 'We'd never matched Dream Weaver with him.'

'Because she was supposed to be meeting Cosmo that night,' said a clear voice as Phoebe stepped into the pillbox beside Juno. 'Except Cosmo cancelled at the last minute. You still tried to drug him anyway, but Juno ate the olives you'd spiked.'

'Exactly!' cried Xanthe.

Phoebe leant down to murmur to Juno, 'This might sound insane, but I believe them. I don't think they've killed anyone.'

'Welcome to madness,' Juno breathed back, 'neither do I.'

Outside, a loud splash came from the direction of the river, followed by breathless, shouty voices; Cheryl Welch screeching, 'Where is he? Where's my River?' Bethany calling, 'Calm down, sis, wait for me!' Mil booming, 'I bloody well fell in!' And

Courtney's familiar caw was shouting from the opposite bank that she couldn't risk getting her phone wet so would keep filming from there.

The two Welch sirens burst inside first, Cheryl hurtling up to River and pulling him to her chest in an embrace that was part maternal, part half-nelson. 'What did you do, baby? What have you *done*?'

Bethany panted inside too, taking in the scene. 'That's my bloody Wonderbra Cosmo's wearing!'

'Getting quite crowded in here,' Juno muttered, squeezing her way outside.

Phoebe followed.

Mil was hastily wading out of the Dunnett through the reeds. It was a very Colin Firth as Mr Darcy moment, Juno felt, trying not to notice how excitingly his wet shirt clung to the muscles of his wide shoulders.

As if reading her thoughts, he squared those shoulders ruggedly. 'What's happening? Do they need help in there?'

'I think they're fine,' said Phoebe, cocking her head to listen to Cheryl Welch screaming at her son inside the pillbox that he was a bloody idiot.

Juno hurriedly brought Mil up to date, watching his mouth open ever wider in shock.

'So you see my detective itch was right all along!' she said triumphantly. 'They *did* slip Wayne Baxendale a Micky Finn, which probably triggered a heart attack.'

'At least he died happy,' murmured Phoebe, which Juno felt was scant consolation.

'*And* they lured Rich to the pavilion, pretending to be Edit the yoga instructor,' she went on. 'Presumably they'd spiked something he ingested while he was waiting for her to arrive. Then they dressed him up and took pictures while he babbled deliriously about what had really happened to Holly. Those drugs work like a truth serum. They also remove all inhibitions and fears, hence he must have done the rest himself.'

'So Rich *did* asphyxiate himself?' asked Mil, squeezing water from his clothes.

'Or somebody else found him like that and took advantage of the situation,' Phoebe suggested.

They all pondered this in silence for a moment. Police sirens sounded in the distance, along with approaching helicopter rotors. Closer to, another engine puttered on the water.

'But what about Don?' asked Juno, hugging herself at the memory of it. 'That was no accident, surely?'

Phoebe sucked her teeth, shaking her head. 'It was a carefully planned murder. Far better thought out than a couple of teenagers hacking an app and drugging middle-aged men to dress up in lingerie.'

'You know who did it!' Juno gasped.

'I know who I think did it,' she corrected. 'The first thing we have to ask is who would gain from Don's death?'

'We didn't really know anything about him, Freddy. He mentioned an ex-wife.'

'I'm stumped,' Mil admitted.

'Rich Bass's life insurance won't pay out because his death was deemed self-inflicted. But if that cause of death were changed to murder, everything would be different.'

'You can't think Debra killed Don?'

'A huge payout like that would solve all her financial woes,' Mil conceded.

Phoebe nodded. 'Debra begged us to prove Rich's death was murder, but we couldn't because it wasn't, at least it's highly unlikely. So what she needed was another, almost identical death, to cast doubt over Rich's self-inflicted one. She knew a lot of the details of how Rich died from the police, and a few more from us: that he'd been roofied with Chemsex on the Beach, that he was wearing clothes from the church jumble – which we now know River must have taken from the Three Decrees' Graveyard Raver stash – and that he'd attached his robe belt to a hook to restrict his airway and enhance his... experience. To have one auto-erotic asphyxia in a village looks like misfortune; two looks like...'

'Murder!' Juno gulped. 'But how on earth did she do it?'

'She must have had to have an accomplice,' said Phoebe.

'Grant! I knew it.' Juno felt even more triumphant. 'Detective itch.'

'Not Grant,' Phoebe dismissed. 'He was enjoying a champagne tea with Zadie Welch at the time of the murder in front of multiple witnesses.'

'First I've heard of it,' Mil bristled.

'There's no way Debra could have lifted Don's body on her own to string him up on the bathroom door hook,' said Juno.

'Exactly,' Phoebe agreed. 'Her accomplice had to be physically fit, and also a hotel insider, or they knew one. Don's room was deliberately switched to the Red Priest Suite to ensure privacy and minimum CCTV – there are no cameras in the tower staircases because they're Grade I listed – along with an escape route. The bathroom windows were unlocked beforehand, and those keys are kept in a secure cabinet in the Maintenance Office.'

'You worked all that out yourself?' Mil looked wildly impressed.

'Brilliant,' Juno agreed, feeling stupid because she still didn't know who the accomplice might be.

Then Phoebe caught her eye with that kind, clever smile, reminding her she'd been largely unconscious at the time. 'My guess is that Debra was already lying in wait in the hotel suite bathroom with the jumble sale booty, while her accomplice followed you and Don up to the room, used a keycard to slip in behind you and bundled Don into the bathroom to despatch him with the same MO as Rich. High risk, but also high stakes.'

Juno thought about the strange, recurring memory she had of a shadowy figure looming past while Eminem was telling her to lose herself to the music.

'But how did Debra roofie us?' she asked. 'She came nowhere near us.'

'The drugs were in the olives,' Phoebe said. 'Cosmo's olives. Probably spiked twice, once by Bonnie and Clyde in there, and once by their intended victim.'

'*Cosmo?*' Juno gasped. 'Why would Cosmo help Debra kill someone in cold blood like that?'

'Debra knew she could never manage it alone, so she chose to ask the only person she knew who had killed somebody. She had witnessed Cosmo step out in front of his wife Holly's car intending for one or both of them would die. At the time he didn't much care which. A true crime of passion. But passions fade, whereas bad reputations scar forever. It's why Rich held such sway over Cosmo, because he knew what he'd done. With Rich dead, Cosmo thought his secret was finally safe. Then Debra asked him to do one last—'

'Stop him!' shouted a voice from the direction of the pillbox.

It was Felix, sprinting around the side of the little concrete outpost, his blue eyes like searchlights raking up around the coppice. 'Did you see where he ran?'

'Cosmo?' Juno asked excitedly.

'River! He just did a – Jesus, there goes the other one!'

Streaking out from the pillbox and away through the trees, Xanthe had disappeared from sight within seconds.

The police sirens were getting closer, the helicopter blades thundering, but not close enough.

The Welch sisters were spilling out of the pillbox now, arguing furiously about whose fault it was the youngsters had run – 'you shouldn't've told him he'll go to prison!'; 'That Xanthe's a psycho like her mum' – and behind them, groggily propped up by his blue-haired daughter, came Cosmo.

Now he was regaining cognisance, his Chemsex cocktail rendered him open-heartedly tearful, telling Autumn, 'Let's not make a run for it. I'll say I bottled it and Debra pulled a gun on me to make me do it.'

'Did she, Dad?' she ask hopefully as she led him away to sit on the bank and await arrest.

Juno secretly rather hoped Debra had, if only to prove she could method act that ruthless *Eastenders* diva after all. She entertained a brief vision of her in Flatpack Mansion right now, frantically stuffing a Louis Vuitton holdall with cash from the sale of a Rolex as she prepared to flee to Ecuador. But she guessed Debra was more likely to be packing her *Fifty Shades* trilogy and gel nail spares in preparation for a long spell inside.

'What I don't understand is,' Mil was asking quietly, 'if Cosmo loathed that app so much, why did he come here to meet a bird off it today?'

'Cosmo was playing detective too!' Juno revealed in an undertone.

'Don't say "bird", Mil.' Phoebe wrinkled her nose, a gesture Juno now knew meant she was about to disprove her theory. 'And are you asking why Cosmo wanted to meet a twenty-something, super-flexible Hungarian yoga instructor?'

'Fair point.' He shrugged. Then, to Juno's delight, he added, 'Prat.'

Juno felt strangely emotional.

The sirens were really loud now, a police Land Rover bouncing along a farm track two fields away.

On the canal, a familiar narrowboat was drawing level.

At the tiller, Eric's handsome, golden-bearded face was wreathed in smiles. Never had he looked more like his father, Juno thought tearfully.

'Hey, Mom!' he shouted across to his mother. 'You have a granddaughter!'

'I what?' She felt herself sagging in shock, stopped from falling over by Mil's strong wet grip.

'It's a girl! You're a grandmother!'

'Ohmygod!' she shrieked, turning to hug Phoebe, then Mil and Felix, then hurry towards the canal to hitch a lift, shouting back, 'Can somebody else tell the police who the killers are? Mother Love has just become Grandmother Love!'

EPILOGUE
PHOEBE

'Isn't this fantastic, Freddy?'

In the darkened church hall, waving glowsticks to high-energy dance music, Juno's teeth glowed ultraviolet bright, her unstoppable smile making it easy to identify her as the most energetic dancer. She was on fire.

Waving her fading glowsticks to 'Pump Up the Volume', Phoebe was feeling too hot and claustrophobic to argue the point. But she was sticking to running along the local towpaths in future.

'*Pump it*, ladies!' On stage, Bethany Welch was giving it her all in a dayglo unitard and headset, platinum dreadlocks whipping from side to side. 'This is the last track of the night, so *feel that burn!*'

Phoebe felt it burn into her very soul, which craved builder's tea and *The Archers*.

Afterwards, a group of Clubbercise classmates walked from the church hall to The Barton Arms.

Cheryl Welch insisted on buying the first round. Tanned

deepest Rodin bronze from another Greek minibreak with 'Hot' Rod, Cheryl looked amazing, a toffee apple face with a big white smile bitten out. She pulled out her phone. 'I have pictures! But first, here's one I got this morning of River and Xanthe together on a bridge over the Danube in Budapest! Don't they look gorgeous?'

The Clubbercise ladies cooed and ahh-ed that they were love's young dream.

'I wonder if they've done any yoga while they're in Hungary?' Juno murmured to Phoebe in an undertone.

'Far too busy counting their lucky star tattoos,' she muttered back.

'Carbs incoming!' Courtney delivered several bowls of pub favourite thrice-fried chips to the table. Reinstated as The Barton Arms' surliest – and only – waitress, Courtney was revelling in her return, bending down beside Phoebe to reveal: 'Just filmed a bloke keying a Merc outside. My true crime channel has ten thousand subscribers. I can offer you advertorials at a good rate. And don't tell Juno, but her Housewarming Party Dance has three million hits. Me and Seph are off to Magaluf on the profits.'

Juno leaned across after Courtney had gone. 'How many views?'

'Three million.'

'I'll throw in a few Clubbercise moves next time. Get ratings up.'

She and Phoebe both looked up at different fixed points in the ceiling, the need to stifle shared, irrepressible giggles a rare, undimmed treat.

Leaving their exercise classmates admiring endless selfies of Cheryl taken on Aegean beaches, they moved away to join Felix and Mil at the end of the bar.

'How are my favourite sleuths?' Mil's handsomely craggy smile greeted them, his arms outstretched.

'I've retired from sleuthing,' said Juno. 'I am truly appalling at it. I had no idea Debra was that ruthless. I can't believe she *really* pulled a gun on Cosmo.'

The police had descended on Flatpack Mansion to arrest Debra Bass within minutes of Cosmo's confession that day at the Chill Pillbox. She remained on remand while Cosmo was now out on bail and lying low in London. According to the many newspaper reports, early evidence pointed at him being heavily coerced, threatened with a firearm and still suffering PTSD from the loss of his wife. Also having very good lawyers.

Juno had just received a long letter from Debra telling her all about the memoirs she was writing. 'Debra says they'll be an unflinchingly honest account of her and Rich's emotional journey.'

'Maybe she'll finally reveal who Zadie caught the Basses in bed with,' mused Felix. 'Someone so scandalous it took a vintage Rolex to buy her silence.'

'Oh, Courtney already put that on TikTok,' said Juno, 'and it was just a dominatrix from Newborough.'

'Zadie told me it was identical triplets Rich found on OnlyFans,' insisted Mil.

'I heard it was hairy rent boy from Swindon who dresses up as a teddy bear,' Phoebe murmured.

'Perhaps they were all there, having an orgy?' suggested Felix.

They shared a brief, horrified silence at the thought.

'I just hope poor Bullet didn't witness it,' said Phoebe, who had been relieved to learn the Basses' beloved dachshund was now living in the lap of heritage thatched luxury with Grant and Tiffany.

'It's bound to come out in the memoir,' Juno promised.

'Which I predict will be a BookTok sensation and *Sunday Times* bestseller that gets adapted into an award-winning Hollywood blockbuster,' was Phoebe's verdict, 'but I'm not remotely bitter.'

'Because DI Carrick Lowe is about to become a household name!' cheered Mil, a huge fan of Phoebe's mountain-hearted, tough-talking eighties detective.

The others raised their glasses, whooping and whistling.

'Don't tempt fate,' she scoffed, swigging nervously from hers. In truth, Phoebe was still reeling that Lucia Vance – Middle England's go-to murder mystery producer – had recently made contact again through Dennis, bubbling over with industry-savvy enthusiasm for what she described as her new 'crime crush'. The television adaptation was in its infancy, and living with filmmaker Felix had imbued Phoebe with a healthy level of scepticism, but Lucia's team had already acquired rights and appointed a producer. And Dennis was busy negotiating his cameo, credit and introduction fee.

Reluctant to remain the focus of attention, Phoebe quickly switched the subject back to Debra. 'Do you think she might actually have murdered Rich?'

'I suppose it'll all come out in the trial,' Felix shrugged.

'Or the memoir.'

'I'm dreading having to be a witness at the trial.' Juno pressed her hands to her pink cheeks, eyes widening. 'What if one day in the future little Luna looks back at the Year You Were Born news headline and sees that her grandmother testified to being found unconscious in a hotel room with a murder victim that she'd just met on an infidelity dating app?'

'She's going to be Gen Alpha,' said Felix. 'They won't read anything as long as a news headline.'

'More likely she'll see that Granny was a part of a brilliant detective team that caught the killer!' said Mil.

'I'm done with all that,' Juno reminded him.

'That's a shame.' Phoebe lifted her glass, looking into her wine, which was as deliciously complex yet transparent as her friend, 'because I was starting to think we're rather good at it. In fact, I was going to suggest you get your branded merch back out and put an ad in the paper.'

'Seriously?' Juno looked thrilled.

'Hoo-bloody-ray to that!' Mil cheered, lifting his beer bottle to his lips.

As Phoebe hoped, Juno was already bursting with renewed enthusiasm: 'Maybe Eric can help too, especially now he's living so close. And he wants to pay you back for your kindness, Freddy. I know, he can build us a website!' She raised her own glass.

Felix lifted his bottle to clink against it. 'Village Detectives dot com.'

'I'll drink to that.' Mil added his bottle to the tinkling medley.

Phoebe smiled, touching each of their glasses in turn. 'Let's just *not* have an app.'

* * *

MORE FROM FIONA WALKER

The next book in Fiona Walker's Village Detective Series, is available to order now here:

https://mybook.to/Book4BackAd

ACKNOWLEDGEMENTS

It's a joy to count myself a part of the Boldwood Books team, who are the hardest working, most enthusiastic and loveliest bunch in the business – not to mention multi-award-winning, as our indefatigable founder would rightly urge me to point out. Publishing director supreme Isobel Akenhead is an editorial genius with a heart the size of Kent, and I am so grateful to work with her, never more so than on this one. Magnificent managing editor Hayley Russell, production hotshots Ben Wilson and Leila Mauger, sales dynamos Wendy Neale and Isabelle Flynn, and marketing gurus Claire Fenby-Warren and the *maravillosa* Marcela Torres are all Boldwood superstars. CEO Amanda Ridout is my industry hero and a true champion of commercial fiction. Thank you all.

Big cheers also to my brilliant, collaborative, patient and oh-so-talented cover designer Rachel Lawston and to eagle-eyed copy ed Cecily Blench and proofreader Jennifer Kay Davies.

Huge, heartfelt thanks to the fantastic team at Curtis Brown, especially my powerhouse literary agent and sounding board, Sheila Crowley and the wonderful Helena Maybery.

Limitless hugs as always to my family and friends, many of whom I listed excitedly and extensively in the first book of this series, and all of whom I love beyond words, so I'll write no more here because I'd far rather tell you in person (but probably not on social media because I'm hopeless at it, as you know).

The greatest whoop as always goes out to you for reading *The Little Black Book Killer*. Whether you read one book a year or one a week, I'm so grateful you made this one mine. To those who have enjoyed my other novels and keep coming back for more, your loyalty means the world. And to all of you kind enough to leave a review and recommend The Village Detectives, I can't thank you enough; it makes a huge difference. Phoebe and Juno – and I – can't wait to tackle the next case...

ABOUT THE AUTHOR

Fiona Walker is the million copy bestselling author of joyously funny romantic comedies. She has grown up alongside her readers, from nineties London party-animal to dog-walking country mum, and her knack for story-telling remains as compelling as ever. Fiona lives in Shakespeare Country with her partner, their two daughters and a menagerie of horses, dogs and other animals.

Sign up to Fiona Walker's mailing list for news, competitions and updates on future books.

Visit Fiona's Website: www.fionawalker.com

Follow Fiona on social media:

 facebook.com/fionawalkeruk
 x.com/fionawalkeruk
 instagram.com/fionawalkeruk
 pinterest.com/fionawalkerauthor

ALSO BY FIONA WALKER

Village Detectives Series

The Art of Murder

The Poison Pen Letters

The Little Black Book Killer

POISON
& pens

POISON & PENS IS THE HOME OF
COZY MYSTERIES SO POUR YOURSELF
A CUP OF TEA & GET SLEUTHING!

DISCOVER PAGE-TURNING NOVELS FROM
YOUR FAVOURITE AUTHORS &
MEET NEW FRIENDS

JOIN OUR
FACEBOOK GROUP

BIT.LYPOISONANDPENSFB

SIGN UP TO OUR
NEWSLETTER

BIT.LY/POISONANDPENSNEWS

Boldwood

Boldwood Books is an award-winning fiction publishing company seeking out the best stories from around the world.

Find out more at www.boldwoodbooks.com

Join our reader community for brilliant books, competitions and offers!

Follow us

@BoldwoodBooks

@TheBoldBookClub

Sign up to our weekly deals newsletter

https://bit.ly/BoldwoodBNewsletter

Printed in Dunstable, United Kingdom